Praise for Beth Overmyer

'Fans of pseudo-medieval fantasy quest tales and authors like Terry Brooks, Anne McCaffrey, and Brandon Sanderson, and those looking for something to read after bingeing the Netflix show *Cursed*, will get a kick out of Overmyer's action-packed series.'
Booklist on *The Goblets Immortal* series

'Fast-paced and can be read in a day – perfect for a long airplane ride.'
SciFiMoviePage on *The Goblets Immortal*

'Overmyer ramps up the action in this suspenseful sequel to *The Goblets Immortal* […] the magic system is innovative as ever and the dramatic chase scenes drive the plot forward. Series devotees will find plenty to hold their attention.'
Publishers Weekly on *Holes in the Veil*

'The book works for any fan of fantasy, but its full embrace of the Faeries means that it would appeal especially to fans of boggarts and sprites.'
SFBook on *Brittle*, the first of the *Blade and Bone* books

'Overmyer has an easy, engaging style that sucks the reader into the story.'
Concatenation on *Tempered Glass*, the second *Blade and Bone* book

'*Brittle* sets the stage for an epic journey of survival, power, and self-discovery. *Tempered Glass* deepens the stakes, exploring the challenges of power, love, and destiny.'
Jlreadstoperpetuity on the *Blade and Bone* books

'I practically lost hours reading this book, barely noticing the time. I will be keeping an eye out for the rest of the series!'
One More Chapter Reviews on *Brittle*

'Well paced, exciting, full of drama and tension, and not forgetting subtle romance.'
Emma Louise Writes on *Brittle*

'Brittle is an easy read, with an interesting world and a story flow that keeps you turning the pages for answers.'
Marie Sinadjan, Vocal Media, on *Brittle*

'This novel is action packed from the first chapter, tons of twists and turns you won't see coming and a unique story line that will more than keep you intrigued. [...] Overmyer knows how to craft a plot that flows seamlessly and keeps you wanting more.'
Titleswtyler on *Tempered Glass*

'This book might be one of my favorite reads for the year! [...] I highly recommend picking up this book! Especially if you enjoyed Once *Upon a Broken Heart* or *ACOTAR*.'
Kaylyn Pautz on *Tempered Glass*

'Beth's writing instantly immerses the reader in a rich and detailed world. [...] The storyline was original and inventive and I flew through this in a couple of sittings!'
Books By Bindu on *Tempered Glass*

'Brilliant, fast paced and action packed.'
Bookshortie on *Tempered Glass*

BETH OVERMYER

FORGED

Blade and Bone Book Three

Following *Brittle* and *Tempered Glass*

This is a **FLAME TREE PRESS** book

Text copyright © 2025 Beth Overmyer

All rights reserved. No part of this publication may be reproduced, stored in a retrieval system, or transmitted in any form or by any means, electronic, mechanical, photocopying, recording or otherwise, without the prior written permission of the publisher.

FLAME TREE PRESS
6 Melbray Mews, London, SW6 3NS, UK
flametreepress.com

US sales, distribution and warehouse:
Simon & Schuster
simonandschuster.biz

UK distribution and warehouse:
Hachette UK Distribution
hukdcustomerservice@hachette.co.uk

Publisher's Note: This is a work of fiction. Names, characters, places, and incidents are a product of the author's imagination. Locales and public names are sometimes used for atmospheric purposes. Any resemblance to actual people, living or dead, or to businesses, companies, events, institutions, or locales is completely coincidental.

Thanks to the Flame Tree Press team.

The cover is made by Flame Tree Studio, working with the fine and wonderful artist Broci who created the illustration especially for this book. The art is © Broci 2025.
The font families used are Avenir and Bembo.

Flame Tree Press is an imprint of Flame Tree Publishing Ltd
flametreepublishing.com

A copy of the CIP data for this book is available from the British Library and the Library of Congress.

1 3 5 7 9 8 6 4 2

PB ISBN: 978-1-78758-950-6
HB ISBN: 978-1-78758-951-3
ebook ISBN: 978-1-78758-952-0

Printed and bound in Great Britain by Clays Ltd, Elcograf S.p.A.

BETH OVERMYER

FORGED

Blade and Bone Book Three

Following *Brittle* and *Tempered Glass*

FLAME TREE PRESS
London & New York

'I do not ask for any crown
But that which all may win
Nor seek to conquer any world
Except the one within.'
– from the poem 'My Kingdom'
by Louisa May Alcott

Part One

Prologue

First, there was darkness. All light Dacre had cast had died the moment Verve left him waist-deep in an encasement of stone. He was still weak from absorbing all the magic he could from the different pools in Ithalamore, the Lands of the Dead. Even now the power pressed against his mind, begging him to do something with it, but he couldn't. Not yet, anyway. His hands were pinned to his side, trapped like the rest of him.

"Hello?" His hoarse voice echoed back at him. Of course no one was there to answer. All of his company had perished fighting the pools' guardians, and those that could not die were banished to other realms. *What a waste of power.*

He attempted to move his fingers and heard a soft *crack*. That sound gave him hope, but he knew better than to push himself. *Verve, what a mess you've put me in.* He smiled ruefully. She had bested him in a fight, something he would never allow to happen again. Not that he wanted to fight her, but the former mortal was sometimes irrational and often unpredictable, and Dacre would do what he needed in order to see her at his side.

The thought of the power they shared between them made him giddy. There was another crack as loud as a whip stroke, and the stone ensnaring his left arm crumbled. That drove him to the brink of exhaustion, and he leaned forward with a groan.

Little good all our power will do me if I never get out of here, he thought upon hearing an otherworldly howl in the distance. It wasn't that he was afraid of dying; he was high fae and couldn't perish...well, except, perhaps by Verve's hand, now that she had managed to sever the bond between them, something he could sense. What troubled him were the many pitfalls in the underworld, holes he could disappear down and never return from. If some creature were to chase or fight him, Dacre could easily be driven into such an abyss.

After resting another moment, he used his free hand to chip away at the stone trapping his arm. This proved tedious work. Dacre allowed himself a minute to recover.

Once he was free of Ithalamore, he would need to regroup, learn how to use his newfound magic, and rally his allies before Verve had a chance to make plans of her own. Not that they would be entirely her own. There was still her husband, Fenn – *Curse him!* – and no doubt he would meddle. The anger Dacre felt upon thinking of that monster with the woman who was rightfully his was blinding. A snarl escaped his lips and magic burst forth from his limbs, obliterating the remaining rock that entombed him.

The force with which he was released pitched Dacre forward, and he lay sprawled on the ground. Again there was a howl, though the more he thought on it, the more it sounded like a gust of wind and not a creature.

Dacre pulled himself to his feet, knees ready to buckle beneath his weight. Then his newly acquired magic fully settled on him like a cloak and sank into his skin with a sigh. It burned terribly and made him feel like he would be rent in two, such was the volume and strength of it. But soon enough, the sensation passed and he forced himself into action. He would head for Death's Maw – the hawthorn tree that would make a gateway back to his realm – and hope he was now able to open it himself without relying on Verve.

Something made him pause, however. He'd left Verve in the chamber by the closed gateway, bound and, at the time, presumably alone. Why had she and his servant Olive, who must have disguised herself and slipped among Dacre's troops, ventured farther inward instead of leaving Ithalamore altogether? Dacre laughed. *Verve made a deal with Igraine and broke the curse I put on her. Clever.* He paused. True, he had slain Olive when he found her watching over what he at the time presumed to be Verve's corpse. When Verve had awoken, she'd run and then attacked him with such fury... But Igraine, the half-dead, half-alive potion-maker, would not have simply *given* Verve the potion she needed. There would have been a price. *For something like that, a high price.* The thought made him move.

He turned to face the howling behind him. If he could get to Olive before it was too late, perhaps he would learn something to his advantage. So it was with renewed determination that Dacre ran back for his former servant's body.

It didn't take him long to find where he had left her. A mere hour had passed, maybe two, and she appeared fairly fresh. Dacre knelt next to the corpse, took his knife, and slit open his thumb. He let six droplets fall into the corpse's gaping mouth and waited.

At once Olive's shell sat up with a rasp and turned its head to stare at him with glassy eyes. Hopefully he had reached her before her memories had fled.

"Olive, tell me what deal Verity Springer made with the potion-maker Igraine."

A great shudder went through the creature. "Olive cannot have been my name." Her breath stank of rot already, and Dacre had to breathe through his mouth.

"What did Verity Springer promise Igraine in return for her help?" He reached out with more magic, pushing his will against the corpse's stupidly stubborn loyalty to its former occupant.

"She promised..." The creature resisted, but Dacre knew it was on the precipice of bending to his will.

"Yes?"

In the distance, the unnatural wind roared once more. Olive's corpse fought his control for but a second longer before something changed in its expression and inflection. "The Fire Queen promised to return to Ithalamore within six weeks' time."

Dacre frowned. "Why will she return here?" Without thinking, he caught the corpse before it could fall over, and it clung to him with a surprisingly strong grip.

"Ought not to have told you. Ought not to have betrayed her to the Traitor King."

He shoved the body away in disgust. What it said was an annoyance, an old prejudice passed around by some fae with no vision or understanding of what the future could be. What the future *should* be. But he couldn't let a corpse of all things get the better of him. "Tell me why Miss Springer is returning to Ithalamore."

"To see – to see her father and sister, the former whom you killed, and the latter whom she slew." The body collapsed back onto the ground, a great gust of wind leaving her shrunken frame as the last of her memories fled into the next life.

With no further use for the body, Dacre pulled his magic out of it and allowed the power to return unto himself. "Poor Verve," he groaned. He knew her sister had died quite suddenly, but had not suspected her of being responsible. It was sad, for her…but oh-so terribly convenient for him.

Chapter One

Whispers of Dacre and his followers had reached Verve's ears. For the first time, she didn't argue when asked to stay within the magical boundary surrounding her and Fenn's home in Etterhea, the mortal realm. The Traitor King had, after all, absorbed much power the last time they met, and he'd shown no signs of giving up his pursuit of her.

A knock at the front door caused Verve to jump. Fenn's knock: one quick rap, followed by a pause, and then a quick succession of taps that made up a code. The first single knock was a greeting. Three quick knocks after would mean 'I'm alone'. Four evenly spaced knocks meant 'I've brought company'. And five rapid raps meant 'I'm alone and fine but I have news'. Any more would mean he was injured or pursued. Verve waited, her heart beating fit to burst out of her chest after the sixth and final knock came.

Fenn's custom then dictated that he would not magically undo the locks unless he sensed she was in peril, so Verve sprinted for the door and drew power into her hand. He had told her to do so every time someone approached the house, even if she was certain it was him. "Fenn?"

"You presume correctly," said her husband's voice from the other side of the door.

She slid back the bolt and undid the many locks that would really only stop or slow down a mortal, but they were left as a test of sorts. Only Fenn and Verve knew he would leave the locks for her. "What's the news?" Verve asked as she pulled the door open and let her magic drop. She blinked when he didn't enter.

"I smell something burned," he said, fighting a grin apparently. "Is everything all right?" He leaned down and kissed her on the lips.

Verve's knees softened as he stroked her cheek and moved his mouth to her neck. "Just a little accident this morning." She cringed when he stiffened.

"You're unhurt?"

She nodded and moved back so he could enter their home.

Fenn set his leather bag inside the door and redid all the locks with a wave of his hand. The air filled with the aroma of citrus fruit, the scent his residual burst gave off. It complemented Verve's own spent magic's smell of vanilla and sugary treats. As usual, his eyes swept over her form and he pulled her toward the settee, where he sat with her pressed against him. His nose wrinkled up. "What happened?" Fenn swept an errant strand of red-blond hair out of her face and tucked it behind her ear.

"Oh, it's nothing, really. I was just practicing magic and a little fire started."

His arm went around her. "How little?"

Verve sniffed. The house really did reek. "Well, it was contained to one room this time. But how was your hunting?" she quickly added, sensing he was about to start worrying.

Fenn turned her face to peer up at him. There was a crease in his brow, and his dark eyes were tired. "We'll talk about my hunt soon. First, I want to enjoy a moment with you." His lips grazed her jaw, discouraging coherent thoughts from forming in Verve's head.

Soon they were both glowing, and magic pulsed deliciously beneath her skin.

"Tell me about the little fire," he murmured into her ear.

Verve shuddered mightily as he pulled her into his lap. "Well," she said, her voice breaking. Fenn had nuzzled into her neck and seemed intent on making speech difficult for her. "I was practicing."

"So you said. What were you practicing?" A kiss landed on her collarbone.

"Foresight," she breathed as his lips moved lower.

He was silent for a moment, tightening his hold on her waist. "That hasn't happened before."

She slumped against him. "No, it hasn't." The pair sat in silence for a moment, their hearts' twin beatings slowing from a race to a crawl. Verve twisted her neck so she could look him in the face. "I did try some other magic before that. Just a little magic to move the kettle, and – I sloshed it everywhere, but—"

"It's all right." He pecked her on the cheek. "You don't have to confess to me. I'm not your minder." Fenn spoke as though he thought there was still some hurt on her part, and perhaps there was a sliver of it. After all, he had pressed her to let him use mastership magic, something that would have given him temporary control of her abilities to keep her, and others, safe. It might have worked, but she was no one's puppet. The disagreement was weeks ago, and he had apologized in more ways than one. He knew she did not do well when she felt trapped.

A confession hung on her lips, as it had every day for the past elf-night. Those five weeks had gone too fast, and she was running out of time to tell him that she must put herself in peril once more.

If Fenn suspected she kept a secret, he didn't say. Instead, he leaned back and closed his eyes.

Verve waited, listening to him breathe, before she stirred. He was currently powering around eight active spells, all of which drained on his energy and magic, and it would be best to let him sleep. But when she moved, he gripped her waist more tightly and his eyes opened.

"Trying to sneak off?"

"What?" She choked down a startled laugh.

Concern marred his features and then smoothed out, his lips lifting into a grin. "Would you care to hear my news? Or were you planning on setting fire to the kitchen first?" He tapped her teasingly on the nose, and she swatted his hand away.

"What's your news?" Verve squirmed in his arms, and after a moment he released her with a sigh. She sat on the cushion next to him and angled her body toward his. "Well?"

"I came upon five of Dacre's Trusted, all of them bewitched. He's giving out more power than he has in the past."

Verve frowned. "How do you mean? Did they attack you?" Verve took his hesitation as confirmation, and jumped to her feet.

"No harm came to me, Verve. They were simply more difficult to subdue than the others, that's all." His eyes followed her hand, which had gone to a strand of hair. "There's no need to pull out any of those lovely locks on my account."

That made Verve roll her eyes. "You should have taken me with you."

His eyes flashed, but when he spoke again he sounded calm. "Not yet. Someday soon, but you're not ready."

"Then let me give you some of my power. I have more than enough and it would help…" The words died on her lips as he shook his head.

"You will need all of your might if you are to face Dacre again. Don't waste it on me."

She stabbed her finger at him and triumphantly said, "Fire."

Fenn cocked his head to the side. "What do you mean?"

"You don't have fire. I could give you that." She clenched her teeth as he shook his head once more. "Or at least *some* of it."

"Verve—"

"Just a few drops. I won't miss it. I'm fit to burst with it, anyway."

He patted the cushion next to him, and when she didn't sit, he held out a hand for her. "I'm not saying I'm not thankful for the offer, but if you were to gift me fire, I could lose an ability I already have. Power usually balances itself out." He rose and kissed her hand. "No gifting magic, love. Please."

★ ★ ★

Later, after consuming a cold lunch, Fenn picked up his coat from the nail by the door. He'd said he hadn't needed it earlier, but the day now had grown cool and if a mortal spotted him, it would seem unnatural for him to be without one. "Would you care to go for a walk?"

Verve frowned. His words were softer than usual, and his eyes were underlined with bruise-like lines. "No, thanks."

Disbelief was written on his face. "It's a lovely day." Even as he spoke, he was obviously stifling a yawn.

"It's going to rain."

Fenn smirked. "Is that an actual prediction or are you just guessing?"

"Rain or not, I'd rather stay indoors today."

Whether he truly believed her or not, relief showed in his eyes as he hung the coat back in its place and ambled toward where she sat at the window, watching the wind pick up. It was mid-autumn now, and the trees were resplendent in their yellows, reds, and oranges. Here in Etterhea, the weather would be quite different from that in Letorheas, where the seasons were always spring or summer. Fenn had not mentioned returning there since Verve's narrow escape from Ithalamore, the Lands of the Dead.

"I think it might snow, actually," said Verve. She shuddered at the thought, her eyes drifting across the rows upon rows of trees that separated them from their nearest neighbors.

"You're making things up now." But he didn't push the issue any further. Instead, he stretched and moved toward the settee once more. Within the span of five minutes, Fenn had sat, picked up a book, and then fallen asleep.

Moving with care so as not to disturb him, Verve plucked a feather from her pocket, where she was always sure to have several tucked away, and transformed the plume into a blanket. The air filled with the smell of brown sugar, and she draped the material over Fenn's lap and up to his chest.

Fenn frowned and stirred slightly, as though he were having a troublesome dream.

Verve contorted her fingers and shoved a stream of golden light into his chest. "Sweet dreams only." She kissed the side of his head, and his face went slack, his breathing deeper. Satisfied, her steps took her toward the stairs; there were repairs to be made on the upper floor, and if she didn't make them, Fenn would expend what remained of his energy doing it himself.

A voice stopped her in her tracks. "What on earth?" She hurried toward the door as the talking grew louder, *angrier*.

"It's your fault, Verity Springer. You did this!" The voice belonged to Verve's youngest sister, Davinia. It sounded...different. Strange, even. But perhaps the girl had caught a cold or Verve's imagination was at play.

Without wondering how Dav had found her, Verve undid the many locks on the door and slipped outside. "Dav?" she called.

There was a mirthless laugh. "You are so careless. I knew you'd be the death of us all."

"I don't know what you're talking about," said Verve, running in the direction of the sound.

"Don't you come near me!"

Verve scoffed. "Dav, can we just talk for a moment? I can explain everything. Where are you?"

Dav began to cry. "W-was Helena your fault?"

That made Verve stop in her tracks. "It's not what you think." She spun around in slow circles, looking for where her sister was hiding. "Come out so we can talk."

Silence.

"Dav?" Verve shook herself and stepped into a clearing. "Davinia, you don't need to hide. I didn't mean to hurt anyone." All remained eerily still as she continued forward in search of her sister. Then she stopped and listened, trying to detect a human heartbeat. There was one, but it was on the neighbor's property.

A woman's scream filled the air, and Verve took off at top speed, dodging trees and leaping over bushes as she followed the terrified sounds. The human's heartbeat all but faded, and in its place was a giant thumping, like what one would imagine to be a giant's pulse. Verve covered her ears and stumbled to a stop.

Their neighbor, a woman Verve had only glimpsed from the safety of the protective bubble surrounding Fenn's cottage, lay on the ground, still. "Hello?" Verve asked. The loud thumping sound had ceased. "Ma'am, are you all right?" Wary, she approached the still form, laundry strewn about her. "Can you hear me?"

The woman did not respond.

A low growl reached Verve's ears, and as she stood there in stunned silence, she felt a hot breeze on her back, and something snapped at her.

With a cry, Verve spun around and came face to face with an enormous, scaled beast with wicked-sharp teeth and glowing orange eyes. It stood on two hind legs, towering over Verve as two leathery wings rose from its back.

Chapter Two

At last Verve recovered her wits and dodged the creature as it reached for her. A frustrated roar left her disoriented and unbalanced, and sharp claws tore into her.

Verve winced as silver blood dripped down her side. Trembling, she raised her hands and lobbed a fireball at the creature. The flames glanced off its scales and flew back toward Verve, who dove out of the way just in time, though the heat of her rebounded attack singed the hem of her skirt.

Yellow fangs were upon her, and Verve kicked one of them. Hot, golden liquid gushed out of the beast's mouth as the tooth broke, and Verve got to her feet, her body swaying and her head spinning from blood loss. Her wounds were already healing, but not as quickly as they normally would. Again she lobbed fire at the creature, this time aiming for its open mouth. Her shot did nothing but annoy.

The beast moved forward, its eyes flickering toward the neighbor woman lying on the ground near the clothesline.

"Oh, no you don't," Verve snarled, meaning to put herself between the monster and the defenseless mortal.

It was much quicker than Verve anticipated. Instead of reaching for the woman, it lunged forward, its long neck straightening to its fullest length, and its front claws grabbed Verve's right leg. Her femur snapped audibly, and her vision blurred as pain shot through her body. She screamed as the creature's wings unfurled and it carried her heavenward.

"Release her!" a fell voice called from below.

Something sailed past where Verve dangled, a metal arrow directed by magic. The missile struck the beast in the jaw, driving it wild. It shrieked and thrashed and came crashing back down to earth.

The last thing Verve saw before her head struck the ground was Fenn forming a magical lasso of light and casting it around the monster, who was attempting to right itself and continue flying off.

A metallic taste filled Verve's mouth. She had bitten her tongue. Her ears rang and her vision blurred while Fenn battled on. The monster's claws tightened around Verve's leg, and she lost consciousness for a moment. When she came to her senses, there was a deafening roar followed by a whimper, which gurgled in the creature's throat as Fenn pulled what appeared to be a spear from its neck. Perhaps for good measure, he thrust the weapon into one golden eye, and the struggling ceased entirely.

In the distance, cries arose. "How badly are you hurt?" Fenn turned his back on his kill and bent over Verve, his face ashen, his clothing coated in golden blood. He tapped her face lightly, as she had begun to slip away from him once more. "Stay awake, please."

Verve hissed through her teeth as she tried to sit up. Her leg was bent out at an odd angle and would not support her weight. The sight of it made her feel even fainter. "Mortals are coming," she said through her teeth. "Hide the carcass." She gasped as he slid his arms beneath her frame to lift her. The movement sent a shockwave through her body and she screamed.

At once Fenn set her back down. "Here." Ignoring the approaching cluster of people, he gathered gray-colored magic into the palm of his hand and shoved it through the skin of her forehead.

The pain in her leg peaked for a moment, and then disappeared entirely. She looked down at the appendage once more, thinking she had been healed, but that was not the case. A whimper escaped her as Fenn turned and sized up the gigantic corpse.

"I'll be a moment," he said. "I'll make you invisible, but you must remain silent. The villagers will blame any stranger they find for the state of things. Do you understand me?"

Verve nodded, and his expression softened. Before she could ask him how long he'd be gone, Fenn cast the magic at her, filling the air with the scent of limes, grabbed the monster's corpse by a leg, and dragged it with apparent difficulty toward their property. Through all this, the woman with the washing did not stir, though a steady heartbeat testified to her still living.

Fenn disappeared from sight not a moment too soon. Men and women from the nearby village arrived, rifles and axes in hand, as though they were ready to fight off an invading army.

"Antonia!" cried a man with a leather apron around his waist. He dropped the gun he carried and threw himself down next to the woman, who didn't stir.

While a few of the women tried to rouse Antonia, the rest of the villagers stared at the spot where the creature had lain but moments earlier. "What happened here?" was the question passed back and forth in worried whispers. A few men broke off from the group and crept into the woods surrounding them, their weapons at the ready. What they thought they'd find, Verve didn't know.

It took what felt like forever for everyone to finish searching the woods and tending to the unconscious woman. Several times, people came perilously close to where Verve lay invisible, but they changed course at the last moment as though repelled.

Finally, the scene cleared and the would-be hunters returned from the woods with confused expressions. They briefly stood conversing and then moved inside where the rest of the villagers had convened.

Fenn's heartbeat and breathing announced his return, though he had apparently cast an invisibility spell over himself as well. "I'm sorry I took so long," he said. Unseen arms slid beneath her frame and lifted her, causing no pain, thanks to the numbing magic he had given her.

Verve leaned her head against where she felt his chest, and they started moving. "What was that thing? A dragon?"

"A wyvern. They normally hunt in packs...but I don't sense any others nearby," he quickly added when Verve stiffened. "They won't be able to get onto our property, so don't worry about that." He tightened his hold on her and increased his speed. When they reached the boundary of Fenn's protective charms, he had to slow, as the magic was a physical force to fight against. It let them through and he ran her inside the house and bolted the door behind them with more magic. Only then did he lift the invisibility spells.

"Where did it come from? We're in Etterhea."

He set her down on the settee and hoisted up her skirts. "Sightings of them in the mortal realm are rare, which makes me wonder if someone bewitched it and sent it." His brow puckered as he felt her leg.

"What?"

"It's a bad break." He probed some more. "I've taken away the pain, but you're not going to heal quickly enough on your own."

Verve's lower lip trembled. "What do we do?"

"Hold very still and try not to breathe." First he straightened the appendage, which felt strange to Verve but not painful, since he had numbed her, then he rested both hands over the place where the bone had snapped. An expression of deep concentration crossed his face, and he closed his eyes.

There was the intense aroma of bergamot, and the spot glowed. Verve's leg grew uncomfortably hot. She tried to remain still but it was difficult, and holding her breath went against all her remaining human instincts, though she knew she could go without air indefinitely unless she needed to talk.

Finally, Fenn removed his hands and slumped backward. His eyes opened and she knew he was using through-sight to peer beneath her skin at the work he had just done. "Try moving your leg gently."

Verve did, and Fenn nodded. "Is it fixed?" she asked.

"Yes." He put a staying hand on her arm when she stirred, meaning to get up. "You shouldn't put any weight on it for the next three days at least. Your leg will be too weak to support you." Unsteadily, Fenn got to his feet and swayed for a moment before propping a pillow beneath her leg.

"What's wrong?"

Fenn shrugged, and the movement caused him pain apparently. "Just a little wyvern venom. It should wear off soon enough."

"You're hurt," Verve said, reaching for him. Indeed, looking more closely, she could see that some of the blood was silver and there were slashes through his clothing. "Can you heal yourself?"

He gave her a wry smile. "You mean speed up healing more than my body already does? That's not something many fae can do." His head cocked to the side and a slight frown formed on his face. "You weren't affected by the venom. Peculiar."

"Can I heal you?"

That gave Fenn pause. "I don't know if you have that ability. And even if you did, it's not a good idea to use so much power right now."

Verve scoffed, knowing full well that she did, in fact, have the ability. "Let me at least try."

For a moment, it appeared as though Fenn was going to say no. He opened and closed his mouth a few times, glanced at her leg, and then nodded. "You can try. But don't push yourself too hard, and if you feel weak or lightheaded at any point, stop." He moved closer, and Verve cringed as she took an even better peep at the wounds.

"Those seem infected already."

"They probably are. Magical wounds go bad quickly." The way he regarded her made Verve believe he was about to change his mind – stubborn, stupid man – so she quickly grabbed his hand and tugged him nearer.

"What do I do?"

His eyebrows rose. "You'll have to touch it." When she showed him no sign of changing her mind, he grimaced. "Imagine the wound ends coming together and flesh knitting itself back together."

"That's it?" she asked.

This made Fenn chuckle as he knelt. "It'll take more concentration and energy, but this type of wound doesn't require very complicated magic."

Verve reached a hand inside the tear of his shirt and found the biggest of the wounds, a jagged-feeling gash that was cold to the touch. "You'll tell me if it hurts?" She closed her eyes and prepared herself to perform the necessary magic.

His breathing hitched and Verve knew she was already causing him pain. "It'll hurt regardless. If you heal it, it will hurt. If it heals on its own, it will hurt as well." He sounded so casual about matters.

Without asking him if he was ready, Verve drew her feelings and magic together and gently fed them into Fenn's skin. The wound resisted at first, and Verve pushed with more force. Her hand grew hot, and his flesh warmed beneath hers. A sharp intake of breath made her open her eyes, and she gawped in horror at the burn mark on his abdomen. "Oh no!" she yelped. Her fingertips were still glowing. "I branded you."

"It's all right," Fenn said, sounding perfectly fine. Even as he stood, the angry mark faded. "That was good, Verve. Especially considering it was your first time performing that type of magic." With a flourish he drew the balled-up blanket from the floor and covered her with it.

Even with his reassurance, Verve thought she might be ill. "Where are you going?"

Indeed, her husband was already heading for the door. "I need to properly dispose of the creature's body and scout to make certain our hiding place hasn't been discovered." Fenn quickly shrugged on his coat and undid the locks on the door. "Please, stay where you are, no matter what."

It was a challenge to remain on the settee, but she knew he hadn't lied about her leg needing to rest. Still, she couldn't help but ask, "Are you certain...?" Her heart dropped when he shook his head.

"That bone will snap in two once more if you put your weight on it. This type of healing magic needs time to properly settle in." Perhaps seeing she was on the verge of panic, Fenn hurriedly crossed back to the settee and kissed her. "I'll be all right. Once I get back, I want to talk about what made you leave the property in the first place."

Verve scowled. "I heard Dav."

Fenn stilled. "You heard your sister?" He studied her, a frown forming on his face. "Did you find her?"

"No. But I think I know what's going on because...well, it happened once before." Verve expected him to tell her it could wait, that he had to leave that minute to secure the area. And while there was a definite air of desperation and concern about him, he instead pulled up a chair and sat in front of her.

"Tell me."

Where to start? She straightened a little and winced. Fenn's numbing magic was wearing off already and there was a dull throbbing in her leg where he'd healed it. "Before I left home, I was in the attic and thought I heard my family talking downstairs about wedding preparations for our neighbor. But when I went down, no one was there. I know it sounds stupid, but I don't think it was a fever dream or my imagining." She forced herself to meet his gaze and found him appearing thoughtful rather than doubtful.

"Had any of this already happened? Were you hearing things that had taken place earlier, perhaps?" He sounded hopeful. "It's not unheard of for a fae to catch echoes of the past. Rare, but not strange."

Verve thought back to that late summer's day and frowned. "I don't think so."

"What happened after you came down and found the house empty?" Seemingly lost in thought, he took one of her hands in his and rubbed circles over her knuckles with his thumb.

Memory fought her for a moment, and she closed her eyes, willing it to resurface. It wasn't like her, not being able to recall information… unless someone had tampered with her thoughts. "It's a little hazy, but I do remember going outside and losing control of my magic." She told him about collecting eggs from the henhouse, how she'd managed to accidentally break one and that it had cooked when it made contact with her flesh. "Then I went to the woods and the trees fell over. You called it an energy burst."

Fenn's eyes widened. "I don't remember you knocking over any trees. Was that when you met Dacre in the woods, pretending to be me?"

A reflexive growl arose from her chest, and Fenn dropped her hand. "Sorry," she whispered.

"No, it's all right. Did anything else happen?"

Verve thought for a moment. "Well, before you— I mean, before *he* arrived in your form, the trees righted themselves and everything went back to as it had been moments before."

"Erasure magic," said Fenn. "That is next to impossible to perform accidentally." He sighed. "It sounds like you were either growing in your powers or new ones were developing." Fenn squeezed her hand and rose. "I think your foresight is different than I first thought."

"How do you mean?"

He pulled the blanket up to her neck and propped a pillow beneath her head. "For one thing, it's audible only…for now, at least. Also, it seems like it's very much out of your control." Fenn pushed his chair back. "Your sister is going to return to your life sometime soon, that is for certain. We'll have to be on the watch for her." Now he made for the door.

"That's it?"

Fenn paused mid-step and turned. "We'll have to come up with a way for you to tell the present from the future. For now, while I'm gone, don't believe anything you hear alone. There should be something visual to back it up." He waved, and it was apparent from the tension in his shoulders and the drooping of his eyes that he was fighting exhaustion.

Still Verve didn't stop him, biting her tongue and offering a halfhearted wave in return as he slipped through the door using magic to bolt it behind him.

★ ★ ★

Fenn had been gone for five hours, and the sun was on its way down the horizon. Verve tried not to worry when five hours turned into six and six turned into seven, knowing well that he could take care of himself. *Unless he came across Dacre.* At length the notion caused her to gingerly sit up and pivot, touching her feet to the floor. Pain shot through her leg, up to her hip, and a whimper escaped her lips.

The hour was late. Darkness blanketed the land beyond the window, and the wind rattled tree branches against the siding. In the fireplace, the embers had long since died down to nothing, and the air in the room had a chill to it, one that might have bothered Verve, had she been mortal.

Terror wormed its way into her insides as something loud thumped against the wards surrounding their property. "Fenn?" she whispered.

There was a pause, and again something or someone struck the wall of power. At once a bolt of fire lit up the night, causing the dome-shaped wall to glow a sickly green. The glow faded and all was still once more. She didn't relax, however, but gathered magic into her hands and attempted to rise. Her leg buckled, but she merely shifted her weight to her good one and waited.

There was a heartbeat outside the door and some ragged breathing.

Verve's eyes went to the doorknob, waiting to see if it might turn, and she jumped with a yelp when there was one quick knock. There were no accompanying knocks informing her of Fenn and his condition. Instead, the locks disengaged and the door flew open, admitting Fenn, who had also drawn power into his hands.

"What's wrong?" he asked, his wild eyes sweeping around the room. He took a step closer, but stopped when Verve hissed through her teeth at him. "You shouldn't be putting any weight on that leg."

"Prove it's you," Verve snarled. She'd been tricked enough times by Dacre masquerading as someone else that she was not willing to take any chances.

Fenn or whoever he was quirked an eyebrow. "Can't you smell my magic?"

Verve shrugged and didn't let her own magic drop. "Residual bursts can change."

"True." He stopped his magic from flowing and slowly raised his hands. "Did something happen here?"

"Don't give me that. You attacked the shield and got through somehow."

The fae seemed puzzled for a brief moment before his expression darkened. "Someone tried to get through? When?"

She tried to hobble away as he approached once more, but the man was having none of that. Without using gestures to enhance his magic, he sent a wall of air at Verve, which lifted her off her feet and deposited her gently back onto the sofa.

Instinct took over and Verve set her magic free. It struck Fenn or the imposter in the chest, burning through his clothes and striking a hand-shaped mark on his flesh.

He yelped and yanked his shirt over his head. "Your aim is getting better," he said, his voice thick with pain. "Please, stay seated. I won't try to come near you again until you know it's me for certain."

Every muscle in her body tensed as he bent over, catching his breath apparently...or perhaps putting on a show of weakness to make her drop her guard. "What was the name of the first story I wrote when I was a child?" she asked. This had been a question Father had composed for her to use before.

Sweat rolled down Fenn's brow. "'The Felicitous Band'. May I approach?"

As she watched, his skin turned from angry red to bright pink before fading to pale white, all but for the handprint. She swallowed. "I'm so sorry, Fenn."

"Don't be." He let out a slow breath and approached her, limping. "I lost track of that particular ward and didn't know a breach had been attempted. It's good that you're wary." At once he was using through-sight on her leg, rechecking her femur. "All's well that ends well. But we'll need to move at first light."

Verve shifted as Fenn all but collapsed next to her. "Move?"

"First a wyvern finds us and attempts to snatch you up, then my ward is attacked? Someone knows we're here. We should return to Letorheas." He leaned against her and closed his eyes. "This much power being expended in Etterhea no doubt drew unfriendly eyes to us. My magic should be almost invisible when we return home."

"Just in time to turn around and leave again," she said, thinking of her impending trip to Ithalamore. She'd have to travel to it from Lovelourn, a treacherous island in Etterhea.

Fenn stilled. "What do you mean?"

Oh dear. "Nothing that we need to think about right now. What took you so long?"

"I had to dispose of the body so no mortal would come across it. Then I visited your family to renew their wards. I'm sorry it all took so long. But what did you mean about leaving?" His voice held a note of sorrow that did something unpleasant to Verve's insides. She'd run away before…not from him but toward a solution for her curse. Of course he would take this all wrong. When she took too long to answer, Fenn grasped her chin in his hand and gently turned her face up toward his. "You can trust me, you know."

Reluctantly her eyes met his and she lost all self-control. "When I was in Ithalamore, I had help breaking the curse. And they wanted something in return." She searched his face but found no clues about what he was feeling or thinking, so she continued. "Igraine was a potion-maker, see, and she can travel back and forth between the realms of the living and dead."

"I've heard of Igraine but had thought her to be myth," said Fenn. "What did she want in exchange for helping you?"

Verve swallowed hard. "Well, she made me promise to return to Ithalamore within six weeks' time."

Fenn's eyes shuttered but not before Verve could see the pain there. "For what end?"

"That part of the deal was more for me. She's going to let me see my father and Helena."

His hand moved to the base of her skull and he pulled her closer as though he was afraid of losing her. "But what did *she* want for *herself?*" When his eyes opened, they were lighter than she had seen them in ages, and she knew he was upset, though she could discern no other signs.

This was the part that had troubled Verve most, and she knew it would trouble Fenn even more. "I'm supposed to seek a man who stole her family's powers for himself."

Fenn stiffened. "That's why you asked me about siphons. Where are you to find this person and what then are you to do?" He released the back of her neck and leaned forward, placing his head in his hands.

"I don't know exactly where he is, but Igraine said it's been foreseen that I'll find him. Then I'm supposed to take his powers back and give them…to their owners. Are you very angry?"

When he sat up, surprise was written across his face. "No, I'm not angry, love. I'm just somewhat shocked." Despite what he said, Verve knew he was hurt.

She took one of his hands in her own and squeezed it. "I wanted to tell you ever so many times, but it never could come out. It figures that I'd ruin everything by saying it on accident."

"It's all right. I'm just glad I know now, before it's too late to do anything about it." Fenn got to his feet and turned to face Verve.

"Do anything about it?" she asked. "What is there to be done?"

Fenn stared at her, looking incredulous. "Well, Igraine might come seeking revenge when you don't return to Ithalamore, and I don't know what an undead being can do to a high fae, even one that is other."

"Fenn—"

"I'll have to research special wards and how they affect the non-living."

Seeing he was in denial or simply not understanding the way things were going to go, Verve got to her feet, putting her weight on her good leg, and held up her hands. "Igraine won't need to seek revenge. I'm returning to her."

His face went blank. "But there is no guaranteeing your safety if you return. You're going to have to break your word."

Verve tried reminding herself that he was simply concerned for her and not attempting to control her every move, but it wasn't easy. Fire licked at her fingertips, and she blurted out, "I don't think I can break my word."

Again he closed his eyes and shook his head. "You made a blood vow, didn't you?"

"Yes." When he shuddered, she reached for him. "It was the only way she was going to help me break the curse. Believe me, I wouldn't have done it if I thought there was another way."

"You should be sitting," said Fenn, lifting her into his arms. Instead of setting her on the settee, he carried her into the back bedroom and closed the door behind him with magic. He took his time in depositing her on the bed, being careful not to jostle her as he propped a pillow beneath her leg and then two behind her head. All the while he would not meet her gaze, paying attention instead to her thighs, her abdomen, and then her neck, which he stroked thoughtfully with his finger pads.

Verve shivered as he turned from her and moved toward the fireplace. "Aren't we going to talk about this?" She tried to sit up, but froze when he gave her a disapproving frown.

"Of course we will talk about things, but not when I'm so distraught." He offered her a weak half smile that did not meet his eyes, and set about building a fire.

"You're angry."

Fenn did not turn, nor did he stop working. "I— Yes, I suppose I am somewhat angry." Before she could open her mouth to reassure him, Fenn shook his head and sighed. "I don't like it when you put yourself in unnecessary danger."

Verve scowled at his back, her hands smoking. "It wasn't like I had a choice, Fenn. This was the only way to break the curse."

"But was it really?"

She groaned. "It was."

"You know this for certain?" Attempts to make a fire set aside, Fenn rose and turned. His jaw was tight, his eyes still lighter than they ought to have been. About him was the air of someone talking to a foolish child, and it set Verve's teeth on edge.

"You can't trust me to make my own decisions? Are you even on my side?"

"I would spill my blood for you, Verve."

"I don't want you or anyone to spill blood for me."

He ignored that. "I would give you anything you asked of me." Fenn moved in closer, his power making a soft thrumming noise, warning Verve that he was not entirely in control at the moment.

"Stop."

"You have my heart." Fenn pulled the blanket down so it pooled around her thighs. His hand came to rest on her breast, and he watched her closely with darkening eyes. "You have my life and my body. Make no mistake: I will never stop looking out for you, even when you try to push me away."

"I'm not trying to push you away," she spat.

"I will fight for you even when you won't fight for yourself. When you won't even think of your own good."

"I am thinking of *everyone's* good."

He cocked his head to the side, and his power's thrumming increased. "Are you?" His lips feathered hers. "If traveling to Ithalamore once more put all of humanity in danger, would you still do it?"

"I have no choice."

"If I had the means to sever your blood vow to Igraine, would you accept?"

Verve didn't get a chance to answer before his lips were on hers, silencing any arguments. The kiss was aggressive, angry. It brought her own temper to the surface, and her fingers sparked fire.

Fenn grabbed her hands and encased them in his own, smothering the flames. With apparent reluctance, he ended the kiss but didn't pull away when her arms encircled his neck. "You need to rest."

"I need you to believe in me."

Carefully he removed her arms from about him and pinned them to her sides on the bed. Once more his eyes lightened. He released her and stroked her cheek with the back of his hand. "Believing in someone does not require a person to sacrifice their concerns." Fenn kissed her on the brow, turned, and moved for the door.

"Fenn, please."

He stilled for a moment. "Give me time, Verve." And then he left.

Verve listened to him retreat abovestairs, tears prickling her eyes. *I'm right. I know I'm right.* Nonetheless, her lower lip trembled and she cried until she fell asleep.

Chapter Three

To her surprise, Fenn didn't avoid her for long, though he was quiet and thoughtful, and she didn't attempt to engage him but went back to sleep. When she awoke from a nightmare after a restless night, she found herself in Fenn's arms. She trembled and cried out as he stroked her hair. After that she lay quietly and waited for him to leave. It was another hunting day, after all. He would search for Dacre's Trusted to restore to their right minds, and she would go through her books and learn as much as she could about magic.

But first light came, the birds sang their morning songs, and still Fenn remained. When she at last stirred and tried to get out of bed, he held her closer and tightened his grip, so she stayed in his arms and attempted to ignore the pain in her leg.

Perhaps he sensed her discomfort after a while, or maybe he had forgotten about her injury until that moment, but whatever the case, Fenn swore softly and poured more numbing magic into her body. Even then he would not release her.

Verve pressed her hand over his heart. "I should get up." Her voice was rough and felt raw, and she knew she must have screamed more than she remembered.

"Aren't you tired? You hardly slept last night."

"I don't want to sleep any longer." Memories of the previous night's disagreement came back to her, and she suddenly wanted to be somewhere else.

Fenn ruined her discomfort by kissing her eyes closed. He rested his cheek atop the crown of her head. "Your dreams seem to be getting worse...not that you sleep much anymore." He sounded concerned and puzzled.

"How is your wound?"

"Healed, thanks to you." He squeezed her. "But I don't think I want to face another one of those creatures anytime soon." Fenn's hand rubbed soothing circles on her back. They lay there for a few minutes, his strokes becoming harder as her thoughts scudded here and there... until he said, "I've been thinking about our argument last night."

Verve tried to pull away, but he was having none of that. "I don't want to talk about it anymore."

Fenn rolled her onto her back and sat astride her, taking care not to jostle her bad leg. "I know, but we're not through."

Her eyes narrowed. "If your plan is to sit on me so I can't leave, you're mad." She watched in amusement as he chuckled.

"Yes, you could throw me across the room with a mere thought. I know. I'm not talking about forcing you to stay, because, quite frankly, I can't and would be foolish to attempt it." Fenn winked. "And it would hurt us both." He crawled off her, sat on the edge of the bed, and said to the wall, "I'm coming with you."

Dread dropped into her stomach and she sat up a little too quickly. The world spun around her. It was hypocritical of her, she knew, not wanting to allow Fenn to go with her, but the island of Lovelourn alone was dangerous enough, never mind what they might face in Ithalamore. While it was true that he had found her on the island and left unscathed, he had not been to the underworld, where she'd been assaulted by unfriendly spirits and forced into a cruel bargain with Igraine. She still hadn't told Fenn all of her experience, and she wasn't planning on reliving it for him or anyone anytime soon. A great shudder ran through her body as Fenn got to his feet and faced her.

"Your thoughts are very loud this morning, wife. What has you so troubled?"

She threw a pillow at him, which he caught with ease. "You know very well what. You've not been to the Lands of the Dead, Fenn. What if you don't come out again?"

At that his eyes sparkled. "It's not easy, is it?" He nodded at the wardrobe. "I'll help you dress, and then we must pack."

Verve groaned and sat up slowly. She wasn't eager to return to Letorheas. It still was so foreign to her, and its inhabitants were strange and dangerous. Besides, at least in Etterhea she could say she was in the same realm as her family.

"I'll be fine. I have you to protect me," he said, misreading her grumbling.

She looked at him to see if he was joking, but he seemed completely sincere. Heat traveled up her neck, and she knew her face was blushing furiously, but neither spoke of it as he helped her out of yesterday's clothes and into a brown dress he had made for her.

Then he carried her downstairs where he set her on the settee and next went about packing food in the kitchen. "Don't put weight on your leg, please," he said when she shifted.

"You might need help."

"I don't, as you know very well." He emerged from the kitchen with a large pack, which he handed to Verve before lifting her once more.

"What about the rest of the house?" Though she had only lived there with him for five weeks, it had begun to feel a bit like home. Her heart thumped painfully as he shook his head.

"I can remake most of what is here, but we'll have to burn what we cannot carry."

Verve stilled as he bore her through the front door for the last time. "Burn? Why?"

"Anything left whole might be used to track us. It's a rare fae talent, but I don't want to leave anything to chance." He stopped halfway down the path, turned, and whispered, "I don't have fire. Would you mind…?"

"The whole house?" She swallowed.

The look he gave her was full of pity, as if he understood that she had just begun to put down roots and he was now yanking them up. "Yes, love. The whole house."

After a moment of waiting, just to make certain he was in earnest, Verve raised her hand and directed her magic at the house. Instantly the little cottage caught fire, and smoke ascended into the sky. She thought he would turn then, not make her watch the destruction, but they remained until flames licked at the upper story and the structure creaked and threatened collapse.

Tears prickled at the corners of her eyes, but she fought them and forced herself to keep her gaze on the blaze. It was, after all, just a house, and could be replaced – *would be* replaced. Yes, a house, not a home. Home was where family was. That thought was not as comforting as it could have been, Fenn being the only family she was now in any form of communication with.

As the house came crashing down and the heat from the fire reached them at last, Verve turned her face away and closed her eyes, willing herself to sleep.

★ ★ ★

The gateway Fenn created brought them to a wood in Letorheas. A chill hung in the air, as if there had recently been a frost. It didn't bother Verve as it once would have, but Fenn shuddered and his muscles tightened.

"You've been away too long," he murmured, carrying her through the mist that clung to them.

Verve nearly choked. "This— this is *my* fault?"

He hushed her and quickened his pace. "Can't you feel it?" When she stared up at him, puzzled and quiet, Fenn nodded at the path ahead of them. "The land has been mourning the loss of its queen and the amount of power she took with her. The weather will grow warmer the longer you remain here."

"So, warmer for a week, then?" *Six days*, she amended in her mind.

Fenn shrugged but said nothing about the impending trip. Instead, he cleared his throat and veered to their left to avoid a fallen tree. He could have easily leapt over it, but Verve suspected he did not want to jostle her leg. "There is a house here, one that I think will avoid detection. There are mighty fae within ten miles in every direction, so any power we expend should seem normal to them. They'll just think it's each other's."

"But what about residual bursts?" She bit down on her lower lip as her leg throbbed, and adjusted the books she held on to so the weight was redistributed to her left side. If she complained, Verve knew they would stop, and that was something she didn't feel safe about, now that they were back in Letorheas. Indeed, there were many heartbeats, all belonging to fae, and residual bursts permeated the air, none of which she had smelled the likes of before: horehound, yeasty bread, roses, and thyme. The magic tickled at her nose and made her want to sneeze.

Fenn's pace picked up as he climbed a hill and a rickety shack came into view. "Not all fae can smell residual bursts, though they might pretend to. And before you ask, no one in the vicinity stands with Dacre."

"Then why are you so tense?"

Fenn's sigh rippled through her hair. "They're not exactly in support of the Rogue Prince either."

Ah, yes. Verve had almost forgotten Fenn's title among the fae who hated him and thought him to be a villain. She patted his chest absently as they reached the top of the hill and surveyed the site.

"Might I set you down for a moment? I need to create a protective boundary."

Verve nodded and was carefully deposited onto the ground. "Can I help?" She'd known before she asked what the answer would be.

"I'll set up a special boundary that masks your magic from the rest of the world. Hopefully my power will be enough to contain the signs of your own." He took a few steps away from Verve, raising his hands in the air before him as though he were resting them against a solid wall.

The thought of him creating and powering more wards made Verve shake her head, but she said nothing as he raised the magic around them. It erupted from his fingertips with a soft roar, and soon the air glowed bright blues and greens and purples while what one might describe as a giant soap bubble formed outward, encasing the hill on which their new residence sat. The air smelled potently of bergamot and limes, and Verve had to hold her breath as her throat began to burn.

Once he had finished creating the ward, Fenn staggered but caught himself from collapsing entirely. This ward must be more powerful than the others he had created. Breathing heavily, he sat next to Verve and took her hand in his as he lay back. His fingers were icy cold.

"You should at least let me power this," she said, gesturing around them. The ward had disappeared from sight, but it thrummed in time with his heartbeat and sang softly in the air.

Fenn yawned and peered at her through half-closed eyes. "We're not going to be here long. I can power it for six days." When she started to argue, his breathing slowed and his eyes closed entirely as he drifted off to sleep.

Gently so as not to disturb him, Verve pulled her hand from his. "Stubborn man." A blanket was easily conjured from a blade of grass, and she covered him before reaching into the sack of supplies and seeing what Fenn had deemed important enough to save. There were food supplies, of course, plus a parcel that Verve suspected to contain feathers so she could have something with which to practice more elaborate transformations. Beneath everything, what made up the bulk of the weight of the bag was a short stack of books, ones Fenn must believe them unable to find other copies of. Verve's hand hovered over them for a moment, as she made sure none of them were conveyable texts – books with magic that she could absorb by touching. None were, so she searched through what he had saved. One was a beginner's guide to magic, another, a study of Second Age prophecy, and the remaining five thin books were about the Lands of the Dead. Having no desire to think about that just then, Verve set the books down and rubbed her leg.

As if sensing her discomfort even in sleep, Fenn shifted beneath the blanket and reached out for something. Verve took his hand again and he relaxed at once and the line on his forehead disappeared.

★ ★ ★

Over the next two days, Fenn set about making the shack habitable. He used magic to stabilize the foundation and repair the sides; the whole structure was leaning something dreadful, and there was a large crack running through it all. Though he didn't say, Verve knew he was exhausted, which was perhaps why repairs were taking so long. She'd seen him put a house right with barely any effort before.

Verve had little choice but to watch him the first day, as her leg continued to ache and was still unable to bear her full weight. They slept that night under a roof riddled with holes, as Fenn hadn't the energy or strength to finish everything that day. Indeed, he had taken many rests and did not seem himself.

On the second day, Verve sat up in bed and was pleased to be able to move without too much pain. Cautiously she swung her legs so they were dangling over the edge of the bed. When her body didn't complain too loudly, she let her right toes skim the cold wood floor. As that caused no further irritation, she stood. A pain shot up her thigh, so she clenched her teeth and sat back down. Fenn had said it would take a few days for the healing magic to fully take hold, so she wasn't too surprised. But there were only four days left before she planned to leave. If she wasn't able to walk by then...

Fenn placed a hand on her shoulder and said, "How are you feeling today?"

Verve jumped, sending another jolt of pain through her body. "A little sore," she said through her teeth.

"Here, lie down." He helped her back into a reclining position and then gathered magic into his hand, which he pushed into her forehead.

At once the numbing magic took hold, and she nearly melted with relief. "Thanks."

He stroked her cheek. "You were having quite a nightmare earlier."

Verve frowned as the dream came back to her. It was much like the usual one she'd experienced since returning from Ithalamore: dead bodies strewn about, her sister dying, corpses dragging her down into a grave. But this one had had Igraine in it. The potion-maker had merely stared at Verve, her flaming eyes narrowed, as though she suspected Verve would break her promise.

Shaking the darker thoughts from her head, Verve lay back on the plump pillow Fenn had magicked the night before. "It was the same dream as usual."

He seemed concerned but didn't question her further. Instead, he surprised her by saying, "We need to have a plan for when you return to Ithalamore." He watched her as though he knew she meant to leave without him.

Verve schooled her expression, though she knew she was a terrible actress and would not fool her husband. "What is there to plan? I—Sorry, *we* go in, find Igraine, and then she lets me talk with my father and sister."

"But what about getting there? Lovelourn is riddled with snares." Indeed, when Dacre had dragged her there almost six weeks ago, the island had claimed several mortal lives. The humans had been turned into mindless slaves and were forced to clear the way for the would-be king and his company.

Verve shrugged. "Erecting shields around ourselves should work. It worked for Dacre."

Fenn studied her, his dark eyes probing. "And the hawthorns are giving you trouble, not wishing to make gateways. It's a good thing you have me to deal with the trees on your behalf." He said it so casually and yet Verve took it as a warning: he knew what she was planning and was trying to remind her of the benefits of having him along.

She took his hand and squeezed it. Perhaps she would have to leave sooner than she wanted. But if she wasn't better by the next day, she might have to reconsider things.

"I've been reading about the Lands of the Dead," Fenn said softly. "The Founts of Gain are down there."

A terse nod was all Verve gave him. That did not seem to discourage Fenn, as he continued.

"I doubt Dacre managed to absorb power from every one of the pools." He squeezed her hand with some force. "I am loath to mention this, but some schools of thought teach that the Fire Queen goes on to absorb even more power as she approaches her ascension to the throne."

Verve grew very still. What was he saying?

Fenn turned onto his side to face her and propped a hand under his chin. "I know you aren't going to like this, but I think it might behoove you to consider taking the remaining power for yourself."

The very thought was revolting. These so-called founts contained the magic that dead beings cast off before departing for the next life. She shuddered. "I'm just going there to see my family."

Fenn nodded, as though he understood, and said nothing more on the matter, though Verve could tell he wanted to press his case. With a grunt he sat up and got out of bed. "I should get started on the house. There's plenty more work to be done." He reached for a book on the nightstand on his side and handed it to Verve.

She frowned as she turned it over in her hands. It was *A Beginner's Guide to Magic*. "You think I should be practicing right now?"

"Your leg is almost healed, so I don't see the harm, as long as you remain seated today."

At that her heart leapt. "That's a relief," she said quickly. "It's been maddening sitting and watching you doing all the work." She opened to the page where someone had left off, the top corner folded over. It was a chapter on protective spells and how to cast them on others.

As Fenn started to get dressed, he said, "Perhaps you should study offensive magic right now."

"What? You mean attacking others?"

He shrugged into a short off-white tunic and went for a pair of tan trousers. "It can never hurt to know how to take the reins of a fight. Reacting comes naturally for you, but I've never seen you attack first." Fenn tightened his belt. "Not that I don't believe you can, but I want you to have the experience."

"I've attacked first." Her voice was soft, and she felt like throwing the book away from herself.

Fenn's eyebrows rose. He didn't say anything.

After a moment she conceded that it had been accidental. Not wishing to relive those moments of sheer devastation, Verve allowed her attention to return to the text in front of her.

"I'll be near if you need me." Quietly he slipped from the room.

For hours she studied as Fenn worked on the house. At one point he was on the roof, repairing the many holes that riddled its surface. He peered at her from his perch and apologized when he accidentally dislodged debris that rained down on her. The air smelled strongly of limes and grapefruit and other citrus fruits as he continued to labor.

Though she read a lot about magical theory, she couldn't apply what she had learned at the moment without a sparring partner. So she kept reading and picturing herself performing the tactics on the page. A few times her hands grew hot. She dropped the book when the pages began to smolder, and put out the fire she had started.

Fenn checked in on her at that point, a tray of late-morning breakfast in his hands. She hadn't even smelled food being prepared, nor had she realized how hungry she was. After thanking Fenn, she accepted the tray and tore into toasted cheese and a sausage link.

"How are you getting on?" He stared at the smudged and sooty blankets next to her, his brow furrowing.

Verve licked the grease from her fingers and shrugged. She suspected he knew. "Well enough. You can see what happened when I imagined the spell-work too intently."

He didn't chuckle as she thought he might but instead frowned. "I smelled the residual burst and wondered. Which spell were you focusing on?"

Though she didn't need to look, Verve thumbed back through the book and pointed at the page she had left off on. "Verbal commands and control." She did not like the thought of controlling others, though she had used the ability defensively several times now...twice on Fenn when they were at odds. Guilt tugged at her stomach, but she tried to ignore it. She might have to use control on him again, should he try to stop her from leaving for Ithalamore. Not a happy thought, that.

Perhaps Fenn was thinking along the same lines, for he held out a hand for the book. "Maybe you've taxed yourself enough for the day."

Her eyes narrowed, but she handed over the text anyway. She hadn't ever needed to verbally control anyone, didn't know such a way existed. Verbal spells were supposed to be easier than using natural methodology alone, which for her was bound to her emotions. Verve wondered if both used together, along with gestures, would be more effective, but she wasn't about to practice…or mention her idle wonderings to Fenn. "I think I'll go mad if I have to sit here with nothing to do the remainder of the day." She traced her fingers over the blanket's soot stains, which grew darker at her touch.

"Then perhaps you should exercise your leg a little. With some help, of course."

As she watched, he plucked a feather from the open slit in her pillow, closed his eyes, and conjured a walking stick from it, which he twirled once and handed to her. She grinned and scooted toward the edge of the bed.

"Don't overdo it, please. Just a few times around the house or else you risk further injury."

"Yes, doctor," she said, giving him a mock salute.

Fenn rolled his eyes but seemed amused. "If you feel any pain—"

"I'll sit right down and let you fuss over me." Without waiting for a response or any more instructions, Verve dangled her legs over the edge of the bed and let her feet come to rest on the floor. Carefully she put her weight on her left leg and pulled herself to a standing position, her right leg bent so that just her toes skimmed the boards.

"If you have trouble with the stairs, just let me know."

In total, she took twelve laps around the house, at first putting a minimum and then a moderate amount of her weight on the healing leg. It hurt, but not too severely. Nothing like it had that morning. If she was healing at the rate she believed herself to be, she should be well enough to travel a-ways the next evening. But Fenn wasn't to know that.

Chapter Four

The next day, as Verve again walked around the house, her leg perfectly healed, Fenn watched her the entire time. He intercepted her when she feigned tiredness and entered the house, taking the walking stick from her and then carrying her into the sitting room, where he deposited her on the chaise longue by a roaring fire.

Verve thought he would surely return to his work on the house, but he surprised her by picking up a book on the Fire Queen, one she hadn't realized he had, and sat with her legs propped up across his lap. Though he seemed intent on what he read, Verve knew he wasn't normally this slow a reader. Each page turn came two minutes apart, and she sensed he was watching her from the corner of his eye. What had she done to arouse his suspicion?

"Do you need something, or am I particularly interesting to watch this afternoon?" He didn't look up from his book as he spoke, his lips twitching upward.

She leveled a teasing glare at him. "Your book's upside down."

"No, it is not." He flipped another page and sighed. "Is something the matter?"

Verve shook her head. "Not really." Perhaps she had been imagining it, his suspicion. Maybe she needn't worry.

As if in answer to her silent musings, blue wisps of light started to leak out of Fenn's pores, his mouth, his eyes. The emotions – for that is what Verve knew them to be – swirled around her husband's body faster and faster, and Verve longed to pluck them out of the air and devour them.

What had her deceased friend called her? *Grief-eater.* But she wasn't supposed to be able to see fae emotions, let alone consume them as fuel for future magic-working. If Fenn found out, his concern, the emotion he was emitting right then, would increase tenfold, so she resisted the urge to consume it. It wouldn't have hurt Fenn. In fact, it would have rid him of the feelings temporarily. With great effort, she tore her gaze away and studied the fire, which leapt at her attention.

Fenn seemed to have lost interest in pretending to read, as he set the book aside and took to rubbing her feet. "I'm going to visit your family tomorrow."

Her eyes widened at that but she said nothing. Fenn had just been to see her family.

"Would you like to come with me?"

She wouldn't be here for that to happen. Did he know and was baiting her? "Wouldn't that be dangerous?" Verve was relieved to see the light had ceased to pour out of him.

His hands traveled to her calves. "You're no longer cursed," he said, "and you've been calmer these last few weeks."

"Except when I lit the upstairs on fire."

A low chuckle rumbled in his throat. "Well, yes, but I wasn't there. I think if we went together, and you let me help you mind your magic, it would be safe." His brow puckered as he traced a finger up to her thigh almost absently.

"Will I be able to walk well enough then, do you think?"

He peered at her from the corner of his eyes. "Why don't you tell me?"

Verve's throat went dry. But before she could open her mouth and lie, Fenn moved out from under her legs and lifted her. "What are you doing?"

The grin he gave her was positively wicked. "Let's retire early tonight." He carried her up the stairs, which he took two at a time.

"The sun's still out."

"It won't be for long."

Her heart began to race as he laid her on the bed. "I'm not tired," she protested.

Fenn closed the drapes, and they were plunged into semidarkness. "I'll take care of that."

* * *

Hours later, she drowsed with Fenn at her side, his arms wrapped protectively around her. Lying there, she felt content and boneless and unwilling to move more than a little finger.

It was dark out now. Wind stirred the tree next to their window, its branches grating against the windowpane. Fenn was deeply asleep now, his breaths slow and even, and his arm atop her a deadweight.

For a while she considered abandoning her plan. After all, they were new to each other, and trust was still being built. If she left him in the middle of the night, what would that do to their relationship? But then she reminded herself of the perils of Ithalamore, of the dead she had heard fighting Dacre, and she knew she could not in good conscience allow Fenn to subject himself to that. So, hardening her heart, Verve tried to ease herself out of Fenn's arms, which at once tightened around her.

"Fenn?" she whispered. "I'm going to get some water. Will you let me up?"

He didn't stir or make any noise acknowledging her words. But when she moved a second time, he relaxed and relinquished his hold.

Verve moved to the end of the bed and waited five beatings of her heart before reaching for the pitcher on the table next to her bed and pouring herself a glass of water. She drank for the charade's sake, in case he was truly awake.

The bed creaked behind her, and Verve looked over her shoulder just as Fenn rolled onto his other side. He sighed after a moment, but his breathing soon grew deep and even once more.

Wasting no time, Verve lowered herself to the floorboards, which groaned ominously. She hardly dared breathe. There was no time for inching her way through the room, and she couldn't risk magic, lest he smell the residual burst and for certain know something was amiss. So instead, Verve whispered, "I'll be back." A truth, if a misleading one. She was hating herself more and more with each passing moment.

Fenn was silent. Verve crept out of the room.

The stairs were loud, but Verve managed to descend them without being caught. She hesitated at the door, wondering if she was mad to be doing this alone. *Don't be selfish.* With that thought, she clenched her teeth and left the house. The well-oiled hinges made nary a sound as she opened and shut the door.

In the dim light of the sister half moons, Verve paused and took in her surroundings. The cobbled path before her was exposed, and the nearest bit of cover was ten yards ahead. Where she stood now, Fenn would not be able to see her, should he peer out a window. One step farther, and she was committed to running, something she hadn't been able to test her newly healed leg on.

An owl hooted, spooking her, and she took off into the night. Verve stopped when she reached the nearest tree, waiting, watching the house for any signs of life. All was silent. She moved forward once more, careful not to disturb the brush surrounding her. Heart pounding in her ears, she darted behind another tree and waited. The ward Fenn had erected was a few yards away, invisible but pulsing gently. She could only hope he hadn't added any special touches, such as an alarm that would alert him to her passing through it.

A moment was all she had the patience to wait before launching herself toward the barrier, which pulled at her as she struggled through it. Coaxing whispers reached her ears, coming from the ward. "Stay," they purred. "You don't need to be alone." Verve ignored them and fought until she was finally free.

She stumbled as though invisible hands had reluctantly yet suddenly relinquished her. Then she ran like the devil was on her trail.

At first she was certain she had made it, having heard nothing pursuing. She was fast. Speed was something the Cunning Blade had gifted her when she had accidentally touched it and absorbed its powers all those months ago. But Fenn was fast, too, and soon she was aware that he was behind her. No...not behind her. To her right? Before she could orient herself, he sprang into her path and grabbed her in what would have once been a bone-breaking embrace.

Verve screamed in surprise and rage, until she had the sense to be silent. Quietly, then, she swore at him.

Fenn laughed. "That misguidance hex worked well."

She would have given him a shove, but he had her arms pinned tightly to her sides. "I can't hear you. What did you do?" Verve had meant she couldn't hear his heart or breath.

Fenn stared at her uncomprehendingly for a moment before saying, "Dacre isn't the only one who can silence his heart's beatings." His grip on her tightened, and she knew she would have trouble throwing him off without hurting him, so she didn't try. In the dimness, his eyes glowed like a cat's. "You didn't actually think I would let you go by yourself, now did you?"

She hissed at him, but he simply considered her as an eagle might its prey. "You're going to put us in danger if you show up with me. Igraine isn't expecting anyone else."

He shook his head, reeling her in toward himself after she momentarily broke his hold. "You really are a terrible liar." The grin he gave her was lazy, confident, and it made Verve want to lash out, something she suspected he was waiting for. When she didn't erupt, Fenn held her close and stroked her hair. "Good. You can't afford to lose control in Ithalamore." After a moment, he loosened his grip, allowing her to adjust to her freedom, only to seize her left hand in his right.

Verve seethed but said nothing about his crushing grip. It didn't hurt, after all, and was only a nuisance. "You really want to go with me to Ithalamore?"

"With you I'd go anywhere." He said it with such sincerity that Verve couldn't tease him. "We shouldn't remain in the open for much longer. I don't fear our neighbors but I don't trust them either." Fenn pulled her along behind him as he looked the trees up and down. Upon coming across a hawthorn, he placed both of their hands against the bark and, much to Verve's surprise, the tree split down the middle into a gateway without asking anything in return. Fenn seemed just as puzzled but didn't question it.

Verve struggled against Fenn as he pulled her through the gateway, but her heart wasn't in it. Guilt tugged at her as they emerged into the dimly lit woods of Lovelourn. How the tree had known to bring them here, she couldn't say. She didn't trust it. "Wards," she murmured, and at once Fenn let one ensconce them. The air filled with the smell of lemon, and the orb surrounding them glowed once before growing invisible.

As the gateway shut behind them, the trees on the island reached for the protective sphere, but pulled away at the last second before they could make contact. One tree branch misjudged its closeness and disintegrated at first touch, filling the air with the smell of burning campfires.

Fenn exchanged a glance with her and they moved onward.

"There was quicksand inland," said Verve. She ducked instinctively as another branch reached for them.

"I encountered it when I came for you." He squeezed her hand and pulled her around a stump. "Tell me about Ithalamore."

Verve swallowed. Hard. "You saw Death's Maw." They leapt as one over a fallen log and landed silently on a patch of thorns, which glanced off their bubble harmlessly. "I-I had to kill a fae to get through it."

"You didn't kill the fae, though, I imagine." His thumb stroked the back of her hand reassuringly, and she silently blessed him for thinking the best of her.

"Dacre used mastership magic to force me to – well, you know."

Fenn swore and stopped her mid-step. "I'm so sorry, Verve."

She shrugged and tried to act nonchalant, though her insides writhed at the memory. "What's done is done. Besides," she said, blinking away tears, "it's not like I hadn't killed before."

He surprised her by pulling her into his chest and embracing her hard enough to drive all the air out of her lungs. "We don't have to go to Ithalamore. We can find a way out of your bargain."

Verve hung her head, and Fenn pulled back to study her. She sniffled. "No, I need to do this. I promised." Her eyes bored into his, and she prayed he would understand somehow, that he wouldn't attempt to hinder her. The thought of having to fight him was not one she relished.

Thankfully, Fenn nodded, released her from the embrace, and led her toward the sound of the roaring sea. "Once you were in Ithalamore..." He grew silent and waited for Verve to find her voice and continue.

"Once I was in Ithalamore, Dacre tied me to a pillar, cast a protective ward, and went to the pools. I didn't see him until after he had taken on more power, but I could tell he had absorbed quite a lot." Now they emerged onto the beach, whose sands were blood-red. The air held the tang of briny water and fish, and Verve wrinkled up her nose as they continued hand in hand.

"Did you encounter any of the dead?"

Verve nodded without looking at him. "Mm-hmm. Two of them attacked Olive and me. The other was Igraine, who gave me the potion to help break the curse." Staring ahead in the early morning light, she could make out the form of Death's Maw, a black beacon of a tree reaching high above the others. She shuddered at the sight.

"Olive was Dacre's servant, yes?"

"And my friend," Verve said more sharply than she had meant to. Her throat was beginning to tighten with stress. Mercifully, Fenn asked no more questions, though his eyes were brimming with them.

They encountered no traps and there were no more attacks from the trees the nearer they came to Death's Maw. Verve's breathing became shallow and uneven, and Fenn murmured a few reassuring words that were lost on her.

"We'll get in, see your father and sister, and then leave. I'll keep watch and power a ward around us the entire time."

She wasn't entirely certain a ward would keep out the dead, but she said nothing as they quickened their pace down the beach and soon entered a copse of trees. After five minutes of walking, the copse opened into a clearing, in the middle of which sat the base of Death's Maw. All had gone deathly still but for the now-distant roar of the sea. It was as though the land were holding its breath, waiting to see what would happen next.

The sight of the enormous tree rooted Verve to the spot while at the same time made her want to flee, to forget about Father and Helena and her deal with the potion-maker. Only Fenn at her side kept her calm, and after a moment of hesitation, she took several large strides toward the hawthorn.

She placed her hand against the smooth, cold bark, and the tree growled before saying, in a deep voice, *"Greetings to you and yours, Firstblood of No Land."*

Verve looked at Fenn for encouragement, but when he offered none and stared darkly at the hawthorn, she said, "We wish to pass into Ithalamore." She swore there was laughter echoing in the back of her mind. Her hair stood on end as the tree seemed to inhale.

"Are you certain?" Fenn asked.

What sort of question was that? Of course she wasn't certain, and yet… "Allow my husband and me safe passage to the Lands of the Dead."

Without further hesitation, the tree groaned and creaked, parting into two pieces, its branches furling overhead to form the topmost part of the gateway. The land beyond was pitch-black, just as Verve remembered it.

She tugged Fenn in behind her, ignited a ball of glowing light in the palm of her free hand, and sent it ahead of them to illuminate the way. One step in and the gateway closed behind them.

At once Fenn strengthened the shield around them, and the cave smelled of his magic. "How far in did you go?" His voice echoed off the walls, and Verve hushed him.

"A room or two over. I doubt Igraine will be hard to find, even though I'm early." The potion-maker had found her and Olive an hour or so into their wanderings that fateful day, as though she had sensed their presence and had been drawn to it. Verve moved on ahead, keeping Fenn close by her side.

They walked in silence for half an hour without disturbance, though there were moans and wails in the distance behind them. As she prowled, Verve felt a prickle at the base of her skull, a sensation like someone was watching her from behind. But when she looked, no one was there. Perhaps she was just being fanciful, or perhaps the dead could make themselves invisible and were watching Fenn's and her progress. Whatever the case, no one stopped the couple as they continued their trek.

After what might have been an hour of walking, the caves grew suddenly cold. Fenn pulled her closer. Through his shirt, she could feel his heart racing against her back. Her own pulse thundered in her ears as the light she had created fizzled and died entirely.

"I don't like this," said Fenn. He turned them in circles, as though he was searching for the source of his discomfort and not finding it.

A breeze blew at them, raising Verve's hair and tugging at her nightgown's hem. She barely dared to breathe as the breeze became a gale and lifted her off the ground.

Fenn pulled her down, though he seemed to be having trouble maintaining his footing. "We should leave."

"No," said Verve above the din. "I have to see this through." As if in response to her words, the winds instantly ceased, and the temperature dropped further still.

Verve shivered when a woman's low voice said, "So, the Fire Queen has returned to Ithalamore, just as she promised." A blue light flared to life not six feet from where Verve stood wrapped in Fenn's arms. Igraine's flaming eyes flashed in their sockets, and her ebony hair blew out behind her. She approached.

Fenn bared his teeth, and the woman stopped, amusement written on her face.

"I do not wish your mate harm, Rogue Prince," she said. "You may let her come forward without fear."

Fenn didn't seem to believe Igraine and tightened his hold on Verve, who attempted to gently extricate herself from his arms, only to be nipped on the back of her neck. He actually dared to growl at *her*, a warning not to move.

Igraine smiled at Verve, all teeth. "Very well. I see where things stand." Her voice brimmed with laughter that raised gooseflesh all over Verve's arms. How could she have forgotten how terrifying Igraine was?

Finding her voice at last, Verve said, "I'm here. Where are my father and sister?"

"All in good time." Igraine flicked her wrist, and a mirror the size of Fenn's chest materialized and hovered in the air before them. The glass showed Verve's face and left out Fenn entirely, something that made Verve instantly uneasy. "What you are going to see is an echo from beyond this world." Igraine stepped back and the image in the mirror clouded over, and Verve's face disappeared altogether. A swirling mist filled the frame, and Verve found herself attempting to lean forward, only to be jerked back violently by her husband. "He is right to restrain you. Do not disturb the glass."

"What do you mean by 'an echo'?" asked Fenn.

Igraine stared at him with her fathomless eyes and folded her hands together in front of her waist. "It was truly impossible to bring her father and sister hence. Once you pass to the next life, there is no turning back."

"You promised I would see them!" Verve struggled all the more against Fenn, rage boiling in her veins.

So strong was she that Fenn was forced to use power against her, freezing her in place. "Careful," he whispered in her ear as she fought to break the magic restraining her like a leash.

"See them you shall," said Igraine.

Tears rolled down Verve's cheeks and she glared at Igraine, who regarded her with pity. "Will they be able to hear me?" She gave Fenn a withering glare as he continued to physically and magically hold her in place, but she ceased fighting him.

Igraine dipped her head. "It will be as though they are here with you. But whatever happens, do not touch the glass."

"What will happen if I touch the glass?"

The look Igraine gave her was disapproving and for a moment she seemed unwilling to answer. "You would bind them both to your being. Their essences would be sucked from their souls and they would be forced to wander everywhere with you, unable to rest, unable to find comfort. You would become their tormentor and the very bane of their nonexistence."

Verve flinched and her eyes shifted once more to the swirling mist in the mirror. That was not something she wanted for Father and Helena. She truly missed them to the point of pain, but forcing them to return to dwell in that state? At length she nodded. "I will not touch the glass."

Behind her, Fenn relaxed, if only a little. He shifted his weight, and the shield around them flickered.

"You will not be able to use the mirror properly if you are shielded," said Igraine. "Physical magic impacts spiritual magic in a negative way."

For an agonizing moment he stood there, unmoved and apparently unwilling to let the protective shield drop. But when Verve sniffled softly, he sighed and let the magic holding her and powering the shield go. "Keep on your guard." He loosened his hold on her but did not let go entirely.

"What must I do?" She kept staring into the mirror, waiting for something to happen.

Igraine held up her hands, palms facing outward. "Patience is the key. I'll power the mirror, and all you need to do is keep your eyes fixed on the images you see. Blink, and they are unlikely to reappear once fully formed."

In the near distance, Verve swore she heard a pebble roll across the ground. Fenn must have heard it, too, for his head jerked around. "What was that?"

"Fenn," Verve breathed. The fog in the mirror cleared and Verve could make out the distinct outline of Father's face, which slowly filled in. She didn't dare blink, nor did she dare move.

"Someone else is here, Verve," Fenn warned. "I'm putting the shield back up."

"Once it is severed, I won't be able to form another connection," said Igraine. "For what it's worth, I've had my ladies standing guard in the outer sanctum. No one should have been able to get past them."

"Verve, if you're going to talk to your father, make it quick. This feels like a trap."

Without having to look, Verve knew Igraine's eyes had flashed in Fenn's direction. Verve ignored them both, focusing on the image of her father, which was beaming at her. "Father?"

"Hello, my bright and lovely girl."

The urge to run to him nearly overcame her, but Verve stopped herself at the last second, remembering Igraine's dire warning. "Are you all right?"

His eyes twinkled. "Why, yes, I believe I am. But, Verve," he said, his tone sobering, "why are you disturbing me from my rest? It's good to see you, don't get me wrong. But this is not natural."

At his words, Verve's face burned with shame and her heart ached. "How else was I to ever see you again?" It took all of her self-control not to let tears fill her eyes.

Father gave her a knowing look. "You won't be joining us in the ever after, I gather."

She shook her head. "No, I don't believe so. Is Helena there?"

"Yes, and she is whole. She doesn't blame you for what happened, my dear child. You need to be gentler with yourself." He reached forward as though to pass through the glass, but his hands stopped short.

Fenn was now practically vibrating with agitation. "Verve, love, I can feel another's power down here. I'm going to raise the shield now."

"No!" Verve screamed.

Before Fenn could do as he had said, a bolt of magic rent the air, striking Igraine, who at once vanished, along with the mirror. Another bolt struck Fenn, causing him to double over, writhing in silence on the ground.

Verve spun around, raising a shield to cover herself and her husband, but an invisible force tore it down the middle, as though it were a paltry piece of paper. She dodged a fork of golden light meant for her and quickly raised another shield, which was also torn apart, so she lobbed fireballs in the direction she assumed the attacks were coming from.

"Verve, run." Fenn's words were tight with pain, and he collapsed in another fit of agony.

But Verve wouldn't leave him there, so instead she placed herself between Fenn's prostrate form and the invisible attacker. "Show yourself, coward."

An amused chuckle rippled through the darkness and the attacks stopped. "Oh, Verve. You left me here when you could have simply killed me. Who is really the coward between us?" Dacre's voice was everywhere. It filled the room, her mind, her soul.

She whirled around in circles, trying to locate the source as she drew power into her hands. "Enough of your games."

"Let me have my fun," he whispered into the nape of her neck, and kissed her there.

Verve brought back her elbow fast and with force, connecting with his stomach before Dacre could move.

There was a grunt followed by another laugh as he materialized in front of her. "Temper, temper." He looked her up and down, whistling. "You're just as lovely as I remember."

Suddenly, Verve wished she'd worn more than her nightgown during her flight from the cottage. She didn't dwell on that regret for long. Drawing more power into her hands, Verve was prepared to incinerate Dacre should he make one move toward her and Fenn.

Fenn finally seemed to be recovering, as he got onto his hands and knees and managed to pull himself up next to Verve. "Run," he urged into her ear, just a soft whisper. "The world needs the Fire Queen."

"Yes, it does," said Dacre, rolling his eyes. "I'm not going to harm her."

"I'm sure you wouldn't mean to," said Fenn. "But you've done enough damage already."

At that Dacre flinched ever so slightly, though it might have been a trick of Verve's eyes. He chuckled and lashed out without warning, pinning Fenn to the ground by the throat in one swift movement.

Verve attempted to pull him from Fenn, but the fae was too solid, too strong. She cursed at and kicked him, but Dacre didn't budge. "Stop!" she shrieked. When he did not, Verve threw herself on Dacre's back and tried choking him in turn.

Dacre reared back as she allowed fire to fill her hands, which she closed around his throat, but he merely shook her off as if she were a flea.

She hit the cave wall and all the air left her lungs in one great rush. Stars swam in front of her eyes, and she saw double as Fenn struggled to reach her only to be struck with a bolt of silver light and then lie still.

"Are you all right?" Dacre asked as he approached Verve, his face paling. "I didn't mean to hurt you." He peered over her shoulder and crouched.

Verve didn't have to look to know she had left a large dent in the wall. She whimpered as he stroked her face, and she tried to pull away. "Why can't you leave us alone?"

Dacre cocked his head to the side. "You and the Rogue Prince? Verve, he's dangerous. I've been trying to save you from him this whole time, and you haven't let me." His hand hovered over her heart and he produced an orb of golden light, which he let drift down toward her bare flesh. "No, don't move. You hit your head very hard, I fear. This will help with the pain."

Though Verve's head felt as though it had been cleaved in two, she still was thinking clearly and she knew the orb was not for her pain. The magic felt…wrong. "Get that away from me." She struck out with power, only to miss and find herself pinned beneath Dacre's weight.

He held her hands above her head and stared deep into her eyes. "Don't fight it, Verve. We're meant for each other."

The orb's glow brightened further still and it hovered just inches above her heart. "I hate you." She kicked and she writhed, but to no avail.

Dacre watched her hungrily as the orb touched her flesh. "Just a few more moments, and you'll be mine."

"I'll never be yours." But the words sounded too much like a question to her ears, and she slowly relaxed as more of the spell seeped into her skin.

He leaned down and kissed her softly. The orb was perhaps half-submerged into her flesh when the air grew unbearably cold. Dacre froze, his lustful eyes hooded.

Sense returned to Verve in that moment and she managed to break his hold on her wrists and shove him off of her. The orb had vanished, and Dacre remained unmoving.

"You don't have much time, child," Igraine warned. She sounded out of breath.

Verve spun around at the sound of Igraine's voice. "You're hurt."

Igraine shook her head. "He should not have been able to maim me, but he is more powerful than I had thought possible. Holding him is – difficult." She bared her teeth, wincing with the apparent effort it took to keep Dacre still.

Verve raced to Fenn and attempted to lift his still form, but magic struck her in the shoulder, causing her to drop him.

She cried out in pain as Igraine shouted, "Run, Your Majesty! If he catches you now, we're all doomed." With that said, Igraine turned all her attention back to Dacre, who was rising, his eyes darkening with rage. Igraine threw up a shield between Verve and Fenn, which sent Verve sailing backward into the wall opposite the one she had already struck. This time, she managed to cushion the impact by creating a wall of protection between herself and the rock, glancing off it with a weak grunt.

Igraine kept Fenn and herself shielded. "Run, fool girl."

Verve drew as much power into her hands as she could before releasing it in a wave of pure devastation. The blinding typhoon of magic ripped through Igraine's shield and moved for Dacre, who hastily erected a shield of his own.

He shouted a warning before Verve's own power rebounded and drove her clean through the cave wall behind her and into the next chamber, where she lay dazed and unable to draw breath. Pain seared through her limbs, and she wondered if her leg had been broken again. Blood clouded her vision, and she blinked furiously. Ears ringing, she attempted to right herself.

"Verve!" Dacre shouted as flashes of light filled the darkness. He was still fighting Igraine...fighting and winning.

Igraine formed shield after shield, which Dacre tore through again and again, drawing closer by the second. Helpless on the floor in the midst of the battle, Fenn did not stir.

Verve mustered what strength she had left and pulled herself to her feet. Her leg was not broken, it would seem, as it supported her weight without buckling. She raised her hands and gathered magic into them as she stepped forward, stumbling over collapsed rocks in her path as she went.

Igraine turned her attention to Verve and their eyes met across the way. The woman jerked her head to the left once, twice, and then she disappeared in a flash of gray light, which hid Dacre from Verve's line of sight.

"Careful where you walk," said Dacre, his voice a thunderous boom. "I'll come and help you." He cursed the haze surrounding them, and Verve knew this was her only chance to make a move.

She stumbled in the direction Igraine had gestured toward, hoping it was a clear path to reach Fenn. The ground beneath Verve shook, causing her to lose her balance and pitch forward into a hole wide enough to swallow her. It narrowed as she fell. Supernatural reflexes allowed her to react and catch a lower edge of the pit by her nails, where she hung, struggling to bring herself up.

Then Dacre was there, reaching down toward her, several orbs of orange light illuminating him. "Take my hand."

Verve glared at him.

Dacre rolled his eyes. "Don't be foolish, Verve. That hole could lead anywhere."

She could have flown but for Dacre blocking the mouth of the hole. He would no doubt snatch her as she attempted to soar past. Calm came over her. The rock beneath her fingertips grew slick and she slid until she was clinging by only one hand. If he caught her... No, she wouldn't think of that.

"Verve!" said Dacre, his eyes bright with panic. "Just wait a moment. Hang on with everything you have. I'm coming down."

That was all the incentive she needed. There was no way up, only down, so she relinquished her hold on the crevice and plummeted. Dacre screamed her name as she was gobbled up by the darkness.

Chapter Five

For hours Verve tumbled. Many times she tried controlling the downward spiral, attempted to use her gift of flight so that she might hover, wait Dacre out, and then return to Ithalamore once he was no longer blocking the hole. But it was not to be. There was a pull stronger than gravity, almost magnetic, that drew her toward it. Soon up became down, down became up and she screamed in frustration as she tried to grab at the walls, only to be knocked about.

The way was pitch-black for most of her fall, but after what felt like ages the world below – or was it above? – began to lighten. Droplets of glowing water brushed against her as she rushed past, soaking her through and chilling her to the bone. Cold she hadn't known since her mortal life overcame her, and she was wracked with violent shivers. *This pit must have an end.* She kept reassuring herself that she could not fall forever. The notion – for she knew too little of magic and other realms to be certain – soothed her, until she thought of what a messy end it would be. *I may be immortal, but every bone in my body is going to shatter when I finally reach solid earth.* She closed her eyes against a sudden blinding brilliance.

Her descent slowed. It felt as though she were being yanked in two different directions, two sets of giant, invisible hands warring over possession of her body. Verve struggled against them to no avail. She was frozen in the ether, floating in an unnatural blue twilight.

All had been silent until this point, but for her own racing heart and her occasional scream. Now there were many heartbeats and the sound of voices. Few words were discernable, except for, "Move!" shouted by a male voice, followed by, "Get the net." There was the sound of footsteps running away and then returning, and Verve waited as her eyes tried to adjust.

The shapes above were dim silhouettes against a cloudy sky. She tried to reach for them, but they were too far away. "Help," she said, though the words were raw and rough.

"Where's the net?" asked the same impatient voice she had heard moments before.

"Sorry, Rillian." It was a woman who had spoken.

Verve tried swimming toward them, only to feel that pull drawing her back downward. Frustration overcame her and she attempted to fly. A shooting pain went up her spine, and she bit down a scream.

"Don't struggle!" shouted the man. "You'll make this more difficult."

Verve did as she was ordered to and waited to be hauled out of the pit.

Something floated near her, and she made a grab for it. But the object swirled around and beyond her, and a rush of wind came at her from behind as what appeared to be a net was dragged toward her. Verve allowed it to sweep around her and draw her upward, and did not fight the current of air pulling against her.

"Heave!" said a woman. Whoever was with her obeyed, and the net moved what felt like a millionth of an inch. "Put your backs into it."

For a long moment, nothing gave, but then everything happened all at once. The forces surrounding Verve released her, and she soared upward before landing face-first on a surface covered in sand. Coughing, she rolled onto her back and drew in the first breath she had been able to take in minutes.

When her eyes finally adjusted to the world around her, she sat up to thank her saviors, but they moved back farther than they already were. She frowned. They were fae, all of them, and terror was written on their faces. Some pointed, others whispered.

"It's the end of time."

"Demon."

"World slayer."

"She's not a world slayer," said a man darkly. "They have ice in their eyes, not fire."

A woman scowled at Verve. "Then what *is* she?"

"She's a destroyer, meant to divide and perhaps unite," said the man from earlier, the one who had yelled for the net. His voice was calm and familiar somehow. "This is their Fire Queen."

Verve winced as she was roughly drawn to her feet, and they bound her with thick, heavy chains. "Wait," she said, though she could barely get the word out.

"Throw her back in," said a woman.

"She's just a child." It was another woman who spoke, one who looked at Verve with wide eyes that might have been mistaken for awe and perhaps pity, had she not just drawn a dagger from her belt. At her words, the mob stilled and seemed torn as to what they should do.

A man said, "Do we now murder mere babes? She can't be much more than twenty of their mortal years."

"You can't kill the Fire Queen. But she could kill any of us."

"And yet she hasn't," said the man from earlier. All attention went to him and the crowd tensed, as though waiting for his verdict with dread. He pushed through the throng, a tall man with light brown hair and tawny eyes. He placed a calloused hand beneath Verve's chin and raised her face. Whatever he saw he kept to himself, simply saying, "Finish binding her and bring her to my tent."

Looks were exchanged, fearful ones, but they did as their apparent leader had ordered. Their chains they wound tightly enough to make breathing difficult. Once finished, so quickly Verve could not orient herself, she was pushed again onto the sand and then hauled into the air by four sets of hands.

"We shouldn't allow her into our encampment," one desperate man said. He ran in their intended path, and Verve couldn't help but silently agree.

As soon as she freed herself of her bonds, she wouldn't care what her fire burned to clear the way. But she said nothing and didn't struggle as they carried her to the largest canvas structure in the middle of a city of modest tents.

Wind whipped Verve's hair in her face, clouding her vision of the twilit land, and then she was inside a well-lit room and dropped onto a carpet gritty with sand. "Set her up properly," said the man. "I want a better look at what we're dealing with."

The hands obeyed, and Verve found herself in an upright sitting position, the chains bending with her – bending and constricting her even more. Furious, she fought the urge to test her muscles against the bonds and attack anyone who might attempt to stop her, but the man shook his head ever so slightly.

"Not yet," he said to the room, though Verve wondered if he addressed her personally. He sat down in a wooden chair in front of her, his eyes narrowing as he silently assessed what he saw. "Leave us."

There was the sound of footsteps making a hasty retreat, but one heartbeat remained behind Verve. "I don't approve of this." It sounded like the man who hadn't even wanted her in their encampment.

The man before her bared his teeth, and Verve heard the other fae back away. "Don't bother eavesdropping. I'm raising a silencing spell as soon as you leave." He turned back to Verve and didn't speak again to his inferior, who left the tent with slow steps. "You're being rather docile for someone who is supposed to possess a notorious temper." His eyebrows rose suggestively. "You can't be comfortable in those." There was a whiff of sweet wine and the back of Verve's neck tingled. So, that was his residual burst. Friend or foe, she would file that information away for later use. "Free yourself."

Verve eyed him warily, unable to read the emotions flickering across his face. "And if I do?" she asked.

He gave her a lopsided grin. "What sort of question is that? You could kill me with a mere look if you wanted to, but you need me, so I'm not worried. Now, show me what the Fire Queen can do." His voice was so familiar, it made no sense.

Meeting his gaze, Verve pushed tentatively against the chains binding her. There was an audible snap as several of the links broke in unison. She had not even been using her full strength. "You might want to put up a shield."

"You're not going to melt them?" he asked, sounding disappointed but appearing entertained nonetheless.

"I don't feel like being coated in molten metal, thanks." Without further warning, she flexed and most of the remaining chains snapped. What was left she easily broke through. As she had expected, a few of the links went flying in different directions, but the man before her deflected them easily.

He regarded her as she rose, wary amusement written across his face, and she regarded him back.

At length she grew tired of the silence and asked, "Where am I? Who are you? And why do you sound so familiar?"

"You – you truly don't know where you are?"

Verve shook her head, her temper smoldering beneath her skin, its warm kisses promising violence if she didn't get herself better under control. She closed her eyes for a moment and dragged in a breath through her nose. "I was in – a place." It wasn't apparent if it would be wise to divulge her trip to Ithalamore, so she decided to keep things vague. "I was running from someone and I fell forever and—"

"Linwood," he said.

She blinked. "What?"

"You are in Linwood. The Sky Realm...or Star Realm, depending on whom you ask. You must have fallen from Ithalamore, judging by the hole we fished you out of." His smile was smug, which did nothing to improve Verve's mood.

"The Sky Realm."

"Yes. If we were outside right now, I would show you the heavens and you would see an orb, thousands of miles from here, where sits Letorheas. We are mere specks of glowing dust to them." His voice was bitter, stirring a memory in the back of Verve's mind.

Ages ago, Dacre had told her about a legend that claimed stars in the Letorhean sky to be banished fae. These particular creatures were said to be dangerous. "Who are you? Why are you here?"

Verve didn't know if she would have gotten a more passionate reaction if she had slapped him. The man stalked toward her, menace in his eyes. Before she could erect a shield, he grabbed her by the arm and threw her across the room. She landed on a chaise longue, but by his looks he might be wishing it were jagged rocks.

"Lesson one, Fire Queen," he purred, "don't bait a powerful fae without having a shield in place first."

She glowered at him as he came at her again. "I wasn't baiting you," she said through her teeth. Her hands started to glow and pulse with heat, sparks spitting from her fingertips and marring his royal-red carpet. Good.

Just as quickly as his temper had flared, it seemed to cool, and he watched her with unbridled curiosity. "Your magic is tied to your emotions too, then." As soon as he had said it, his expression darkened once more, as though he felt he had said too much. "You really are a middling, mortal." He said the word 'mortal' with disgust. "Well, *former* mortal, I should say."

Verve allowed the rude remark to go without comment. At least she knew what she was dealing with now and could act with the proper amount of caution.

"What is your name?" he asked. "I didn't catch it before."

"That's because I didn't give it to you."

His lips quirked and he took his seat once again in the wooden chair. "Be careful not to talk to the others like this. They're ready to throw you back whence you came."

"Is that possible?"

He shook his head. "No. You would simply drift there in the 'Tween until the end of eternity. And since eternity never ends, I'd imagine that would get quite boring." He laughed at his own statement or the look on her face, Verve couldn't decide which. "Come, tell me your name."

"Tell me *yours*."

"Names do not have as much power as some might have you think." Lazily, he brushed an invisible speck of dust from his tan tunic. "You needn't fear giving me yours."

Still Verve did not respond. His voice...where *had* she heard it before? She stared at him, willing herself to dredge up his image from a memory, but there was nothing there, just the voice. The thought caused her to jump to her feet, and the man drew a dagger as soon as she moved. "You were the one who helped me in Etterhea. It was your voice guiding me."

He smirked and sheathed the dagger, though his hand remained on its handle. "Very good, Verity."

"So you *do* know my name."

"Of course I know your name. Your friend, the halfling, said it enough times for me to hear." He sat up a little straighter. "How is the old crone, by the way? Hopefully quenching her thirst with something more satisfying than tree sap these days."

Verve cringed. "Olive is dead."

The man paused and nodded. "I see." He drummed his fingers on the chair's armrests, seeming more and more like he was a restless soul, unable to sit still. "You're welcome, by the way."

"For what?"

His brows rose. "For risking everything to guide you to safety. For rescuing you just now from the others who wanted to dispose of you. You're welcome." He smirked when the flames in the lanterns jumped in response to her irritation.

"How did you do it? See me all the way from here and communicate, that is?"

"We all have gifts, Verity. Nothing should surprise you anymore." At once he was on his feet, prowling around the perimeter of the tent, relighting candles that had guttered and stealing not-so-covert glances at Verve as he went. "You may call me Rillian. Or sir, if you like." He peered over his shoulder at her.

"And how do I get back?"

Rillian's smile faded. "To Letorheas? That isn't an easy question, and I'm afraid you won't like what I have to say." Absently his hand went once more for the dagger at his belt, as though he were afraid of her and what she might do if she didn't like his answer.

There was no time for this. Fenn was most likely Dacre's prisoner, if the latter wasn't capable of killing fae now, which she suspected he might be. The realms hung in the balance, and she would do what she must to return and set things right. "There is a man right now, a very powerful fae who is going to take over Letorheas and possibly Etterhea – maybe every realm, if he feels like it. He is cruel and vengeful, and he has no respect for mortal lives."

Rillian yawned. "What has this got to do with any of us here? We're banished, little queen, by the very ones you would rule."

Verve blanched but did not back down. "I don't want to rule anyone." When he laughed, she lost control of her magic once more, and his rug caught fire, but she didn't put it out. Instead, she watched in puzzlement as the flames died without her aid. The air reeked of wine, and Verve hissed. "You have fire."

"I don't have fire, Verity. Just air." To demonstrate, he blew a gust in her direction, one that knocked her off her feet and back onto the chaise. "And you've scorched my carpet. Between that and the help I've offered you that you practically spat at, I'd say the scales are not tipping in your favor."

"Please—"

"Ah, there's a pretty word. Throw in a few compliments, and I might hear you out."

Her mouth worked soundlessly as she tried to figure out the strange man. His moods shifted relentlessly, causing her to wonder if he in fact would make a suitable ally after all. Then again, no one else appeared willing to help. Although, the hour seemed late and others might be abed; perhaps she would find someone willing to tell her how to get home. "Rillian."

"Verity."

"Innocent people – *fae* – will suffer, possibly *die* if we don't do something." She watched him for a sign that he cared, but his face remained unreadable. "Well, if you aren't willing to help, perhaps I'll find someone who is." She turned to leave, but he at once was there, blocking her.

"You're not leaving my sight."

She gave him a pointed glare, but he didn't show any inclination to get out of her way. "Move or I'll burn your tent down."

He held up his hands, not in surrender or placation, it would seem, but to physically stop her if necessary. "You only just arrived. There are many things you will need to learn if you are to face this threat."

"And what has that got to do with you, a man who obviously cares so little for his own brethren?" She lifted her chin, a challenge.

"Easy," he warned. "These fae here? *They* are my people. *You* are an intruder, and I will not have you wandering around, harming a single one of them."

"I wouldn't."

"Oh, you wouldn't mean to. But you're young and new to power. You wouldn't be able to stop yourself." His eyes closed as he warred with himself, and he pinched the bridge of his nose. "Stay in my tent tonight. Let me – let us *both* cool our tempers a bit and we will discuss what is to be done on the morrow." The tone he used brooked no argument. Rillian watched her as she turned over his offer in her mind, his hands twitching before he lowered them to his sides.

Verve looked over her shoulder, where she heard the excited chatter of the other fae in the near distance. Some wondered if she had come to liberate them. Others still wished to chuck her back into the pit they had fished her out of, just like Rillian had warned. He was right. She had only been here half an hour, if that. Time was precious, but what harm would there be in staying the night and sorting out her next course of action in the morning? Surely the whole world wouldn't go to hell in the meantime. "One night." There was no fight in her words, just exhaustion.

Rillian dipped his head and ceased barring her way. "A wise decision. There are creatures here, more dangerous than some fae, even, who wouldn't think twice about devouring you." He moved about, gathering blankets and a pillow from the wardrobe in the corner and tossing them one at a time to Verve, who caught them and set them down on the chaise. Part of the tent was curtained off, and it didn't take through-sight for Verve to see that it housed his bed and some other personal furnishings. "I'll bring food and drink in a moment, but first

I need to address the others. You will stay here while I'm gone and will speak to no one. Try not to burn the place down."

"Fine."

He didn't acknowledge her again as he strode out of the tent, throwing up a visible ward around the place as soon as he set foot outside. It felt as though the air had been sucked out of the place, and Verve found herself unable to breathe. All of the lights at once went out.

Panic was alive and rearing its ugly head within Verve's breast. Not only was she trapped, but she couldn't make a sound about it. Gritting her teeth, she tried to remain calm and wait until he returned, restoring air to the space. It wasn't that she needed to breathe to live, it just felt wrong and uncomfortable not to do it. Still, the room spun as she stumbled for the tent flaps, only to find the ward impassable.

Whatever Rillian was telling the others, Verve couldn't be certain. Her heart's beatings thundered in her ears and she could hear nothing else as she lay down, writhing and shaking.

★ ★ ★

How long she lay there, she wasn't certain. Verve knew she couldn't afford to show her weakness to these people, so she blinked away tears and pulled herself into a sitting position. It had been weeks since she'd last experienced an attack.

All at once air returned to the tent, and she greedily sucked it down. "What are you doing on the floor?" Rillian asked, hesitating at the mouth of the tent.

Verve tried to arrange her features to appear neutral. If he guessed at how much anxiety plagued her, he might wield it as a weapon. More unbidden tears formed in her eyes and nausea tore at her stomach.

Rillian swore. "You don't need air, Verity. I was afraid you'd light the place on fire while I was gone."

She nodded and he watched her closely. Her traitorous lower lip trembled.

His face softened. "You've not been immortal long. It must be strange for you, this new form." Rillian came to her and held out a hand, then pulled her to her feet. "Be careful whom you show weakness to, especially in the Sky Realm. There are those here who would exploit it." With care he had not shown earlier, the strange fae led Verve back to the chaise and eased her down onto its plush surface.

There was much she wanted to know, and the thought of resting while Fenn was in peril made her miserable, but she didn't fight her host as he made her lie down and covered her with a thick blanket. "I—I have dreams. Bad ones."

Rillian's eyes widened. "Oh?"

Verve swallowed and tried to keep her voice from shaking. "I scream a lot in my sleep." It was important that she warn him so he would not attack her out of surprise, as Fenn almost had that first night back from Ithalamore.

His eyes flickered with some emotion that she couldn't identify and he shrugged. "Do sedatives help?"

She shook her head. Fenn had given her one during her second night back from Ithalamore. It had only succeeded in making it more difficult to wake her from the night terror that time.

"Well, then, I will keep the silencing spell up, so the others do not hear." He handed her a pillow, laid out a blanket on the floor, a respectable distance away, and settled down, himself.

Chapter Six

In the deepest part of the night, when the land was cloaked in a severe darkness, Verve gave in to sleep. The day had taken its toll on her mind and body, and she knew she would need all of her strength to get through the next day. Hopefully, leaving the Sky Realm would prove to be easier than entering it.

Her mind wandered to pleasant places at first, lulling her into the false security of a nightmare-free sleep. First she was in bed with Fenn, snuggled against him as he held her tightly and whispered nonsense into her ears. His grip was powerful, and as her dreaming-self attempted to move, she was surprised that he had grown stronger than she. She stared into his eyes and they were darker than she had ever seen them before, full of barely controlled power. Ere she could figure out why, the dream shifted.

Verve was kneeling before a throne, upon which Dacre sat, staring down at her with poorly disguised lust. He held his hand out to her, and she rose before slowly sauntering toward him. The dream shifted.

Now there was a dungeon. The air was cold and rank, and a cloaked man moved with purpose between the rows of cells. Behind him was Fenn, bloody and bound between two fae, who dragged him past other prisoners, some who jeered, others who stared at him in numb silence. Fenn didn't struggle, didn't seem to have an ounce of strength left in him.

"Don't let those get infected," said Dacre, pulling down his hood. He gestured to the lacerations on Fenn's back. "When the queen returns, she'll come for him, and I don't think sickly bait will be as enticing."

The men dragging Fenn threw him into a small cell and ran out, afraid of their charge, it would seem. They shut the cell door and cast ward after ward upon it, filling the air with the potent stink of coffee and hot metal.

After they left, Dacre lingered and stared at the unmoving body. Power crackled around him, and it was apparent he was not in full control of it or his temper. "I'll ask you again, do you know where she went?" When Fenn did not respond, Dacre lashed out with a whip made of magic. The ribbon of darkness passed through the bars and struck its mark on the prostrate fae's back.

Fenn shrieked and convulsed and vomited silver blood onto the straw of his cell. Once the fit had passed, he attempted to draw himself up, only to fall face-first into the puddle of sick.

"Tell me, Rogue Prince. Where is my Fire Queen?"

At that Fenn laughed, and Verve wanted to warn him to cease, to tell Dacre the answers to anything he asked. But she was a silent witness now, and no matter how hard she tried, she couldn't break through the barrier she felt blocking her. It was thin in places, that invisible wall, and she pounded her fists on it, but it did little more than make a ringing noise that set her teeth on edge.

"I don't know anything about where my wife went, Dacre. And even if I did, why would I tell you?"

Dacre lashed out again, eliciting the same reaction as before. The attack seemed to last forever, but at length, Fenn grew silent and lay still, panting through whatever residual pain he was experiencing. "You're a very good liar, unfortunately. I'll have to get more creative about extracting the truth." Dacre scrubbed a hand over his face, and it was with some pleasure that Verve noted how exhausted and anxious he looked. "Perhaps I can help her. Would you really deny her any aid in her most dire of hours?" He kicked a loose stone, which skittered across the prison floor and disappeared into the darkness.

Fenn coughed and managed to roll over onto his side. "Aid *her* or aid *yourself*? Your plans for her, whatever they might be, are no doubt selfish and will not be to her liking."

It was Dacre's turn to laugh. "*I'm* selfish? You are the one who took her away from my home, tried to prevent her from becoming the Fire Queen, all so you could keep her in her fragile, mortal state." Each word he spoke was spat through his teeth, which he bared at his prisoner.

"You almost killed her," said Fenn, earning himself a bolt of blue lightning in his chest. "You tortured her, just so you could have a claim to the very power you—" Another bolt hit him and another. Now his screams were silent.

Verve fought against the barrier, tore into it with her nails, but that yielded no other result than pain for herself. She didn't need to be in Letorheas to know a storm was raging without, one of her making from all the miles that lay between them. The ground shook from a nearby lightning strike, and Dacre relented, having lost his footing.

When he spoke, his voice was thick with rage. "I would kill you, but I know that would break her heart. She's fond of you, for some reason I can't begin to understand."

Fenn didn't stir. Verve hoped he had lost consciousness so he might be free of pain, but his labored breathing made her think otherwise.

Dacre kicked dust in his direction. "When I break whatever bond you forged with her, she'll be mine and you'll be nothing. The Fire Queen and her power belong to me alone. Do you understand?"

If Fenn could answer, he didn't bother. The last thing Verve saw of him before the dream shifted was of him coughing up more blood.

Now her sleeping mind bore her to Etterhea, to her mother's home. There was little joy and no music, for that had died with Helena. Mother sat at the kitchen table, wading through stacks of paper, a puzzled expression on her face. Nearby, Anna, their housekeeper, stirred a fragrant pot of jam on the stovetop. "What's wrong?"

Mother shook her head and rifled through one of the stacks and, coming up with another paper, sat back with a great *whoosh*, as though all the air had left her lungs. "How is she doing it?"

"Who did what now?" Anna stopped her stirring, wiped her hands on her ratty apron, and joined Mother at the table. The plump old woman peeked over Mother's shoulder and frowned. "Those are bills?"

"All paid. We don't owe anyone a single cent. In fact..." Mother handed over the piece of paper in her trembling hands. "Apparently Verity has done so well at her job, they've given her a pay raise."

Anna frowned. "Well, that's a good thing, innit?" She took the paper from Mother, as though she could make sense of it better than her mistress could.

"We've been living well since she left, and now we'll be living as queens."

"It's somethin' to do with that fellow who's been helping us so often. He's strange like Verity."

Mother clicked her tongue. "You're overly suspicious. He has been nothing but good to us."

"But why?" Anna took the chair across from Mother. "He's got your girl in mind somehow, you mark my words."

"Who's got her?" asked Dav as she strolled into the room, her face smudged with charcoal from her drawings. "Are you talking about that man who's sweet on Verity?"

Anna waggled a finger at the youngest Springer girl. "You mind your words now, little miss. We don't know what sort of fella this man might be."

Dav wasn't listening. She wrapped her arms around herself and sighed. "Isn't it romantic? I bet they'll get secretly married, which is something Verity would do just to annoy us all." Grinning like a fool, she went to the stove and stirred the neglected pot of jam.

"Whoever invested money in our name, may they be blessed," said Mother, resting her head in her hands. "I only wish that Helena were alive and Verity would return home so she could enjoy it with us." Her voice broke and tears spilled down her cheeks.

In her dreaming state, Verve longed to reach out and wipe them away. "I'm here, Mother." No one heard her. The barrier between them remained intact, and perhaps that was for the best. Disembodied hands reaching through the ether would terrify them, no doubt. Verve sighed, and the curtains over the sink flapped.

"And you're going to accept the money?" Anna sounded incredulous, as though they were stealing.

"Yes, Anna. I am. *We* are. It's about time something good happened around here, and I am not going to look a gift horse in the mouth."

Again the vision changed, returning to the usual nightmare. When dream-Verve fell, however, something cold clamped down on her mouth and no sound could come out. She thrashed and writhed as she fought to return to consciousness so she might fight off whoever was attacking her. Her eyes flew open, and she was staring straight into the eyes of a strange woman, who slowly raised a finger to her lips.

On the floor across from her, Rillian stirred but didn't wake. That was when the woman's hand went to her belt and she produced an onyx-black knife, which she slashed toward Verve's throat.

Verve easily bucked the woman off and kicked her in the stomach. The knife went skittering across the floor, and now her host did wake.

"What in the name of the third moon—" said Rillian.

The woman tried to flee the tent, but Rillian reached out with magic and drew her back irresistibly, his teeth clenched and his eyes dark with rage.

"What is wrong with you?" he bellowed as the woman struggled against his power's hold. "I knew one of you would be foolish enough to thwart me, but I did not expect an attempted kidnapping right under my nose." Rillian spared Verve an assessing glance. "You are all right?"

Rubbing gooseflesh from her arms, Verve nodded. "That knife…"

"That knife could have done some serious damage to an immortal, even one as powerful as you are. It blocks a fae's abilities for a time, including healing ones." He continued to detain the attacker with his magic as he retrieved the weapon and held it up to the orb he had just conjured. "It wouldn't kill you, but you wouldn't be at full strength for a few days. Just enough time for them to lug you out into the wilderness and dump you down a hole where they think I wouldn't find you. Isn't that right, Mercedes?" He used the tip of the blade to pull the cover from the woman's head and face.

Still she didn't respond but continued to fight, until Rillian held the blade against her throat. Then she ceased all her striving and watched Verve with the wildest dark eyes Verve had ever beheld. Something was wrong with her. It had to be.

Verve meant to intervene, but Rillian lashed out before she could, cutting the fae across her cheek. Silver blood poured down the woman's face, and she collapsed onto the carpet, crying out.

"Verity, I suggest you move into my quarters and put up a silencing spell. This isn't going to be pleasant."

Instead of doing as he asked, Verve approached the terrified and bleeding woman. Pity filled her breast as she studied the creature, and she said, "She didn't hurt me. Put the blade down." Her words were not received kindly.

Rillian turned to her, his eyes narrowing. "You dare tell me how to rule my own people?" A pulse in his throat ticked noticeably, and his face grew red as he stalked toward her, blade still in hand. "Perhaps I should use this on you. Everyone's terrified enough of your presence. One cut might make it a fair fight." As he approached Verve, her would-be attacker took advantage of his distraction and ran from the tent.

Verve snarled at him instinctively and reached out with magic, causing the knife to glow white-hot with fire. Rillian gasped and dropped the blade, cursing her and shaking his hand out. The palm was an angry red, and his fingers were already blistering.

"Get out," he said through his teeth.

She didn't move but continued to hold her ground. "Tell me how to leave this miserable place and I will gladly go."

He made a fist, as though he would very much like to strike her. "Let me calm down first, and then maybe I'll tell you."

Verve nodded at his hand. "You're going to make it worse." She approached Rillian, who backed away. That did not deter her. Verve reached into the air, as she had seen Fenn do on many occasions, and pulled moisture from seemingly nowhere, letting it cool and crystalize in her palm. Then she thrust the chunk of ice at Rillian and marched out of the tent.

Many had gathered around Rillian's residence, no doubt having sent the attacker – Mercedes, Verve recalled. Not feeling particularly charitable toward any of them at the moment, Verve glared at them until they cleared a path for her.

Hot with rage, she strode toward a cluster of hills in the distance. It was perhaps morning here, but the sky was closer to that of a spring's twilight back in Etterhea. What was wrong with Rillian? What made him so angry and impossible? Perhaps he thought she meant to undermine him, to rule his people. Well, Verve had no interest in ruling them or those back in Letorheas…or anywhere, for that matter.

If Rillian would not help her find a way home, then perhaps she would discover one for herself. As she walked at the same impossible speed, however, her temper cooled, and she pondered something that had been niggling at her: if these people were exiled here, why hadn't they returned home? There were no guards that Verve had noticed. What was to stop them from finding a hawthorn and making a gateway back to Letorheas? Or maybe there was an already existing portal, like the one she had fallen through in the Lands of the Dead, that would lead there. If so, why were there so many fae still here? Verve had counted at least fifty the night previous.

Her eyes scanned the endless horizon. There was not a tree in sight. Again her pace slowed, this time to a near crawl. There were trees in the Sky Realm; there had to be. She focused and peered into the distance, spinning in slow circles as she scanned for miles and miles around. Using through-sight made it possible to see beyond the city of tents and the hills that she had been walking toward. She couldn't find any trees, but that didn't mean they weren't out there. That was the hope she clung to as she once again pressed onward, aware of a small group of fae following her at a distance. Though she tried to ignore them, she could hear their voices as though they were speaking directly into her ear.

"Where is she going?" asked a woman.

"Fool girl. She doesn't even know what's out there," said another.

"Should we bring her back?" It was a man who had spoken. He

sounded farther behind the others, as though he were having trouble keeping up.

"Let her find out for herself."

Well, that sounded ominous. But they must have known she could hear them and were trying to intimidate her. Verve picked up her pace again and was delighted when there was cursing behind her as the others tried to keep on her trail.

The longer she walked, the more her temper calmed and common sense returned to her. If she expended all of her energy trudging forward without water or food, she might not be able to fight off any fae who made another attempt to dispose of her. She stopped walking. Behind her, the others paused as well. One laughed, a sound that made Verve grind her teeth and want to shout curses at them. But she needed allies. Just as she thought that, the air filled with a loud shriek and the flapping of giant wings. A shadow passed overhead, but by the time Verve looked heavenward, it was gone.

A barbed tail swiped toward her, and she only just managed to fly in the air to avoid it. The wyvern was orange and twice the size of the one she had faced in Etterhea. It roared as it charged.

Foolish, foolish move to come out here without weapons. Verve encased herself in a thick magical shield, and the land filled with the scent of burned sugar.

The creature charged, and Verve tried to remain calm as a small crack formed in the protective bubble on impact. Powering the shield still, she searched for something she could transform into a sword, but there was only powdery sand and rocks, which were impossible to make into anything new. Another crack formed and another. Desperate, Verve plucked three strands of hair from her head and willed herself to calm so that she might successfully work her magic.

Another crack formed, this time allowing a claw to pass through. Verve shouted in frustration as she reinforced the shield and then did what went against instinct: she held one of the strands and closed her eyes, willing herself to relax.

The first strand of hair caught fire, as did the second and third ones. There was no time to form a weapon, as the wyvern was making even quicker work of her defenses.

She darted away, letting the shield remain. It took the creature a moment to realize it was clawing at an empty shell, but when it understood it had been tricked, it roared and took off after Verve at top speed, wings unfurling behind.

"She's asking to be eaten," said one of the fae who had followed her.

"This should be entertaining."

The words were exactly what she needed to stoke her rage, the emotion that fed her magic best. Verve allowed the anger to smolder, to build, and then the whole world seemed to catch fire.

A ring of flames formed around her and the creature, which took one look at her and hesitated. It let out a low growl and charged.

Verve raised her hand and nearly screamed when all she saw was fire. It was as though she were made of flames, her whole body one human-shaped torch. She marveled for a moment. That moment cost her. The wyvern swiped a claw at her side. She bled fire onto the ground, cried out in agony, and jumped back.

Again the creature paused, watching her with dark eyes. It grunted as it sauntered toward her, ready to finish its meal off at its leisure, apparently. But as soon as its mouth opened, Verve raised her hands and fed an endless stream of golden light down its throat. This was not as easy as controlling Fenn. With him, the magic had wrapped itself around his mind and forced his body to obey. For this creature, the light was slippery and did not grasp on as it ought.

The wyvern shook its enormous head, its tail whipping to and fro as it fought Verve's hold. At least the beast didn't charge or snap at her any longer.

Around them, the flames sputtered and soon went out, even as her body continued to burn. But forcing the creature's will to bend to her own was growing exhausting. Her knees buckled and she sank to the ground. The fire that had consumed her fizzled out all at once, and she was left naked and vulnerable before the giant beast.

It snuffled once, and then licked its chops. It nudged Verve with the back of its claw, knocking her over. Cold and exhausted, Verve could only lie there, trembling as the wyvern gently picked her up in its talons and unfurled its massive wings.

"Put her down!" shouted a fell voice. It was Rillian standing alone, a whip of white light in his hands. The other fae men and women stood far behind him.

The wyvern bared its teeth and snarled, crouching over its prey possessively. It started to fly off, but Rillian moved quickly, ensnaring the creature around the neck with the magical whip. At the contact, a few of the wyvern's scales loosened and fell to the ground. The beast roared as the fae shoved a fistful of forked lightning down its throat. It started to fly off, but Rillian held fast to the whip. He lashed another whip around Verve's waist, releasing the one around the wyvern as he gave Verve's a firm jerk.

Verve flopped around like a rag doll as the creature was thrown off-balance by the sudden absence of restraint. It dropped her, and she plummeted to the ground, striking her head quite hard. Stars swam before her eyes as the beast flew away.

"Yes, just stand there and do nothing, you useless lot," said Rillian, running to Verve and releasing her from his magic. He removed his cloak and covered her naked form. "Are you all right?"

"I think so," she said. Her voice rang in her ears, she could barely move, and she ached, but the wound in her side was already healing. The worst damage that had been done was to her dignity.

"You should have never gone out here alone." His voice was calm but there was anger sparkling in his eyes. "Beasts half that size have taken some of our more powerful fae."

"They died?"

Rillian scooped Verve up and carried her back toward the village of tents. "When a fae is eaten by a creature such as that, they are not killed but simply absorbed into the creature's body. That creature must have had some fae influencing it, as it hesitated before attacking you. We're not their preferred food for that reason: they know we would end up eventually invading their minds and wills that way."

She wrinkled up her nose. That sounded like a horrible way to spend eternity, as part of such a monster.

The others smirked at her as they approached, save for the one who had objected most to her presence. He was pale and wide-eyed.

"That is why we stick together," said one of the women, a short fae with pale blond hair. "And stay away from the hills."

"No one told me that," Verve said wearily, though she wanted to snarl it. "How did the creatures get here?"

The crowd turned their backs on her and walked ahead of them. "What do you mean?" asked Rillian. "This is the realm wyverns made their home."

Verve shook her head, which made the pain spike. She groaned. "One attacked me in Etterhea a few days ago."

"You made it out of that uneaten as well." He sounded reluctantly impressed and then cleared his throat. "Wyverns are interdimensional beings. They can come and go from whatever realm they please."

She took that information in for a moment before asking, "Can they take people with them to these other realms?"

"I'd imagine so."

"Then why not ride them out of here?"

One of the men shook his head. "Why didn't we think of trying that?"

Rillian growled, and the other man tripped over his feet trying to get away. "Some attempted riding the beasts and were consequently devoured. No one can control them." When he spoke again he lowered his voice, and his residual burst told her that he was using magic to hide his words from the others. "Your technique today was too haphazard and wild. If you're going to return to Letorheas and face the Traitor King, you need proper training." The look he gave her was pointed, and while she waited for him to offer to help, he simply turned his attention to the horizon.

Too tired and proud at the moment to ask for training, she kept her mouth shut. If she was going to learn how to better control her magic, Rillian was not her first choice for a teacher. His moods were more unstable than hers even, and she didn't like him. But if he had the same way of manifesting his powers that she did, he might be the perfect choice. Later. She would worry about that later when she did not feel so weak and her head and side were not throbbing.

"I take it you didn't mean to turn into a human bonfire earlier." He peered down at her once more, his lips quirking upward.

Verve grimaced. "No, I didn't. I didn't know that was even possible."

"You're going to have to learn more about your magic and its limits."

She bobbed her head in reluctant acknowledgment as he carried her into his tent without a word to the others. If only he would stop talking and let her rest. As soon as he set her down on the chaise, Rillian used magic to call a pillow from across the room into his waiting hand and tossed it to her.

"Make some clothing for yourself. The others won't want to share anything with you." He watched her, his face unreadable as she stared up and over at him. "You do have transformative magic, don't you?"

"Yes. Do *you*?" It came out grumpier than she had meant it, but Rillian didn't seem to grow angry.

"You can't have others doing everything for you, Verity. If you are to become queen, the sooner you learn that, the better."

His words chafed, but Verve did not let him see how much they bothered her. As he continued to stand there, watching her, she at length said, "I'm not doing it now."

"Oh?"

She rolled her eyes. "I feel like I've had the life sucked out of me."

He stilled. "What did it feel like, expending that much power?"

Verve opened her mouth, ready to snap out a saucy retort, but then she thought about it. At the time, it had been terrifying. Seeing herself as a living flame was disorienting and...exhilarating. But it had drained her quickly. She thought she'd have recovered somewhat by now, but the trip back had exhausted her further still, even though she hadn't made the journey with her own two legs.

When she didn't answer his question, Rillian merely turned and left the tent.

* * *

She drowsed for a few hours. There were whispers of terror and pain from Letorheas that reached her in her unconscious state. More than once someone desperately moaned her name, crying out for the Fire Queen. The land was unbearably hot, she knew on instinct, though lightning thundered in the distance, offering the promise of rain but not delivering. By the few glimpses she caught of the land, Verve knew days, weeks perhaps, had passed since her departure, though it felt like it had barely been twelve hours here. It was dry and overcast. Trees shed their browning leaves, and flowers wilted on bronze stems.

But there was nothing she could do for them – not that she could think of – though she felt their insistent tug on her mind. She waved them away with her thoughts, and a light breeze kissed treetops and stirred the wildlands.

When she roused herself, tears had formed in her eyes, and she knew it was at last raining in Letorheas. Where she was now – the Sky Realm, she reminded herself – the tent was buffeted by mighty gusts of wind. Raindrops pattered against the canvas, and lightning lit up the room like full daylight only to plunge her once more into dimness. Hastily she plucked a feather from the pillowcase and transfigured it into a simple green dress, which she pulled over her head. It was huge on her form, but she ignored that. She really needed to practice precise magic to better get the hang of it.

All of the candles guttered, and judging from the eerie stillness around her, Rillian had not returned. Verve cursed herself for letting her guard down as she had. Anyone might have attacked her with that wicked blade while she rested and recovered from her ordeal. But they hadn't. That's what counted. In the future, she would be more careful, even with Rillian watching her back.

As if summoned by her thoughts, the fae himself slipped in through the tent flaps. He was ashen and unsmiling as he stared at her. "No one can control this tempest."

Verve frowned and sat up, rubbing the gooseflesh on her arms. "You make all the weather here?"

Rillian nodded. "Yes. Did you make this storm?"

"I-I don't know."

He sighed and gestured for her to follow him out of the tent and into the deluge, which she did, albeit reluctantly. "It started about thirty minutes ago," he shouted over the wind and rain. "If someone doesn't stop it within the next hour, we'll be flooded." His attention turned to her, an expectant expression on his face. "Young weather-makers often create weather by accident but not storms like this. Look."

She obliged him. Tents had blown over and fae scrambled around, trying to gather their belongings, which were no doubt near-ruined thanks to the heavy downpour. The back of Verve's neck tingled as she peered up at the sky, and a bolt of lightning shot straight for her.

"Verity!" Rillian screamed a split second before it struck her.

As one dreaming, Verve caught the bolt in her hands and let it dissolve into nothingness. Her skin glowed as she watched it with curiosity. Then, sense returned to her and she quickly raised her hands to the heavens and, pushing her magic and feelings together, yelled at the sky, "Stop!" At once, the winds died and the rain ceased. It was not sunny now, not in this realm, but the sky was kissed with a soft glow that provided enough light to see by.

Beside her, Rillian sighed in relief. "You do have some control. That is good. That is very good." Of all things, he clapped her once on the back and turned to the chaos surrounding them. He left Verve standing alone and on the receiving end of many nervous glances.

She approached three fae trying to erect a brown, weather-beaten tent. At the sight of her, two of them dropped their sides of the tent and backed away, their eyes wide. The third fae, the one who had advocated for her banishment, shook his head. "Don't admit to all you can do, Fire Queen. There are those among us who would use it to their advantage."

The other fae turned to each other, looking confused.

Almost two years ago, Dacre had gifted Verve with a translating spell, one that would allow her to understand any language spoken to her and, in turn, allowed her to speak it back. If she wasn't paying attention, all languages sounded one and the same. This, however, was spoken with such a thick accent, Verve knew at once that he was not speaking a tongue common to him.

"What do you mean?" she asked in the same language.

The man merely grunted and walked away, leaving Verve alone with the two nervous fae. She tried offering them a smile, but she knew it came off as a halfhearted grimace, and they left her in a hurry to help some of the others.

There was much to be done to repair the tent village. They raised structures that had been knocked over and blown away by her tempest. Belongings needed gathering and airing out. Some things – such as papers and food items – seemed ruined beyond repair, but a few fae went around using erasure magic to undo the damage, and were in most cases able to restore objects to their original state.

As they worked, the waters receded – they had reached Verve's anklebones – and the powdery grit that covered the realm was turned into what felt like clay. It squelched and stuck to her bare feet. Wiser fae had built their homes on raised platforms, with the poles coming down the sides to touch the ground. Rillian's, Verve noted, was untouched by the winds or rain, so strong were the wards he kept up.

She tried helping where she could, though most would not let her anywhere near their property without aggressive posturing.

One particularly nasty fellow attacked her with an ancient-looking sword, which she only just managed to avoid by dancing out of the way. "Unnatural creature," he snarled and seemed ready to attempt another attack.

"Enough of your theatrics, Jaq," said a slight she-fae with dark brown hair. "Stop trying to frighten the girl. She's not impressed." Without warning, she slid an arm through Verve's and pulled her away from Jaq, who cursed them as they left.

Verve started to thank her, but the woman held up her hand. There was obviously something she wanted to say. Her posture was tense, her eyes wide and alert. But at length she merely shook her head and said,

"That was some display with the fire. You'll want to be careful who you show all your tricks." She nodded in the direction of the very man who had said the same thing to her earlier. "My advice? Stay away from most of the males. They're territorial and will try to use your powers to further their agenda."

"Which is?"

The slight creature shook her head and patted Verve's hand before unthreading her arm from hers. "Not here. Too many traitors in our midst." She waved at two females who were folding a quilt together. When she spoke again, her voice was soft and a residual burst the smell of chamomile accompanied it. "Put your trust in Rillian. He has a temper, yes, but he is a good leader. You will need each other's support in the days to come." The woman turned to help a fae who seemed to be injured, leaving Verve more confused than she had been before.

Chapter Seven

It took much effort and working together, but the tent village – which had been named Caverille by its occupants, Verve soon discovered – was at length restored. The real problem was going to be the mud. Apparently, the weather-makers in the Sky Realm only made it rain on the outskirts of Caverille, and just to fill the water troughs. One or two fae there had water-manipulation abilities, so storms were their main source for drink. She thought about offering to dry the land, but decided against it; no one wanted to see another display of fire. Knowing her lack of control, she could set everything ablaze.

No one outright accused Verve of creating the catastrophic storm, but she could see the hatred in their eyes. She would have to find a way to redeem herself, were she to get the information she needed to leave.

Rillian was in extra good spirits after they had finished laboring, but Verve still approached him cautiously, having remained on the outskirts of the village and helping where she could do so unobserved. As she picked her way toward him, Rillian looked up from his spell-casting. From the appearance of things, he was patching holes in the ward he had created around his home. "You don't do things by halves, do you? I'm surprised you didn't turn into a whirlwind yourself." He laughed as she fought to hide her scowl.

"I would apologize for losing control," she said as evenly as she could, "but I don't think that would make a jot of difference with you or any of your people."

His eyebrows rose at those words but the smirk didn't leave his face. "We're going to see how good your transformative skills are here in a moment. I also want to test to see if you have creative abilities as well." When she didn't respond but stared at him, her thoughts churning, he laughed once more and raised his hands to continue his work. "Can you?"

"Can I what?"

"Make something out of nothing?"

Verve thought back to the time she had formed a knife out of nothing and used it against Dacre. Then she had formed gloves to protect others from touching her skin while she'd been cursed. "I don't know."

The smirk Rillian gave her told her he knew she was lying, but he didn't accuse her of being dishonest. Instead, the fae shrugged and finished his magic. "Clean your feet before coming inside. You've done enough damage today as it is." He didn't remain to see the grimace on her face.

Verve sat just inside the entrance to his tent, her back to Rillian, and reached into her pocket for a feather she had tucked in there earlier. It was obvious he was watching her, waiting to see how skilled or unskilled she was, but Verve tried to ignore him while she attempted to turn the feather into a towel to clean her feet off with. But before she could even alight upon a feeling, Rillian sighed and approached her.

"You're fighting for a feeling when you should be melting into one."

Her hand closed around the feather just as it went up in flames. "I don't have trouble with this when people aren't watching me only to criticize." She didn't need to see him to know his eyes had flashed with annoyance at her tone.

Instead of snapping back at her, Rillian took in a slow breath before saying, "Your emotions must always lie on the surface if you are to grasp them quickly enough to perform combat."

"All I'm combating right now is mud." She knew she ought to be thankful for his help, but irritation continued to flare within her breast, blurring her vision and making her fingers itch with the need to burn something.

"You build on this sort of magic, the mundane. If you cannot master your most simplistic abilities, you have no right wielding fire."

The air smelled strongly of burned sugar as she fought to control herself. He was just trying to help…as arrogantly as anyone possibly could have. Verve's temper continued to simmer as she plucked a hair from her head.

"Don't fight your anger with me. Push it into your transformative magic."

"Who says I'm angry?"

Rillian chuckled darkly. "I know when someone is angry with me."

Verve looked over her shoulder at him. "Anger always ends in fire." It was painful to admit, but maybe it would cause him to back off and stop pushing her to utilize the emotion.

"Interesting." He folded his arms across his chest, his brow wrinkling. "There are different levels to anger. Irritation, annoyance, fury, rage… I wonder if you advance so quickly to fury or rage that your magic simply explodes from you, out of control. Perhaps if you acknowledged that you are almost always angry, you could feed the fire within in a way so that the pot simmers without boiling over, so to speak." He regarded her, and apparently seeing he wasn't making sense, he tried again. "If you add straw to a fire, the material combusts quickly. Short, hot, but fairly harmless if there's nothing else to catch. Tinder and kindling create and feed a fire…but it is a dry log that sustains it and lets it grow." He drew a circle with his foot. "Properly contained and maintained, the heart of the fire will be hot for days. Straw, little irritations, cause flare-ups. But it's expected and dealt with by the boundaries set around the blaze. You need to learn to choose what irritates you."

"All of those words for that?" she said, jumping to her feet, his precious rug be hanged. "I've been fighting my temper my whole life. You don't think I haven't thought of this?" Why was she so angry? No, not angry. She was furious, so furious the world around her blurred. Verve grew still and blinked the haze from her eyes. He was making her angry, but not in a normal sense. Yes, how had she missed the residual burst? The tent reeked of wine and spices. "Are you trying to burn this whole place down?"

Rillian grinned, all teeth. "You finally figured out what I can do. Bravo."

Verve rolled her eyes and in the space between breaths, she was holding a white towel instead of a hair. "So you're not a complete hothead. You were pushing emotions at me?"

He nodded smugly. "If it makes you feel any better, I had to work twice as hard to manipulate how you feel as I do with a regular fae. Throwing my victims off-balance with my own vacillating emotions usually works when I'm having trouble finding a way into their emotions. Who knew that it would take boring you with bad analogies to get the reaction I was looking for?"

"And do you manipulate people often?" Even as she said it, she felt herself calming down, though she knew she ought to be more worried. If he could influence or control emotions, no wonder he had so much support here, and that very much left her at his mercy. She fought the feeling of peace tooth and nail, and the air smelled quite suddenly of vanilla.

The twinkle in Rillian's eye told her that he was indeed responsible for the change in her feelings. "I only step in when I think someone's about to harm me or mine."

"I'm not here to harm anyone," Verve said.

His head bobbed in acknowledgment. "I wanted to know what I'm dealing with. So, magic tied to emotions, rage as your main trigger for fire and perhaps successful spells, and you raised a shield against me just now, unconsciously, I believe." He uncrossed his arms and disappeared into the back room that comprised his personal quarters. When he re-emerged, he was carrying a pad of paper and a pencil. Instead of taking notes, however, Rillian snapped the pencil in two and held it out for her to see. Then, he placed both ends back together and performed erasure magic. The tent filled with the smell of wine, and the pencil halves fused back together. "Can you see where they were joined?" He handed the pencil to Verve, who took it and at once noted a red line where the erasure magic had taken hold. When she handed the pencil back to Rillian without saying anything, he nodded, thoughtful. "You are powerful enough to see the after-effects. Don't bother lying; it's plain as day on your face. You must have the potential to take on much more magic."

Verve frowned as he now jotted down a few notes. "What makes you say that?" She tried to see what he was writing, but to her eyes, no words appeared on the paper. She smelled mulling spices and knew he was using magic to prevent her from perceiving his words.

"Seeing magic is often an indicator. We don't know why, but those who can often go on to be more powerful." He frowned. "Are you a siphon?"

The hairs on the back of her neck rose at the word and she regarded him warily. "I don't know."

"There is one siphon here," he said, ignoring her discomfort. "Him you'll want to avoid."

Verve's heart raced. "Who should I avoid?"

At once Rillian's expression darkened and he shook his head. "You've met him already. Finley doesn't want you here, Verity. He'll warn you about me, too, because he knows I need you. Be careful that you are not left alone with him."

"And he's a siphon." Could this Finley be the man whom Igraine wanted her to divest of powers or kill? "Does he have any family left in Letorheas?"

"Little, if any. It's hard to keep track of our families at this distance."

"But there is a way." She waited, her hands clasping and unclasping in front of her. When he did not answer, she asked, "If there was a way for you to see me in Etterhea, then there is a way to return to Letorheas, isn't there?"

Rillian sighed. "There's a reason no one leaves the Sky Realm, and that is because someone has to kill a high fae and offer their blood for a hawthorn to drink in order to make a gateway. No one here is capable of dying, Verity, of shedding their life's blood. That is, they *weren't*, not until you arrived." The way he looked at her chilled her to the marrow. "No one's going to agree to die so that everyone else might return to Letorheas. That is why most hate you and some covet you. You could decide for us."

Verve turned away. "I'm done killing."

"You might think that," he said barely above a murmur, "but life has a way of surprising you. If you were cornered, I can see you easily taking out whoever stands in your way." It wasn't said with malice, but it made Verve cringe nonetheless.

Was that how people saw her? A viper poised to kill? "There has to be another way. I won't consider the alternative." Even as she said the words, her insides twisted and she thought she might vomit.

"If there were another way, it's already been attempted." He set his papers and pencil aside and sat across from the chaise longue, one ankle crossed over the other. "We can worry about that later. For now, I want you to try a few things." Rillian gestured to the chaise, meaning for her to take a seat.

Verve hesitated but complied, wondering what he was about to ask of her. "I'm not a dog that does tricks," she said as he nodded at the feathers.

"Well, as long as you're stuck here, you're going to need to contribute something to our society." Again he pointed at the feathers. "I'm running low on bedding and clothing. You're going to make and unmake a few things for me."

"Unmake?" She didn't take her eyes off him as she reached for a feather.

"It's a good way to learn magical theory, while at the same time discovering what you can and can't do. I'm assuming you have erasure magic like a normal high fae would."

She didn't react, but Rillian nodded as though she had just confided in him.

"So, if I'm able, you want me to make something and then make it go away? Is that it?"

"Not just make something disappear. I want you to return it to its original state, unless I say otherwise. Young magic-wielders struggle with getting fabric and materials to feel right against the skin. And sizing is often an issue as well." He nodded at the giant dress Verve wore, making her flush.

"This isn't going to solve any of my problems."

"No, but it will solve a few of *mine*. My blankets are wearing thin and need replacing." He leaned back and gestured toward his room. "Make a proper one for me and you can have lunch."

Incredulous, she stared at him. How could he so casually tell her that their means of escape would yet again make a murderer of her, and then expect trivial tasks to be performed on his behalf? This time he didn't have to manipulate her feelings by magical means. The feather in her hands burst into flames as she glowered at him.

Rillian shook his head. "I'm not trying to be cruel or heartless, Verity. The facts are simple: you can choose to leave at any time you wish now. But you have a conscience…a wonderful yet terribly inconvenient thing, which I know you will listen to until every other hope has been extinguished. So, in the meantime, I ask for domestic aid in exchange for food, shelter, protection, and training. Do you think I ask too much? If anything, I ask for too little."

"Are you always so mercenarily minded?"

He shrugged. "Perhaps I was born thus. Or perhaps spending three hundred years here has made me this way."

"Three hundred years?" The man didn't appear to be any older than thirty. When he didn't respond, Verve took her lower lip between her teeth and gave what he had said some thought. It would be wise to keep in Rillian's good graces, if she wasn't going to murder someone so that they all might leave. The secret to leaving had to lie in the wyverns, since they were interdimensional creatures. But how to communicate with them… without being eaten, that was? Something prickled at the base of Verve's skull as a memory resurfaced, the words an ally had once said to her:

"The No Lands refer to the paths between realms. These you should be able to traverse once you part with your mortal ties."

Since her early days as a fae, Verve had often been called 'Firstblood of No Land' by the hawthorns she encountered. But the ally in Verve's memory had been mistaken. Verve was not able to travel between worlds now, even though she was no longer mortal, save for her heart, the essence of who she was.

Sitting there with the feather in hand, Verve became aware that Rillian was staring at her, as though he had spoken and was waiting for a response. A shiver shuddered through her body and she asked, "What do you know of the No Lands?"

"They are the paths between realms, in theory," he said carefully. "No one's ever seen them, save for the hawthorns, and they don't share their secrets." He sat up a little straighter in his chair, his eyes narrowed into slits as he stared at the feather. It would seem no more answers would be forthcoming at the moment.

With a sigh, Verve turned her attention to what was in her hand. She might as well get this over with, if she wished to eat that day. It was difficult, ignoring Rillian's attention as she attempted to work her magic. Thankfully, though, this feather didn't burst into flames. Her eyes closed as she focused on emotion – weariness – and pushed it, along with her magic, at the plume, which trembled and then grew in length and width until it took up most of the tent.

Rillian roared with laughter even as he disappeared from Verve's view. "You lost focus."

Verve attempted to salvage the gigantic mistake and turned it into an equally large down-filled quilt. That, at least, stopped the impossible fae from laughing.

"Smaller."

Again Verve reached for a feeling – she passed over irritation and alighted on hope – which she shoved at the blanket, focusing with all her might on it shrinking to a normal size. Surely that would be acceptable.

Once the quilt wasn't so large, Rillian held out his hand, forcing Verve to approach him with her work. He took it from her, rubbed the material between his fingers, and shook his head. "Too rough."

Verve quirked a brow at that but said nothing. She also rubbed the material between her fingers and had to concede the point: it felt like burlap. So she closed her eyes once more and focused on how she thought it should feel, feeding her feelings into her magic until the fabric softened in her hands. Surely Rillian wouldn't object to this.

"If you close your eyes while you work," he said, taking the quilt from her and weighing it in his hands, "it may help with concentration now, but don't let it become a crutch. If you can't learn to focus with your eyes open while you perform magic, you will be easily attacked and taken advantage of."

She didn't bother to correct him. Even with her eyes closed, Verve could perceive everything around her in the back of her mind, but perhaps he shouldn't know that. "Does that pass the test?" Verve nodded at the quilt, which he at once handed back to her.

"Too thin. Fae in this realm become cold, as you no doubt have observed. Try once more."

Though she felt like throwing the quilt in his face, Verve closed her eyes again and focused on the fabric thickening. But before she could get very far with her magic, Rillian interrupted her.

"Stop. I want you to keep your eyes open this time. And don't worry about making the fabric heavier – don't deny that was your aim; focus instead on the empty places." When she stared at him, he smirked. "Tighten the threads so that there are no gaps. Like so." Rillian reached out and caught Verve's right sleeve in his hand. The room smelled at once of wine as the fabric of her dress shrank before her eyes so that she was no longer swimming in it. "See?" His hand roamed up her arm as he inspected his own work, and then his fingers slithered back down, brushing the inside of her wrist.

Verve jerked away with a surprised yelp. It felt as though he had just kissed her there.

"Sorry," he murmured. "Sometimes, my power gets away from me." Rillian cleared his throat. "Try once more. Eyes open, and melt into the emotions, don't fight for them."

"I don't know how much more magic this can take." She shook the former feather out for emphasis.

"Token. An object you manipulate into another is called a token."

"Fine. This token is about spent."

He gave her another lazy grin. "Then you'd better make this attempt count."

It took her a moment to regain her concentration, but when she did, Verve cleared her throat and tried once more, keeping her eyes open as he wanted. Her focus narrowed onto the quilt's threads, the magic pulsing in her veins, and the mixed feelings she had about the fae who sat before her. The result was twofold: the threads knit themselves more closely together, but they also turned the most disgusting shade of yellow. Frustrated, Verve tossed the quilt back at Rillian, expecting him to at once reject it.

Instead, he nodded, folded the quilt and set it aside. "All right. Can you do that eighty-eight more times?"

★ ★ ★

For the next three hours, Verve made, unmade, and remade dozens of blankets. Some turned out better than others. All had to be adjusted on some point. There were a few that wound up with holes in them, which Rillian blamed on her lack of focus. Others were too small, too big, too thin, too thick, or just the wrong object altogether. Verve produced a pillow once by accident. Rillian didn't know what had caused that, but he set it aside and said she could make more of those another time.

Finally, exhausted and head aching, Verve produced the eighty-ninth quilt and made the necessary adjustments. "There. Finished." She threw it onto one of the stacks and sat with a grunt back onto the chaise.

Rillian yawned and got to his feet. "Not just yet." He picked up the stack nearest him and headed for the mouth of the tent, but paused to say over his shoulder, "I know you're tired, but this should be rewarding for you to see." With that said, he disappeared, leaving Verve to struggle to her feet and stumble after him.

A crowd had gathered outside Rillian's tent. There was much chatter – *happy* chatter, something Verve hadn't heard from any of them since she'd arrived. She stood a-ways behind her host, who began passing out blankets to those nearest him. Soon a line formed, and Rillian ran out of blankets.

"There are more," he assured the other fae, gesturing at Verve, who ran back inside for the next stack.

They went on like this for a good twenty minutes, and although folks didn't smile or thank Verve, a few gave her a respectful nod before turning and going on their way. It was going well, until there were only three fae and two blankets left. At the end of the line was Finley, the man Rillian had warned her was a siphon and to be avoided. He didn't seem pleased, not one bit.

He pushed his way to the front of the line and pointed an accusing finger at Rillian, who simply smirked at him, as though used to this behavior. "Don't think this will change anything, Rillian. Tigers cannot change their stripes." He looked at Verve. "Everyone knows what you are, what you are capable of."

Verve frowned, uncertain if he was addressing the words to her or to Rillian. Instead of answering, for she was much too tired to match wits at the moment, she turned and walked back into the tent. She sat on the floor, for the chaise seemed too far away. She had not felt this weak since she was human. Was it possible that she was ill? Her whole body ached and her head felt feverish. At least she hadn't had a fit in front of everyone else; it would not do to show weakness. But just as quickly as the faintness had come on, she felt herself regaining strength and managed to sit up as Rillian entered the tent.

The fae gave her a puzzled glance, walked past her, and moved toward the back of his tent. When he turned, he was holding a plate filled with bread, cheese, and some withered grapes, all of which he handed to her before returning to the back of the tent and filling a plate for himself.

"How—"

"Some take pity on those in the Sky Realm and send a weekly offering through the portal hole next to the one you arrived in. That's how we found you so quickly; we were waiting for another delivery. That particular portal originates in the wilds of Letorheas and is how fae were sent here originally. Until it stopped accepting living beings, that is." He sat across from Verve and nodded at her plate. "Eat. It's not poisoned." As though to prove it to her, Rillian tore into the brown bread on his own plate.

Feeling half-starved and still weakened from the magic she had performed, Verve took a tentative bite of white cheese and had to suppress a moan. It was the best she had tasted, though perhaps it was a bit tough and a little saltier than she normally would have preferred. "You've been here for three hundred years?"

Rillian nodded as he bit into a grape, pulling a face. "I was among the first to be sent here, which is perhaps why I was easily appointed leader. The other two, my predecessors, were half-fae and quickly succumbed to the cold." He shuddered.

"What did you do that you were sent here?" It was a question that had been bothering Verve since he had first helped her and then shown her his temper.

If the question offended Rillian, Verve couldn't be sure. When he spoke, his voice was even enough. "Starting about four hundred years ago and up until recently, fae were less...enlightened when it comes to those who wield great power. Your mate – Fenn, is it? – he was meant to be sent here as well but some kind or foolish soul gave him a warning and he fled, I am told. But when confronted with the old prophecies of the Fire Queen, well, I hear many have changed their hearts and minds. Your mate should no longer be pursued, given what you are."

That was a relief. Verve had always wondered why Fenn was a fae on the run, though she had never asked him about it. "So, you're very powerful?"

Rillian merely shrugged. "It's all relative. Compared to some, yes." He gestured vaguely in the direction of the tent flap. "And yet compared to others..." His brows rose meaningfully.

Verve ate, and she at last started to feel more like her new normal, not so weak and tired. Perhaps she had overtaxed herself and was paying the price.

"What we did today – or, rather, what *you* did, will build some goodwill with the others."

"Except for Finley."

Rillian inclined his head at that. "We don't need that man's approval, anyway. Every group has its malcontents and troublemakers. Avoid him, and we'll avoid many difficulties."

They finished eating in silence, each lost in their own thoughts, judging from the preoccupied look on Rillian's face. She was about to rise, but a spell of dizziness overtook her.

"*Verve.*"

Verve sat up, even as the world in front of her grew hazy. She blinked her eyes. "Did you say something?" she asked.

It seemed she had startled Rillian from his thoughts, as he jumped slightly. "What? No." He frowned. "Are you all right?"

Her head bobbed and the room grew dim before her eyes.

"*Verve.*"

The voice was familiar, albeit tortured, desperate. Dread clutched Verve's heart even as she allowed her mind to sink into the intruding vision as though it were a hot bath.

Chapter Eight

Alone in the bowels of the earth, abandoned to fate and time, a power gathered. It was raw and wild, but its call to Verve was like that of an old friend.

"*Find me. Claim me.*"

In her fevered vision, she felt magic reaching for her, stretching its stiff limbs and searching for her, probing the darkness. Unthinking, she grasped for it as well. It was so near she could smell the tang of its potency. The aroma was heady, earthy at first until it began to take on her own magic's scent, but it was stronger than she had ever noticed before.

"*You are an empty well. Come, be filled.*"

Wind roared in her ears, and she continued to reach out blindly. Crazed, she fought against her body, as though she could escape its confines and be elsewhere – *everywhere*.

And just like that, the power retreated, as though beaten back by an unseen force. Tears formed in her eyes. She wanted that power, needed it to the point of pain. With a gasp she curled in on herself, all too aware of its loss.

"*Verve.*"

Her head jerked up at this voice, or rather, tried to. She was aware of her body lying on the floor of the tent, sensed Rillian trying to rouse her from her state, but her spirit wandered to Fenn's cell in Letorheas.

He was alone this time, chained to a wall, his face thin and bruised. The manacles around his wrists, she observed upon closer examination, had strange runes etched into them, and they radiated a great magic, one that made her power want to retreat. Gritting her teeth, Verve's spirit squatted down before her husband.

As if sensing her, Fenn looked up, but his eyes were so swollen, she wondered if he would have been able to see her, even if she were actually there. His head turned this way and that, but he stilled once she placed her now-translucent hands on either side of his face.

There was a barrier between them, one separating the physical from the spiritual, and she fought against it. This time, she managed to squeeze her fingers through and pushed healing magic into Fenn's flesh.

He groaned in apparent relief, and Verve realized the manacles restraining him must also be restraining his magic. Why else had he been unable to escape?

Furious, Verve stood and placed her hands on the metal bonds. They burned, and it took much self-control not to pull away. She closed her eyes and fed her rage into them, mindful to keep the magic from reaching Fenn's vulnerable flesh.

The manacles fought her and merely absorbed her magic. That did not discourage her. Verve found the slot where a key was meant to fit and sent her power sprawling into its depths, feeling around until she heard a satisfying click. The manacles opened, releasing Fenn's wrists.

Fenn fell face-forward onto the ground and lay there panting for some time. When it seemed he hadn't the strength to move, Verve went to him and placed a hand on his shoulder.

"Get up," she murmured. Why was he so still? He was free of the bonds, so that shouldn't be an issue. Unless... Unless he had been hurt too much to heal quickly. Verve laid a hand on the back of his neck and reached out with power, exploring him with her eyes and her magic to see what needed to be done. When that revealed nothing, she used through-sight and saw that damage had been done internally. His lungs were full of fluid and infection swam in his blood. Slowly his own magic was attempting to heal him, but it seemed it needed some help. "Fenn, can you hear me?" His skin was cold and clammy to the touch, but she clamped down on the nape of his neck as he stirred, holding him still as she started to heal him. This time, she made certain to work at a steady crawl so she wouldn't burn him. A new mark from her overeager hands was the last thing he needed.

She envisioned the infection being flushed from his body, the fluid leaving his lungs as she pushed her magic and feelings of love for him together into his flesh. Beneath her touch his skin grew hot, as though he were suddenly running a fever.

Fenn cried out softly and once more attempted to stir. With little difficulty, she held him down, continuing to heal him bit by bit until, with a cough and a mighty shudder, he sat up.

Weakened, Verve stumbled back and into another vision. The ground beneath her spirit was cold and smooth. Magic thrummed in the air. She straightened and blinked against the sudden light that met her.

The vast room in which she now stood was lined with rows upon rows of books. A large chandelier glowed overhead, and many candelabras rested on tables, all giving off an unnatural rosy light. Spots formed in Verve's vision, and she looked at her bare feet, hoping to regain her full sight and orient herself.

"Have you tried over there, Your Majesty?" said a man, his voice bouncing around the room.

Two fae hearts beat from the other side of a bookcase, and Verve picked her way toward them, though she was weary. Twice she stumbled, knocking into the stacks without making a sound, though the wood felt solid beneath her touch.

"Yes," said Dacre. "But the books have a tendency to switch themselves around. Check the ones there against this list." There was the rustle of parchment, and the scent of coffee as Verve rounded the corner.

Fear tugged at her as she hesitated. Was this a vision of the past, present, or future? Fenn seemed to think her future visions were audible only, so perhaps that might be ruled out. If it were the past, she doubted she could disrupt anything, but if it were the present... She would have to be careful not to alert anyone to her presence.

Dacre startled Verve by throwing the book in front of him across the room. As it connected with the shelf in its path, the text shattered into dust and knocked over the entire unit. "Fix that," he snapped at his servant, who scurried over to the mess.

The scrawny fae stretched out his hand, and the shelf righted itself. His magic reeked of Dacre's. "Let me just reshelve these—"

"Didn't I tell you to check the books over there against the list?" Dacre threw the parchment, which sailed toward the other fae and struck him in the face.

The servant hastily peeled the list away from his face, his brow wrinkling. "I'm sorry. I thought I should—"

"Take those thoughts and apply them to finding my queen."

"She's not among the stacks, surely?" It had been the wrong jest to make.

Dacre didn't need to use gestures to aid his magic anymore, it would seem. Without batting an eye, he struck out with a whip made of silver light. It lashed the servant across the face, opening a deep wound that caused the fae to cry out and leak silver blood. Then, perhaps regretting his action, Dacre used magic to repair the servant's face. "There will be time for laughter later, when she is home and safe by my side. Until then, I suggest you refrain from making any stupid jokes like that. Understand?" He stood, and the other fae cowered.

"Yes, Your Majesty." He bowed low, and Dacre rolled his eyes. "If I might suggest interrogating the prisoner once more..."

"Questioning the Rogue Prince is on my list of things to do, but now is the time for study. Besides, I doubt he knows much or anything about the Lands of the Dead that I have not already gleaned from my reading." Dacre rose, looking over the texts on the table in front of him. "There has to be a quicker, more efficient way to search for the information I seek."

Now on the other side of the room, several bookcases dividing them, the servant called out, "There are some books here on the Lands of the Dead."

Dacre's head shot up. "Bring them at once." He placed a marker in the book he had been perusing and closed the pages shut with a snap.

"There are many of them, You Majesty. I might suggest you come here."

He surprised Verve with the speed at which he moved, though she was capable of keeping a great pace herself. Dacre was very much a blur as he closed the distance between him and his servant, and Verve knew that the average fae eye wouldn't have been able to note any movement at all. In his wake, papers scattered and the many shelves shook and swayed, as though ready to topple over.

Verve followed, curious to see what the servant had found. She crept, though she was fairly certain she couldn't be heard or observed, and arrived in time to see Dacre pull a large black book from the stacks. The tome was so thick it had to be at least two thousand pages long. There were so many leaves, it was a surprise the binding hadn't snapped. Magic must be holding it together.

"This seems promising." With care, Dacre set the book on a table abutting another shelf. "Yes, I will start with that. Bring the rest over and set them by me. Then fetch a few of the other librarians, and make them swear to secrecy. I want as many trusted eyes as possible going over this information." When his servant didn't move but continued to stand there, frowning in apparent concern, Dacre turned and regarded the fae with a disapproving eye.

"If I might, Your Majesty. You killed half the librarians and banished several others when they refused to submit to your reign." The servant cringed when Dacre folded his arms across his chest, amused, it would seem.

Verve blanched. It was a good thing she had gotten to Fenn when she had. No doubt Dacre would have killed him also, whether by design or in a fit of rage.

When he spoke, Dacre's voice was a deadly purr, making Verve's hairs stand on end. "Are you telling me you are all that is left?"

"N-no, Your Majesty. There are three remaining, but they are on holiday."

"But they will be happy to cut their holiday short to aid their king."

The servant was silent for a moment, and then bowed low once more. "If that is what you wish." He turned and seemed ready to leave but paused.

Footsteps approached, along with the odor of spent magic – hot metal, what Dacre's residual burst used to be. Verve wrinkled up her nose as the newcomer came nearer.

Dacre bristled noticeably at the fae's approach. "Tell me you've come bearing good tidings."

At his master's words, the tall, reedy fae stopped in the shadow of the nearest shelf.

"No more of the nonsense you told me yesterday," said Dacre.

The clearly older fae sighed. "Your Majesty, as your adviser, there are certain things I must say, even if you don't wish to hear them." When he was not rebuffed, the man's spine straightened and he cleared his throat. "You've made some excellent moves, using the foresight and resources of others to the best possible advantage. The alliance with the northern lands, the use of mastership magic on certain parties, and even how you went about your attempt at creating the Fire Queen: all triumphs." He watched his king as a mouse might watch a hawk circling overhead.

"I do not keep you around to feed my vanity, Àed. Say what you mean to say." Even as he spoke, Dacre moved back to the new book his servant had found and pored over the words within.

Àed's Adam's apple bobbed. "You have achieved everything you have set out to do and have an ungodly amount of power at your disposal."

Dacre tensed. Magic visibly rippled through his hair and along the outline of his figure. He crackled with pure power as he said, "Go on."

Ignoring every instinct it went against, Verve approached the table where Dacre worked. She wanted to know what was in that book and would, if she could find a way to cross between worlds without being discovered, destroy the text and perhaps even the whole library. At the thought, fire pulsed in her veins and she had to shove it down with some effort.

"Perhaps you should take what you have and forget about certain… *assets* you've long coveted."

All grew very quiet. A fly that had been lazily buzzing around ceased its racket. The mice Verve had heard playing in the walls stilled. The servant, who had been making his way to the exit, froze where he stood, as though unwilling or unable to move. Àed the adviser seemed to shrink, or perhaps Dacre grew suddenly.

"And what coveted assets am I meant to give up?" Dacre turned and prowled toward the adviser, electricity pulsing through his being.

Verve darted for the book and looked at the page that lay open, the title page, which read: *Portals in the Darkened World*. Hastily she reached out and managed to turn the page. Her eyes scanned words that made her blood curdle. The text spoke of ways to recall a person banished to another realm.

Behind her back, she knew Dacre was glaring at Àed, but she didn't dare glance over her shoulder even; she needed this text for herself...but could she bring it with her to the realm her physical form now lay in? She could touch it, feel the texture of the pages beneath her hands, but when she tried lifting it, the book remained stubbornly still.

"Well, the, er, asset I refer to is the Fire Queen herself," said the adviser. "I believe that you must find a way to rule without her."

A chill ran down Verve's spine. The temperature in the library had dropped significantly, and the air was charged with an unseen storm. She hastened her reading, scouring the text for any information that might aid her, since she apparently was unable to bring the text back to the Sky Realm.

"You mean leave my queen to whatever fate she might meet?" Dacre asked, his voice low, menacing.

The adviser swallowed loudly. "Your Majesty, she might very well be beyond all aid. It would behoove you to move on and find another woman to replace her. Surely you have enough power to run the realm on your own."

Back where her body lay, Verve felt herself beginning to wake. The words before her eyes were swimming, fading, and she knew she didn't have much time. So she reached out with her power and attempted to light the book ablaze. Even if the book couldn't aid her, she wouldn't allow it to be used by Dacre.

"What do you take me for?" Dacre grabbed the elder fae by the throat as Verve continued in her struggles to ignite the pages. "The Fire Queen is mine and I will have no other."

At last fire erupted from the tips of Verve's fingers, licking at the pages as she reached through the barrier separating her soul from this realm. Thankfully, the men didn't notice, and the book was quickly engulfed in flames, something she knew erasure magic could not fix.

"You could have any woman you desired. We could find a real princess, someone with royalty in their blood," said Àed when Dacre loosened his hold on his throat. "This so-called queen is of mortal beginnings. Why her?"

Dacre growled. "I don't expect an insect like you to understand the bonds of love."

"And power," said the adviser, earning himself a blow across the face.

"Your Majesty?" said the servant who still remained frozen by the door. "Behind you."

The Traitor King sniffed the air. "What is that smell?" He swore as he turned at last, too late spying the book, which had set the table it sat on ablaze. It took no apparent effort from Dacre to extinguish the fire, but the text seemed beyond saving. "What the devil...?" His spine straightened.

At once Verve felt the pull of her body weaken. It was as if something were suddenly holding her spirit in Letorheas and attempting to reel her in.

"Hello, Verve." He spun around too quickly for her to react and cast a net of light around her in the blinking of an eye. His eyes swept over her as she struggled and snarled, and he seemed thoroughly amused and perhaps a touch relieved at whatever it was he saw. "Get out," he said to the adviser and the servant, who didn't need telling twice. "You shouldn't have started that fire."

"Why not? So you can have your precious information?" Verve snapped, looking around for something, anything, she might use against him.

Dacre folded his arms across his chest and smirked. "No, because that lifted whatever invisible quality you had cast on yourself." He frowned and approached her. "How are you here?"

The more she thrashed, the tighter the netting became. Fire lit up her fingertips as panic flowed through her, and Dacre tried taking her hands as though to enclose the flames raging there, but his flesh passed right through, much to her relief. "I'm not here," she said as though compelled.

"Fascinating." Again his hand passed through her, though she felt the whisper of it. "Tell me where you are so that I might rescue you." Again the words were laced with compulsion, and Verve had to fight the urge to tell him. "Firstblood of the No Lands. Your spirit already has found the way through, though your body has not yet. How long have you been so able?" These words had a stronger hold on her, and it was pure agony keeping her mouth closed against what she suddenly needed to say.

The truth was, she had experienced this phenomenon since the first night after her transformation into the Fire Queen. Then she had witnessed her sister Helena being held captive by the king, had seen Fenn confer with his cousin and once-ally, Tilda, and had witnessed Dacre rummaging through papers in his room. At the time, she had thought herself to be mad, or at the very most a vivid dreamer. Now she knew better.

His eyes searched hers, as though he could plumb her secrets from their depths. When he stepped forward, she managed to raise her hands, the fire building higher still. "I'm not going to harm you, Verve," he said. "You must know this by now."

"Stay back."

Dacre lunged at her suddenly, placing his hands on either side of her head, which she could not move this way or that. "Try to quiet your mind, otherwise this might be uncomfortable."

Verve raised her hands and attempted to push fire at him, but he merely stepped behind her and managed to reposition himself in such a way that she could not reach him. She cursed at him as the netting tightened to such an extent that her hands were now pinned to her sides.

"Try, Verve. Try to be at peace for a moment." Without warning, something cold and foreign slithered into her ears, her nostrils, and crawled through her senses until it filled her mind. "Show me where you are."

Unwittingly, her mind conjured up the image of the hole she had fallen down that had led to— No, she would not even think its name, lest he hear. She felt his breath on the nape of her neck.

"I can help you, Verve," he whispered. "Show me where you are, and I will come for you myself."

It occurred to her to feed him the wrong word or the wrong image, but the magic in her mind betrayed her to him, and he simply chuckled. "Get out of my head." Back in the Sky Realm, her body convulsed with the effort she was expending to resist.

Dacre's hands moved slowly but steadily against her temples, teasing and coaxing information from her. "There. Almost…"

The image of a wyvern unfurling its great wings filled her mind, and Dacre latched on to it. Verve wanted to scream in frustration as he continued sifting through her thoughts. She could feel his presence in her mind, gently brushing up against the walls of her consciousness.

"You're in the Sky Realm." He withdrew his hands and pulled his magic out of her head.

Unsteady suddenly, Verve stumbled forward and the netting released her. "If you come for me," said Verve, her voice shaking more than she would like, "I will kill you."

Something flashed in his eyes, and Verve could not decipher whether it was excitement or rage. "Oh, you might be tempted to try. But in the end, you'll realize that you need me more than you think you hate me." He took a small step toward her, his lips twitching. "Why don't you return to your body now? This can't be easy on you." Dacre surprised her by drawing power into his hand, a tiny, glowing sphere. It hovered above his palm, and he put it to his lips before blowing it into her face, where it shattered and passed through her.

Verve's spirit left the scene and she woke up in her body in the Sky Realm. "He's coming," she said with a gasp. But when she opened her eyes, it was not Rillian leaning over her. Weakened from her sudden excursion, Verve flailed and attempted to crawl away from the man kneeling next to her.

It was Finley, the fae who did not want her there one bit, and he was whiter than chalk. "We don't have much time." He put a hand over her mouth as she made to scream, but Verve batted it away easily enough.

"Are you here to throw me into a pit? Because that's not going to end very well for you."

The fae frowned. "No, you misunderstand. I came to give you a warning."

"Where is Rillian?" She scooted backward, and Finley had the sense to give her space.

"He's dealing with an unfortunate accident." His cold half smile chilled

Verve to the marrow. "You need to leave. No one wants you here. Choose someone to kill and return to the miserable realm whence you came."

Someone cleared their throat at the tent's opening, and both Finley and Verve looked to see Rillian standing there, his face red with rage. "Have you said all that you wished to say, Fin?" His fists clenched and unclenched at his sides, and the other fae gave them a wary glance.

"She doesn't belong among us."

Rillian cocked his head to the side. "Is that really what you came to say?" He took another step closer and then another.

Wisely, Finley circled away, his focus intent on the exit. "I meant no harm, Rillian." He continued in his slow, deliberate retreat as the other fae placed himself in front of Verve. "I'll leave now."

"You spilled the water supply."

Finley was nearly to the exit now. "I don't know what you're talking about."

"You will clean up the mess you made, and then you will help replenish the supply."

The fae made a small half bow and fled.

Rage and power radiated off Rillian in tangible waves, and he raised his hands, casting more magical wards that Verve knew no one would be able to break through. "You're unharmed?" The air smelled strongly of wine and mulling spices, setting Verve's nerves on edge and riling up her own magic.

"Yes, but—"

"What did he say?"

Verve blinked as Rillian stalked slowly toward her. His voice was calm enough, but there was something in his eyes that told her he was on edge still and would likely remain so until she set his mind at ease. "Finley? He told me I don't belong here and that I should kill someone so that I might return to Letorheas." She studied him as he took his chair and peered down at her.

"When I left, you were having a fit of some kind. Do you think it was manufactured?" He held up a hand before she could answer. "Please, I know you're kind, and perhaps that is a strength among mortals, but here and now it might put you and others in danger. Regardless of what you think I might do to Finley, you need to tell me if he cast a spell over you."

She shook her head, causing his frown to deepen. "I have...*visions* sometimes. It wasn't anything anyone did to me."

At that Rillian seemed to relax a little. He drummed his fingers on the armrests of his seat. Then he leaned forward, eyes flashing. "If he hurt you or took anything from you, I want you to kill him."

Verve blanched. "He didn't hurt me. Nor did he use his siphoning abilities against me."

Rillian's brows rose. "And you know you would be certain of this? Think carefully, Verity. Are all your powers intact?"

"There will be time to talk of this later," said Verve, not wishing to have to sift through her known magical abilities at the moment. "Dacre is coming." The words did not have the effect on the fae that she thought they would.

Of all things, Rillian laughed. "Oh, he plans to throw himself through a portal? Good luck to him, freeing himself from one of those without aid. Relax, Verity. Your would-be king isn't the main thing you should be concerned about right now." He got to his feet and held out a hand for her, before dropping it. "You really don't need to worry. It's not like he can hop on a wyvern and ride here." His magic was slithering around her, poking and assessing, perhaps trying to see if he detected any missing power.

Verve bristled and attempted to shield herself. There was a whiff of toffee, and Rillian drew his magic back to himself as her magic swatted his away. "He's more powerful than I think you realize, Rillian. Dacre is coming, and— Oh, everything's gone to hell." She rested her head in her hands. Panic bubbled in her stomach, and her breaths became labored.

"Don't throw yourself into another fit. Or, if you cannot fight it, use it to your advantage."

She snarled. "You think I can control this?"

Rillian shook his head. "Perhaps you can't, but you can control what you're focusing on and that's half of the battle." He approached Verve slowly and sank to the ground nearby as her breathing became more and more ragged and the room spun. "He isn't coming, Verity. It's not in the prophecies. Besides," Rillian said hastily, "we really do have much bigger problems on our hands at the moment. Finley is up to something. He— Verity, slow, deep breaths."

Verve shuddered mightily. "What prophecies?" She blinked rapidly and tried counting backward from twenty in her mind.

For a moment, he hesitated, his expression blank, before saying, "There are some prophecies I remember reading about the Fire Queen and the Traitor King, and none of them mentioned him traveling to any other realm besides Etterhea, Letorheas, and Ithalamore." When she opened her mouth to spill out more doubt, he gently but firmly said, "No one is coming, but we can leave. Any time, Verity, *you* can leave. Remember that and maybe it will help keep your attacks at bay." He reached out as though to take one of her hands in his own, but whatever he saw in her face must have made him change his mind, for he pulled back at the last moment and sighed. "I have to help oversee the cleanup. The weather-makers are exhausted from the winds they had to create to dry up your mess."

If she had not been so caught up in her own anxiety, she might have flinched at his words. As it was, she simply gave her head a small jerk in acknowledgment.

Rillian nudged her with his foot. "Instead of wallowing in your own misery, it might behoove you to come to our aid once more. Since you have water, you can do us a great service right now." He got to his feet and padded toward the tent flap. He hesitated there as he waited for Verve to pull herself together.

"If I help, you'll tell me more of these prophecies." It wasn't a question, though they both knew she would help no matter what he chose to tell or not tell her.

He dipped his head and held the tent flap open. "Fine. I must warn you, though, that you might not like everything I have to say." And with that, he left.

Chapter Nine

Verve agreed to restock their water supply. First, however, the troughs that would hold the water needed repairing. Someone or something had gouged deep holes in all ten, and it took Rillian's skill to repair them. As he worked, Verve noticed his eyes kept finding Finley, both their expressions grim, though the latter fae did not acknowledge or look at Verve or Rillian.

Wyverns roared in the distance, making Verve jump every time, until the fae next to her said, "The beasts rarely come any closer to Caverille. The only reason they attacked you was because you entered their domain and they felt threatened." She nodded at Rillian. "And if any get too close, he is the one who protects us from them. It's said he's killed forty in the last hundred years."

As the women watched, Rillian finished using his magic to patch the tenth and final trough. The air stank of sweet wine and spices, and Verve wrinkled up her nose in distaste. Her family was made up of teetotalers, and she never had learned to like the beverage, especially after she'd been forced to drink wine to calm her nerves.

Rillian gestured to Verve, and the small crowd parted, allowing her through. "Fire and water don't normally mix," he said below his breath as she moved to his side. "This should prove to those who doubt that you're an asset and not all a liability." He gestured to the troughs and stepped back to give her room to work.

Verve put her hands over the first trough. She was still fatigued from her visions and making all those blankets, but she simply calmed herself and searched for water in the air. It wasn't hard to find, thanks to the recent downpour she had caused. Soon enough, droplets formed in the bottom of the first trough, a slow, steady trickle. She smelled vanilla and hot spun sugar as she worked at increasing the speed of the water flow, pushing her feelings and magic together. By the time the container was full, a dull headache had formed behind her eyes and she had to stop herself from stumbling into the second one.

The second and third filled up quickly enough, and Verve didn't have to expend nearly as much energy, as she was already in the right mode to find water. From time to time, she looked up from her work and noticed that much of the crowd had lost interest and was leaving. That was a relief.

While she filled the fourth, fifth, and sixth troughs, she saw that only five fae remained: Rillian, the woman who had comforted her about the wyverns, two other she-fae, and another male. Thankfully, Finley was nowhere to be seen.

She all but fell into the seventh trough, and Rillian had to catch her. There was a burst of wine smell as he leaned in to say, "Can you manage to fill the rest? Or do you need to take a break?"

Verve gently but firmly shrugged him off. Now she felt cold and clammy, and it took great effort to fill the remaining four troughs, and when she finished she sank to the ground in relief and closed her eyes.

"Dear me," said one of the women remaining. "The poor thing is completely drained." The she-fae hurried toward them, ignoring Rillian, who raised a hand as if in warning for some reason. She knelt next to Verve and put her fingers against the ticking pulse of her neck. "Rillian, I'll help her back to your tent, if you don't mind. I think the others would like a word with you." Before the other fae could object, the woman scooped Verve up and carried her back toward the tent village, her steps smooth and slow.

Peeking over the she-fae's shoulder, Verve saw Rillian watching her with a concerned expression before he turned and began conversing with the fae now surrounding him. "I can walk," Verve said, but the woman carrying her merely sniffed.

"I hear you wish to train so that you might better face the Traitor King." The she-fae's voice was low and her pace increased slightly. "There is a network of caves that you would be wise to visit."

The headache that had been a mere annoyance before was now a pounding menace, and Verve wished the fae carrying her would simply be quiet. Still, if this woman was friendly, Verve knew she couldn't spit in the face of a potential ally. "Is it a good place to practice combative magic?" Her eyes flickered closed and she allowed the rocking motion of the woman's body to soothe her.

"You've felt it, haven't you? The distant call of some great power, tempting you to claim it?" Her steps slowed once more. "You cannot face the evils here and back in Letorheas until you've seen the Ahkoshwa."

Verve peered up at the woman. "What do you mean?"

The she-fae looked around them, a hunted air about her suddenly. "I live in the blue tent on the outskirts of the village. Come to me tonight, but do not bring anyone with you. I will tell you of the cave and what you must do." She carried Verve into Rillian's tent and set her down on the chaise longue. "Whatever you do, do not speak of the Ahkoshwa with anyone and do not allow yourself to be left alone with Rillian. He is not what he seems."

A frown tugged at the corners of Verve's mouth and she nearly went cross-eyed trying to keep her focus on the woman. "I don't understand." By now she could hear several fae approaching the tent. Verve marveled at the woman, whose expression and manners at once changed as she covered Verve with a blanket.

"I am called Yoshabet. Yosha for short, if you please, Majesty. But my, you are still so drawn and pale. Has the master not fed you anything today?" Before Verve could answer, Yosha bustled toward another room in the tent, humming a strange tune as plates clicked against each other and the aroma of heating food reached Verve's nostrils.

Rillian entered the tent at that moment. His eyes went first to Verve and then flickered in surprise to Yosha, who hustled toward them with two bowls of the most delicious-smelling soup and a hunk of bread. "You didn't have to go to this trouble, Yosha." Though he said it kindly, Verve detected a flash of annoyance crossing his face.

Yosha waved his words away after she thrust a bowl and the bread into Rillian's hands. "It's no trouble." She approached Verve and handed the other bowl to her, then sat cross-legged on the floor.

Rillian seemed ready to protest but instead took his usual seat and started eating. "That was some display with the water." He nodded at Verve.

"You shouldn't have let her drive herself to the point of exhaustion," said Yosha, sounding more like a fussing mama than someone who was very upset by what she had witnessed. "Aren't you hungry, dear? You should be replenishing your strength."

Verve forced a polite nod and took a sip of the soup. This woman appeared to be kind, but Verve didn't know if she should mention her concerns about Dacre in front of her. She didn't want to alarm anyone. Though Rillian didn't seem to think it was anything to worry about. But could she trust him? Everyone seemed to be warning her either against him or Finley. Verve didn't know what to think or whom to believe.

They spoke at first of matters that did not touch on Verve. It was mostly Yosha speaking, going on and on about the disagreement between two weather-makers, the fae couple whom she suspected of stealing rations from others, and other affairs that one might find even in a mortal village.

Throughout it all, Rillian appeared to be giving attention to her words, making the occasional sympathetic noise and speaking where he would be expected to. But Verve could read the tension in his shoulders, like he was trying to be polite but was struggling.

"—And then there's the matter of Finley," said Yosha. At once the atmosphere in the tent changed.

Rillian leaned forward, his grip on the bowl tightening enough that the pottery cracked. He looked at the mess he had created, before causing the bowl to fuse back together with an audible snap. The air smelled of mulling spices, and he set the repaired crockery aside. "You have news?" His eyes darted to Verve and then back to Yosha again.

Yosha blushed. "Well, you know me. I don't mean to hear things I oughtn't. And I really shouldn't gossip." It sounded like she very much wanted to gossip. She got to her feet, and moved coyly toward the adjoining room.

"It's not gossip if it's helping the people of Caverille."

Verve, who wasn't hungry, set the bowl aside, leaned back, and watched the two through half-shuttered eyes. All she wanted to do was rest, but she knew she should be finding a way to leave the Sky Realm before Dacre figured out how to travel there. She didn't care what Rillian thought he knew of prophecy; if Dacre got a hold of her, she would have to kill him before he bent her to his will, which he had already attempted to do in Ithalamore.

"Well," said Yosha after a long pause, startling Verve, "I suppose it would be best if I told you. You are, after all, in an authoritative position and could do something about this dangerous nonsense."

It would seem that Rillian was nearing the end of his patience. Irritation poured off of him in visible waves of vapor the color of a murky pool. "What dangerous nonsense?" Rillian asked.

"Oh, well, I might have overheard some plans of his." She had her leader's interest and she obviously knew it, milking it for all the attention she could get.

Why, though? She wasn't at all like this earlier. Verve closed her mouth when she realized belatedly that it was gawping.

"Tell me what was said, please," said Rillian.

Yosha let out a nervous hum. "Well, Finley has moved to the southern hills. He plans to remain there until he has what he wants."

Rillian raked a hand back through his hair. "And what he wants is...?"

"Why, the wyverns, of course." She said it as though it were the most obvious thing in the world. When Rillian didn't react but sat there in apparent puzzled silence, Yosha twisted the hem of her left sleeve in her slender hands. "I was right in telling you, wasn't I?"

"What does Finley want with the wyverns? He's terrified of them."

Verve recalled the look on Finley's face when she had faced the orange beast. He had seemed terrified and unwilling to approach a step closer.

Yosha shrugged. "He saw me eavesdr— *listening* at that point and didn't finish saying what his plans were."

Now Rillian was on his feet moving for the tent flap. "You were right in telling me this, Yoshabet." He paused mid-step and turned to face her. "Who was he speaking with? You saw them, yes?"

"They were veiled. But there is a possibility it was Mercedes."

Verve's blood ran cold at the mention of the she-fae who had attempted to slice Verve's throat open with the magic-canceling blade.

As if following her line of thought, Rillian gave his attention to Verve. "Those two in league with each other can't lead to anything good." He reached for a long walking stick by the tent's entrance. "Verity, you are to stay here until I return. And don't look at me like that; it's not safe wandering with those two potentially stirring up the packs." He turned to Yosha. "I would advise remaining in the safety of your tent until this is all over."

Yosha bobbed her head and followed closely on Rillian's heels. "Should I tell the others anything?"

Rillian hesitated for a moment before speaking. "There's no need to alarm anyone at this point. He surely wouldn't drive the creatures into the encampment. There's nothing for him to gain from that." With that said, the pair left the tent.

What could all this mean? Verve sat forward, resting her sore head in her hands. Perhaps Finley guessed she had been contemplating how to utilize the wyverns to free herself – and possibly others – from the Sky Realm. Maybe he had simply run away, afraid that Verve might select him as the person who should be sacrificed in order to make a gateway. It made sense he might think that. Not that she was going to kill anyone. But the wyverns...there had to be a way to control them. Verve knew she had better figure it out, and quickly.

But the more she thought about it, the more convinced she became that Yoshabet had been lying. If Rillian was preoccupied with Finley's comings and goings, then that would free Verve to sneak out and visit the she-fae's tent. That must have been Yoshabet's intent. Why did she not trust Rillian, though? Verve had been warned against Finley, yes, but that was mostly from Rillian himself and perhaps a few supporters. It might be wise to look into her mysterious host as well.

Verve picked up her bowl and spoon, rose, and carried them toward a pile of dirty dishes that had accumulated in a haphazard stack in a corner. With a shrug, she deposited her bowl and spoon onto the stack, which thankfully did not come crashing down around her ankles.

With Rillian gone and her wits sharpening, Verve prowled around the perimeter of the tent. She felt magic there, and when she squinted, she could see it faintly. Power limned the walls in near-transparent hues of red. It made her skin tingle and her hair stand on end. Once she had walked around the tent's edges – as much as she could with furniture in the way – she decided to poke around more closely.

First Verve went for the small enclosure within the tent, the curtained-off quarters that made up Rillian's bedroom. There she found a cot covered in a pile of quilts, all thrown back as though the occupant had risen hurriedly, and a small desk with a stool seated before it. She reached out with magic, hoping to discern if any spells guarded the desk. At once her power ran into a visible wall surrounding the desk, and the room filled with the smell of vanilla and wine. A warning tickled the back of her mind, something telling her she should not tangle with this type of magic. Reluctantly, she backed away and left the room. *I have no reason to suspect him of anything devious. Sure, he tried to manipulate my emotions before, but he might have just been trying to get a better feel for who I am.*

She hoped the smell of her magic would dissipate quickly enough so Rillian wouldn't know she had been in his personal quarters. If he could smell magic, that would lead to awkward questions. With nothing else to do, Verve sat back down on the chaise and waited for nightfall.

★ ★ ★

There was a dampness in the air, one that permeated Verve's clothing and sank into her bones. She shivered and grabbed a yellow blanket, and draped it around herself like a cloak as she moved toward the tent flap.

What little sun they got in the Sky Realm had faded, and the land was covered in a creeping darkness and unspooling mists. Verve was about to venture out but paused. The yellow of the blanket would surely attract attention of those watching Rillian's tent, and Yoshabet had seemed to want her to leave unobserved for whatever reason, so Verve took the corner of the blanket in her fingers and willed it to fade to a deep slate-gray. Almost instantly the fabric turned jet-black. *Well, that works too*, she mused as she stepped out into the night.

Orange and yellow lights bobbed in the distance, magical orbs set out to illuminate the way of late wanderers. The sounds and smells of the evening assaulted Verve more intensely as she walked onward, searching the dimness for the outskirts of Caverille. There was laughter and music, men and women chattering and debating over the din, creating an ambiance of comfort and familiarity. Aromas of magic and cooked food reached Verve's nostrils, and it felt like that afternoon's soup had been ages ago.

Thankfully, no one appeared to observe her as she walked. That or she wasn't so very out of place for anyone to take notice of.

The fog thickened, and Verve wondered if it was a weather-maker's doing or perhaps just a creation of the realm. She rubbed her hands together with vigor and moved past a cluster of larger tents that were lit up brightly within and practically vibrated with life and laughter.

On the outskirts of the tent village, there were white tents, tan tents, yellow tents, and one red tent. Verve circled around the perimeter of Caverille. It was quieter here, save for the occasional distant roars of a wyvern and a few howls that reminded Verve of the dire wolves she had encountered months ago. At last, after having prowled for half a mile, she came across the only blue tent she had thus far seen. All was dim and silent within, save for the steady beating of a fae heart.

Verve hesitated. Was this some sort of trap? Had she been a fool for venturing out on a night like this, when Finley was up to goodness knew what?

She was about to turn around and leave when a soft voice said from behind her, "Were you followed?"

Startled, Verve drew power into her hands and spun around to face Yoshabet. The fae had silenced her heart's beatings and Verve had not heard her approach. "Don't scare me like that."

Yoshabet hastened toward her, a finger to her lips. "You must remain silent. Douse your power and do not use it until we're out of camp." Something in the distance roared, and the fae jumped, clutching a hand to her heart. "You did not say if you were followed or not."

"I-I don't think I was." Verve let the power in her hands drop, though she remained wary and ready to summon fire at the slightest provocation.

Someone stirred within the blue tent and a light flared up within. "Who's out there making so much noise? I'm trying to sleep." Moments later, a woman in a nightgown appeared, clutching a lantern in her right hand and holding a shawl closed with the other. She was the exact image of Yoshabet.

"What the devil?" Verve drew back, her fingertips itching.

"Twin," was all that Yoshabet offered.

The identical woman nodded at Yoshabet, bowed slightly to Verve, turned, and sat in the sand outside her tent flap. "It's tonight, then? I'll keep watch," she said. The woman stretched her hand in front of her and waved it around a few times, stirring up a slight breeze that smelled of pine. What appeared to be a small funnel cloud materialized before her, and the image of three men appeared within, poking around a cluster of hills. "Green sparks for a ten-minute warning. Golden sparks mean they are using great speed and their return is imminent. Red sparks mean stay where you are."

"Thank you, Estelle," said Yoshabet.

Estelle grunted and continued to stare into the whirlwind before her. "Be mindful of the skies."

Without warning, Yoshabet took one of Verve's hands in her own and tugged her toward the hills in the east, her footsteps silent and sure. "I know you have many questions, but it's not safe yet. There are those who would stop us." That did nothing to dispel Verve's unease.

"What—"

Yoshabet hushed her and increased her pace. Soon they were at least two miles outside the encampment, which disappeared behind the sand dunes. "We're almost there," the fae reassured her. "When we're there, we'll assess how much has been lost."

"What has been *lost*?"

Again the woman silenced her. Once she apparently thought it safe enough to speak, Yoshabet cast a spell, filling the night air with the aroma of mint. "I'm an assessor," she said, keeping her voice pitched low. "It is not a rare gift, not even here. When I helped you out of the portal hole, I sensed great magic within you. I want to see how much has been lost since then." Without asking for Verve's permission, the she-fae squeezed Verve's hand between her own and closed her eyes. The smell of mint intensified the moment Verve's fingers started to burn, but Yoshabet dropped her hand as though startled. "Child, you have been quite drained."

"What do you mean?" Verve demanded.

Yoshabet motioned for Verve to follow her around a looming black wall of rocks. "Do you know what a siphon is?"

The words made her blood turn to ice. "But I haven't been around Finley hardly." Either this woman was lying about being an assessor or the fact that Verve had been drained of power. "I would have known if I'd been siphoned off of."

The fae stopped walking, and Verve ran into her. "You feel at your best and at your full strength?" She didn't wait for Verve to answer before approaching the wall of rock and raising her hands.

Verve frowned. Now that the woman mentioned it, hadn't she, Verve, been feeling more and more tired lately? Weaker? Wasn't there a bit of hollowness where there once had been a mighty thrumming in her chest? "I don't know."

Yoshabet didn't respond to the lie but focused instead on raising a barrier of magic around them. It was a great amount of power that she expended, and the air reeked of her magic. Panting, the woman motioned for Verve to follow her to the wall of rocks. "There is but one way in, and only one person may enter at a time. Touch the wall, and it will appear. The door will seal itself to me, once you are inside." She looked at Verve expectantly.

"Why should I go in there?" Something didn't feel right, but Verve couldn't quite place what that might be.

"Please, we don't have much time. If you are to succeed, you must enter now before anyone can stop you."

But Verve didn't move. "You're going to have to give me a better explanation than that if you want me to co-operate."

The fae shook her head. "Some of the words have been cursed for me, but let's see if I can't find a way around them." She drew in a deep breath and looked to the skies, perhaps watching for a sign from her twin. When none appeared, Yoshabet relaxed noticeably. "You know there is a siphon. You know who they are. They have – made it difficult for me. If you are to enter the cave and it accepts you and you accept its gift, you will be able to—" The she-fae's face turned gray as she tried to get the words out. She stopped for a moment, panting, before trying again. "You can – leave here. Free us all."

Verve searched the woman's face, trying to decide if she believed what Yoshabet said. It felt too good to be true, and as Mother had always taught her, such things almost always *were* too good to be true. "And if the cave does not accept me?"

Yoshabet made a face. "It will."

"But if it doesn't?"

That made the woman pause, a war in her eyes. "You will be stripped of all your powers." Before Verve could protest, Yoshabet held up a staying hand. "But this cave was meant for the Fire Queen and the Fire Queen alone. It is obvious you were brought here for this."

The words rang true in Verve's mind, but she couldn't shake a sense of foreboding. "I was brought here because I fell down a hole." She ran her slick palms down the sides of her dress.

"I know you feel it. There is something more you are meant to do, not spend the remainder of your days here because you refuse to commit murder." Again Yoshabet's eyes went to the heavens. All was still. Fog continued to roll in over the land, and the sky remained clear of any display of colored sparks.

"How do I know this isn't some sort of trick?" Verve asked. "I have no reason to trust you."

"You also have no reason to *distrust* me." Her gaze returned to Verve, pleading. "You are meant to save us all."

"I—"

"Not just this realm, but all the realms. You think the Traitor King is only a threat to Letorheas? You do not know the prophecies. And if you believe the Traitor King is the only problem before you, you are sorely mistaken. There is the siphon."

Verve threw up her hands in warning as the woman approached. "There's something that — I don't know. There's something that rings false about you." She waited for the woman to deny it, but the woman nodded.

"I sensed that one of your underdeveloped gifts is discernment." She looked at the sky again and shook her head. "We really don't have time for this. Do you want great power, to return to the home realms to overthrow the Traitor King, or do you wish to be killed for your power?" Apparently Yoshabet had not meant to say so much, as she recoiled and took her lower lip between her teeth.

"Are you planning on trying to kill me?"

"No, of course not. I'm trying to help you reach your potential. I have nothing to gain by your death."

"Except escape from this realm."

Yoshabet tilted her head in agreement. "But I would benefit from anyone's death, for that matter. Think. Who would want your own power to wield against you and free his people?"

Verve took another step away. "Don't come so close."

"Verity, it's not that difficult to figure out. You've allowed yourself to relax too much. Your guard has dropped and you've been willfully deceived. You are in grave danger."

"Perhaps from you." Verve drew power into her hands and was ready to release it if she must. "What are you hiding?" Her power flared as Yoshabet raised her hands, but the fae quickly lowered them.

"Fine." She sounded more resigned than annoyed. "I will show you. But know this before you strike: you've been misled about me, Your Majesty." With those words spoken, the night air filled with the aroma of peppermint, and Yoshabet's skin began to bubble and expand. A faint light seeped out of her pores, and with a soft hiss, the transformation was complete and Finley stood before her.

Chapter Ten

"You!" Verve reared back, though the man neither approached her nor made any sign of attempting to use magic. "You're the siphon! Yoshabet isn't real, is she?"

The fae she had believed to be Yoshabet simply shook his head. "Estelle had a twin, but Yosha died at birth. You and I are the only ones here who know this, Your Majesty. So much that has happened since your arrival was a distraction from a master manipulator." Green sparks lit up the sky. "Please, this is your one and only chance. Do you think the siphon is going to let you out of their sight again? You must do this." He pointed at the rocks. "Place your hands on the surface and a doorway will appear for you. Once inside the cave, you will know what to do."

Still Verve hesitated. "If this is a trap…"

"It's not. I swear on the twin moons it is not." Again the sky lit up with green sparks. "Ten minutes is all we have. *Less than* ten. I beg you, Your Majesty." The man got to his knees and clasped his hands in front of him, his eyes full of terror.

Nothing about his actions rang false. But since when was she the best judge of character? Nonetheless, a sense of dread had come over her and she knew without knowing how she knew that her next move was crucial. "I need a blood vow."

Finley reached into his belt, and before she could stop him, he sliced his palm open. "Do as I have done, then take my hand." He extended the knife to her, and she accepted it and sliced her own palm.

Verve took his hand in her own and felt magic flow between them. "Vow that I will come out of there unscathed by your hand." She nodded toward the cave.

"I vow it." At his words, the smell of mint intensified and the magic from his blood made Verve's hand tingle.

Now she knew beyond a shadow of a doubt that Finley was speaking the truth. Yellow sparks lit up the sky, and Verve hastened toward the wall of rock and placed both her hands on its cold surface, just as Finley had instructed her to do. At once the rock writhed beneath her touch and a narrow opening formed where her flesh had met unyielding wall. Verve conjured three orbs of light and stepped into the unknown.

At first, she experienced a tugging sensation, one much like she'd felt when she fell through the hole leading to the Sky Realm. She stumbled onward and she knew without having to look that the entryway had indeed disappeared, just as Finley had said. But she would worry about that later.

Cautiously Verve stepped forward. Puddles littered the path before her, and soon she stood in the middle of a great room, indigo stalactites frozen mid-drip from above. She spun in slow circles and let her light orbs dance around her. *What am I meant to do? Finley said I would know.*

Uncertainty ate at her. What if this had been a trap and Finley had managed to circumvent the blood vow?

"*Psst.*"

She stopped revolving and froze. "Hello? Finley? Is that you?" Of course it wasn't him. He had said he would be unable to follow. But if not him, who?

There was no immediate response, though Verve now had a strong feeling of being watched, not by one set of eyes but many. As she ventured ahead, her arms broke out in gooseflesh and her hair stood on end.

Someone inhaled, and a soft voice tickled her ears and bounced off the walls.

"*To gain much...*"

"Who's there?"

The whispered words, not her own, echoed around her, growing slightly louder with each iteration until they repeated again,

"*To gain much...much...MUCH...*"

Verve slammed her hands over her ears, though that did nothing to block out the noise.

"*She must lose much…much…much.*"

Power thrummed around her, as though dozens of fae were preparing an attack. But the air smelled of nothing, no residual burst except for her own. At once her lights died out with an audible *pop*, pitching the cavern into complete darkness. Verve reached out in front of her, feeling the way toward where she remembered the one exit being.

"*What do you seek, Firstblood of the No Lands?*"

A wall of green fire materialized in front of Verve, staying her retreat. Slowly it traveled toward her, driving her back to the far wall.

Verve swallowed. "I want to return home."

"*Home?*" Now two voices spoke as one – one male, one female – and the sound was lilted with mirth. "*Where does the Fire Queen call home? Everywhere…and nowhere.*"

"Please, I wish to return to Etterhea."

"*And?*"

And what? What could they be after? "Um, I wish to return to Etterhea and Letorheas?" The wall of fire ceased driving Verve away, just as her back slammed into cold, unyielding rock.

"*And what do you need?*"

Verve spun around to face the wall, from where the voices seemed to be coming. "I need to leave this place."

"*No, what do you really need?*"

"I don't know what you want me to say."

"*Don't you, though?*"

"I really don't."

A great sigh rippled the hair on her head, and Verve took an automatic step back. "*Power.*"

"Power?"

The wall in front of her took on a golden hue. "*Much power. It is yours for the taking. But it will cost you. Oh, yes, it will cost you dearly.*" As if to highlight its words, the fire behind Verve flared up once more, making her sweat profusely.

"I don't want or need more power. I just want to return to my family."

"That is why you shall have more power."

Verve took another step back. "I would just like the power to leave here and take as many people as I am able back to Letorheas with me."

"Long have we waited for you, child." It was now three voices speaking, possibly more. The effect was strange. It felt as though the words were going to make Verve's chest burst open, like her heart were some drum wildly beating to escape its cage. "Take...take... take." An invisible force reached out and grabbed Verve's wrists in their grasp and drew her irresistibly toward the glowing rock wall.

In vain Verve struggled. Pain shot through her arms to the point where she thought she might sprain something. "Just tell me how to leave here."

The force pulling at Verve slammed her open palms against the wall, and something cold and sharp sliced into her fingertips. It burned. Verve clenched her teeth, fighting a scream, as the voices chanted strange words she could not comprehend.

"Choose now, Fire Queen," several voices said over the din.

"Choose what?" Verve cried.

A whirlwind of light and color swirled around her, whipping her hair about and lifting her feet from the ground. "To gain much, she must lose..."

Images floated across the wall, sights of home. There was Mother sitting at the kitchen table, sipping her morning cup of tea. She looked so sad and yet Dav sat across from her, rambling on without a care as she drew with her charcoals on a pad of paper. Outside, Anna hung clothes on the line to dry, her face more drawn than Verve remembered it being. Then the scene changed, and Verve was gazing upon her elder sister, Ainsley, and her husband. Ainsley's stomach was swollen with child, and when Markus pressed an ear against her, his face split into a heart-stopping smile. "She kicked!" he crowed.

"*He* kicked," Ainsley countered with a laugh.

"Choose."

"I don't understand!" Verve yelled above the roar of the wind. "What am I meant to choose?"

"To gain what you need, one life must be taken in exchange."

Terror seized at Verve's heart and she tried to pull her fingers away from the wall. "You're lying. They're back in Etterhea. You can't touch them there."

When the voices spoke again, they were tinged with wry humor. "Oh, can't we?" The images before Verve changed, though this time they held a ghostly, almost transparent quality. Mother slumped forward onto the table, her eyes open and glassy. Dav collapsed in a heap on the floor. Anna was sprawled out on the lawn, a trickle of dark blood running from her pale lips. And then there was Ainsley, lying so very still as her husband wept over her. *"Magic is everywhere, Verity Springer. It touches everything and everyone. Therefore, I am...here. And there. And over there as well. Choose who will die."*

"You can't have any of them."

"A balance of power must be struck," the voices insisted. *"You cannot expect we would part with this power for free."*

"Keep your power, then. I'll find another way out of this godforsaken realm." But the more she struggled, the more the rock seemed to pull at her.

"You will choose. Or we will take them all."

Tears burned Verve's eyes, clouding her vision. There had to be some way around this. She couldn't sacrifice a family member for anything in the world. Mother – dear, sweet Mother; what would Verve be without her? And Ainsley? She was with child. There was no way she could choose her. Then there was Dav. As much as Verve didn't get along with her, it would hurt everyone to lose her. And Anna was as much family as any of them.

"If you will not choose now..."

"Stop it! I understand. But you can't have any of them." She looked around her desperately, as though the solution would materialize before her. "Take – take me instead."

Of all things, the voices laughed, a terrible sound that made Verve want to curl up in a ball. *So brave. So selfless. But no, you are not an option. The realms need their Fire Queen.*

Verve cursed and kicked the rock. She couldn't very well not choose and then lose *all* of her loved ones. Desperation loosened her tongue and she at last stopped struggling, slumping against the wall. "Dav. Y-you can have Dav." The moment the words left her lips, she regretted them, and great sobs shook her body.

The unseen force dropped her like she had burned it, and she fell to the ground with a bone-jarring thud. *"You would withhold your best from us? Interesting..."* The voices did not sound happy. *"We had come to expect more from you, Firstblood of the No Lands."*

She rubbed away the tears blurring her vision and tried to back away from the source of the voices, but bumped into an unseen force. "What did you expect me to say? I offered myself, but you would not have me, so I chose the most logical option." Her voice wobbled over the words, and the cave trembled, causing rocks to tumble from the high ceiling. A stalactite lodged itself into the ground inches from Verve's left leg, and she let out an involuntary yelp.

"Every choice has a consequence. She who chooses poorly loses even more than what she expected."

"Please, don't harm any of them."

The voices weren't listening. *"And yet a deal is a deal. You must take the power of the Ahkoshwa. Return to Letorheas a woman with less and yet so much more."* Five bolts of colored light – crimson, ocher, gold, emerald, and silver – burst forth from the wall of rock and struck Verve in the chest.

For a moment, Verve's soul hovered over the scene, watching as the light poured forth from her mouth, from her eyes and ears, from every strand of hair. Then her soul soared back into her body, which convulsed, and all grew dark as wave after wave of power washed over her, filled her, threatened to drag her down into a deep, dark nothing.

"You possess the elements, but we amplify the gift of fire."

Verve took a burning blast to her heart, which she thought might explode at contact. Light returned to her vision, painfully bright.

"*All things must have balance, and thus we impart the gifts of darkness and emptiness. They are the Fire Queen's to wield as she sees just and right.*"

Again she felt her body take the impact of the Ahkoshwa's gifts, and she writhed and whimpered. Soon enough, though, that pain passed and she tried to sit upright, thinking the cave was finished. It was not.

In quick succession, Verve was forcefully given the ability to physically walk the paths between the realms, the gift of communicating with all living creatures, and a dozen other magical talents that she could not hear over the sound of her own screams. Finally, the voices quieted, and with the newfound stillness, Verve's pain ebbed and she lay sprawled out on the cave floor, panting and shaking.

A powerful light spilled out of her every pore, but with each throbbing beat of her heart, it dimmed. She tested her fingers to see if she could move them. There was a great roaring sound in response, and the ground beneath her trembled. Verve fought to sit up as rocks tumbled from the ceiling, crashing down around her ears and on top of her. The air left her lungs in one great *whoosh*, and she was unable to call for help or to move out from under the weight of the boulders.

Chapter Eleven

In the near distance, outside the now-collapsed walls of rock, there were cries of dismay and confused voices demanding to know what had happened to their 'sacred monument'. The mound of rocks shifted as someone attempted to move a few. Others shouted for them to stop, that they would bring the rubble sliding down on themselves.

Verve groaned, using up what little air she had left in her lungs. Exhaustion weighted her down as much as the rocks. She hadn't been this tired after absorbing the Cunning Blade's power. What she had been gifted this time must have added up to so much more. She tried again to rise, to push the rocks off her, but it proved fruitless and she continued to lie there while fae speculated as to what had caused the cave-in.

"It must have been a wyvern," said one fae, her voice rising above the others. "One lash of its tail could have taken the Ahkoshwa down." To this there were a few jeers and other noises of dissent.

"The beasts don't come this far north."

"But it has been known to happen."

If only Verve could draw attention to herself, then perhaps the fae would start digging for her. Or maybe they would simply leave her to be buried until the end of days. *Nonsense*, she chided herself. *I will soon have enough strength to free myself. Besides, it might be better to be left alone until I'm able to fight.* The thought of facing the real siphon left her feeling uneasy.

As if in response to her silent worries, more of the rocks shifted and a voice called out to her. "Your Majesty, are you able to move?" It was Finley, and Verve could have melted with relief. What had taken him so long to ask?

Verve pushed against the rocks that had landed on her chest and succeeded in drawing in a few gulps of air. "I'm barely able to move an inch."

The ground trembled as more rocks were lifted and cast aside. The fae voices that had been chattering were now raised in alarm and it sounded as though many hands had begun digging. "I'm sorry it took me so long to come to your aid," said Finley. "I had to send a certain someone on a fool's errand to buy you more time." There was a pause followed by the whispered words, "Were you able to take it?"

A sob tore itself loose from Verve's chest. She needed to get out of here, to make certain the magic didn't take any of her family. Gone were the thoughts of saving the realms, of defeating Dacre. If something had happened to any of her loved ones, she didn't know what she would do.

Finley must have heard her cry for the rate at which he dug increased. "We'll get you out, don't you worry."

"What was she doing in there in the first place?" asked a man's voice that Verve didn't recognize. "It is forbidden."

"Fool, it's in the prophecy," a woman who might have been Mercedes snarled.

Others grunted their assent. "That's not all the prophecy said, I'm sure. It is a shame what information we have here has been lost." A shame, indeed, though Verve doubted very much it had been an accident like this man seemed to believe.

Again Verve tried moving, feeling some strength slowly yet steadily pour into her body. How long it would take all of the magic to fully absorb into her being, she couldn't say. With the Cunning Blade, it had been nearly instant. This power hovered around her, as though waiting for what had been taken in to finish settling into her bones so as not to overwhelm her body. She wiggled the fingers on her right hand, and there was a deep rumble as more rocks went sliding.

Outside, several fae shouted and ran away, judging by the sound of things. "Your Majesty, please try not to move. You're going to trap yourself worse and possibly harm some of us," said Finley.

Verve opened her mouth to apologize, but again her lungs had emptied, making speech impossible. Panic pushed down on her. When she was a mere child, Verve had fallen down a well and hadn't been found for days. Would she be stuck in the crushing darkness here for just as long or perhaps longer? The memory of the cold and loneliness of the well caused Verve to break out in a cold sweat. Air. She needed air.

In obvious response to her increasing anxiety, the mound trembled. Men and women screamed as the rocks shot away from where Verve was buried and exploded in clouds of black powder. She could see it happening all around her without having to open her eyes, which she had shut.

Now light shone through gaps in the rocks, and Verve thought she might be able to pull herself out, if only her whole body wasn't trembling. She tried to suppress the tremors as she pushed against the boulder that had landed on her chest. The rock moved a few inches before collapsing once more on top of her.

"What happened here?" The new voice belonged to Rillian and he sounded furious. "Did you allow this?"

"Your days are over, tyrant," said Finley.

Verve used through-sight to see what was happening around her.

Rillian lunged at the man and pinned him by the throat to the ground. He'd moved so quickly, Verve had hardly been able to take it in.

Assessing herself and her magic, Verve was alarmed to discover that her speed ability had been greatly diminished. That would be a great loss in a fight, but she needed to find a way to get it back from the siphon. She wished Finley hadn't made the declaration he had; she would need the element of surprise in order to attack Rillian successfully, and she had the feeling she would only have one chance. Verve pushed against the rock pinning her down. "Help," she croaked.

The males stopped fighting and turned to her. "Are you in there, Verity?" asked Rillian, his tone cautious.

Aware that he might read her emotions easily, and also hear her racing heart, she took a slow, calming breath before continuing. "I'm stuck."

"What are you doing in there?" Rillian didn't make a move to help her and held Finley back from coming to her aid.

Verve sighed the sigh of the tired and attempted to sound embarrassed. "I was hoping to find answers about the prophecy you mentioned." She added a wobble to her voice.

Rillian tightened his hold on Finley, who didn't even bother fighting against him anymore. There was a tightness in Rillian's shoulders, and his eyes had narrowed into slits as he stared at the general area where she had been buried. "And did you find any answers?" His voice was calm, though Verve could feel his tension, see it emitting from him in waves of nauseating green.

She shoved against the rocks once and let frustration enter her voice as she sobbed, "It d-didn't let me get far."

"What didn't?"

Verve sniffed. "It called itself the Ahkoshwa and it said I wasn't w-worthy." Those words rang true to her own ears, and she could but hope they rang true to Rillian's as well.

Next to the siphon, Finley frowned. "You mean it didn't work?"

"No," Verve snapped. "It t-took—" She thought of her family and wailed. How much time would she have to buy herself? Even now, any one of her family members could be meeting their end at this magic's hand and it was all her own stupid fault. "It took everything." Her breaths came in gasps, and she allowed panic to radiate from her in physical waves that she knew would reach her nemesis.

Rillian released Finley and stepped forward. "Are you hurt?"

"Y-yes."

Finley started digging, but Rillian crossed his arms over his chest. "If it took all your magic, then how are you still alive?"

Blast. I should have thought of that.

"What does it matter?" one of the women in the crowd said. "Maybe some powers were left to her as a mercy. She can't harm us anymore, so we might as well dig her out and see what is to be done next."

Free of Rillian, Finley and several others started to move the rocks piled above where Verve lay. All the while, Rillian watched, tension in his posture and apprehension in his eyes. Still, he didn't stop anyone from digging.

Verve lay still and closed her eyes. If only she could absorb all the power more quickly. It hung around her like a cloud and, bit by bit, it shrank as she pulled it in through her skin. Thankfully, she didn't think anyone could see it, otherwise they would probably leave her.

Progress was slow at first, until more fae joined in. Soon more soft light touched Verve's face, and she hastily muted her magic before anyone could notice it.

At last the final boulder was removed and Finley thrust out a hand, which Verve grasped gently, aware that she had taken on more strength. "You gave us quite a fright." His voice was rough and by the reddening of his face, she realized she had still grasped him too hard.

Verve offered her ally a smile as he pulled her up. "Thanks."

"She's all right!" Finley called out.

Rillian was on the outskirts of the group, observing and waiting.

She ought to have known he was the siphon from the beginning. But if he was the one that Igraine had foreseen Verve meeting, that would make him a Larknott, and that would most likely mean he was related to Fenn. Squinting at him, Verve thought she could see it in his face, some features that might belong to her husband. She would have to be quick about absorbing his magic, if she was indeed now a siphon like she suspected. If she failed, the bargain she had made with Igraine dictated that she must kill him.

Finley carried her slowly down the mound of rubble, his footing unsure as rock shifted beneath him. "Do you think you can stand?" He adjusted her, and his hand brushed against the skin of her elbow.

The sensation prickled, and Verve realized she had felt this before when in contact with Rillian. Sure enough, she assessed her magic, and noted that some of her new abilities had been drained. She momentarily threw up a shield around herself, forcing Finley to drop her, and landed in a crouch. The air smelled not of mint like Finley's residual burst, but of wine and spices. But that couldn't be. Rillian stood at the bottom of the rock pile.

"What's wrong?" Finley backed away as Verve growled at him.

She looked around her, trying to make sense of what had just happened. Finley was a siphon too? Why did his magic smell like Rillian's now? Wanting to save her energy and strength, Verve let her shield drop.

"Slowly putting it together, are you?" said Rillian, a smirk settling onto his face.

Verve looked from him to Finley. Was Finley a projection? No, that couldn't be. A projection wouldn't have been able to lift rock or have a feel to it. "What are you exactly?" She fought to keep the fear out of her voice.

The crowd surrounding them backed away.

"I told you I could control emotions, but I wasn't completely forthcoming with you." Even as he spoke, Rillian drew a shield around himself.

"You don't just control *emotions*. You can control *people*."

Rillian dipped his head in a mocking bow. "The lady *can* learn."

Despite her growing apprehension, Verve picked her way down the remainder of the rubble, aware all the while that Finley stood behind her and might attack at any moment. "That's why his magic smells like yours right now." She needed to buy herself time – time to gain more power and time to figure out what on earth was happening. "You're both siphons?"

Before Verve could think of any more ways to stall, a bolt of azure fire hit her in the chest and knocked her onto her bottom. She attempted to raise another shield around herself, but Rillian struck out again, too quickly for her to react.

Again and again magic fire pummeled her. Rillian maintained his distance, but others did not.

Apparently under Rillian's control, Mercedes and Estelle drew magic into their hands and joined with him in his attacks, their magical waves of torment pouring into her body. Behind her, Finley approached, a rope made of poisonous green light in his hands.

Verve screamed in pain and frustration. This wasn't how it was supposed to go. Why was her new magic taking so long to absorb into her body? At this point, everyone besides the four surrounding her had fled.

"Give it up, Verity." Now Rillian did approach Verve, lashing out with a fire whip. "You can't handle all that power."

Something brushed up against Verve's consciousness, but Verve swatted it away with a thought. "Stay away from me."

The hateful fae laughed, but at least he had ceased his attacks, as had the others under his control. He crouched in front of her, rightly thinking she was currently unable to do anything about her predicament. "Magic is not for mortals, former or otherwise." He brushed a strand of sweaty hair behind her right ear, and Verve tried to bat at him, but she was too weak.

Again she felt something brush up against her mind, a cat begging for attention. "Stay out of my head," she spat.

Her words seemed to have startled Rillian, because his hand jerked away, having only absorbed a small amount of power from the contact. "Give your power willingly, and I'll let you live. I'll kill another fae, and even let you return to Etterhea. Resist me, and you'll be the one I sacrifice to open a portal."

"Mistress..."

Verve shuddered as a presence in the back of her mind pushed into her thoughts, its voice foreign and inhuman.

"Don't give him your power."

In the distance, there was an animalistic screech, which caused Finley to jump and back away, the rope still in his hands. "That wyvern sounds close," he murmured.

"What will it be, Verity? Renounce this nonsense and live, or die a horrible, needless death."

Bleary-eyed, she looked around her, but Rillian snatched her jaw in his hand and jerked her face upward. Verve winced as he sucked more power out of her. She tried to shake him off. When that didn't work, she attempted to block him. But it was no use. Her newly acquired magic was minutes away from being fully realized, but she didn't have that much time.

Rillian glowered at her. "I take your silence for stubbornness. I will ask once more, and then I will take what I want. Give me your magic."

"What? So you can be the Fire Queen?"

He struck her across the face. "Remember, you brought this all on yourself." Rillian's right palm glowed silver as he brought it down and clamped it around her throat.

"Fight just a moment more, Mistress."

Pain burst behind Verve's eyes as Rillian drew out her creation ability thread by thread, taking it into his own magical stores. She attempted another shield, but that's the ability he went for next. Now she writhed, using all her strength...which Rillian at once stole as well. The remainder of her speed went after that, her endurance after that, quickly followed by transformative magic, and flight.

As he pulled ability after ability out of her, Verve desperately clung to the ones she thought might aid her when the full force of her new magic surfaced. But he ripped each away like she was a garment he was unmaking.

A mighty roar resounded, and the earth trembled as clouds of dust rose and cloaked the scene.

Closer to human than she had been since Dacre transformed her, Verve coughed and sputtered as she tried to draw breath.

Rillian's hand tightened around her throat. "You called the wyverns, did you?" He leaned in. "Two can play that game." With that said, he took one last ability from her: the magic that allowed her to communicate with animals. She felt it leave her with a small tug, and the back of her mind went quiet.

The first wyvern to land was a small blue one. Verve stared at its yellowing teeth, which snapped in her direction. All around them, beasts of varying sizes and colors flew in and landed, their wings furling and unfurling.

There was nowhere to run, no gap to squeeze through unnoticed. Verve pushed herself into a sitting position and reached deep inside herself, plumbing the depths of what little magic she had left for something, anything, that might aid her. All she could sense, however, was a little fire and an overwhelming sense of what she at first mistook for thirst. The more she studied the feeling, however, the more certain she became that Rillian had failed to absorb her siphoning ability. Perhaps it was because he already had that sort of magic, or maybe he hadn't sensed it in her. Whatever the case, it was too little too late: Rillian had already released her throat and was moving toward the animals. Skin-to-skin contact was needed for siphoning, from what she understood.

It was with a small amount of satisfaction that Verve noted Rillian was handling the magic poorly. Though he didn't seem weakened by the quick absorption like she had, it wasn't staying in his body. In fact, the power kept drifting back toward Verve, as though it understood who its true mistress was. Rillian paid this no mind as he raised his hands to the wyverns, no doubt issuing the silent command for the beasts to attack her.

The first wyvern, the blue one, snorted, and the others roared in unison. Rillian took a half step back, and the creatures tightened the circle they had formed.

"You are *mine* to command." Rillian sounded annoyed, and there was an edge of panic to his words, but he held his ground, hands still raised as though he could manipulate the creatures that way. But when the wyverns stomped their large feet, he shot up into the air like an arrow and attempted to fly away. The beasts were not having any of that. Though Rillian was fast, the blue wyvern was faster. Before the siphon could flee, he found himself clamped in the wyvern's claws. He fought against the creature and managed to free himself, but then the other wyverns were there, dragging him down between themselves.

Fearful of being trampled, Verve staggered to her feet and looked for a way out. The wyverns were so preoccupied with subduing Rillian, she might just have a chance of freeing herself.

She made it a few steps toward the rock mound, but at once a yellow wyvern with brown stripes blocked her path and snapped its teeth at her. Verve raised her hands – as if *that* would do anything to save her – and the beast stopped, its eyes twinkling as though it would laugh. But that had to have been Verve's fancying. Surely these monsters didn't have human emotions. She took an unsteady step backward as it took a step toward her. Behind her, Rillian continued to scream and struggle. The air reeked sharply of wine and spices.

It would seem the beast meant her no harm, so with one last wary glance, Verve turned her back on it and faced Rillian, whose limbs each found themselves in a different wyvern's mouth, his body drawn out taut as though they meant to quarter him.

Verve jumped when the wyvern at her back nudged her in the rump. She didn't need telling twice. Her hand went to her bruised throat as she picked her way toward Rillian.

Upon seeing her, the fae kicked and writhed, but the beasts seemed to have bested him. "You were not meant to have this power." His eyes bulged and spittle flew from his mouth even as the stolen magic curled away from him once more and snaked around Verve.

Though it was a tight fit, she managed to squeeze between the wyverns and, with the magic calling to her, Verve grasped Rillian's left forearm in her hand. At first she felt nothing and wasn't sure what to do.

Rillian tried siphoning more magic off her, but she drew on her closest emotion, rage, envisioning power flowing from his veins and into her own. There was no resistance as the magic responded to her silent commands. Her body drank it down in deep gulps, filling the well that she was until she was nigh drowning. At that point, Verve tried to release him, certain she had taken all the power she could, but it were as though her hand had become attached to his skin. More and more magic left him and entered her. She gritted her teeth and closed her eyes. *Stop! Enough!* It had to end. Surely no fae was meant to have this much magic.

Thankfully the pain was more bearable this time around, and when she had siphoned every last drop of his magic, Verve let out a painful gasp. Raw power coursed through her veins, and it threatened to explode onto the landscape surrounding.

"You could have left me something," Rillian spat, going on to call her every filthy name she had ever heard.

Perhaps sensing the fae was no longer a threat, three of the four wyverns ceased holding him still, but the one remaining, the small blue beast, licked its chops. In the back of Verve's mind, it said, *"This wretch is responsible for over two hundred deaths of my kind. I ought to tear him apart right here and now, but as a truce between our races, I will offer him to you to dispose of as you see fit."* The wyvern tossed Rillian at Verve's feet.

Verve regarded him with a shudder as gooseflesh rose on her arms. "I'm sorry he took so many from you."

The creature's black eyes narrowed. *"Your mate took the life of one of our more misguided calves."*

That had only been a baby that had attacked her in Etterhea? Seeing a touch of ire in the beast's eyes, Verve swallowed and hastily attempted to make an apology for Fenn, for fear he might find himself the object of vengeance. But the wyvern cut her off before she could get a word out.

"There is no need for you to be sorry. The calf meant to bring you to our realm against the council's advisement. It was a misguided attempt to hasten the fulfillment of prophecy."

Between them, Rillian had started to crawl away, but the wyvern brought one of its claws down on his thigh and held him in place. "Curse you."

"One more word and I might just fillet him myself."

"Your kind has prophecies?"

The wyvern tossed its massive head and made a gurgling noise that Verve swore was a sound of amusement. *"No, but there reside within many of us the likes of you and the likes of immortal races from other realms. We may lose most of our humanity and memories, but we remember the day foretold, when the Fire Queen will free the Sky Realm from its oppressors and submit it to its rightful and sole denizens."*

Verve swallowed. "And you will promise to leave fae and humankind alone?"

The creature seemed to consider this for a moment, its head cocked comically to the side. *"This will take some convincing. I can foresee no* objections to leaving the fae alone, but humans are plentiful in many realms and make easy prey."

"If I am to fulfill this prophecy and give you the realm, then I think it more than fair to demand fae and humans alike to be declared off-limits." At her words, power thrummed beneath her skin, which glowed a brilliant gold.

As though it were uneasy, the creature shifted its weight slightly. "Very well. But make no mistake: if fae or human alike hunts one of my kind, they forfeit their life."

Verve nodded. "That sounds fair enough."

Rillian had kicked at the beast during the exchange, his desperation palpable. He now managed to free his right arm and produced a dagger, which he slashed toward the wyvern's claw. The weapon glanced off the creature's thick skin, and Rillian cursed as it skittered away.

"Are you going to end him or am I?"

She regarded Rillian, and shook her head. "I don't know if I should be the one to decide his fate." Verve turned and faced Finley, who had stood in the near distance. "Finley, are you yourself again?"

The blue wyvern and its fellows growled as the fae approached, his steps slow and cautious.

"I am sorry, Your Majesty. I didn't mean to—"

Verve held up a hand. "It's all right. You could've told me he can control other people, though. And the fact that you're also a siphon." She quirked an eyebrow at him and smirked.

Finley cleared his throat. "I didn't know for certain about his manipulative ability, to be fair." He lowered his gaze, which he trained on Rillian. "What are you going to do with him?"

"My opinion is that we should take him back to Letorheas and let him live as a mortal there."

That made Finley laugh. "You're not serious? Ve— Your Majesty, he has done nothing but stolen others' magic and benefited from their hard labor."

"I know."

Finley threw up his hands in apparent disbelief. "And yet you would show him mercy? He tried to kill you."

"I—"

"It shouldn't be up to her to decide," said an unfamiliar male voice. A group of fae came forward, Mercedes and Estelle among them.

At the group's approach, the wyverns snorted and backed away toward the mound of rocks, as though guarding Verve from behind. The blue one left Rillian where he lay, chest heaving.

Mercedes glowered at Verve. "He should die for what he's done." Many fae shouted their agreement. "After you've given back what's been taken from each of us." Murmurs rose up among the thickening crowd, and Verve's heart fluttered nervously.

Finley surprised her by speaking up over the throng's growing restlessness. "She'll return your gifts in due time."

"When?" a male fae demanded. "What's to stop her from doing so *now*?"

"If she's to free us from this realm, she's going to need her strength. Gifting temporarily weakens the giver."

She dipped her head in acknowledgment. "I will return to each fae what was taken from them...after they join me in Etterhea." When many cried out in anger and dismay, the fire in Verve's veins threatened to erupt through her every pore. "I need every one of you to help me overthrow Letorheas's Traitor King. You can either swear a blood oath to me here and have your magic returned now, or you can prove your loyalty by waiting until we're in the mortal realm to receive what was taken." She didn't know where this boldness came from, but she knew she would most likely fail without allies.

"Majesty, is that wise?" Finley shook his head.

"Why Etterhea?" asked Estelle, sounding more curious than upset.

Because I have to protect my family. Because I might have already signed their death warrants. "You are all wanted creatures in Letorheas. The moment you set foot in that realm, you will be hunted for your past crimes or for your power."

No one argued with that, though the feeling the crowd gave Verve made her uneasy. She knew if she gave them their power now, she would never see them again. Strangely enough, no one took her up on the offer of making a blood oath.

"Very well," said Mercedes, as though she spoke for everyone. "If you mean what you say, kill Rillian to prove you're serious." She nodded at the wretch, who had only just pulled himself to his knees.

The look Rillian gave Verve was smug, as if to say, 'I know you don't have it in you to take my life or any life, for that matter.'

There had to be another way. She had no love for Rillian, even though he was related to Fenn, but killing him seemed extreme. Verve was about to refuse to perform the deed, but Mercedes interrupted.

"You haven't the stomach, have you? Weak and useless. Why would we follow someone so powerless?"

At those words, Verve's temper and magic rose to the surface. "How sporting is it to kill a mere mortal who can't rise to their own defense?"

"Your Majesty." Finley's tone was laced with a warning.

Verve went on, power thrumming beneath her skin as she began to glow blue. "He is harmless now. Why would you have me kill him? Isn't losing his power punishment enough?"

"Prove your worth!" someone in the crowd shouted. Others echoed with their agreement. The mob moved toward her, as though to force her hand.

Verve bared her teeth, which caused a few to pause. "You can return to Letorheas and be free of him. Why do you need—"

There was a flash of red light, and the smell of mint and iron filled the air. Where Rillian had been sitting a moment before, he now lay spread-eagle, blood dribbling down his chin, his eyes wide and glassy. *Dead.*

Verve could only gawp in horror.

"Enough of this pointless bickering," said Finley as he lowered his hand. "The Fire Queen had no right to take Rillian's life. The honor belonged to one of us, one who has truly been tormented by him."

"What have you done?" Spots formed in the corners of Verve's vision. She should be used to death by now, but it still came as a terrible shock to her system to see the lifeless corpse lying there.

Finley sniffed, his chin jutting out. "I did what had to be done." Here he turned his attention to the crowd. "Let the Fire Queen prove her worth another way. Follow her to Etterhea and reclaim your powers there." He frowned but said nothing about the tremors which now wracked her body as he put a steadying hand on the small of her back.

It was Estelle who spoke next. "How does the magic work? Does she just speak a few words and we end up back in the mortal realm or...?"

"Or she could control the wyverns to give us a ride back," another fae mused.

Verve shook herself out of her stupor. "No. I don't know if that would work." She felt a nudge at the back of her mind, the agreement of several of the creatures behind her.

"Wait here," said Finley. He ran through the crowd, which parted for him. They all stared at Verve in silence for a few minutes, flinching and backing away every time a wyvern growled or moved. Minutes later, Finley returned, a small red book in his hands and a grin on his face. "I knew he hadn't destroyed all the sacred books." He opened the book to the very middle and held the text out to Verve, who accepted it with apprehension.

There was a subtle magic in the pages, one that set her teeth on edge and made her blood sing. She took the book with care and did not fling it away, even though it whispered her name and raised her hackles. Confused, she flipped through the text. Every page but the middle one was blank. "I don't understand." Verve squinted as she leafed through it once more. She thought something might be faintly etched on the paper, but there was nothing. Just the middle page that said, *She who is worthy buries. And from the corpse I shall rise.* She tried handing the book back to Finley, but he simply stepped back, his grin twisting into a grimace.

"It's a touch macabre and dramatic for my taste, but I think you're meant to..." Here he pointed from the book and then to Rillian's corpse. "He's not what is considered high fae since you took all his magic and immortality, but his blood and flesh might work anyway."

Verve thought she was going to be sick. "Do I have to put the book inside him?"

Finley tugged at the hem of his tunic. "You can use magic to do that, if doing it by hand makes you uneasy." There was no mistaking the look on his face: he wanted out of this realm as much as she did.

"Right." Verve closed the pages and approached Rillian, and laid the book on his chest. Then, shutting her eyes, she swallowed her disgust and pushed the feeling of sorrow together with magic, imagining the book seeping through the corpse's flesh and coming to rest inside his rib cage. To her surprise, her magic's residual burst had disappeared. There was no scent, no sign she had used magic at all but for the warm feeling of release from her body.

She didn't have time to wonder at the change before the ground rumbled and the sky darkened as clouds rolled in from the far reaches of the land. The earth where Rillian lay swallowed him into its depths, and from the sandy soil that covered him there rose a golden sapling, which grew as they watched in awe to the largest hawthorn tree Verve had ever seen.

Relieved laughter spilled out around her, and the fae rushed the tree. The first one to put her hand on the bark didn't have to barter or threaten for her passage, for the hawthorn simply split in two, the boughs overhead twining together to form the top of the gateway it had made. The she-fae hesitated for a moment but then touched her hand over her heart as she looked Verve in the eye and ran through to the land beyond.

Fae after fae went through, and the tree allowed them safe passage. Soon it was just Verve and Finley. His eyes searched hers, and then he approached the gateway.

"Where in Etterhea should we meet you?"

Verve ran through the possibilities in her mind. She couldn't have them meeting her at Maplehurst or on the neighbor's property; a group that large would attract unwanted attention. Besides, the area was most likely being watched by Dacre and his allies. "Caldron Banks. There is a large wood there on my aunt's property. It's south of a small town, the only civilization for miles. But I can show you myself." Verve hastened to his side and peered through the gateway that had been made. All the fae that had passed through were nowhere to be seen, and the world beyond…it was unfamiliar.

"Of course. But it seems you and I will have to track down the others." Finley extended his hand, and the two gripped forearms and shook. "Don't worry." With that said, the fae stepped through the gateway.

Verve made to follow, but the gateway closed in her face. "Hey!" She placed her hand on the bark, which shriveled beneath her touch. "I need passage too." The tree didn't respond, so she struck it once with her fist. In response, there was a giant ripping sound and the hawthorn crashed to the ground, its trunk having split clean in half. Her breath caught. "That was my way out of here!" Panic dug its claws into her gut, and she closed her eyes tightly.

"You are Firstblood of the No Lands," said a soft voice in her mind.

That made Verve open her eyes. "Yes, but I thought—"

"If the prophecy holds, and it has so far, you don't need a tree to make a gateway." When Verve continued to stand there in stupefaction, the blue wyvern snorted and stomped its right claws impatiently. *"Don't you feel it? The possibilities?"*

There was something, she had to admit, that felt different about the world around her, something that she hadn't felt until the Ahkoshwa had given her the new abilities, but it could be anything. She was still so new to being a fae. Verve shook her head and paused. "You're an interdimensional creature."

"As are you," a green wyvern countered.

"How do you do it? Travel from realm to realm without a tree to make a gateway?"

The creatures made a gurgling noise, which now Verve was certain had to be laughter. Then the blue wyvern stepped toward her. *"You must feel for the fabric of reality, hold it in your power, and rip through it. Really, it should be second nature to you, youngling."*

"But I'm not one of your kind. I wasn't born with this ability."

"Ah, but you were reborn into it." The beast dipped its head. *"I will give you a quick demonstration, and then you must be on your way. I sense*

your fellow fae are not going to patiently wait for you in the mortal realm." It unfurled its wings as if preparing to take flight, but simply used them to balance itself as it reared back and reached forward with both claws. There was a flicker of white light, and where there had been clear air there was now a growing patch of rippling gray.

Verve's fingertips tingled as she watched the tear grow under the wyvern's guidance. She raised her hands and felt for something to cling to, until she brushed against an object not solid and yet velvety. The contradiction baffled her, but she didn't question it. "So I tear through this?"

"*Yes. You rip a hole in the fabric of reality and then you walk the paths of the No Lands. Keep your destination in mind at all times and your feet will guide you.*" The creature relinquished its hold on the fabric, and the hole that had been rent in the air at once repaired itself. The wyvern sat on its haunches, its tail flicking like a cat's as it watched Verve attempt to grip on to the fabric.

For a moment she lost the sense of reality beneath her fingers. Frustration overcame her, and fire erupted from her fingertips, which caused the wyverns to growl and back away. "Sorry." She shook her head, gritted her teeth, and willed the flames to dissipate before reaching out once more for the fabric and successfully grasping a fold of it in each hand. Reality solidified in her grasp, and she hastily tore through it ere it could elude her again. Blue sparks spit from the edges of the hole she created, a hole that expanded as she dragged her hands outward, the fabric still pinched between her fingers.

"*Goodbye for now, Firstblood of the No Lands. And good luck.*"

Verve nodded her thanks and stepped into the paths between.

Part Two

Chapter Twelve

The paths between worlds were a rippling, inconstant gray, like a watercolor painting that was overly wet and running, with flashes of color appearing beneath her feet as she moved. Instinct drove her forward at a steady pace, and she was unwilling to stop for fear of her nerves taking over as she realized she had indeed stepped outside the realms of reality. Verve kept her hands raised and let magic course through her body.

It had been easy, ripping a hole in the ether. Now, with nothing familiar to orient her, however, Verve found it difficult not to give in to panic. It didn't help that there seemed to be little breathable air here. Slowly, she dragged in one breath, held it, and then let it out.

All was eerily silent. Verve couldn't even hear her own breathing or heartbeat, which she had grown so accustomed to. The skin on the nape of her neck prickled, and she felt at once that she was being watched. "Hello?" she called out or, rather, she meant to. No sound escaped her in this place. Verve stopped walking and turned in a circle, hoping to catch a glimpse of whoever or whatever might be stalking her.

Silver tree roots writhed in her peripheral vision, but when she turned back to face them head-on, there was nothing there. *"Hello, Firstblood,"* said one voice, which was echoed around her by numerous others.

Verve turned back to her intended path, shaking her head. It had been a tree's voice that had spoken. How she knew, she couldn't say, but it did make sense, as trees – hawthorns, that was – were the only other creatures she knew that could create portals between the realms besides wyverns. The thought made her feel less alone, and she walked now with more confidence in her steps.

All at once, something inside her screamed for her to stop, and she did. Verve brought the fingertips of both her hands together and felt for the fabric that made up this non-realm. In the Sky Realm, the fabric had been easier to grab on to. Here it was slippery, and she lost it several times in her attempts to rip it open. As she had seen Father do numerous times before he turned a newspaper page, Verve licked her fingers and that allowed her to gain purchase on the material, which she rent in two, admitting a near-blinding light. Squinting, she stepped through the hole she had created, and the tear sealed itself behind her.

It took Verve a moment to adjust and take in her surroundings, and when she did, she hastily ducked behind a thick tree. There were several mortals nearby. If they came upon her now, glowing with power, they would be terrified and rumors would spread.

Where she stood was just outside the town near her aunt's house. The fae she had freed should have been close enough to sense, to hear, but all she could pick up on were the comings and goings of mortals in the near distance. Her heart sank. There wasn't much she could do by herself, what with the little experience she had with her magic. Perhaps she was close to being evenly matched with Dacre, but *he* at least had many allies. She had expected some of the fae from the Sky Realm to back out of the agreement, but she hadn't thought it would be all of them.

The moments ticked by, and she warred to bring herself and her power under better control, lest she be observed. It was an odd thing, no longer smelling her own magic, but stranger still to see it leaking out of her every pore when she had even the slightest shift in her mood. Fenn's lesson on muting her magic seemed like eons ago, but Verve closed her eyes and recalled it as she stuffed down her apprehension. She dragged a hand over her face, willing herself to appear normal to the mortal eye. Sensing it had worked, Verve peered around her and listened in hopes of detecting a fae heartbeat nearby. All she heard was the mortals working in her aunt's fields.

How long should she wait? Her family was possibly in peril and every minute she wasted waiting could cost her dearly.

Verve took to pacing but stopped almost as soon as she started. It wouldn't do for the Fire Queen to appear distraught and impatient.

Who would follow that sort of leader? The thought made her pause. She wasn't a leader and was fooling no one. No wonder none of the fae she had freed were loyal.

Her face heating and her spirits sinking, Verve took one last look around the empty woods and prepared herself to make a portal. Maybe she could find her family and Fenn – had he escaped – and they could hide until Dacre forgot about her...or someone more capable dealt with him. Yes, that sounded like a much better plan. She found the fabric that made up the reality of Etterhea and was about to tear it, when she heard the telltale sounds of a gateway opening not two miles away. Verve hiked up the skirt of her dress and ran toward the noise. When she arrived, the gateway was still open and Finley was only just emerging.

At the sight of her, the fae's eyes widened and he took a half step back. "Who are— My, you look completely mortal. Forgive me, Your Majesty, but I didn't recognize you for a moment." He shuddered as the gateway closed behind him.

The smile Verve had felt tugging at her lips melted downward. "Where are the others?"

His suddenly erratic heartbeat betrayed the news he was about to deliver. "I'm sorry. By the time I had emerged from the portal from the Sky Realm, more than half had already fled. And the others... Well, some listened, but most want nothing to do with the fae of Letorheas. Not after the way they treated us." Something he saw in her face must have made the fae uneasy, for he pulled at the collar of his shirt and would not meet her gaze.

"But *you* came." She took a slow step toward him and held out a hand. "Thank you."

Finley eyed her outstretched hand, shivered, and took it in one of his own. They shook, and then he didn't seem able to release her fast enough. "They might change their mind yet, if given time." He sounded doubtful.

Verve's magic was threatening to rise up and lash out at something, anything. She hastily mastered herself and pointed to the hawthorn. "Would you be willing to make another stop before we find shelter?"

"Somewhere in Letorheas?" He sounded so hopeful that Verve cringed.

"I'm afraid the stop is in Etterhea." She motioned to the tree. "There's a wood outside my family's home. There are at least two hawthorns there."

Understanding lit up Finley's eyes. "Will the Traitor King not be waiting for you to make a move like that?" It hurt to hear, but the fae was right. If she boldly approached her home from the Woodhouses' property, she would most likely find herself in a trap. But she needed to make certain her family was all right.

Verve regarded Finley for a moment, an idea forming in her mind. "Dacre doesn't know your face. At least, I'm *assuming* he's never met you." She watched him for any signs of recognition. "Dacre. Dacre Starside. Did you ever cross paths before you were banished?"

"The Starsides are of noble blood – or, at least they were during my time in Letorheas. We moved in very different circles. I doubt I ever crossed his path when he was a youngling, though the name does sound familiar." He regarded Verve for a moment. "I will scout out your family's home and make certain your loved ones are all right. Then we will talk about your returning what Rillian stole from me."

Relief bloomed in Verve's breast and she nodded. "Thank you." She cleared her throat and gestured to the hawthorn. "There are hawthorns on the outskirts of the town near my homestead. Could you make a portal there? To Brecksville? Avon's the province, if the tree needs to know." It was true Verve could create a portal there herself, using her newfound ability, but she was uncertain whether or not she could bring Finley safely through, and she didn't fancy traveling through the No Lands again so soon.

"Very well. Why don't you wait here? I shouldn't be long." He reached into his boot and produced a dagger, but Verve stopped him from slashing the tree.

"Yes, but why don't you let me make the gateway?" Perhaps the tree would allow her to make a gateway now that she was an interdimensional being.

Frowning, Finley stepped out of the way and replaced the blade in its sheath. "You do it the compassionate way." He sounded impressed. "As a youngling, I never had the patience for that sort of thing."

Verve didn't respond as she placed her palm against the hawthorn's trunk. She was prepared to offer the tree something in exchange for Finley's safe passage, or for it to ignore her entirely, but the hawthorn, which must have read her mind, at once opened a portal, trembling and sputtering nonsense as it waited with obvious impatience for Verve to unhand it.

"Ask someone in town for Maplehurst, and if no one knows that, say you're looking for the Springer family," Verve told Finley. "You'll need to mute your magic. Mortals still don't know of the fae."

"They will soon, if prophecy has anything to say about it." With that said, Finley hastened through the gateway, which shut with a *snap* behind him.

There was nothing left to do now but wait for Finley to return. Once he had made certain it was safe, she would reunite with her family and find a way to put protective spells on them.

Mortal workers in the near distance were taking their break around the watering hole on Aunt Springer's property. Their boisterous laughter set Verve's nerves on edge as they talked and joked, and she had to keep a tight leash on her magic.

The land was in the throes of winter, though it had been autumn when she'd last been in the realm. If she were caught out here with no coat and no chaperone, there would be some interesting questions to answer. The thought amused her, as her situation would no doubt have distressed her youngest sister. Verve ran her slick hands down the length of her dress.

What felt like hours passed, though it couldn't have been more than forty minutes, judging from the position of the sun, when the hawthorn she had been watching split down the middle, forming a gateway. Finley emerged, his face pale and his magic still muted. He stood in the portal's mouth and gestured for her to come closer. "You need to see this." His tone was grim, and his expression hardened.

Verve didn't hesitate but threw herself through the gateway, which mercifully let her pass – something she was uncertain it would do – and emerged with Finley not in the woods outside town but on the Woodhouse property. Bile rose in her throat. "You were supposed to use the same tree outside town. These woods—"

"There are no fae for miles and miles. I thought you'd want to return as quickly as possible without being seen." He gestured toward her property. "It's not a pretty sight, I'm afraid." His tone was softer, apologetic, but there was a note of fear in his voice, and Verve realized belatedly he was afraid of her reaction to whatever she was about to find.

Without sparing him another glance, Verve took off at top speed and arrived outside Maplehurst's back gate in half a second. Only, there was no gate, just the remains of one. It had fallen over as if it had been struck by a great wind, and the house… "No, no, no." Verve ran for the house, ignoring Finley, who had just arrived on the property.

"There's no one in there," he said as Verve picked through the charred ruins. "I can't smell anything."

Verve continued to dig, throwing aside siding and beams and anything that stood between her and the heart of the house.

"Your Majesty, you're going to draw unwanted attention to us."

She sank to the ground with a sob and ceased searching. "This is all my fault." If she had offered a different family member in exchange for power, would the outcome have been the same? Verve cursed below her breath and wiped away a few angry tears. How would she have known? It wasn't fair.

Finley cleared his throat. "Maybe your family wasn't home when this happened."

"This is the Ahkoshwa's doing. Of course they were home." Vibrating with rage, Verve rose and cast a glance back over her shoulder.

The other fae's face paled and he stepped back. "W-what would you care to do now?" He lowered his gaze as Verve fought to master herself.

That was a very good question, but it was one she didn't have the strength to answer. Her lower lip trembled as rage gave way to grief.

Verve hugged herself and turned away from the wreckage. She sniffed and her head jerked up. There was the tinge of stale magic in the air, and it smelled like sweets, her old residual burst's scent. Tears clouded her vision, and she did not resist when Finley took her by the arm and drew her away from the site.

The fae led her to a hawthorn tree and released her in order to make a gateway. But when Verve sank to the ground and rested her head in her hands, he shook his head and moved nearer. "It isn't safe to remain here. Come, Your Ma—"

"Don't call me that," Verve whispered.

Finley swallowed, hard. "As you wish." He looked around them as the birdsong quieted and the air crackled with barely suppressed power. "Careful."

Verve's magic was barely under control, and she was having trouble making herself care. First Helena, then the rest of her family. What would be taken from her next?

"Verity," he said sharply. "Stop wallowing and control yourself."

Her head snapped up at the sound of his voice. Around her, a few of the trees had uprooted and were hovering in the air. If a mortal came upon them now... With difficulty, Verve reached for her power and spooled it in toward herself. The trees collapsed back to earth in response, causing the earth to quake beneath them.

Finley hastily went about righting the trees that had landed with their roots outside of the soil. "I know you've lost much, Verity. But there are many left who still need your help." The air filled with the scent of peppermint as he worked. Once he had finished, he held out his hand for her, which she took with reluctance. "We must return to Letorheas before we are noticed here." He spoke sense, but Verve couldn't bring herself to leave so soon. It felt almost...callous.

"I want to know what happened. How they— How my family perished exactly."

The fae nodded. "All right. Where would we learn such information?"

Verve thought for a moment. "We'll talk to the neighbors. They should know."

"And then we leave this realm." There was no question in Finley's voice, and Verve knew his loyalty would only stretch so far.

"Of course. And I'll give you your power back."

Finley seemed to sag with relief at these words and squeezed her hand. "Lead the way."

There was no one in the open for a mile, of that Verve was certain. Still, there were mortal heartbeats inside the Woodhouses' manor house, so she kept her pace close to something expected of a human and advised Finley to do the same.

When they arrived at the house, Verve rapped her fist once on the servants' quarters. She remembered too late that she was barefoot and wearing something this realm wouldn't consider appropriate. "Oh, hang it all," she murmured as the door swung open.

"Hello, how may I help— Goodness, Miss Springer! What happened to you?" The maid's wide eyes went from staring in horror at Verve to narrowing in suspicion at the male fae behind her. She continued to bar the door. "Are you hurt?"

Verve shook her head. "No. I've just returned from…" What lie had been spun to keep her family safe? It seemed to have been ages ago since she left her family estate after accidentally murdering Helena. Tears formed in her eyes and she let them spill.

Compassion overtook the maid's apparent survival instincts, as she reached out and embraced Verve. "I'm so sorry for your loss."

Behind Verve, Finley tensed. Verve could feel the shift in his mood and see it in his posture.

The maid scowled at him. "You may come in, but I ask that your foreign friend remain outdoors." She moved aside for Verve to enter.

"He's all right," Verve assured her. After rubbing her eyes and clearing her throat, she turned to the other fae and said, "Please keep watch out here. I shouldn't be more than half an hour."

His eyebrows rose. "Did I not mute my magic well enough?" He'd spoken in a different language so the maid wouldn't understand.

"We— they're very suspicious of foreigners in these parts. I'm sorry, Finley. If I take too long, knock and have them fetch me."

Finley waved away her apology and walked off. "I won't be far, should you need me."

"Miss?" the maid asked. "Please, it's cold. We don't want the warm air escaping the house."

"Right." Verve sucked in a deep breath and followed the maid, who shut and barred the door behind her.

"I shall take you to Mr. Woodhouse."

Verve didn't follow but stood in the small kitchen, which was empty of people but full of the smells of baking bread. "The Misses Woodhouse are...?"

The maid frowned slightly. "They've not been found. Mrs. Woodhouse keeps to her bedchamber. You see, she hasn't been the same since they left."

"Right." Verve had all but forgotten about the missing middlings from her area. More of Dacre's doing, no doubt. *I need to stay on task,* she chided herself as she ran a hand over a flour-covered counter. "Do you know what happened to my family?"

"You mean you haven't heard? Well, I-I don't know I'm the one to say, Miss Verity. Mr. Woodhouse has heard plenty. I can bring you to him, if you'll just follow me." Her heart had taken off at a run, and the blood drained from her face as she stared at Verve.

"You know what happened. Please, tell me everything." The words Verve spoke were laced with persuasion, and the mortal had no chance of resisting.

The maid's face went slack and she recited what she knew. "Mrs. Springer and her maid, Anna, were found dead after their house caught fire. It was an accident, the fire. The town constable believes someone left their knitting too close to the kitchen stove."

Verve drew in a shuddering breath as the news she had feared crashed over her. She let the loss sink into her bones, but did not succumb to it as she wished to. Now was not the time to give in to despair. Ainsley, her eldest sister, might still be alive. If she was, Verve would go to her and place protective charms on her and her household, with Finley's help. "What happened to Davinia?" Verve sniffed as she tried to control her tears, and was surprised to smell the aroma of limes.

"The youngest Springer child escaped the fire and is staying with family overseas." There was a powerful burst of citrus, and the maid's eyes glazed over as she spoke.

It made no sense. This woman couldn't have a drop of magic in her body. Verve would know...wouldn't she? Tentatively she reached out with her own magic and probed her, feeling for anything that might indicate she was other than what she appeared to be. Verve's power brushed up against something, and the maid flinched, so Verve withdrew it. "Has anyone strange been to visit you recently?" If the maid didn't have magic, then Fenn had been there and had tampered with her memories. But why?

Again the woman's eyes glazed. "I don't know what you mean."

Verve decided to try asking something else. "Do you know any news of Ainsley Springer – I mean, Ainsley *Weatherby*?"

Now the maid's distant expression faded and was replaced with sorrow. "You haven't heard about her either, then." She gestured to the chair by the kitchen table. When Verve didn't take the seat, the maid sighed and hugged her arms around herself. "She went into premature labor and... well, there was nothing that could be done for her or the babies."

That news almost bowled Verve over. She stumbled backward, reaching for something, anything, to support herself. Instead she accidentally knocked over a metal mixing bowl, which clanged to the floor with a deafening ringing noise.

"Oh, my dear. I am ever so sorry for your losses. It's too much for one to bear."

As one in a waking nightmare, Verve nodded and drifted out of the kitchen, leaving the door open to the elements behind her. She sensed rather than saw Finley approach her, his very being trembling with questions.

Thankfully, he didn't speak but followed Verve back to Maplehurst, where she sat on the stump of the old oak and closed her eyes. For some time she remained there, silently trying to bring herself under better control. If she had been quicker in returning to Etterhea, she might have reached her family before the Ahkoshwa had taken its due. Then again, the magic had said it was everywhere. "They were dead the moment I made my choice," said Verve, resting her head in her hands.

Behind her, Finley cleared his throat. "I don't know how much daylight we have left. I've never been to this realm." He shifted from foot to foot, waiting, apparently, for Verve to say something. When she didn't respond, he persisted. "You have many enemies, Verity. It would not do for us to remain here exposed thus."

Verve sat up straight at the words. "Fenn was here."

"Who...?"

"My husband." For some reason, her voice broke on the words. "He tampered with the maid's memories." Verve dried her tears and got to her feet. Then, after brushing herself off for something to do, she turned to face the other fae. "I need to find him and discover why. Also, I don't know what became of my youngest sister."

Finley stiffened. "You promised to return my power." He would not meet her gaze when he spoke, and he flinched ever so slightly when she moved toward him.

"What was taken?" She produced a handkerchief out of thin air and used it to dab at her nose.

"Shouldn't we return to Letorheas first?"

Verve sighed. "I'm going to trace Fenn from here. I'll try talking to some of the hawthorns, to see if they know anything. But first, I want to keep my promise." She did not, in fact, want to keep her promise, but she knew that if she waited any longer to return Finley's stolen magic, the fae's loyalty to her would waver, and she needed him more than she wished she did.

"Rillian took most of my foresight, but please keep that. Male fae don't handle it as well as females do. He also took a measure of strength and speed."

She felt her brow wrinkle. "How much?"

"There should be a signature attached to the magic, one that you can sense in me...if you look for it." He reached for her hand but hesitated. "May I?"

Verve gave him her hand, and the fae brought her fingertips to his forehead. She was about to ask what she ought to do next, but a measure of the magic within her responded to her physical contact with Finley and wriggled its way toward him.

The fae gasped as it pressed up against the tips of Verve's fingers, striving to reach him. "Hold on to foresight and let the others pass through." His voice was taut, excited.

Verve felt her body weakening but grabbed on to what she discerned to be Finley's foresight and released the rest into the other fae. There was a strong burst of mint, and Verve's knees wobbled as the magic left her.

Finley caught her before her head could hit the tree stump and lowered her slowly to the ground. His eyes were bright, more alert than she had ever seen them. "Are you well?"

Shaking, Verve attempted to sit up, but it felt as though a lead weight had settled onto her chest. Gifting magic to a mortal in the past hadn't cost her this much energy. It must have been more magic that she had parted with this time. "Why...?"

There was a flash of blinding white light, and Finley disappeared from view. The air smelled of mint and orange as two powerful fae clashed against each other.

Chapter Thirteen

Verve coughed and rolled over onto her side as she fought to stay awake. Sleep was all she wanted to do at this point, but she knew she couldn't afford to lose consciousness for one minute. "Stop," she croaked. She didn't have to sit up to see Fenn and Finley tussle.

The two males threw wave after wave of magic at each other, deflecting and dodging whatever came their way. Fenn was trying to reach Verve, but Finley proved a difficult foe. He balled up the magic that Fenn threw at him, gathered it into a sphere and sent it flying back at Fenn, who swore and only just managed to get out of its way. The destructive wave of power hit the remains of the house, which dissolved into dust.

Verve tried again. "Stop it, both of you!"

"Are you all right, Verve?" Fenn demanded as his fist connected with his opponent's jaw.

Finley responded by putting Fenn in a headlock, and the two fell over in a heap.

"He's with me," Verve gasped. "Fenn, get off him."

At once, Fenn backed away, his dark eyes narrowed into suspicious slits. "He's not with you. This is the siphon you sought." He prowled toward Verve, but Finley continued to block his way. "Isn't that right, Uncle?"

Finley blinked. "Who are you?"

Fenn took advantage of the other's stupefaction to reach Verve, placing himself in front of her. "You set off my alarm five minutes ago, but... Where have you been? How did you—"

"Later. What do you mean this is your uncle? He was killed back in Linwood."

"No," said Fenn slowly, pointing. "That is my great-uncle Finn. I was named for him." He helped Verve to her feet and put a supporting arm around her waist. "He siphoned magic off you just now. Couldn't you feel it?"

"He didn't siphon," said Verve. "I gave—"

"Now that we know who everyone is and what they can do," said Finley, making Fenn growl, "we should move this conversation somewhere safer." He nodded at where the house had stood. "Whoever burned the house down might still be out there. I know your wife – Fenn, was it?" The fae gestured toward the woods and began walking. "I mean neither of you any harm. Come. It really doesn't feel safe here in the open like this."

"Trust me, the person who burned the house down is *not* returning." Fenn scooped Verve into his arms and kissed her temple. "Do you trust him?"

"I-I think so. But I don't understand. He's really your uncle?"

"Later," he murmured into her ear, causing gooseflesh to rise on her skin. Fenn increased his speed and soon caught up with Finley.

Still feeling weak, Verve rested her head on Fenn's shoulder and watched the land blur by through half-shuttered eyes. She couldn't help but feel grateful that she hadn't had to part with more magic all at once, as she would have needed to if the other fae men and women had kept their word.

Before either could stop him, Finley produced a dagger and cut a slit in his finger. He then stabbed the tree, which trembled beneath his touch. "Allow us safe passage to—"

He looked at Fenn, who said, "Croweshyde in Letorheas."

"Croweshyde," Finley echoed, twisting the blade in farther when the hawthorn resisted him.

Fenn said nothing of his uncle's behavior, but Verve knew he was frustrated and annoyed. The emotions left him in staggering waves that she could both see and sense, and Verve fought sudden nausea at the potency of them. She patted his arm reassuringly as the hawthorn relented and allowed them to pass. "Listen," he said as the gateway shut behind them, "there is something you should know."

He stopped when Finley turned and gestured widely. "Where to now?"

A growl rumbled in Fenn's chest. "It's not three miles from here, but in that time, I need to warn you both of—" Twigs snapped in the near distance, and Fenn cursed. "This isn't ideal. Verve, promise me you won't let her provoke you."

"It's your fault, Verity Springer. You did this!" said a female voice that was at once familiar but at the same time strange and wild.

Verve blinked as Fenn set her on her feet and tried to place himself between her and the approaching fae. "What's going on?" she asked while Fenn raised a shield around them.

Finley raised a shield as well, placing himself in front of Fenn and Verve as a blond-haired creature darted out of the woods before them, her eyes glinting in the midday sun. She looked Verve in the eye and pointed an accusing finger at her.

Verve squinted, trying to make sense of what she was seeing. "Dav?"

Mirthless laughter filled the air around them as Verve broke free of Fenn and approached the edge of the shield. "You are so careless. I knew you'd be the death of us all," Dav said.

"What happened to you? How did you… This makes no sense." She turned to Fenn, who wouldn't take his eyes off Verve's youngest sister. "She's not a middling. How did she get magic?"

"I was hoping you might have an idea."

"Stop talking about me like I'm not here," Dav shrieked. Tears ran down her face. "The voice said you did this to me. You killed Mother and Anna, not me. And I bet, you witch, I bet— W-was Helena your fault?" Her voice broke and she collapsed onto the ground sobbing.

Verve made a move toward her, but Fenn placed a staying hand on her shoulder, his eyes hard. "Careful. She's powerful and spiteful." He gestured to the space in front of Davinia, where water bubbled up from the ground as she wept uncontrollably.

"Oh, Dav."

Dav glared at Verve with such hatred, Verve knew the new fae would kill her if she were so able. "Don't look at me like I'm the monster here.

You're the monster, Verity. Anna knew. She tried to warn us." She ran at Fenn's shield, which Fenn let drop at the last minute so she wouldn't be harmed, and then he caught the youngest Springer woman by the throat and lifted her off the ground.

"Enough," he said, and he shook her.

Dav's fingers went to her throat as her legs kicked out furiously. She moved her lips as if to form words, but she must not have been getting enough air to make noise.

"Fenn, you're hurting her." Verve stepped forward, but her husband gently yet firmly held her back.

"I am *not* hurting her."

Dav writhed.

"If you can't behave," Fenn said, his voice soft and deadly, "I will lock you in the pit. Do you understand?" When Dav ceased kicking, he dropped her to the ground, where she lay sprawled out, coughing and cursing.

Verve gawped at Fenn. The last time she had seen him so angry was when he fought Dacre. She placed a hand on his arm, and he whirled toward her, his teeth bared. Instinctively, she bared her teeth as well. A growl escaped her throat. "Don't treat my sister like that ever again."

Fenn shook his head, his features softening. "Young fae like that need to be handled with a firm grip, Verve, or else they will grow to be a harm to others."

She scoffed and shrugged him off, nearly sending herself sprawling. Fenn caught her before she could topple to the ground, though she fought him. "You didn't handle me like that, and my temper is twenty times worse than hers."

"You were different," said Fenn. He managed to pin her against his chest and tucked her head beneath his chin.

"Because...?"

He kissed the top of her head. "Because you are my mate and you have no hatred in you."

Finley, who had been silent until that moment, cleared his throat. "He's right, Verity. Fae filled with that much power and hatred are a liability. It might be wise to put her down."

"No," said Verve and Fenn at once.

Dav now sat with her knees curled to her chest. She rocked as magic visibly coursed through her, barely under control. "Stop talking about me like I'm not here." The poor girl sniffled and hid her face. "Why did this happen to me?"

Verve swallowed. "Well, I have a theory."

Dav looked up. "What did you *do*?" Her voice was like icy needles, digging into Verve's heart.

After taking a fortifying breath, Verve explained about the Ahkoshwa and the terrible decision she'd been forced to make in the cave. While she spoke, Dav's expression darkened further still, and when Verve got to the part about the power entering her, the girl hissed. "I'm guessing that since the magic thought I had chosen selfishly, it took who I didn't think I could spare and kept who – well, it spared and empowered who I least get along with." The look Dav gave Verve made her wish she could sink into the ground right there and then.

"So first you try to have me killed, but then you get my entire family killed instead. How selfish and stupid can one person be?"

Fire licked at Verve's fingertips at the girl's words, and she had to fight to master her own temper. "I'm sorry. I tried to choose no one, but it wouldn't let me."

Dav scoffed.

"Don't say you wouldn't have chosen me to die rather than the others, Davinia Springer. Don't you dare."

That made Dav quiet for a moment, and her expression smoothed over somewhat. A burble of laughter left her.

Fenn tensed, his right arm tightening around Verve as he raised his left and formed another shield around them. "She does this before she loses control. You might want to raise a shield as well, Uncle."

Light exploded forth from Dav, toppling trees and pushing against Fenn's shield with such force that it rippled in places. Finley had only just managed to raise a shield of his own when a thick branch collapsed upon it; the wood at once sizzled and dissolved into ash on contact.

With a mighty shudder, Dav hiccoughed and again rested her face in her hands. "This isn't fair."

Pity tugged at Verve's heart, but it warred with irritation when her youngest sister looked up and said, "I hate you, Verity Springer. You will pay for this."

Finley was the first to let his shield drop. He regarded Dav for a moment and then reached out a hand for the girl. "I can help you, miss."

Dav hissed at him. "Don't touch me. You just said I ought to be killed." She crawled away as the older fae closed in.

"Don't touch her," Verve warned.

That made Finley still. "I'm not going to hurt her. But I think it would be best for all if her magic was taken away."

"And you're the one to do it, are you?" Verve eyed him shrewdly. If she had known this was the fae and not Rillian who had stolen magic from so many, would she have spared him? Why hadn't Fenn mentioned his siphon uncle before?

Fenn let the shield surrounding him and Verve drop. "Careful." He gripped Verve loosely by the shoulders, whether to stay or comfort her, she couldn't say. "We should take this conversation indoors. I have some wards here, but they will not have disguised Davinia's magic-use. Any nearby creatures will want to know who produced that energy burst." He released Verve, and she stumbled from the sudden loss of restraint.

"But her magic—" Finley began, but Fenn placed himself between Dav and him.

"We'll discuss if a siphon such as yourself should be allowed to handle that much power, but later. If you can't behave yourself, Uncle, I suggest you find somewhere else to spend the night."

Finley nodded tersely and fell behind his nephew, who scooped Dav up and carried her around fallen trees and into the fast-darkening woods surrounding. "I did much wrong in my youth," Finley said to Verve as they followed in Fenn's wake. "But I learned my lesson when Rillian stole most of what I had from me. Being banished to Linwood drove him to madness. It forged me into who I am." He eyed Verve as they continued onward. "I daresay your short time there helped forge you as well."

"If you're trying to get me to trust you so I drop my guard, you're wasting your time." Verve turned her focus to the path ahead of them. She stumbled over a fallen log and refused help when it was offered to her.

"That's fair. But you'll learn I *am* trustworthy…in time."

They walked for ten minutes at a moderate pace for a human but a relaxed pace for a fae. Verve suspected Fenn was moving more slowly to accommodate her current weakened state. Strength was slow in returning, though it did so at a steady rate.

Low-hanging branches reached down to her, only to rear back at the last moment as though afraid. As none of the trees did this to her three companions, Verve couldn't help but feel uneasy. The woods were quiet but for the crunch of fallen leaves and the beating of individual hearts. Shadow was fast falling over the land, and the air's temperature dipped with the setting of the sun.

Finally, after Verve thought she might have to sit down and beg for a break, Fenn slowed and came to a stop by a hill. "Let me raise a few more wards."

"I'll do it," said Finley. Before Fenn could stop him, the fae lifted his hands and the air rippled turquoise beneath his fingertips. Wave upon wave of magic left him, and all smelled potently of peppermint. Panting, Finley lowered his hands and gestured for Verve to walk ahead of him.

"This residence is all I could come by in this part of the world," Fenn said. He set Dav on her feet, and the girl wobbled slightly.

Finley and Verve exchanged a short glance. "Residence?" Finley prompted.

"It's on the other side of this hill." Fenn held out his hand for Verve, who approached him warily. Noticing her sudden standoffish manners, perhaps, he came to her, took her hand, and said, "I'm sorry I treated your sister so. I forget you weren't born into this way of life."

"And it won't happen again."

"Indeed, it won't." Fenn squeezed her hand and led them around the large mound of earth. On the other side sat nothing.

"Um," said Verve.

Fenn turned her around to face the brick-and-clay shanty that had been built into the side of the hill. "It will be close quarters, but it should keep us dry and warm as we sort things out."

Her knees nearly buckled beneath the weight of all she had borne and would now have to relate. The thought of recounting her time in the Lands of the Dead alone made Verve want to lie down and take a long nap.

The room within the little house was as Fenn had said: tight but dry. There were the remnants of a fire in the grate toward the right of the hovel, and to the left sat a tiny bed with a faded brown quilt crumpled in a heap, as though its occupant had risen and left in haste. In the middle of it all sat a small table with three chairs around it.

Pushing past Verve, Dav made her way to the bed, where she plopped down and glared at the others, as though daring them to take the bit of creature comfort she had obviously claimed as her own.

Fenn's left eye twitched. He said nothing of the girl's aggression but moved toward the fireplace, Verve in tow. "My wards are strong, and the one Finley put up is powerful as well. They might keep out the enemy, but they could also draw their attention. I should keep an eye on things." He stroked her cheek. "Will you be all right for a while?" His eyes narrowed as he peeked over at Dav.

"I'll take first watch," said Finley, obviously surprising Fenn as well. He smirked as he looked between the two of them. "You two have a lot of catching up to do." Eyebrows raised in a knowing fashion, he ducked out of the house and shut the door behind him.

The door had been shut not five seconds before Verve found herself crushed into Fenn's body. "I thought I'd lost you." He spoke in a tongue different than the one they had been speaking, and Verve guessed he was doing it to keep his uncle – and perhaps Dav – from eavesdropping and understanding. His lips brushed the crown of her head and trailed down to her forehead and then her nose.

"How long was I gone?" she asked, a bit more breathlessly than she would have liked with her sister in the room.

Fenn didn't answer at first, his attention on her throat, which he caressed with his mouth. The moan that escaped him made Verve certain he had forgotten about Dav, so she put her hands on his chest, shoving him gently. Fenn merely moved lower, flicking his tongue over her collarbone.

"My sister is here."

"She can go outside." His lips rose to Verve's, swallowing her complaint.

Behind them, Dav sighed. "You get all the good things in life."

That seemed to bring Fenn back to the moment. He drew in a deep breath and shuddered as he put an inch between Verve and himself. "I'm sorry, my love. You must be exhausted."

Verve nearly stumbled at the sudden distance but righted herself before Fenn had to intervene. "How long was I gone?"

"I heard you the first time. Sorry." He brought her hand to his lips and led her to the fireplace. There were two cushions sitting there, and Fenn lowered himself down onto one, never releasing Verve's hand. When she had sat next to him, he stirred the ashes with a stick, as if that would bring a fire to life. "You've been gone for five months, two days, and six hours." He watched her, concerned.

The air rushed out of her lungs. Five months? That was a long time. Not as long as it might have been, but a decent amount of time for Dacre to make all sorts of trouble. "And when did my family...?" She couldn't bring herself to say the words. It was still too fresh a wound. Behind them, she knew Dav was trying to understand every word they were speaking, her oval face scrunched up in concentration.

"An elf-night ago."

Five weeks? She had just made the deal with the Ahkoshwa for power the night previous. Time did indeed move differently in other realms. "And how long were you in the dungeon?"

Fenn's expression darkened. "Long enough," he said, and she knew she would get no more out of him on that. "How did you do it? I'm assuming it was you who freed me."

Verve told him about her ability to physically walk between worlds, and the fact that her soul had been able to do it long before then.

The news surprised Fenn, that much was obvious. "I need to brush up on my Second and Third Age prophecies." He leaned in, relinquishing his grip on the stick and his attempts to mend a nonexistent fire. "Are you very hungry? I have enough supplies to last the four of us for another two days, but then I think we should forage or hunt."

"I'm a touch hungry." In truth, she was too keen on getting more answers to think much of food.

Fenn released her hand. "All right, Fire Queen, you mend the blaze and I'll tell you what has transpired in your absence while we put something together." He reached next to the fireplace and produced a moss-covered log, which he set in place, and then a few sticks that looked too wet to possibly ignite.

When Verve raised her hand, Fenn quickly seized her gently by the wrist. "You have way too much power now to use gestures for anything other than a crisis." He released her, and she felt her fingertips tingle, itch, and burn.

She nodded tightly. "Right. I'm both the powder keg and the match."

He did not argue with that assessment. "Do you have air? The ability to manipulate it, I mean."

Verve almost shook her head, but then she remembered that Rillian had and that she had taken all of his power. "Yes, I do."

"It might be wise to use that to dry out the log and sticks before you use fire." While she went about trying to work out how to do that exactly, Fenn scooted away and rummaged through a small footlocker near at hand.

"I'm hungry and bored," Dav said. She had moved toward them so quickly, it made Verve snarl a warning. That caused the girl to take a few steps back, her face draining of color.

"Yes, Davinia, your sister is very powerful. I suggest you use more care in how you treat and speak to her." Fenn removed four apples, a quarter loaf of white bread, and a large hunk of questionable-looking cheese from the footlocker. He tossed one apple to Dav and then another, which she caught with ease. "Please take some out to Finley. We'll know if you don't."

Trembling and yet glowering, Dav approached Fenn and took the chunk of cheese and the bread. "I'll learn your secret language sometime. I'm good with foreign tongues." With that said, she left them.

Now Verve didn't need to reach deep inside for an emotion. She let the fire flow through her and it all but exploded into the fireplace. At once, the log lit up as though it had been dry all along.

"We'll work on air," he promised.

Verve didn't argue. She knew she would need every advantage against Dacre that she could get. "What has Dacre been doing?" Her stomach clenched in knots as she waited to hear what she might be facing, impatience setting her teeth on edge as Fenn seemed to take his time in answering.

He drew two sausages out of the footlocker, threaded a stick through them, and held the stick over the fire. As they began their slow cook, his eyes flickered to Verve. "Dacre had himself crowned king over the inhabited lands of Letorheas, including the wildlands, which used to be outside the royal governance during Midras's two-hundred-year reign. He's lethal now, more so than before. He can kill high fae, just like you can."

So, it was as she had feared. Still, she couldn't help but recoil at the news. "He could have killed you."

"But he didn't."

"If I had been too late, he could have. He still might try."

Fenn took her hands in his free one. "He's too smart for that. He needs me alive. Controlled and alive, mind." His lips turned up in a parody of a smile. "He wants you to co-operate with him, and having something to bargain with is his best strategy. Dacre Starside isn't going to kill me."

His assurances sounded good, but they brought Verve little comfort. She knew the extent of Dacre's obsession with her and with power. If he caught Verve and took control of her through mastership magic – the sort of magic that allowed one fae to manipulate another's power – Fenn would be in graver danger than ever. Instead of telling him so, she simply stared into the blaze and tried to calm her inner turmoil. "What else?"

"He's made a grab for a few other realms – Tootaryn, Avari, Glast. Thankfully, the trees are terrified of him now and aren't co-operating. And he can't walk between worlds as you can, so he's reliant on others to make gateways for him." Here Fenn's lips turned down and a crease formed on his brow. "Those who resist him have started destroying hawthorns. Anyone caught has been executed." He swallowed, looking away from Verve and into the blaze. "Many fae and elves have died. Etterhea has been left alone…for now. But I understand that he would use it as another way to bargain with you." He turned the stick in his hands, and the smell of cooking meat made Verve's stomach rumble.

"If he gets ahold of my power, he'll have access to any and every realm."

Fenn did not argue but his grip on the roasting stick tightened noticeably. "That is why we have to keep you far away from him and his Trusted." Behind them, the door opened and Dav stalked back inside.

She said not a word to either of them, but sat back down on the mattress and stared at the roasting sausages. With gusto she tore into a green apple that had been given to her, then stuffed the remainder of the cheese into her mouth.

"Is he still taking middlings from Etterhea?" Verve squirmed on her cushion, unable suddenly to be comfortable.

"Not at such a great rate as before, now that he has the power he sought from the Lands of the Dead. But there are still many missing from your home area, and the disappearances haven't gone unnoticed by the mortals. There is talk of a serial kidnapper or killer." He peered over his shoulder at Dav before looking back at Verve. "I returned to Etterhea to get your family to safety. I'm sorry."

They sat in silence as the meat continued to cook, sizzling and popping and filling the small house with delectable aromas. Fenn gave one of the sausages to Verve and the other he tossed to Dav, which she caught and devoured as though she hadn't eaten in days. Juice dribbled down her chin, and she looked positively feral. "How much longer are we staying here?" Dav wiped her chin with her torn sleeve.

The glance Fenn gave Verve was full of meaning, but when he spoke, he directed his words and attention at Dav. "You need to learn to master your magic, Davinia. As I have other priorities, finding you a suitable tutor will be important."

Dav pulled a face. "That doesn't answer my question as to how long we'll be living in this hellhole."

Verve's spine stiffened at her sister's tone. "Dav."

No doubt sensing that a fight was about to break out, Fenn placed a staying hand on Verve's arm. "We'll be able to leave here soon enough. No more than three days hence."

"You promise?"

"No, I don't," Fenn said simply and procured a small hand pie for himself.

Chapter Fourteen

That night, after the scant supper had been consumed and the fire was fed as well, everyone settled down for sleep. Outside, in a tent he had magicked into existence, Finley's distant deep and even breathing soon filled the silences between the logs' popping in the grate. He had promised to check the wards around midnight, confident they would be alerted of any intruders.

Like a true gentleman, Fenn allowed Dav to sleep on the bed, and Verve didn't argue. There was no room on the small cot for two, and she wanted to be as near to Fenn as she could. The couple stretched out by the fire, all belongings having been vanished to give them more room.

They lay entwined while the wind picked up outside and the fire died down to embers.

Dav coughed once and rolled over on her mattress, her back to both of them. It didn't take long after that until her breathing slowed and deepened, and Verve knew the girl was at least half asleep.

Around her, Fenn's arms tightened and he buried his nose in her hair. "You put on a very good disguise, Verve." He sniffed. "I can't even smell your magic."

Verve had forgotten that she had muted her power. "I didn't want to scare the Woodhouses' maid."

"Hmm." He kissed the nape of her neck.

She closed her eyes as his hands began to wander. "I don't have a residual burst anymore." For a moment, she wondered if Fenn had heard her over his own racing heart.

He didn't respond at first as he tasted the flesh of her throat and then moved to her lips, moaning into her mouth before pulling away an inch or so. "You can use that to your advantage," he breathed into her ear.

"You could go anywhere and fool anyone that you are mortal." Fenn stroked her face and then rested his brow against hers.

"If I could shape-change I could fool people. Dacre knows what I look like."

At the mention of their mutual enemy, Fenn let out a heavy breath and stiffened. "Verve, my uncle has shape-changing abilities."

"What has that got to do with me?"

"You said you were a siphon now."

"With lots of power to return to many individuals, if I am to keep my word to Igraine. I'm not taking anyone else's magic from them."

Fenn rubbed soothing circles on her back. "Maybe you don't have to. Maybe you already have shape-changing in your repertoire." He kissed her nose and rolled with her so that she was straddling him.

Verve's heart pounded as he slid his hands under her dress, pulling it up to her waist. Her eyes searched his in the semidarkness, incredulous that he would be so bold while her sister was still in the room.

He cleared his throat softly. "Shape-changing, I am told, is easier when one is naked." He'd said it so seriously, that Verve had to laugh. "Aren't you tempted to try?"

For one wild moment, she was uncertain what he meant by that. "I'll assume you mean shape-changing." She wriggled, and Fenn allowed her to roll off of him.

"I know a few assessors. They can tell you whether or not you have the ability before we begin experimenting."

"Finley's an assessor."

Fenn let out a slow breath, as though relieved. "They are fairly common, but I'm glad we have someone close at hand. My allies are scattered, and those I thought I could trust have either said no word to me since before our trip to Ithalamore or have turned and put their support behind Dacre." He stared at the low ceiling, his expression bleak.

"Can we trust him to help us? Your uncle, I mean."

"That, dear wife, is yet to be seen."

As if in response to the statement, the door creaked open and the fae himself ducked inside. "There's someone out there, in the woods. We need to leave. Now."

Verve listened. There was no breath, no heartbeat, no footfall that would indicate anyone was less than six miles away. "I don't sense anything."

"My alarms didn't go off, and judging by your expression, I'm guessing yours didn't either," Fenn said, springing to his feet. He reached for the makeshift fire poker and moved toward the door. "Are you certain you didn't have a vision or perhaps imagine it?"

At once Finley was shaking his head. He held out his hand for Verve and helped her to her feet, though his nephew glared. "I saw her, plain as day, flaming eyes and all. She saw me staring and vanished, but I doubt she went far."

"Verve, stay inside. No one needs to know you're back from the other realm."

She wanted to argue, but Finley did it for her.

"If some woman is out there with flaming eyes, I'll take the equivalent of a mortal bomb over a throwing knife, however sharp."

"I'm not a bomb," Verve snapped. "And if they have glowing eyes, I have a very good idea who it is."

Fenn looked at her and together they said, "Igraine."

They searched the immediate area, starting from the perimeter where Finley had set up his wards and moving inward. There was no trace of the non-living elf, not even a footprint.

It would have been wise to divide and conquer, and Verve had said so, but neither male was willing to leave her alone. So Fenn stuck by her side, and Finley ventured farther beyond the circle.

"There are no hawthorns within the perimeter," said Fenn as they watched his uncle disappear into the night. "Not that we know if Igraine even needs one."

Verve shook her head. "Do you think she can do what I can?"

"World-walk without a hawthorn? I doubt it." His breath clouded the air in front of him and he shifted his weight so he was leaning toward Verve. "If Igraine can walk through wards, though, that could mean trouble."

"You don't trust her."

Fenn stared into the darkness, and she followed his gaze, which alighted on Finley, who was picking his way through the barely lit path. "She said her family members were robbed of their magic by a siphon. Having my uncle close, presuming he is truly the guilty party, is dangerous. Igraine might mistake it for an alliance and see that as a betrayal of trust on your part." He looked down at her grimly.

"I don't need any more enemies."

"Agreed." When he spoke again, the words were accompanied by a burst of lime, meaning he had probably put up a barrier around them so no one could eavesdrop. "We should shun him and soon."

Verve stiffened. She didn't trust the fae, not quite, but if he was Fenn's only remaining relative, she didn't know if she could bear making him a stranger. "I'll think about it."

A wail pierced the night, a high-pitched cry that sent shivers down Verve's spine. At once the stick in Fenn's hands elongated and transformed into a bow, and onto that he nocked an arrow he created out of nothing. "Someone has breached the perimeter."

Footsteps ran toward them. Finley had just crossed into a beam of moonlight when there was an explosion behind them. It lifted Verve off her feet and threw her several yards, and fire lapped at the hem of her dress as she soared. The heat of the blast had caused the grass to wither for yards beyond them, and where the house should have been visible, there was now a thick curtain of black smoke.

"Dav!" Verve ran to the hovel in the hill, which had been destroyed, and started lobbing mounds of rock and earth away even as fire shot up through the ruins of the hill and the house. "Can you hear me? Davinia!"

Fenn was by her side now, digging through the rubble. It took them less than three minutes to come to the realization that nothing of her sister remained. Verve closed her eyes and sank back onto her heels. Cold crept over her being but she didn't shiver.

"That was the breach," Fenn said beside her. "Verve? Love, she wasn't in there." He grasped Verve by the shoulder and gave her a gentle shake. "Davinia must have caused the explosion after she fled, a parting shot, if you will."

At that moment, Finley reached them and looked pointedly at Verve, who could see the whole scene without having to open her eyes. "Is she all right?"

The woods surrounding had been leveled. They glowed a sickly green and still burned in places. Verve drew her first breath in minutes and used Fenn's help to get to her feet. "We need to leave." She glanced once more at the scene to reassure herself that she had left no stone unturned and that her sister had not in fact been blasted to smithereens.

"Traveling at night in these parts isn't advised," said Fenn. "There are were-creatures that roam in packs. Bog sprites that are under *his* control. Any one of them could waylay us and cause damage to our plans."

Plans? What plans, other than keeping my return to the realm a secret? Verve thought wearily. "We're going to lose any element of surprise if we don't risk it." She told him about the fae she heard stirring.

That made Finley's brow wrinkle and he cocked his head to the side, incredulous. "No one would have heard or seen that explosion, not through the extensive wards your mate and I put up."

"What about Igraine?" Fenn angled himself more toward Verve. "Do you sense anything?"

"No."

"The potion-maker?" said Finley sharply. His eyes grew wide, and his heart rate increased. "We do need to move now."

Verve knew why Finley wanted to flee, but she didn't protest since it would get her the result she wanted. "Fenn. Please. We need to go."

"All right. But I would like it if you remained here a moment longer while Finley and I make certain the path to the nearest hawthorn is safe, all right?"

"Will you look for Dav?"

Fenn cleared his throat, but it was Finley who spoke. "Your sister's gone the pixie's way, Verity."

"Come again?"

"She's not waiting for you in the woods anywhere. The lass has fled."

★ ★ ★

It didn't take long for Fenn to confirm that the woods were quite empty of any fae besides the three of them. Not that Verve needed to do more than listen to know that the girl was nowhere nearby. "Did she use a gateway?" Verve asked as Finley returned from his hunt for a hawthorn. "Or is she just a really fast runner?" The last part she addressed to Fenn.

"She's fast," Fenn confirmed.

Why did Dav have to behave like an ill-tempered child? If she would have given Verve a chance, Verve could have siphoned her powers or had Finley do it. Verve kept silently telling herself that magic was the problem and not her own horrible decisions.

"The area is clear…for now." Finley motioned for the two of them to follow him and began to run.

Fenn took Verve's hand and they both ran after him. "Wait, Finley. Let me," he said, just as his uncle had produced a dagger from his boot. "We need all the allies we can get."

"The compassionate way is going to see us all caught one of these days." Finley swore as Fenn pushed past him and laid his hand upon the tree.

It took the better part of five minutes for Fenn to make a deal with the tree to let them pass. All the while, Verve practically vibrated with anxiety beside him, and Finley seemed ready to rip his hair out. When the agreement had been reached between tree and fae, a gateway opened into a wood bathed in sunlight, a place whose name made chill bumps break out on Verve's arms.

"Why are we in Thistleback Wood?" she demanded.

After Finley passed through, the gateway shut behind them. "We ought to destroy the tree so no one can follow us." He looked from Verve to Fenn and then back to Verve again. "What is wrong with this wood exactly?" He sniffed. "We're back in the mortal realm." His tone was approving.

"'Markson roams Thistleback Wood. Extract the burial site.' And we are not destroying the tree." Fenn took Verve's hand once more and led her and his uncle around the back of the tree, heading into the sun, which had risen to its zenith.

"Sorry?" asked Finley, clearly baffled by the exchange.

Verve ignored him. "The Cunning Blade has been destroyed. Dacre knows that, but how many don't know and might be still seeking it?"

Fenn appeared amused. "Markson buried the blade before he went insane, and then I restored his sanity before planting a false memory in his mind. He's living in hiding as a hermit in these woods."

"Fenn," Verve protested, "anyone could have found him. He was a deserter. He could have been executed ages ago."

Fenn shook his head. "I put a repelling charm on him."

Finley let out a low whistle. "You gifted him that?" He turned to Verve, reading her puzzled looks correctly. "Some charms can be gifted only once, and the caster had to have sacrificed something great in order to do so." His attention turned to his nephew, whom he seemed to be regarding in a new light.

"The extent of the charm," said Fenn as though Finley hadn't spoken, "covers a five-mile radius. It will repel every human and fae that Markson doesn't want near him, besides me and those whom I grant access." Clearly he seemed to think this was explanation enough and kept walking.

Verve turned the matter over in her mind. "So if we're in that five-mile radius…"

"No one will be able to reach us unless I give them permission to." Fenn gestured to the woods surrounding them. "If we can find Markson and remain within the spell's range, we'll be safe while we take the necessary time to form a plan." He shot another glance at her over his shoulder. "You should get a better handle on your magic."

"Why didn't you put the repelling charm on me or one of my family?" The words came out before Verve could stop them, but it was a good question. If Fenn had, she wouldn't have been kidnapped by Dacre and turned into the Fire Queen in the first place. Something akin to hurt bubbled up in her gut, along with anger.

"Your Maj— *Verity*," said Finley softly, "a fae can only impart that gift one time."

Still she looked at her husband, waiting for his answer. "That was the sacrifice I had to make," Fenn said quietly. "I suspected what you were to me at that point, even though we had only met once, but I gave priority to the Cunning Blade and its secrecy. Markson was with me when the blade was retrieved. If it was known for certain I had it, he could have been tortured for its whereabouts."

He chose Markson over me and my family. The realization made her head spin. If he had chosen differently, this all might not have happened. Dacre wouldn't have kidnapped her, wouldn't have almost drowned her to turn her into a fae, and the Cunning Blade – well, she might have accidentally touched it and turned into the Fire Queen anyway, but *still*. "When were you going to tell me?"

Fenn's brows rose in obvious surprise. "I didn't know it was something I *should* tell." He stopped walking and held up a hand for them to do the same.

Verve was not done with her questions. "Why not hide with Dav here, though?"

"Because I don't trust your sister." He put a finger to his lips, and Verve reluctantly saved her questions and accusations for later.

A tense silence fell over the three of them, and it did not break until Verve became aware of a mortal's beating heart in the distance. She heard it for a moment, and then it disappeared. Beside her, Fenn had grown tense.

"We're close," he said.

"Was that the man we seek?" Finley asked, running a hand down his face to mute his magic. He did a fair job, but Verve could still tell that he had power.

Fenn followed in his footsteps, and his muting was even less impressive than his uncle's. There was no way that Markson wouldn't realize Fenn wasn't different. "Let me explain a few things about Markson." He took off at a brisk walk, and his traveling companions kept pace. "The man is utterly suspicious. I tried to instill some peace, but his mind was severely damaged when he touched the Cunning Blade."

"You said you repaired his mind." The words came out sounding like an accusation, and the look she got from Fenn was startled.

"I did," he said, a note of defensiveness in his voice. "But some things could not be fixed." He ducked behind a thick tree and pulled Verve over with him. When he spoke again, it was in low, urgent tones. "We can use magic around him, but only once I've reintroduced myself and am able to reassure him that we'll never use it against him. The man has been through enough, and we don't want to give him a heart episode."

"He won't seek someone out and betray us?" Finley demanded, keeping his voice down as well.

"I trust him as much as I trust you."

Not much, then, thought Verve.

"We'll clear his memory before we leave him." Fenn peered around the tree. "I gave him some magic so that he could silence his heart and breathing, should he feel the need or desire to. He knows we're here and is hiding."

Verve frowned as they continued to wait. "If he knows we're here, why are *we* hiding?"

"We're not hiding so much as staying out of his line of sight." That was as clear as mud, and she told him so. Fenn grimaced. "You don't think I left him here weaponless, do you? He may have a repelling charm on him, but that doesn't work on most beasts."

"I take it you gave him something magical," said Finley. He did not sound happy about that at all.

Fenn shrugged. "A bewitched bow and some hexed arrows."

Finley swore and seemed ready to swat Fenn for his perceived stupidity. "Boy, you cannot trust mortals. They are unstable creatures and should have no contact with magic."

"Watch your words, Uncle. I trust some mortals more than I trust most fae." Fenn's tone brooked no further argument, his body pulsing with dangerous magic.

The last thing Verve needed was the two males fighting. She none too subtly put herself in the middle, separating them as best she could. "How long do we wait here?"

"We wait until he approaches us. And judging from what I remember of the man, we won't be waiting long."

As if in response to Fenn's words, an arrow shot through the air and embedded itself in the other side of the tree. On contact, the bark rippled with purple fire, and Fenn grabbed Verve, threw her to the ground in front of him, and shielded her with his body as the tree exploded.

Verve's ears rang and the world around her filled with sunspots. Dazed, she tried to rise, but Fenn gently pushed her back down and spun around to face the threat.

"Markson, we come in peace!"

Beside them, Finley pulled tree shards out of his body. Fenn's back had suffered just as much, and Verve rose, despite Fenn's low warning to stay put, and started pulling debris out of him.

The voice that then spoke was hoarse, and it came from not three yards away. "Comes in peace." He spat. "That's what I would expect someone who means me ill to say." There was the sound of a bow being fitted with another arrow.

"You don't remember me?"

There was a pause. "Left me this bow and them arrows, you did, laddie. But don't think for one moment I won't kill the lot of ya if'n I don't like what ya has to say. Ken?" The bow made a low-pitched *twang*, but the man didn't release the arrow.

"If you truly remembered, you would know that I gave you that bow to defend yourself from animals. That I never intended you to turn and wield them on myself and my wife." He winced as Verve yanked out the largest piece of wood from his back.

"You brought your wife into these woods, eh? Ne'er took you for the marrying type, Baer."

'Baer' was the name Verve's father had called Fenn by. Father had left Verve a note before his death, telling her to look for Mr. Baer and give him a cryptic message about Thistleback Wood. The name, of course, had been a pseudonym, and none of the humans Fenn worked with had known he was fae.

"You can tell your missus to stop hiding behind your back and come out with her hands high."

"That won't be necessary," said Fenn, posturing. How had he ever managed to pass as human using these manners?

Verve cleared her throat and stepped around him, slowly, her hands raised. "You'll have to excuse my husband."

At the sight of her, the withered old man's eyes widened and he dropped the weapon in his hands. He stared at her for a long, uncomfortable moment and then ran at her, arms open.

Fenn placed himself between the two of them with such speed, Markson had to know he was fae. "Careful," Fenn warned.

"Oh, get on with you. I was just going to give Springer's daughter a hug."

The words knocked the air out of Verve's lungs, even more so than the man's ensuing embrace. "What?" she gasped, eyeing Fenn for an explanation.

A smile stole over Fenn's features as the old man pulled back to better see her. "I forget. You have people in common," Fenn said.

Markson grinned at her. "Verve, isn't it? You look just like he drew you."

This all was a bit much to take in. The ground beneath her feet felt suddenly unsteady, and she had to grip on to Fenn for support. "You knew my father." Unbidden tears filled her eyes, but she didn't let them fall, because she knew they would be silver.

Something she had said made the old man frown and pull back. "What do you mean by 'knew' him?" His eyes searched Verve's face and weight seemed to settle on his back, his posture sagging beneath it.

Verve swallowed and was about to explain, but Fenn cut in. "Three days. We just need a place to stay for three days and then we'll be gone."

"And you thought I would take you in, is that it?"

Fenn said nothing but waited. Nearby, Finley had finished plucking splinters out of himself, his residual burst alerting Verve to the fact that he had used magic. Thankfully, Markson didn't seem to be able to smell it. Or, if he did, he didn't think anything of the sudden aroma of mint.

The old man's unwavering gaze turned back to Verve and his eyes softened. "For Fredrick's daughter," he said, as though answering some unspoken question. He turned to his left and motioned for the others to follow him. "It's not much, but you're welcome to stay as long as you need to hide for."

"What makes you think we need to hide?" Verve asked.

Markson chuckled. "I know what a hunted person looks like, Miss Springer." He picked up his pace, snatching a tall stick from next to a tree as he strode toward a destination that Verve had to use through-sight to see: a wooden hut, three miles off, with a fire pit out front. "People going missing around these parts. You wouldn't have any ideas about what happened, lad?" The words had been directed at Fenn, who was walking side by side with Finley.

"It's an enemy's doing," was all Fenn said.

The old man grunted. "Very well. You'll tell me eventually and in your own way, just like old times." He cleared his throat and spat into the bushes on his left. "That fae's repelling gift or whatever it is you gave me, why doesn't it work on you? I didn't want you to find me, Baer, and you did so anyway."

The tension in the air was palpable. The quick thudding of Markson's heart told Verve he suspected something and was afraid. *Terrified*, she thought as puffs of a green light swirled out of the man. It took all of her self-control not to pluck the feelings out of the air and devour them. "You don't need to be afraid of him," she said softly.

"Who says I'm afraid, girl?" he demanded. His tone was steady, but Verve knew her eyes weren't deceiving her.

"He fought beside you, helped you. He's still the same man."

Markson stopped walking and turned to face Verve. "You don't know what I've seen, Miss Springer. Your husband is and has always been dangerous. It just took me until now to realize how very dangerous." He reached behind him, drew an arrow from a quiver Verve had thought was a satchel until that moment, and threw it at Fenn.

The arrow soared toward him as though drawn by a magnet, and it pulsed with violet-colored light. Fenn's eyes widened for a brief moment, before Verve intercepted the arrow ere it could reach her husband. It felt as though all her nerve endings were on fire, but with a thought she sent the magicked object flying up far and away from herself. The sky filled with forked violet lightning, accompanied by a terrible roar, and then all was still.

All three men stood stock still, watching her. Two were terrified, one was in awe. "Verve," Fenn murmured, putting his hands up as though attempting to not startle her. "That should have rendered you unconscious."

Verve blinked rapidly, wondering why her husband was talking to her like she was a bomb. "Why are you looking at me like that?"

"She – *it* must be a shape-changer," said Markson. "You're all here to torture information out of me, aren't you?"

Fenn ignored Markson and pointed to Verve's hand. "You're holding a spell in your palm."

She looked at her right hand, which was still raised, and sure enough, a white orb of light rested there. Baffled, Verve studied it. "What should I do?"

"Stay away from me," said Markson. "I have more where that arrow came from." The old man was backing away and fell over a thick tree root. There was a great *snap*, and he screamed.

"What do you want to do with the magic?" Fenn asked Verve, ignoring Markson. His voice was patient yet strained somehow, as though he wasn't quite certain of what he was dealing with. "Verve? Tell me what the spell is."

Verve drew the orb close to her eye and studied it. Deep down she knew it wasn't for knocking someone unconscious. That was the spell she had released into the sky. No, this one felt like it was for paralysis. She said so aloud.

"Very good. You can do one of two things, love. Either release it into the sky or, if you are able, absorb it."

"Do you want to explain why you're staring at me like that?" she asked.

Finley had gone to aid Markson, who was attempting to crawl away from them, his leg twisted oddly as though he had sprained or broken it. "Whatever you're going to do, Verity, I recommend doing it quickly. I can't heal, so one of you needs to mend his bone."

Fenn's eyes were wide and dark. "If you can absorb magic like that – magic cast against you – your chances of facing Dacre and winning just tripled."

Now Finley turned his attention back to both of them. "In theory, siphoning magic that way shouldn't be possible." He shrugged. "But why don't you do what your instincts are telling you to do. The worst that can happen is you keel over and we have to administer an antidote."

At that Verve nearly dropped the spell, and Fenn backed away. "Will it hurt?"

Finley snorted. "Hurt? No. Paralyze you temporarily? More likely."

Fenn glowered at his uncle. "She's already touching the magic," he argued. "It would have taken effect by now. Go ahead, Verve. Make your choice." He backed away some more, either giving her room to work or afraid that she would accidentally release the spell on his person.

"All right." *I can eat feelings, why couldn't I eat magic as well?* She raised the orb to her lips, but instinct screamed against her, so she stopped herself at the last minute and closed her fist around the magic, willing her skin to absorb it. Nothing happened.

"Maybe it takes time to master," Finley offered. "Or maybe the girl has a shield containing the spell." He threw up a wall behind him, effectively blocking Markson's attempts to crawl away. "I suggest you lob it to the heavens, dear. We don't need to have that thing explode and put us all out of commission."

It was obvious that Fenn wasn't convinced of his uncle's words. His mouth opened, as though he were about to offer advice, but Verve's mind was already made up.

She threw the spell heavenward, where it exploded in a burst of brilliant white fireworks. Whether or not her husband was disappointed, Verve couldn't say. "What are we going to do about him now?"

No doubt wishing he was invisible, Markson cringed at her words. "You lot, stay away from me."

"Markson – *John*, we're not going to harm you," Fenn said firmly yet gently. He approached the man, who was fumbling for another arrow. Without any show, Fenn caused the satchel containing the missiles to fly off and away into the woods, and the air stank of lemons.

"You were fae all along."

Fenn inclined his head. "Not all fae are bad."

The old man licked his lips, his eyes still wide with fear. His attention turned to Verve, and his face paled further as his left eye started to twitch.

"Some are very powerful, yes. But it does not follow that they use their might for evil." He didn't seem to be getting through to the man, who couldn't tear his gaze from Verve's face. Fenn sighed and turned to Verve as well. "We might have to clear some memory before we proceed. Also, your disguise is slipping a bit."

Verve didn't pay the words much mind, but looked down at Markson's leg. "Does that hurt terribly?" Slowly she moved toward him, what she hoped was an encouraging and non-frightening smile on her face.

"Careful, now," said Finley. "His heart is fit to burst out of his breast."

"I know." Her eyes never left Markson's. "Would you let me help you with that?" She nodded at his injury, and the old man trembled.

"Maybe I should do it," said Fenn. "If he has a heart episode and dies, the repelling magic I put on him will dissipate and we'll be exposed here, especially after those two displays of fireworks you just put on."

She shut out the rest of Fenn's and Finley's objections and knelt next to the man. "I'm not going to hurt you."

"You're a changeling. A shifter." The words that came out of the man's mouth were barely above a whisper.

"I might be," she admitted, "but I'm still Fredrick Springer's daughter, and I want to help his friend. Will you let me?" Verve ignored

Fenn's hand, which had gripped her by the shoulder, as she reached out and placed her open palm on the old man's leg.

Markson hissed at the contact but did nothing else except stare into the depths of her eyes, as one mesmerized. "Are you really Verity?" His voice was tight with pain.

"I am, and I need you to sit very still while I mend this." She nodded at his leg, which was now swelling to twice its normal size.

Fenn's grip on her shoulder tightened, warning her. "Healing them is different." He didn't need to say 'humans' for Verve to understand what he meant. "Your emotional push should be gentler – much, much gentler than what you're accustomed to."

Verve nodded as Markson continued to stare at her like he had never seen such a sight in his life. She waited for Fenn to continue.

"First, assess how bad the break is. If it's in two pieces, it will be an easier mend. If it's broken but still connected…"

"It'll be more difficult," she finished for him. Adjusting her eyes, Verve used through-sight to examine the injury. It took a moment for her to assess, and when she did, she was concerned to see that there were two breaks in the bone, making for one separate piece that was unattached. She told Fenn of her findings. "Maybe you should do it." She started to get up, but Markson's hand shot out and grabbed on to her with surprising strength.

Fenn hissed, but the old man didn't seem to notice. "I wouldn't handle her like that," he said to Markson, who either didn't hear or care.

He groaned. "You do it, Miss Springer. You do it or no one."

Behind them, Finley let out a string of soft expletives. "If she gets this wrong and kills him…"

"It'll be fine," she said. "What next?"

"Now that you've assessed the break," Fenn said to Verve after shooting a stern look at his uncle, "you'll need to place your hand over the loose bone. But first, try to numb him."

Verve did so, and Markson flopped back in apparent relief. Then she followed Fenn's remaining instructions, placing her hand on the middle of the wound, grasping on to a calm feeling, and gently reaching out with what he told her to imagine was a thimble's worth of magic into the leg.

There was at once an audible *bang*, and Markson's leg glowed brightly for a brief moment. The man went entirely limp, and his eyes closed.

"Do we need to run?" asked Finley, apparently thinking the old man was dead.

Verve barely allowed herself to breathe, listening to the man's heart slow and then speed up once more before settling on a normal beat. "Did I hurt him?" Her voice trembled on the words, and Fenn pulled her to her feet.

"No, but he's had a rough day. The average human mind can only handle so much exposure to magic before it shuts things down." Fenn gestured to Markson's rising and falling chest. "He'll be unconscious for a few hours, but he's fine, Verve. He's truly going to be fine." Fenn stooped, lifted the human, and carefully draped him over his shoulder. "I can see the hut in the near distance. Finley, would you mind running ahead to check for traps?" The two males exchanged a look that did not go unnoticed by Verve.

As Finley ran ahead of them, Verve peered at Fenn from the corner of her eye. "What was that about?"

"I wanted a moment alone with you."

Verve glanced at the unconscious mortal and snorted. "I see that. For what reason?"

Fenn let out a low sigh. "It's about your sister."

Somehow, Verve doubted that was what the look had been about, but she couldn't be certain she hadn't imagined it. They started walking at a leisurely pace, their eyes on Finley, who was disabling some harmful trap that had been raised near Markson's hiding place. "You're debating about which one of us should search for her." It should be Verve. She knew he would argue – and win, no doubt – but Dav was *her* family. Perhaps the only family she had left besides cranky old Aunt Springer and a cousin.

"I don't trust Finley alone with you," he said after a moment.

"He hasn't hurt me, though. Besides, I can handle myself."

He frowned. "He wouldn't be with us still if I thought he might hurt you. No, that's not the problem." Fenn readjusted his burden and picked up his pace slightly.

"I could go after Dav."

"Absolutely not."

Verve's eyes rolled heavenward. "Then...?"

Fenn let out a frustrated breath. "I don't know. I *could* send my uncle after her." He looked at Verve, as though for approval. When Verve offered none but continued to turn the matter over in her head, Fenn came to a stop and lowered his voice, which was accompanied by the telltale signs of a spell that would give their words privacy. "He's a selfish man, Verve. Everything I've ever heard of Finley has shown him to be entirely absorbed with his own affairs. He stole power from many fae and gave a lot of it to those he knew he could call in favors from."

"He's your mother's uncle?"

Fenn quirked an eyebrow. "Verve, are you listening?"

"I am listening, but I'm not certain what we should do either. If we send him after Dav, he could betray us." She let out a huff. "There aren't any good options."

"Which is why I propose a gamble," said Fenn, moving forward once more. "We should let your sister go...for now."

Verve opened her mouth to protest, but then closed it once more. It was a risk for certain. But her youngest sister was powerful and could most likely take care of herself. Besides, Dav was the one who had run away in the first place. Maybe she just needed time to calm down and get used to the idea of being fae.

"You're not angry." He sounded surprised. "You're not going to try to pull off some heroic feat, are you?"

"Like what?" Her eyes flashed to his.

Fenn's lips twitched. "No running off to save the day without telling me first, all right?"

"All right." *This time.*

Once Finley had finished clearing the area of traps, Fenn carried Markson into the small shelter, which was comprised of crudely nailed-together boards and some tar paper. He set the man on a bed of blankets, and then settled down to sleep himself just outside the makeshift door. Their night in Letorheas had been interrupted, and he was no doubt exhausted.

"Shouldn't someone keep watch?" Verve asked as Finley lay in the shade of a great oak.

Finley was already asleep, his deep, even breathing giving him away. Fenn, on the other hand, gestured for Verve to join him. "The repelling charm will keep unwanted parties away. And we'll hear Markson if he wakes up." He held out his arms for her.

Reluctantly, she gave in to the notion that the others weren't going to make any plans until they had rested, so she lay down next to Fenn and allowed herself to be pressed once more into his chest.

Though Verve didn't think she could rest, she lay there and tried to quiet her mind. Fenn melted into her. His grasp on her tightened and then went slack before he succumbed to sleep, his warm breath tickling the nape of her neck.

A gentle breeze enveloped them as the sun disappeared behind a bank of clouds, casting the land into a sudden and unnatural dimness. The air around them grew cold, and Verve had the distinct impression that she was being watched. At first she thought it was her fancy, that her mind was playing tricks on her. No one could find them here, after all. Fenn's repelling charm was at work because Markson was still alive. But the longer she lay there and tried to forget her troubles, the more it became impressed upon her that she should extricate herself from Fenn's grasp and find out what was causing her to feel so on edge.

Fenn stirred. "What's wrong?" he murmured.

Verve probed with her magic, but whatever she had sensed was gone. "Nothing." She settled back down and, soon enough, weariness overcame her and she fell into a dreamless sleep.

Chapter Fifteen

The company slept well into the late afternoon when the shadows began to fall. There was a nip in the air borne on swift breezes, whispers that winter had yet to move on. Verve was first to rise. It came as a surprise to her that she had been unconscious for more than three hours. Perhaps absorbing more power as quickly as she had was to blame. She stretched and sat up. Something was amiss, but she couldn't put a name to her unease.

As if sensing it as well, Fenn jerked awake and was on his feet in a fraction of a second. His brow wrinkled and he looked at Verve. "What is it?"

Verve shook her head. "Something's wrong. I just don't know what." She closed her eyes and Fenn prowled around the camp, reaching out with magic as he probed for answers. There were no sounds beyond what the three of them plus the mortal would make. Verve used her power to scan the area around them and arrived at the conclusion that there was nothing to be *seen* either, nothing to raise alarm.

Fenn inhaled deeply. "It smells of death here, very faintly." He turned to Verve. "Can you smell it?"

"I don't— Oh, that is wretched!" She must have forgotten to breathe until that moment.

At her proclamation, Finley rose as well, his eyes sharp and alert. He said nothing as he peered into the woods. Then, without warning, he took off at a run.

"Finley?" Verve asked, meaning to run after him.

"Stay where you are, Verve," Fenn said with magical compulsion in his voice. It worked on her somewhat, only enough to make her hesitate.

"What is it?" she said, irritated that he had used power against her.

"A moment, Verve." Fenn held up a hand for her to wait and then raced out of sight.

She frowned at first, keen on knowing what was going on and not wanting to be left in the dark. But as the minutes wore on, apprehension tickled at her nerves and she took to pacing. When she thought she could bear it no longer and would have to use through-sight or some means to discover what had the males so upset, both Fenn and his uncle hastened into sight, their hands dirty and reeking of decay. Verve took an automatic step back and plugged her nose. "What did you find?" she asked after a moment.

The two men looked at each other. Finley spoke first. "A warning, to either you or me or the both of us."

Well, that made nothing clear. She turned to Fenn, who said, "The ground outside the repelling charm was just littered with bodies."

Verve gawped at him. "Bodies?"

"Of animals," Fenn said quickly. "It's meant to frighten someone. We buried everything before it could attract predators."

Finley shook his head. "It's a message that Igraine knows where I am and that she will bide her time until she can get to us." With some force he threw away a stick he'd been holding, and he then turned his intensity on Verve. "What did you promise her exactly?"

Fenn put himself between the two. "Don't talk to her that way."

Verve rolled her eyes. "My deal with Igraine was that I restore the magic that *you* stole." She jabbed her finger in his direction.

That seemed to take Finley aback. "Then why haven't you?"

"When, exactly, would I have had time to return to Ithalamore to do so? Hmm?" She hoped the look she gave him made it clear how she felt about that question.

"We're trapped." Finley backed down. Some of the fire left his gaze. "There's nowhere we can go that she cannot reach." His voice had taken on a resigned quality.

"What can she do to us, though?" Verve wondered. They were immortal; Igraine was dead. But then Verve thought of her loved ones in the next life and her heart seized. Could Igraine make things difficult for them? She didn't care to find out. Yes, she would have to return to Ithalamore as soon as possible to receive the names of those she was supposed to give power to.

"She will get what she wants," said Fenn evenly. "She just might not get it as quickly as she would like to." He straightened, stretched, and then went about collecting wood to add to the ashes of a fire pit.

Verve followed his example, though her eyes kept seeking out Finley, who seemed to be fast sinking into a quiet despair.

Once the two of them had collected enough branches and twigs, Fenn dusted off his hands and stepped back. "If you are up for the challenge, I would like you to dry out the logs, using air alone. No gestures, eyes closed, only your senses telling you what to do. Can you do it?"

"Why?" she asked.

"You're good with matter, passable with water, from what I've seen. But your fire is out of control and I haven't seen you work much with air. As for the gestures…you're too powerful for them now."

"What about verbals?"

Fenn made a face. "They're almost as potent as gestures, but I don't want you to become reliant on them. Say Dacre takes your voice and has you immobilized. Practice the elements without crutches, and you could drown him, quarter him, suck the air out of his lungs, and then set him ablaze without batting an eye." It sounded very much like Fenn was looking forward to her doing these things to their mutual foe, but Verve couldn't bring herself to even offer a small smile.

The first thing she did was find her balance, her legs spread apart and her knees slightly bent so they wouldn't lock. Fenn had taught her this stance during one of their mock battles, and it had served her well so far. She closed her eyes and focused as the scene around her came into view in her mind's eye. Then she reached for a feeling, the first one that always lay simmering beneath the surface: anger. It wasn't a stable emotion, and fire wanted to leap out of her with the magical blast of air she attempted to release. As it was, the blast of wind was hot, and the plants surrounding them withered. Her eyes flew open.

At once Fenn was there, throwing a protective shield around the shelter. "Careful. We don't want to cook Markson." His tone was light, but Verve knew it was an all too real possibility.

She let out a great huff and shook out her arms. "Right." Again she closed her eyes.

"You've dried the logs out," Fenn told her. "There's very little water to pull from the air now, so I won't try to soak them. Why don't you try fire, but this time, find a positive emotion to use."

She sneaked a peek at him. "What makes you say it wasn't a positive feeling I reached for?"

He shook his head and crossed his arms over his chest. "Your face is an open book sometimes. That's another thing to work on. Now—"

"Close my eyes and focus. But why focus my eyes if I can still see everything with them closed?"

That made Fenn still. "You're using through-sight?"

"No. It's...it's like I'm over and around and in everything. Doesn't that happen to you?"

"Soul-walking?" Finley said from nearby. He sounded mildly curious but didn't look any less full of dread.

"You have to lose consciousness for that, I believe...judging from what she's said." Fenn was looking at Verve like she was some marvelous puzzle that he was trying to piece together but was having a challenging time doing so.

Amusement was the emotion Verve then coupled with her magic, shoving them both together at the dried twigs and logs. At once the wood ignited, the flames rising sky-high. The heat must have been oppressive for the others, because they quickly stepped back. She cringed. "Sorry."

Once the fire had calmed and had been fed some more logs – Fenn saw to drying those out – the three of them searched the camp for something to eat. Markson had a few supplies hanging from a net in a tree and others buried in the compact soil beneath a rock. Altogether, they found five strips of smoked and dried venison, half a loaf of hard-as-nails bread wrapped in a shawl, and a canteen that was half-full of wine that smelled more of vinegar than anything.

A few times throughout the late afternoon, they had checked on Markson and made sure his pulse was still strong. But the man didn't seem ready to wake from his ordeal.

Verve's stomach snarled in protest as Fenn put the provisions aside, save for the canteen, the contents of which he sloshed around three times. "We can't be far from a town," she said as Fenn passed her the canteen. The sour wine smelled much sweeter now and had increased in volume. She took a quick gulp and passed it back to Fenn.

"If we're to get more supplies, we'll have to forage within the perimeter of the charm." Fenn took a swig of the wine and passed it to Finley. "Visiting any civilization isn't a good idea at this point."

Finley chuckled and gulped down a few mouthfuls. "Too bad the carcasses Igraine left us were rotten through and through. We could have eaten them otherwise." He screwed on the cap of the canteen and tossed it back to Fenn.

From within the shelter, there was a soft groan. "What in the blazes…?"

Verve froze but Fenn made for the hut, tension showing only in his shoulders. "You're awake."

Markson mumbled something unintelligible then let out a string of curses Verve had never heard in all her days. He sat up and looked through the doorway directly into her eyes. When he spoke, his voice trembled. "That was…" Of all things, tears ran down his ruddy cheeks and he shook his head. "My pain's gone. All gone." He wiped at his eyes and pulled himself to his feet.

Verve was about to tell Markson to be careful, to not walk on the damaged leg. But he seemed so steady and sure, she knew her healing had taken hold completely. The man was as good as new.

Though Markson seemed grateful, Fenn none too subtly put himself in front of Verve. "I'm glad you're feeling better. We're sorry about the break."

"Never mind, never mind." Markson cleared his throat, which had grown hoarse with some emotion. "I'm sorry for being so quick to attack you and yours."

Verve waved away the remark, and noted the man cringed in response. "You've been through a lot. I don't blame you for wanting to protect yourself."

"This in no way means I trust you," he quickly added. "But perhaps we can come to a truce of sorts? You don't use your magic tricks on me and I don't try to harm you." He held out his hand, but Fenn continued to block the way. Markson cowered slightly.

Instead of pushing Fenn away or telling him to move, Verve reached around him. The man gripped forearms with her and they shook on their agreement, however temporary it might be. Relief flooded Verve at the contact, and as they dropped hands, she was hopeful there might be a chance for her to win over other mortals.

Markson cleared his throat and stepped back. He surveyed his camp, nodding when he spied the supplies they had unearthed. "Well, I see you've found my provisions. Or, rather, what's left of them. Been meaning to go into town and replenish my supplies." Here he addressed Fenn. "Would it be possible for you to, er – you know." He waved his hands in the air, suggestive of what he must think spell-casting looked like.

"Food cannot be created from nothing, nor multiplied, only salvaged. I can restore moisture to your bread, and draw water from the air to fill your canteen when it empties." Fenn passed the wine to the old man, who unstoppered it and took a deep pull. "We'll forage tomorrow."

No one argued.

Chapter Sixteen

When the sun had disappeared over the horizon and the land was plunged into a starless night, Markson retired into his hut after offering a few furs to his guests. Finley declined, but Fenn accepted two.

"I'll keep first watch," said Fenn's uncle. He winked at the couple and then gazed into the fire, his expression thoughtful.

Fenn took Verve by the hand and led her to the other side of the shelter, where he laid one of the furs on the ground. The soil was smooth there, free of rocks. Even though she wasn't tired, Verve lay down, and Fenn quickly followed suit before covering them both with the other fur.

They lay on their backs next to each other, their eyes on the swaying treetops above. From inside the hut, Markson snored, and beyond him, the fire crackled merrily.

Verve broke the silence, her voice frail. "Do you think she's all right?" She felt Fenn's gaze move to her face.

"Your sister? I don't know. I hope so." He took her hand in his and squeezed it. "Davinia has a ridiculous amount of power."

"But she's untrained."

"Mm," Fenn concurred. The following moments passed by so silently that Verve wondered if Fenn might have fallen asleep. When he spoke again, she jolted, her fingers burning. "Do you wish to go after her?" His voice was reluctant yet willing, making it obvious he thought it a bad idea.

She considered that for a moment. Did Dav *want* to be found? Had she simply acted rashly? It was true that Dav had been irritated – well, not *irritated*. *Irate* was more like it. But what if she was somewhere lost and cold and afraid, regretting her decision to flee? "How would we find her now?"

"Honestly? I don't know if either of us is able. I lost her once, after I took her from the ruins of your home. It was she who returned to me, and that was only because she was hungry. Davinia is...*gifted* at hiding."

Verve sniffed, stifling a sob. "W-well, that would mean she could hide from anyone or anything bad, right?"

Fenn moved closer and drew her into his arms. "Yes, of course."

"But we can still look for her?"

"On the morrow." He kissed her cheek, and she relaxed...somewhat.

The air cooled considerably as the hour grew later. Soon snow fell from the heavens and clung to her hair. The wind picked up. Leaves skittered here and there. At one point, Verve swore there were glowing eyes of an animal in the near distance, only for them to disappear by the time she mentioned it to Fenn.

Fenn did not respond to that, so she shook him a little. "Fenn," Verve breathed. "There's something out there."

He didn't make a sound nor did he stir. Perhaps he was more tired than he had let on. But he was no longer powering wards around them nor spells to protect her family – they were all dead, save for Dav, and Verve didn't believe one spell would tire Fenn so much. She pulled back a little to better see his face, which was relaxed in sleep.

A log popped in the fire beyond the hut, and again Verve jumped. There still was no response from Fenn. "Fenn? Wake up. There's something wrong." She maneuvered out of his grasp easily, and his arm fell back limply at his side. "Fenn." He was still breathing and his heart was beating at a steady rate. What had happened to him? "Finley, something's wrong with Fenn!"

Finley didn't respond either. The light from the fire died in that moment, plunging the immediate area into an even greater darkness.

Verve slapped Fenn across the face. "Wake up!" There was no reaction. "Finley, help me." All grew eerily quiet and still. The temperature dipped once more, so much so that the furs could not keep out the cold. She stumbled to her feet and ran to fetch Finley, hoping he could help her rouse Fenn. It was little surprise when she saw the fae sprawled out on the ground by the now-dead fire, a dagger resting just out of reach of his fingertips.

"Such a pity that I have the rogue in my power and yet I cannot find the courage to exact revenge," said a hauntingly beautiful voice. It was coming from above and near at hand.

Verve scanned the woods first and then looked up. There, in the branches of the great oak, sat a woman with raven-black hair and eyes that flamed in their sockets.

"Igraine," Verve said, loudly enough that it should have awakened the entire camp.

The undead potion-maker drifted downward until she hovered inches from Finley, hatred marring her features. "I will not kill your ill-advised ally, Firstblood. Not now, anyway. Time may prove that you need him yet."

"How did you find us?" That had been the wrong thing to say.

The flames in Igraine's eyes leapt. "You thought you could hide from me? That a simple charm would fool the queen of the dead?" She laughed, and it was not a pleasant sound.

Verve remained calm, however, and said, "We weren't hiding, not exactly. We were…temporarily avoiding you."

That made Igraine's brows rise. "I see. You have what was stolen, and now is the time to return it. Every last drop." She stared at Verve, *into* her, daring her to object.

Dread prickled at the base of Verve's neck. She had not asked for all this power. But what if she needed every bit if she was going to defeat Dacre? The Traitor King had taken on a lot of magic as well, and she knew it would most likely rival her own.

Igraine didn't react well to Verve's hesitation. She swooped toward her, bringing her nose a fraction of an inch from Verve's. "If you refuse to return the power to their rightful owners, I will take your husband into my service as recompense – just as the deal we struck said." The queen of the dead had not specified whom she would take, but Verve ought to have known it would be someone very important to her.

Verve raised her hands, hoping to placate Igraine. "I will return the power. But you have yet to tell me how to find the owners."

"For you, it will be easy to get there; it's getting them all *out* that will be a trick." She studied Verve, backing away a few feet, much to Verve's relief. "All twelve fae are locked in the dungeons of Strattavus Palace. You will need to create a gateway there and safely shepherd each fae to a safe location before you return the magic."

"Strattavus Palace," said Verve, and a dull headache started to throb behind her eyes. "Is that where—"

"Yes, it is where the Traitor King rules from. I know you have soul-walked there before, so you should find it in your physical form as well. If you are quick and stealthy, you might just succeed. If you fail, you might not get another chance until your ascension, in which case I will consider our agreement in partial breach."

The words fell like a physical blow. Verve winced and backed away. "What would that mean for Fenn?"

Igraine showed her teeth. "Partial breach, partial servitude. Half the year your mate would serve me, reaping souls, while the other half he would spend with you."

Verve gnawed on her lower lip. "Is there any possible way we could renegotiate the terms of the bargain?"

Again Igraine laughed, though this time she sounded truly amused. "You think I make blood oaths so lightly? No, the deal's the deal. I will not amend."

That left Verve no choice whatsoever. She glared at Igraine, angry tongues of fire licking her nailbeds. "Whether I fail or not – and I won't – you'll soon be sorry for the day you made a deal with me." With that said, she turned her attention from Igraine and focused on finding the fabric that made up the mortal realm.

"I will meet you outside the ruins of the Larknott family estate. Try very hard not to lose anyone on the paths between realms. Your mate is depending on you." A cloud of darkness descended where Igraine stood, swallowing her up and then dissipating to reveal that she had gone.

After sparing one last glance for her poor husband, Verve found the fabric and tore it asunder. Once the rip was large enough for her to step through, she did so and followed her soul's memory toward the dungeons of Strattavus.

As she traversed the silent paths of the No Lands, Verve tried to formulate a plan. She would find her way to the cell that had held Fenn first, in order to orient herself, and pray that there were no guards at hand. Her loss of residual burst would be an advantage, if perhaps her only one. No one would smell or hear her coming, but there were other possible ways of alerting Dacre to her presence. For all she knew, there were hidden spells set up, rigged to alert Dacre or his men if the prison walls were breached. What could she do about that? Her nerves jangled and her stomach churned, making concentrating next to impossible, so much so that she nearly missed the pulsing sensation in her chest. This was where she needed to exit the paths and hopefully land where she meant to.

Verve skidded to a halt, felt for the fabric of the No Lands, and tore a hole through it, just large enough to peer through. The world beyond indeed opened into a cell, one that was occupied by a male fae, chained to the wall. Was he perhaps one of the fae who needed his magic returned? She hadn't thought to ask Igraine how she would know whom to save. *Blast*. Then, knowing she would most likely have to empty the prison, Verve gritted her teeth and widened the hole enough for herself to step through. When she had fully emerged into the cell, the gaping hole mended itself behind her.

The male looked up, his mouth opening as though to yell, but he hesitated when Verve put a finger to her lips. She listened. There were many fae heartbeats near at hand, and many more above, mingled with some mortal ones as well.

"There are no guards down here," said the man, his voice strained and above a whisper. "How did you get in?" He tensed when she approached him.

"I'll explain later." She reached out and sent her magic spiraling down into the lock of his manacles, and was at once rewarded with a distinct *click*.

Unlike how Fenn had fared, the male seemed to be in decent shape, though it took him a moment to get to his feet as his magic visibly surged through him. "Who are you? How did you find me?" He rubbed his wrists and moved toward the bars, as though ready to break through them.

Verve held up a staying hand. "There might be an alarm. We'll have to portal." Was that the word for what she could do? The way the fae looked at Verve made her doubt.

"Portal? You mean make a tunnel? These walls are too thick to tunnel through, and they're reinforced with magic. I'll have to take my chances with the bars." He tried to move around Verve, but she grabbed him by the shoulder and pulled him back with more force than she had meant to. The fae went flying back toward the wall and landed with a bone-jarring *thud*. He swore at her and jumped to his feet, fear rolling off him in waves.

"I'm sorry," she said. "I forget my own strength sometimes." She raised her hands, preparing to make another gateway, but the fae seemed to misinterpret her intentions.

He flew at Verve, knocked her onto her back, and pinned her hands above her head. "What do you want with me?" he demanded. Before Verve could get back up, he slammed her head down against the floor, leaving a large dent in the rock.

"I really don't have time for this. Sorry." She freed her right hand from his grasp and bent her thumb in toward her little finger, then sent a wave of golden light into his chest.

At once the fae rolled off her and got to his feet, his face strangely blank.

Verve needed both hands to make a portal, so she simply said to the man, "Sleep," lacing the word with compulsion. She let him crumple to the ground in a dead faint while she went about making a gateway. Once she had made a hole large enough, Verve slung the male over her shoulder and carried him through the paths of the No Lands toward where she hoped Igraine would be waiting. Repeating this process not once but at least eleven more times was daunting. She tried not to think too much about it as she arrived at her destination and made to rip another hole, this time to exit. The male fae, though he was light, proved cumbersome, and Verve set him down so she could work her magic. That was her first mistake.

As soon as her skin ceased to touch his, the world beneath them both lurched. Verve righted herself and looked down, only to find that the male had vanished. "Where are you?" she tried to scream, but the sound was dampened and came out as the softest of whispers. Frantic, Verve surveyed her immediate area. There was no trace of him, not even an imprint on the flickering light that made up the ground.

Verve got on her hands and knees and felt around, still calling for the fae. She crawled and she cried out but soon realized he was lost and beyond aid. All was silent in the No Lands.

Panic seized Verve. Her chest tightened and she tried to suck down air, but there was little to be had. Since the male was a lost cause, Verve ripped a hole and entered Letorheas, right outside the ruins of Fenn's family estate.

Igraine was waiting there, her arms folded across her chest. But upon seeing Verve's face, something shifted in the woman's demeanor and she ran to Verve, eyes wide. "You lost someone on the paths. Who did you lose?"

It took Verve a moment before she could speak. She stooped over, resting her hands on her knees, eyes closed. "I don't know. He was a male with bright red hair and blue-gray eyes." Verve composed herself and looked once more at Igraine, fearful of how she would react. When she didn't, Verve snarled at her. "You didn't tell me I could lose them on the paths that easily." Her voice was pitched high, and Igraine put her hands over her own ears.

"Calm down. Think, Firstblood. Think. You are the only one who can traverse those paths. You must use flesh-to-flesh contact or extend some of your power if you are to safely transport anyone through the No Lands. Surely this should have been obvious."

"No, it wasn't." Her shoulders shook now with silent sobs, and it was then that Igraine's features softened.

"He will spend eternity lost there, whoever it was. You owe it to him to finish this."

Verve drew in a shaky breath and nodded. "All right." She sniffed and all but sank back down. "How do I do this?"

Igraine's jaw tightened and she said through her teeth, "You know quite well now what to do. I suggest you get to work before the Traitor King discovers he has a prisoner missing. Hurry!"

With those fear-inducing words echoing in her mind, Verve once again created a gateway and this time followed the path with what was hopefully a good guess of where to land. The cell next to the now-lost fae's had been silent, but Verve aimed for it nonetheless and was pleasantly surprised when she emerged from the No Lands. Unlike the previous cell, this one held not one but three prisoners, all of them chained together with magic-canceling manacles.

The trio was alert already, no doubt having heard the earlier rescue. They didn't ask any questions, thankfully, as Verve worked on the bonds restricting their wrists and then their ankles. "Whatever happens, do not let go of me. You must remain in skin-to-skin contact if you wish to emerge on the other side." Verve rolled up her ratty dress's sleeves so that her flesh was bared, and the males at once gripped on to her. This made moving her arms clumsier, but she managed to tunnel through the No Lands and this time emerged on the other side with the three males intact.

Their faces were wan, and it was with relief that they collapsed onto the ground in Letorheas and kissed Verve's feet, of all things. "How can we repay you?" asked one fae with the sandy blond hair.

Igraine was there at once, pulling the other two males to their feet before drawing them into an embrace. "I thought I'd never see you again," the potion-maker said between sobs.

Verve didn't linger for the remainder of the reunion but portaled back to the dungeons, this time freeing five in one fell swoop, albeit with much awkward maneuvering to ensure everyone remained safe. Igraine claimed three of them and informed Verve she had now freed five of her kin.

Seven yet remained.

The next two rescues only yielded three prisoners, all of them Igraine's family. On her following trip back, Verve became aware of some commotion overhead, but didn't stop to worry about it. Instead, she increased her pace. She freed four fae from their shackles and brought them back safely to the estate. One of them were Igraine's. The ones who were not with the potion-maker quickly left the group, after bowing low. There were only two prisoners left who she needed to save.

When Verve emerged this time in the dungeons, the palace above them was in an uproar. Shouts echoed off the stone walls, fast approaching the cell which Verve had portaled to. She made hasty work of the one prisoner's bonds, prayed he was one of the two remaining that she needed, then hissed instructions and created another gateway. Verve all but dragged the male through the No Lands, at a punishing pace. What felt like an eternity later, she ripped another tear in the ether, swung the fae around herself so that he landed on his bottom by Igraine, and let the rip close behind her as she raced toward what she hoped would be the final prison cell.

Something had changed. She knew it before she lifted her hands to the fabric, and thus she hesitated, fingertips itching as she contemplated what she ought to do. Was someone else in the cell that awaited her, someone who shouldn't be? The thought snuffed out any rage she felt toward Igraine. Dread filled irritation's place. It was true that she could find her way to another cell, listen, and work her way from there. But time was of the essence. If she waited, the prisoner – or *prisoners* – might be better guarded and her only chance would have been seized from her. Verve ceased to teeter on the edge of indecision. She tore a hole in the fabric and emerged, poised to fight.

There was one prisoner in the cell she had entered, and a look at him told Verve something was very wrong indeed. He was too calm, too ordinary.

Before she could move, the male said, "Please, you have to help me." The words froze Verve to the spot. The slight fellow craned his neck, desperation in his eyes.

Verve's mouth went dry. No matter what she tried, she couldn't bring herself to move. She knew this was Dacre in a different form.

Belatedly she even smelled his magic hanging in the air: burned coffee and chocolate. Why couldn't she move her feet? Her magic retreated deep down, as though frightened.

The male didn't stop his charade. "Please. You've helped the others. Don't deny it, I've heard quite a commotion down here."

Then why was all so still now? *Get out. Get out. Raise your hands, make a gateway, and get out.* Though her feet would not obey, her hands did. Verve raised both arms and tore a hole through the ether, only to be unable to walk through it. The gateway soon fizzled and the rip sealed itself.

"Let. Me. Go," she said through her teeth.

"What do you mean?" He seemed completely baffled. But why keep up the game?

Something struck Verve in the back, a powerful freezing spell that made movement altogether impossible now, but for her eyes. She closed her lids and viewed the room around her from an aerial perspective. There were two of them in the cell, and the man in chains continued to gawp at her, even as he struggled against his bonds. Cold ran down Verve's spine when a finger traced down the length of her back. That was when Verve detected the third heartbeat in the room, one that had been silent until then.

"You found your way back," said Dacre. "I knew you were clever enough." He stepped around from behind her as he dropped the invisibility he had enveloped himself in.

Mercifully, the spell he had cast on her was starting to fade, though she didn't dare make him aware of this fact until she was completely free of it. She glared at him as he studied her.

"You look entirely mortal. What happened to—" Understanding dawned on his face and he staggered back a step.

Movement returned to Verve's fingers, though she fought to keep them absolutely still. She didn't even dare move her mouth, which she felt regain its freedom. Magic tingled in her fingertips and slowly trickled back through her veins, filling her with the sensation of pins and needles.

"You've grown more powerful." He stared at her in wonder for a moment, before nearly startling Verve out of her wits by shouting, "Bring it – no, bring *both*!"

Verve didn't like the sound of that. Still, she fought to remain motionless, her hands and arms now free of Dacre's spell. If only her feet and legs would be next, but the spell was fading from her head downward, releasing one body part at a time as her blood pumped sluggishly from her heart.

Dacre moved in closer, sniffing. "You've lost your residual burst too. That's useful to know." He stroked her face with the tips of his fingers and then cupped her cheeks in the palms of his gloved hands. "Where were you? How did you— Well, I know that you can create gateways, thanks to your brilliant display just now."

Her feet were free, but it felt as though she had been sleeping on them in a strange way, and she wasn't certain they would bear her any distance. Footsteps thundered overhead, fae shouting, doors slamming, and all the while Dacre watched her. It was agony to stand there, but Verve let her power rise, pulse in her veins as she waited for the right moment to release it. He would have to unhand her or she would have to remove his hands from her person if she were to attempt anything, otherwise he might follow her into the No Lands. *Could I lead him and lose him there? I wonder...*

"We have them, sire!" The voice was close, and Verve knew her moment to act was now.

Dacre's eyes never left hers as he dropped his hands. "Hurry," he called out to his men. "I don't know how much longer I can hold—"

Verve released her magic on Dacre in one mighty wave, which sent him crashing through three cell walls. Then, moving more quickly than she knew herself capable of, she freed the final prisoner, be he friend or foe, and ripped open another gateway. "Hold on to my arm!" she shouted.

The freed man obeyed, only to be struck with a bolt of black lightning. He crumpled to the floor, silver blood leaking from his parted lips. There was no heartbeat or breath from the poor soul, and Verve knew she must leave without him.

For good measure, she sent one final spell flying back over her shoulder, one made of fire and loathing, before throwing herself through the portal. With a strangled sob she picked her way blindly through the No Lands, fearful of what would become of Fenn now that she had failed. Her husband, a servant to the queen of death? No, she couldn't accept that. But— Oh, what if she had truly lost him to Igraine? Verve's hatred for Dacre doubled, tripled, and she became a wild thing of fire and rage there in the way between all lands. For a long while she simply stood there, burning, and she ceased to hear the trees call to her.

When Verve opened another gateway back into Letorheas, there was screaming in horror. The ten fae she had saved stared at her, and almost as one dropped to their knees, unable or unwilling to look upon her face.

The undead woman managed to raise her gaze to Verve's, though the fire in her eyes faltered. "You did not bring anyone else, I see." Her words resounded in Verve's mind like a guillotine's blade striking its mark.

Rage slowly gave way to terror, and the fire she was made of guttered, leaving her standing in her fae form adorned with smoldering rags. At least this time she hadn't been weakened nearly as much. Verve glared at Igraine. "I will return the gifts to their rightful owners."

Igraine gave her a curt nod.

"But since our original bargain did *not* include my rescuing your kin, you will absolve me of not being able to return the magic to them all."

The fae opened her mouth, but Verve raised her hand.

"My husband is free. You must declare it, or so help me, I will return the gifts to all of your kin and then I will kill them." She put as much frustration and anger into her words as she could, but she wondered if the undead creature knew what she really was thinking.

The ten fae continued to kneel, their eyes on Igraine. "She owes you nothing," said a she-fae with wide brown eyes. "Igraine, you must see that—"

"The deal is the deal," said Igraine. "You only have ten fae to whom you can and must restore powers, so either you will render your husband to my service for two months out of every twelve, or kill the one who stole the magic in the first place."

"Igraine," warned one of the males.

Verve's heart was beating more quickly than it ought to, and she knew the undead being could hear it as well as her relations. "Two months?" How could she ask that of Fenn? No, it wasn't possible. And yet the bargain they had struck weighed on her, and she knew that something very bad would happen if they didn't come to some agreement.

"Two months," said Igraine, "or you can kill the siphon. You know very well that this is the way it must be. The blood vow isn't going to release you until you have fulfilled your part. Little by little, it will wear at your sanity. The Fire Queen without a steady mind is a dangerous thing, not only for herself but for her people." She tilted her head to the side, showing her teeth as she grinned. "You're not going to kill my kin when you cannot even bring yourself to kill the siphon. Don't deny it. Your heart still hurts from all the other deaths you've already caused."

Verve screamed at the woman, lashing out with enough power to send Igraine flying. Trees were leveled, and the fae men and women she had rescued toppled as well. Chest heaving, fingertips shooting sparks, Verve struggled to bring herself under control. "I will think on it, you horrible woman – curse you."

Igraine picked herself back up, her grin having faded into a slight smirk. "Very well. Don't take too long in deciding. Your mental stability will only last for so long."

Ignoring the taunt, Verve went to the closest fae, took his hand, and started the process of returning power. Just as it had been with Finley, the fae had a magical signature, and his power within her recognized its owner and flowed through her to him with ease. As soon as the transfer had been completed, the fae rose, kissed her on the cheek, and departed. She stumbled to the next in line and repeated the process. The second transfer didn't take as long, little power having been stolen. This fae kissed her cheek as well but went to stand by Igraine once it was finished. Eight more times Verve repeated the process, her movements becoming clumsier as the world spun around her more and more with each transfer.

Finally, when the last fae had their magic returned to them, Verve sank to her knees. Down was up and up was down, and she couldn't form a coherent thought as Igraine – a mere blur of light and color – collected her into her arms and carried her away from the ruins.

Verve was wracked with shivers. Nausea ripped at her insides, so she closed her eyes and tried to find sleep.

"Losing that much power that quickly will make you ill," said Igraine, her tone pitying and yet mocking at the same time somehow. Where there had been light there was now a dimness, as though someone had blown out a lamp. The imprint of the now-absent light caused her vision to fill with sunspots.

The temperature dropped once more, and Verve felt herself being lowered to the hard, cold ground. She tried to sit up but couldn't find the strength. Igraine could do a lot of damage to her, should she choose. Perhaps it had been unwise of Verve to provoke her.

But instead of harming Verve, Igraine laid a hand on her brow and murmured, "Careful not to burn the world down, little queen." And then she was gone.

A whimper escaped Verve's lips, and she continued to shake violently. Fire within her rose to meet what had been taken, and she burned... not with flames but with fever. "Help me." The words were a desperate whisper. All that power, gone. The loss made tears cloud her vision. Perhaps the Ahkoshwa had been right. Perhaps Verve *was* an empty well, needing to be filled. Her heart ached for more magic, even as she loathed the thought of possessing it. If only she could stop trembling.

"Verve!" shouted a familiar voice.

"Verity!" a second voice called. "She shouldn't have been able to sneak past my wards."

"Don't underestimate her."

They were a-ways off, true, but why couldn't they hear her frenzied heart beating? Now that she thought of it, *she* couldn't even hear it beating. Was she dead?

"I'm here," she tried to say. It came out more as a grunt, but it was enough to alert the men to her whereabouts.

Footsteps crashed and crunched through obstacles to get to her.

"Is she dead?" asked Finley.

Fenn growled at him. "No. But something's wrong. I can't even *feel* her heart beating."

When Finley spoke, his voice was grim. "It's almost as though she's reverted to her mortal state and— You'd better work on her."

Swearing a rainbow of curses, Fenn laid her out on the ground and pumped his hands on her chest over her heart. At first he was gentle, but soon he was pounding on her with enough force to break ribs. "Verve, can you hear me?" He pinched her nose and breathed into her mouth, filling her lungs with air.

She shuddered with such a violent seizure that Fenn was thrown from her prone form. Her heart thudded once, albeit weakly, stopped, and then picked up to a sluggish rhythm as though reluctant to keep beating.

"What the devil happened?" Finley's ashen face came briefly into view before Verve's vision clouded over once more.

"I don't know," Fenn snapped. He tapped Verve's face lightly. "Verve, what happened? If you can talk, tell me so I might help you." He waited a moment and then took her wrist between his fingers.

Finley sighed. "I think I know what's wrong."

"We have to get her cool. She's burning up." Fenn set her down once more and started to rip through her dress.

"Leave it. She'll be all right; you just need to put out any flames as they appear so they don't cause a forest fire."

Something icy cold rested on Verve's brow, and she let out a relieved sigh. Again she tried talking, but it proved too tiresome so she simply drowsed as Fenn tended to her.

"What is wrong with her?" a third voice demanded. *Markson.*

"Fever," the other two said at once.

"She's going through withdrawal," said Finley. "We need to put her someplace where she won't cause any damage to herself or to us."

"Withdrawal?" It was Fenn who spoke, his tone suspicious. "What is that supposed to mean?"

"There's an abandoned well not half a mile from here," said Markson. "It's been boarded up. If you'll follow me..."

Verve tried to scream in protest, but all that came out was a tiny squawk as Fenn lifted her once more and hastened after Markson. As a child, she had fallen down a well, where she had remained lost to her family for several days. Fire erupted from her fingertips, which Fenn at once extinguished, as though he had anticipated it.

"What do you mean by withdrawal?" Fenn repeated, this time through clenched teeth.

"It simply means that she is experiencing the loss of much magic. Verity must have returned the stolen powers she took from Rillian and—"

"But is she going to be all right?" It came out a strangled sob, and Verve felt her heart break for her husband. His grief and terror almost made her forget what they were about to do to her.

The four of them slowed, stopped, and there was the groan of boards being moved.

"I told you, she's going to be fine."

Fenn drew in a gasping breath. "How do you know? How could you possibly know for certain?"

There was a pause, and when Finley answered, the words obviously pained him. "Because I have seen many fae lose all or most of their power, and I have lost much power myself. It makes one quite ill. But she's strong, son. Don't worry for her. She'll pull through. Remember, she's high fae."

"It's about ten feet down," said Markson. "Should I find a rope to lower her with?"

Stop! Please stop. Her vision cleared and she watched helplessly as she was carried nearer. "N-no," she managed to choke out. No one listened to her.

"I'll go down first, brace myself toward the middle of the structure, and then you will lower her down to me," said Fenn, passing her to Finley.

"It's not going to harm Verity if we let her drop. Think about this. *She* can't die, but she can kill you…maybe even by accident." He followed Fenn to the well, and Verve strained against him.

Fenn didn't listen to his uncle but leapt into the well. There was a great splash, the sound of some sediment striking the water, and then he called for her to be brought to him. "Hurry!"

The fever burning in Verve's veins was starting to manifest visibly. Her body took on a red glow and fire licked at the remains of her clothing.

"This is madness," said Finley. But he nonetheless set her on the edge of the well, took her by the wrists, and let her dangle into the abyss. "If she becomes violent, get out."

"Verve, it's going to be all right. I'm going to be down here with you the whole time." He grabbed her and cradled her against his chest, even as her breathing became labored and the world spun before her eyes. All at once he ceased bracing himself against the walls of the well and they plummeted a few feet, landing with a splash in the frigid water below.

They didn't land a moment too soon. The tongues of flame that had broken out all over Verve's body briefly died and then erupted from her in waves that shook the foundations of the structure and caused the soothing water to evaporate.

Fenn let out a mighty yelp but held her closer still.

It was too hot. She panted and writhed as he drew water from the earth below and brought it up to her neck. Almost at once it was depleted, so again he drew more.

"T-trapped," she sobbed into his chest.

He stroked her hair. "No, you're not. We'll climb out once you get better, all right? It's only a little while more, love."

"Please don't leave me down here." She clawed at him, tried freeing herself from his grasp, but she was too weak.

"I'm not leaving you down here. You can't get rid of me so easily." He brushed a strand of hair out of her eyes and then dipped his face down so that their lips touched. His skin was frigid compared to hers, and the contact soothed her momentarily.

Wave after wave of fire burst forth from her body, and each time Fenn drew water from the earth to try to extinguish or control it. Each time, it evaporated almost instantly. At long last, after Verve thought she could take no more of this, her fever broke and the flames in her veins ceased to burn so brightly. Sweat poured down her neck, and Fenn sank with her to his knees, holding her close through a final seizure.

Chapter Seventeen

After what felt like an eternity, Fenn conjured clothing to replace what had been destroyed – hers and his own – and, with his uncle's help, raised Verve out of the well. In the near distance, Markson sat with the canteen of wine, his hands trembling.

Only when she had been wrapped in a blanket and set down in Fenn's lap did it became apparent how angry her husband was. His skin was flushed, burned from the flames she had produced, but she realized some of the color had nothing to do with physical injury.

Verve tried squirming away, but his arms folded around her and held her firmly in place. She yowled at him as he nipped her. "Don't you bite me like you're some wild animal," she snarled.

"He almost lost you, child," said Finley. "What you deserve is a good thrashing, not a love bite."

Fenn's tongue skimmed the skin where his teeth had touched her, as though offering an apology. "You promised." His voice broke on the words. "No more leaving me behind. No more doing things needlessly on your own." Before she could defend herself, Fenn smashed his lips against hers, his fingers weaving into her hair and pulling her nearer. The kiss was not a gentle one. Through it she felt his rage and hurt, but she remained wooden against his demanding mouth. He hadn't even given her a chance to explain, maddening man!

It wasn't until she felt the tears running down his face and onto hers that she softened and laid a tentative hand over his heart. "Fenn," she said. He pulled away a fraction of an inch.

"What am I to do, Verve?" He kissed her neck.

"You can let me explain what actually happened, to begin with."

"You left." He shuddered violently when she placed a finger on his lips. "I woke up and you were gone."

She rubbed away a few stray tears from his cheeks and looked him in the eye. "I didn't have much choice."

Fenn scoffed.

"Igraine can walk through wards and isn't repelled by Markson's charm," Verve said. When Fenn started to look away, Verve took his chin in her hand and turned his face back to her own. "Fenn. I had to go with her."

His eyes flickered back to hers, and her heart broke all over again when she remembered how badly she had messed things up with retrieving the prisoners. It was her turn to cry.

Fenn swore when she started to sob, and pulled her head under his chin. "I'm not that angry. Truly."

"Y-you should be." Unable to stop herself and unwilling to keep any more secrets, Verve told him everything that had transpired while he had slept that unnatural sleep. Or rather, almost everything; she left out the part about Dacre almost catching her, not wanting to upset Fenn any more than he already was. When she mentioned the bargain, Fenn simply sighed as she broke down into more tears and gasped for air. She knew he didn't have to guess the outcome of her adventure but she forced herself to say the words, that she had lost two of Igraine's family members, thus dooming Fenn to two months of service out of every twelve.

Instead of shouting as Verve thought he ought, Fenn surprised her by getting to his feet, scooping her up, and carrying her away from camp. "Mind the wards while we're away," he called over his shoulder to Finley.

Though bewildered, Verve didn't dare ask Fenn where he was taking her or why. Whatever he had in mind, she most likely deserved it. Maybe he would cast her out or give her a thorough yelling at. Now she didn't dare meet his gaze, which she felt intent on her face.

They walked for a-ways, until the sounds of Finley and Markson were softer, and then Fenn threw out a sound barrier that blocked outside noise altogether. "I think you need a reminder," said Fenn, setting her on the ground.

Verve tried sitting up, but he lowered himself astride her hips, pinning her between his thighs. "A reminder?"

"Of what you are to me." Fenn drew a thread of silver magic into his right palm, and the air filled with the aroma of citrus. "You are my friend." He played with the power, letting it weave in and out of his fingers. "You are not just my friend, but my wife. And not just my wife, but my mate. Do you know what that all means?" A smile tugged at the corners of his lips, which he brought to hers once, softly, before pulling back slightly. "You are mine. Mine to cherish, protect, love…enjoy." He spoke the last word barely above a whisper and into the shell of her ear. "I can manage the cherishing and loving part, and in moments like these, I can more thoroughly enjoy. But to protect when you won't let me?"

She parted her lips to protest, but instead got a mouthful of his tongue. This kiss made her mind go pleasantly blank, and she tried in vain to remember why they were both so upset.

He moaned shamelessly, sending fire skittering across her bones. "I'm going to mark you, Verve," he said, pulling back half an inch, eyes hooded. "You, among others, need to remember who you belong to." His lips were back on hers for a moment, as though he were having trouble controlling himself and his desires. The magic in his hand flirted with her neck, and she spied it out of the corner of her eye, pushing him back at the last moment. "What?"

"I *am* yours, Fenn. But I don't need a mark to remember that."

The grin he gave her was positively wicked. "If you think this will hurt, you're wrong. And don't worry, you're going to mark me as well once I'm through." Fenn kissed her cheek, hesitating as he looked her over. At length, he peeled down the neckline of the dress he had created for her, and let his hand hover there.

Verve sighed. "All right, do it, but I don't think I need—"

Fenn pressed the magic into the skin over her heart, causing Verve to yelp in surprise. He was right: it didn't hurt, but it felt…strange, like Fenn was kissing her everywhere all at once. Warmth flooded her cheeks as he rubbed the spot where there was now a silver mark in a foreign script, which she realized represented his name.

"I had wanted to do that as soon as we were soul-bound," he confessed. "But I thought you might not want to be even more unbreakably tied to me." His thumb skimmed her lips, making them tingle.

"What does it do exactly?" Every part of her being thrummed his name. Never before had she wanted Fenn quite this much. The intensity of her feelings startled Verve but didn't stop her from throwing her arms around his neck and pulling him nearer.

His eyes darkened considerably. "It doesn't create. It simply amplifies and protects what is already there."

She stroked his face. "Protects? Were you afraid I would stop feeling for you?"

He leaned into her palm and his eyes fluttered closed. "Perhaps, but not for the reasons you might think." Fenn didn't elaborate, and Verve didn't ask him to, caught up in the sensations she was still experiencing from the mark.

It was quickly becoming apparent why he had marked her. Now she couldn't imagine leaving him behind for any period of time. Verve fisted his shirtfront and pulled him down so that their lips met once more. She was surprised when he was the first to pull away, his face radiant.

"It's my turn." Fenn rolled off of her and onto his back, and then took her left hand in his. "Think of your name. Your true name, not what you were given at birth."

Entranced, she watched his lips move, and he chuckled darkly. "What do you mean?" Verve asked, giving him a playful shove.

"It's a name you've given yourself, one you've probably never spoken to another."

That made Verve's brow crease. "I'm confused. I don't have a name like that."

Fenn smoothed out the crease with his fingertips. "It is what you would call yourself now that you have been remade. Not after what Dacre attempted, but when you touched the Cunning Blade." He looked at her expectantly. "You feel it, deep down…the name, that is."

At those words, something tugged at the back of Verve's mind. A word, not one that she had ever consciously thought of, nor one she could voice now. Perhaps 'name' was the wrong way to describe it; it was more of an impression, a feeling. "I think I know what you mean. But I don't know how to say it."

"You don't have to speak it. Feel it, let it fill you, and then push it into my skin."

Verve snagged her lower lip with her teeth, nearly tearing the skin. "But what if I burn you again?"

Fenn coiled a strand of her hair around one of his fingers. "I'm not afraid of you, Verve." His eyes searched hers. "Powers help me, maybe I should be. But I'm not." He freed her hair, then took her hand and flipped it so her palm was facing downward.

With him watching her expectantly, Verve knew she had to at least try, so, closing her eyes, she searched once more for her true name. It was slippery at first, and she had difficulty cornering it in her mind, but when she did, she latched on to it and let it fill her. An overwhelming sensation of power made her hesitate as her hand lit up like the midday sun.

"It's all right," said Fenn. He pulled down the neck of his own shirt and waited, his body quivering with what she recognized as anticipation and not fear. "Don't worry about hurting me. I trust you."

If she didn't do this soon, Verve knew she would lose her nerve, so gently she brought the magic in her hand to the space over Fenn's heart and pressed it down into his skin. With a sigh, the mark settled into his flesh. It glowed golden, a looping script in some ancient tongue that Verve knew she would never be able to pronounce. She let out a relieved breath. "That wasn't nearly as terrible as I—"

Fenn was astride her again in a flash. Frenzied, he kissed her as though he were afraid she would disappear.

Verve rested her palms on his chest, and he sighed happily.

His lips trailed down farther and farther until they came to rest on the mark he had given her, then his tongue traced over the script. Quite suddenly, though, he ceased and nestled into her bosom. "I forget. You need to sleep."

With her heart now racing as it was, Verve didn't think sleep possible. But he rolled off of her and didn't respond to the suggestive hand she trailed down to his hip. She huffed, causing him to smirk.

"We'll have plenty of time for that later." He bussed her left temple and took her hand in his own. "Rest."

Though Verve didn't feel tired, she closed her eyes and was unconscious moments later.

★ ★ ★

She awoke what might have been minutes later, as the sun seemed to be in the same position in the sky. Her throat was parched, however, and she felt magic building up inside her, begging for release, as often happened when she went too long without using it. She blinked and sat up.

A quilt she didn't remember from before pooled in her lap. Verve stretched her arms toward the heavens and sparks formed in her empty hands. Empty. Frantic now, she searched for Fenn. There was no one within her normal range of vision, but two immortal heartbeats thudded in the near distance, one of them instantly recognizable as Fenn's. Relief washed over Verve as she staggered to her feet and made her way to the fire pit, which was now not ten paces from her. Confused, she better took in her surroundings and noted she had been moved.

"Good, you're awake," said Fenn from behind her.

Verve yawned as he handed her a canteen full of what smelled like plain water this time. Gratefully she took a few deep gulps. "How long was I asleep?" She wiped her mouth with the back of her hand after he'd taken the canteen back from her.

"A day."

That startled her. "That long?"

Fenn shrugged. "You gave away quite a bit of magic, Verve. Finley says it's normal for fae to sleep for days on end after such an event. All things considered, you weren't unconscious for long." He reached into a knapsack on the ground and produced a bright green apple. "Here. You must be hungry."

"She's awake, is she?" said Markson. He ducked outside the shelter. "Late to rise and early to bed, makes a gal unruly, foolhardy, and dead." He'd said it jokingly, but Verve knew at once Fenn had taken issue with the rhyme.

"Easy," she murmured.

It was apparent Markson didn't notice any shift in the mood, his lips twitching as he approached. "You gave us all a fright, Miss Springer. That fire was..." He whistled. "I never did see such a thing in all my days. That other fellow, he picked me up and ran after the first eruption. Nearly singed my eyebrows off." Strangely enough, the man didn't seem as though he'd been frightened by the event. Rather, he sounded quite amused.

Verve grimaced, which only made the man laugh more. "I'm sorry if I frightened you."

Finley cleared his throat, and Verve turned her head to look at him. He appeared nervous and somewhat upset, his left eye twitching as he nodded at her. "I'm glad to see you've reentered the land of the waking. We have a lot to do." With a gesture to both her and Fenn, Finley reached into the pouch around his neck and produced a crumpled-up piece of parchment.

At once Verve smelled the aromas of chocolate and coffee. A growl tore itself from her lips as her heart took off at a sprint. Why did that parchment reek of Dacre? "What is this?" she demanded as he extended the crumpled ball to her. Fingers tingling, she did not accept the offering.

"While you were sleeping, I ventured into Letorheas to pick up more supplies. Your mate let me go, though reluctantly, for we both could foresee the lack of food provisions fast becoming a problem. This," said Finley, smoothing out the parchment in his hands, "was hanging in the shop I ventured into, and I'd imagine it's hanging in every other business in Letorheas as well. It reads, and I quote:

'To celebrate the coronations of His Majesty, King Dacre Starside of the Realms, and his queen, the palace will hold a fete for the first three nights of the Middling Season. All classes of high fae are expected to attend.'"

A swooping sensation filled Verve's stomach, and she could have laughed with relief. Dacre had found his queen, had he? He would now not dare upset the lady by pursuing Verve. "This isn't terrible news, is it?"

Finley cleared his throat.

"Verve—" said Fenn.

"He's found his bride. All we have to do is keep him in check. Maybe I don't even need to take the throne from him." She felt giddy suddenly, lighter than she had been in ages. But why were the men still so concerned?

"You haven't seen the way the announcement is ended," said Finley. He handed the parchment to Verve, who glanced and then dropped it as though she'd been burned.

Indeed, after a few pompous declarations, the announcement had a close-to-life drawing of Dacre hand in hand with her own likeness. She was about to set fire to the parchment, but Fenn hastily snatched it up and tucked it in his pocket. "I'm sorry, Verve. He's not given up on you. In fact, it seems his obsession is only increasing." He sounded rather calm for someone with fire burning in his eyes.

Verve tried to make sense of the news. Why would Dacre have gone to the trouble of having those announcements created and distributed? The whole thing was a lie. He hadn't caught Verve, and even if he had, she was married...not that Dacre would let the latter stop him. She shuddered. "I don't think I understand what's happening."

"He's either being overly optimistic," Fenn said, "or something has happened to make him think he's close to realizing his objective." He gestured to Finley, whose face was stony and unreadable. "Before you woke up, we were talking about one of us going to Strattavus Palace for reconnaissance."

She was already shaking her head. "No. You're not going." How could he even entertain such an idea, especially after he had scolded her for running off? Now that they had marked each other, Verve knew separation would be all the more difficult.

Fenn raised his hands in truce. "We need to know what Dacre's up to. One of us at least will have to return to Letorheas to listen for rumors and rumblings."

"And that leads to another problem," said Finley. "Your husband's allies have gone silent. Any person he has ever worked with seems to have disappeared."

Beside them, Markson grunted. "I don't know who this Dacre fellow is, but it sounds like he believes Miss Springer will be at the fete. He must have something he knows she either wants or needs."

Another concerned glance passed between Fenn and Finley. It was the latter who spoke first. "It's definitely a trap. But what is the bait?"

"She all but exploded with fire before," said Markson, still caught on a different point of the conversation. "Perhaps you only need to get her close enough to the palace and let her…well, you know." He made a whooshing sound and threw his hands up in a great arc, in imitation of an eruption.

Fenn shook his head. "There would be perhaps hundreds of innocents inside. Explosions are out of the question."

"You must be trained, and quickly, Verity. Sooner or later, your path will cross with this would-be king, and you'll need to be ready. Until we know what the bait is, you are going to need to learn as much as you can about all that magic flowing through your veins." Finley moved closer and held out his hand. "And to start, we need to know everything that's there."

There was no arguing with that, Verve knew. Gone were the days when she had the luxury of ignoring and neglecting her power. Tensing her jaw, Verve reached for Finley's hand, only for Fenn to stop her with a look. "What?"

"He's a siphon. I don't know how wise this is."

If Finley was hurt or surprised, he didn't let on. "She's a powerful siphon as well, boy. You didn't see her drain our common foe in the Sky Realm. Verity can protect herself from the likes of me, if I wanted to steal."

Still Fenn didn't seem convinced. But instead of objecting or insisting that he wouldn't allow it, he turned to Verve and waited, his eyebrows raised in question.

"We'll never know if we can fully trust him until we're put in a situation like this." Verve studied Fenn, and to her relief, he nodded.

"If you feel your magic fading, quickly pull away. If you can't pull away, I will deal with him."

Finley rolled his eyes. "Now that that's settled..." He held out his hand once more, and Verve took it. As soon as their skin made contact, he frowned. "Strength, immortality, extraordinary speed, flight, spell-casting, illusion-casting, animal communication...shape-changing." His face lit up on that last one. "That will be useful. World-walking, siphoning, assessing, mind reading – that's very underdeveloped – of all of the elements, strongest is fire, which we already knew..." He went on and on for the next few minutes, naming abilities that were practically dormant or so weak they had little chance of growing enough to be of use. At last he released her hand and shook out his own as though it had been burned. "There is a lot there, but I'm surprised to sense you have only world-walking and no transporting."

"There's a difference?" asked Fenn.

"Oh, yes there is. World-walking, from what I understand of it, rips a hole in the fabric of reality and takes much more effort to perform, whereas transporting is as easy as stepping from one room to the next. It's true you can only transport up to half a mile, but that could have been more useful in making a quick getaway, should the need arise." He rocked on his heels, his gaze calculating. "We'll need to assess which abilities will prove the most useful and develop those first, as well as work on managing fire. I can tell you're not in full control always."

Verve gave him a slight nod. "Right. How do we know what's going to be the most useful?"

Finley turned to Fenn. "I know you don't have fire, but why not work on that with her while I return to Letorheas? I'll see if there are any new developments in the kingdom, and report back what I find."

"Why are you helping us?" Fenn demanded. "You have nothing to gain."

"I don't?"

Fenn's eyes narrowed. "Not from my perspective, no."

The older fae's shoulders heaved slightly. "Can you believe I'm simply doing this for the greater good?"

"No, I don't believe that. Not for one second."

"Then do you need me to make a blood vow that I won't betray you?" Tension hummed in the air like electricity before a lightning storm. No one spoke or moved for a forever moment. When Fenn failed to respond, Finley reached for the sheath at his side and produced a small knife, the same one he had made the vow to Verve with. "My reasons, I admit, are selfish. I crave redemption."

Fenn snorted, his eyes never leaving the blade.

"Blood of my niece's blood, flesh and bone of our shared ancestors, does not this mean something to you? Have you ever committed a wrong so heinous, you would stop at few lengths to right it? Come, take the vow with me and let me blot out my ledger." The blade moved nearer the flesh of his palm, but before he could slash it, Fenn grabbed him by his shirtsleeve.

"Blood vows can be twisted by skilled and powerful fae," said Fenn. "Curses, however, are a much more potent assurance."

Finley's ensuing difficulty swallowing was audible and visual. For a wild moment, Verve thought Fenn was doing something to his uncle, but then she realized he was simply terrified.

But instead of going into further detail of what he meant to do or making further threats, Fenn released Finley. "Put away your blade. You're upsetting our host."

Markson sniffed. "It will take more than a simple knife to rattle this old man." He, however, continued to eye the blade warily.

"I will try to return within a few hours. If I am gone longer than five, move your camp and burn everything here so that you cannot be tracked." Finley thrust the knife back into its sheath and used magic to change the length and color of his hair. "No one should know me by sight in Letorheas."

"You're quite sure of that?" Verve asked.

Finley shook his head. "I'm not. But taking another's form is a last resort. I could end up running into the fae I'm imitating or someone who knows them."

Markson surprised Verve by asking, "What about a mortal's form?"

"I've not known many mortals. Even if you described someone to me, I would have to see them before changing."

"Too many of our kind know your form, Markson," said Fenn. "He's not going to shape-change into you."

With a nod to each of them, Finley took his leave. Soon he was outside the repelling charm and disappeared from sight.

Verve turned to Fenn. "Did you curse him?"

He appeared amused. Fenn held up a finger until the telltale sounds of Finley leaving Etterhea reached them, and even then he kept his voice low. "I'm not able to perform a true curse. A mild hex? Yes, as you well know. Cursing is a form of binding magic, and it's too slippery for me to master." He gestured to the dying embers in the fire pit. "Now, since time moves quite differently in Letorheas, we might have just minutes to practice before he returns. Or we could have hours. Why don't you see how much you can master yourself?"

"What should I do?" She reached out for the fire, and Fenn quickly stopped her with a shake of his head.

"Use no words, no gestures. Just make the fire grow to the height of your waist and cause it to linger there as I count to ten. Then extinguish it by depriving it of air or ordering it to cease with a thought." He glanced at Markson, who took another step away.

"And if I can't control it?" The thought of fire pouring out of her body once more, of her becoming a living flame, made her hesitate. What if she set everything and everyone ablaze?

Fenn gave her a nudge. "I'll be here, and it won't be so out of control as it was when you were suffering withdrawal." His voice broke on the second to last word, but he hastily cleared his throat and gestured for her to begin.

Verve didn't. "Why didn't you put out my flames before?" It wasn't an accusation, and she hoped he knew that.

"I tried depriving the fire of air, but they... Those flames were self-contained. This will be different. You're the master of flame in this situation. It does not master you."

"I hope that's true," she murmured as she balled her hands into fists and reminded herself to keep them still and by her sides. As soon as she entertained the idea of creating fire, a blaze higher than their heads shot up from the fire pit, which startled her and Markson but didn't seem to catch Fenn off guard.

At once he deprived the flames of air and they ceased to be. "Your left eye twitched."

Verve let out a huff. "So I can't move anything at all while I'm using magic?"

"Did you use an emotional shove when you blinked?"

"No." Irritation bubbled inside her, and her veins pulsed with light.

"Really? You just formed a thought and fire appeared?"

A tight nod was all she gave him.

Instead of being terrified as Verve knew he ought, Fenn appeared intrigued by a new mystery to solve. His head cocked to the side and he stroked his chin, eyes unfocused for a moment. "You don't need gestures for creating flame, but you might need to use them to control it."

By now, Markson had moved away from where they stood. He no longer looked vaguely amused, but neither did he seem quite as alarmed as he had when they had first arrived.

"Try thinking of a gesture – a small gesture, mind – to use immediately after creating fire."

Verve rolled up her sleeves. "Should I time that with my emotional push?"

Fenn's grin spread once more. "I think your magic has changed again. If you simply thought of fire, magic should be right at your fingertips."

"That's terrifying," said Verve.

"Yes, it is. And it doesn't mean emotions can't trigger or strengthen your magic, so be sure to keep them in check." This time, he took a step closer. "Why don't you try again?"

No sooner had the suggestion been made than Verve thought of fire and it leapt twice as high as before from the pit. She was about to reach out to stop it from growing, but remembered what Fenn had said about a small gesture. Her right fist opened and she imagined the fire shrinking. At once, it died.

"Very good, but this time, try to shrink it without putting it out entirely."

On and on practice continued like this. Verve created, maintained, shrank, grew, and extinguished so many fires that she quickly lost track of how long she had been at it. She was improving, Fenn said so, but it was obvious she would need a lot more work to keep accidental sparks from forming at her fingertips. That wasn't getting any better. In fact, with all the work she had been doing with the element, it seemed more readily available. As soon as she pictured flames in her mind, her fingers would light up.

"Why don't we work with water for a little while?" said Fenn. "We only have a few hours of daylight left. Better to have dreams of trickles of water on your mind than fire when you sleep."

Verve blinked in confusion. She peered up at the sky, and sure enough, the sun was on its way down. "Water."

"I want to see how strong it is with you. Finley didn't say how much control you have over it." He caused the canteen to fly into his outstretched hand and then tossed the vessel to Verve, who caught and unstoppered it. "Take a pull, hold it in your mouth, and think about its taste. Wait a moment and then swallow."

Verve did so. It felt strange, experiencing water after working with flame. She could tell it warred against the fire in her veins, and that water manipulation was quite a weak ability in her repertoire.

As though reading Verve's thoughts – though, more likely, her face – Fenn said, "It is strange, I'd imagine, having both of those contradictory elements, but water should help temper your fire. Look at it as a blessing." It was obvious he was about to say more, but there was the sound of a gateway opening in the distance, and he was suddenly rigid and alert. "I don't recognize the heartbeat."

"Could it be Finley in disguise?" She drew power into her hands moments after Fenn had, dropping the canteen to the ground in the process.

"It probably is." Fenn put himself between Verve and the approaching footsteps, then went about casting all sorts of wards.

Markson stirred from the nap he had been taking at this point and got to his feet. "Is there someone out there?" He yawned widely.

The smell of peppermint wafted toward them on a breeze, but still Fenn did not relax. When Verve asked why, he said, "You've said it before yourself, residual bursts can change. We have to be absolutely certain it's him before I let him back through the charm and wards." He lowered his hands and moved in the direction of the gateway. "Stay here and protect Markson. Flee without him if it comes to that." He said the last part in a different language, and Verve knew it was so Markson wouldn't understand.

"I'm coming with you."

Fenn shook his head but didn't make any further objection as she followed him.

They ran at top speed toward the approaching footsteps and beating heart, which now sounded familiar. Outside the repelling charm, which was visible like a glowing bubble to Verve's eyes, prowled Finley – or, at least, someone in his form – and he appeared to be looking for something. It was obvious he couldn't see them or hear them, the way his eyes kept slipping over where they stood.

"I think that was the same tree," he murmured. "Fenn? If you're there, let me know. I have news for Verity."

Verve made to step forward, but Fenn held up a hand in warning. "What? He said he has news for me." Why she whispered those words, she didn't know.

"It could easily be Dacre in his form." He made a face, one that told Verve he was going to regret his next words. "Verve? If Dacre is as powerful as we believe him to be, there's really only one way to know this is truly Finley."

"Oh?" Her stomach clenched at his tone.

The hair that had gotten in Fenn's eyes blew out and up in a puff of air as he exhaled. "I'm afraid you're going to have to try to use another gift on him."

"What?" She waited.

"Try to read the poor man's mind."

Verve could only stare at him for a moment before blurting out, "B-but I've never even *tried* that before. And Finley told me it's a dormant ability."

"Dormant, but not dead." He turned to Verve, perhaps sensing her rising panic.

Again Finley called for Fenn, pacing just inches away from the repelling charm, which continued to glow strangely in pulses of green and purple. "Should I go back or…?"

"If he *is* Finley, we need to get him to safety," said Verve. "Anyone could follow him through that particular hawthorn."

"But if it's not him…" Fenn's brows rose meaningfully. "At least try."

Verve frowned. "What if I can't?"

Fenn crossed his arms across his chest and shrugged. "Then we'll figure something else out, but this is a quickest and surest option."

"If you're debating about if it's me, I know a secret about Fenn's mother that only he would know."

That caused Verve to hesitate, looking to her husband for guidance. "Should we at least listen to what he has to say?" Her heart sank when Fenn shook his head.

"Close your eyes." He waited until she had done so before continuing. "Don't listen to what he's saying. Listen for what he's *not* saying." Well, that made about as much sense as an armadillo in a chemise, as her eccentric Uncle Arthur used to say.

Still, Verve tried to do as Fenn said even as Finley continued speaking.

"His great-grandmother – my grandmother – was the first fae to discover our realm."

That startled Verve out of her attempt. She opened her eyes and stared at Fenn, who simply groaned. "Is that true?"

"It's true, but not important. Dacre could have easily found that information in one of his books. I understand he has many at his disposal these days." He gestured in such a way that told Verve he meant for her to keep trying to read Finley's mind.

Finley swore. "I know you're there, you two. I used the same sister tree to bring me back. Don't think I don't recognize the markings. Please, let me through. I don't know if I was pursued or not." He waited. Verve kept trying to reach his mind, but all she experienced was a dull throbbing in her temples. "Oh, for love of all, we should have come up with a special word or signal before I left." Finley kicked at a clod of dirt that went flying forward and struck Fenn in the knee. Of course Finley didn't notice this but continued to look desperately around him. Then, his face lit up and he nodded. "Verity, if you're there, you can read my mind. Try that."

"I am trying!" Verve shouted in frustration. She gave Fenn an imploring look, but he was unmoved.

"We might need to move our camp."

"No, he's your family. We're not leaving him behind, especially not over such a stupid mistake."

Before Fenn could argue with that, Finley held up a hand as though he could see them. "If you're having trouble reading my mind, I can make it easier for you. Do you remember how I said you have a mental shield? Well, I have mental projection. If you allow me through, I can assist you in hearing my thoughts."

Fire licked at Verve's fingertips, as her frustration and anxiety were continuing to build to a crescendo. "How?" she asked Fenn. "I can't hear his thoughts. Why should I be able to lower a shield I've never even noticed? And how is this different than talking to each other using, you know, our voices?" She closed her hands into fists when she noticed the fire was going to erupt.

"Mental voices have a signature that is not possible to counterfeit," he explained with a sigh. "I have experience lowering my shield. Let me do this." It was apparent Fenn didn't relish the thought of Finley feeding thoughts into his mind, but he closed his eyes and the air filled with the scent of grapefruits and limes.

After a moment, Fenn nodded, opened his eyes, and used magic to allow Finley to see through the charm. The fae seemed ready to collapse in relief and hurried toward them as Fenn extended a hand to help him through.

"They have someone," Finley said as soon as he was in the protective bubble. "They're going to kill her if Verve doesn't surrender herself before the fete."

"My sister?" Verve tried and failed to keep her voice from rising in panic. At least the fire inside her calmed down as terror rose.

"No, not your sister. Though I know the Traitor King is looking for her."

Relief only lasted for a brief moment. "Who does Dacre have, then?" she demanded.

"A woman. Elderly. The notices were stuck fast with magic to doors all over the city. I copied the woman's likeness, though I fear I am a poor artist." Finley reached into the pouch around his neck and produced a carefully folded scrap of paper. He handed it to Verve, who snatched it from him and stared at a drawing of her last living great-aunt.

"Your sister must be well hidden," said Fenn after a moment. "Dacre would have used her as more tempting bait than this if he were able."

Though she didn't much care for Aunt Springer, Verve didn't want her to die. "She is family."

"I bet he's bluffing," said Finley as they walked back toward the camp at a slower pace. "Not that he has your aunt, Verity, but that he would actually kill her."

Fenn nodded slowly. "He has been reluctant to hurt you in the past."

"But this isn't *me*. This is *my aunt*."

"Yes, but it would hurt you greatly, wouldn't it?" Fenn watched her. "Verve?"

Verve wrung her hands. "Yes. I mean, not really. Maybe. But— Oh, how dreadful am I that I would consider leaving my aunt to the mercy of that monster!" A breeze picked up around them as her control slipped.

"Easy," warned Finley. "He must think you're in Letorheas, since he put all those posters around. Well, unless that's what he wants us to think he thinks."

The only sound Verve could make was a soft moan. What was to be done? She couldn't very well hand herself over to Dacre and ruin her own life and possibly many or all of the realms. If he was half as powerful as she thought he was, they would need many more allies. Unless...
"What if you sneaked into the palace and freed her?" she said to Finley. "You could take the form of a guard or keep your own form."

Finley was already shaking his head. "We would need a great distraction for that to work. But what if you world-walked into her cell and out with her again? The Traitor King would never anticipate that."

"I'm afraid that might not work." She shot a sideways glance at Fenn, her fists clenching and unclenching.

"Why?" Fenn asked. "Verve, what aren't you telling us?" For a moment the men stopped walking, though she continued onward, afraid to admit what had happened.

Lying and making excuses were not options anymore, she realized, so instead of marching onward, Verve turned and faced her husband. "He knows I can world-walk. In fact, he caught me doing so."

Fenn's face paled. "He caught you?"

Verve raised her hand. "No, no. *Almost* caught. There is a difference. I am here, aren't I?"

"Did he touch your skin?" Finley demanded.

"I-I don't know, but— Does it matter?"

Finley groaned, and Fenn shook his head as Finley said, "If he's an assessor, he could have done a reading on you. If he knows all of your abilities..."

"Then there's no way for me to surprise him," Verve finished, her face flushing with shame and anger. If only she had been able to siphon off Dacre. Unfortunately, the thought hadn't occurred to her.

★ ★ ★

Silence fell over the group as they returned to camp, where Markson was happily oblivious to the tension. He scurried here and there, tending the fire, which he'd rebuilt since their departure, laying out the supplies Finley had brought them, and preparing the beginnings of a meal. Soft brown bread and pale butter, a variety of orange and white cheeses, green apples, red grapes, a trout, and many herbs and seasonings were spread out across a fallen tree serving as a table.

Fenn gave Verve a warning squeeze on the shoulder, and she looked down to see her fingers glowing a bright orange. "We'll figure something out." He stooped to kiss her right temple and then approached the human.

She tucked her hands into fists and willed the fire to die. "Did I ruin everything?" Verve spoke to herself, but Finley answered.

"No. The Traitor King might not be an assessor. And even if he is, he can't predict everything we might try. But we'll have to form a good plan, either way." He lowered a pack he'd been carrying on his back and rifled through it. "Have you had any visions since returning from the Sky Realm?" Finley pulled out some more produce to add to the pile Markson had begun.

"I haven't," said Verve. "I never thought I'd come to miss having insight into the present."

"But have you had any visions of the future?" Finley straightened and turned his pack upside down. A lone grape plummeted from its depths, and he caught it with lightning-fast reflexes.

"My visions have always been of the present. The future has been sound only."

"Strange, but not unheard of," he conceded. "Do you ever try to have visions – visual or audible – or do they just interrupt your dreams?" Finley tossed the grape into his mouth. He took a knife from Markson's unsteady hands and went about deboning the fish on the log.

Verve picked at a loose thread on her dress as she watched him work. "They interrupt dreams and waking moments. I've never tried to experience a vision before."

Fenn tossed another log onto the fire. "That is something you might want to do. But I'm afraid a male would be little help in that department."

"Foresight is not a gift many men can handle," said Finley, perhaps noticing the confused expression on Verve's face. "We tend to not have that gift or, when we do, it slowly drives us insane. But if you can attempt to peer or listen ahead, you might give us an advantage."

It was hard to not feel overwhelmed, especially having just finished struggling with fire and mind reading. "I'll try."

Finley grunted and threw the fish, skin side down, into an oiled skillet. "You have most of my foresight, and though I rarely use it, I might be able to at least give you some advice. Would you mind lowering the flames? I don't want this to burn." He sprinkled the fish with something that looked like pink salt flakes and then a pinch of black pepper.

Fenn watched intently as Verve closed her eyes and focused on causing the flames to die down. "Nice work."

They finished preparing the rest of the meal without speaking of their dilemma, each caught up in their own tasks and talking only of what was before them. Soon the savory aroma of cooking fish filled the camp, and Verve squeezed half a lemon over the flesh.

By the time they sat down to eat, Verve's stomach felt ready to rip itself apart, so hungry was she. They tore into the meal without preamble, between the four of them devouring the fish in minutes, along with buttered bread.

Markson was the first to finish eating and watched the three fae in apparent amazement as they ate the rest of the food. "I thought fae didn't need food to live."

Finley laughed. "High fae don't need it to live, but we do need it to sustain our energy and use it as fuel for magic." He snatched a pear from the pile of fruits and chomped a large bite out of it.

"What happens if you go without food? I mean, how long can you go without before…bad things happen? You ken?"

Verve knew he was making polite conversation, but she stopped listening. She didn't like to think of how long Fenn might've gone without food when he was imprisoned by Dacre. Absently, she produced a spark of magic between her fingertips, as she had seen Fenn do, and focused on weaving it back and forth, back and forth. To her surprise, she found it soothing, and soon her thoughts drifted.

There really was only one solution to their problem. If Finley's reports were correct, and she had no reason to doubt them, they wouldn't be able to use force to rescue Aunt Springer; Dacre simply had too many men at his disposal. So, if not by force, they would have to do so by cunning.

The magic in her hand changed from white to red. She squinted and let the world go out of focus.

If Finley could find out enough about the guards, he could kidnap and impersonate one, and then free Aunt Springer while she, Verve, caused a distraction. Maybe not a distraction. She sat up a little straighter. What if *Finley's* part was the distraction? Or maybe…

"Verve!" Fenn shouted, snapping his fingers in front of her face.

The magic had gone out of her hand and she was being shaken by Finley. "Still with us?" he asked.

Verve blinked and her surroundings came back into clearer focus. "W-what happened? Did I miss something?" She looked from Fenn to Finley, and then at Markson, who stared at her with a frown.

"I thought you were having a fit," said Fenn.

"Aye, the fire died," said Markson. "And the air grew very cold."

Finley searched her face. "Were you trying to have a vision or…?"

"No," said Verve. "I was just…meditating."

"You said something about a switch," Fenn prompted. "Were you thinking over our problems?"

Weary, she rubbed her eyes. "Yes, but I seem to be no closer to a solution. Unless." Verve turned to Finley. "Unless you can teach me to shape-change before the fete."

At this, Finley's frown deepened. "You wish to free your aunt yourself? I think I might have a better chance of doing that successfully. It takes a lot of practice to impersonate a person perfectly. And if you're caught, it could spell doom for many people, if I remember my prophecy correctly."

"Your going is out of the question," said Fenn. "Please, Verve. *Don't.*" He placed a staying hand on her arm, as though she were thinking of running off right then and there.

"I'm afraid my idea's a little more dangerous than that." She forced a smile onto her face, one that was not mirrored by any of the others. When no one asked her to elaborate, Verve simply sighed and pressed on. "What I'm suggesting is that Finley free my aunt and cause a bit of a disturbance while doing so."

Finley's brows rose. "You want me to get caught?"

"I want you to *almost* get caught. If you cause enough chaos, Dacre will be distracted. Then I can slip in as someone else and siphon as much of his magic as I am able."

To his credit, Fenn didn't immediately object, but he did let out a mighty groan before poking holes in her plan. "How would you get near him and touch his skin without raising suspicion?"

That was a good point. Verve at once felt the air go out of her lungs and her plan. But still she couldn't let go of the idea. "What if it was someone he always kept close?"

"Or wanted to interrogate?" Finley asked, animated suddenly. "If I could take one of your family member's forms, I could get close enough to him."

"But if you siphon from him and he figures out what you're doing, do you have enough power to thwart him?" Verve gave him a moment to form his answer, but his suddenly closed mouth provided the information she needed. "It has to be me. If he figures out I'm siphoning, I can at least buy you and Fenn some time to get my aunt to safety."

Fenn opened his mouth, ready, no doubt, with his objection. Verve didn't allow him the chance to express it.

"Can you shape-change?"

He glared at her. "No."

"We could disguise him as a guard," said Finley. "Some palace guards are helmed, from what I saw. We could sneak him in as a servant, along with ourselves, steal the necessary clothing and armor – or magick copies, should it come to that. Fenn can stay near you in case things go awry. It's a good plan."

"There's one large problem." They all looked at Fenn, who then finished with, "I won't allow it."

Verve fought the ensuing wave of irritation that swept over her. She watched as Fenn's feelings visibly danced around him. Terror like a living snake coiled out from and around him, tightening and tightening to such an extent, Verve feared for his safety. She reached out and snatched it away from him. The living emotion writhed in her hands as Fenn's face smoothed of care lines, leaving him with a rather blank yet peaceful expression. It didn't last long. Worry followed the terror – the latter of which Verve tore to vaporous pieces and let float away. This emotion was more sinister-looking, and as she reached to grab it away from her husband, Finley put out his hand and stopped her.

"Grief-eaters need to learn when to step in and when to let things go. Your mate has many good reasons to worry, not the least of all that he could forfeit his life helping you."

Verve cringed. "Then he can stay behind." At once she hated herself for saying it, and knew herself incapable of leaving him behind. Curse the marking! She should have never allowed it.

As one waking from a sudden slumber, Fenn jolted and then shook his head with great force. "You know my thoughts on that, love. Where you go, I go. But you are not going there."

"I won't let my aunt die because of my inaction."

"Dacre is bluffing," said Fenn, taking up Finley's tune. "You said so."

Finley's shoulders rose and then dropped. "What I said is that he *might* be."

"He might *not* be," said Verve. "Please, Fenn. Don't make me beg for your help."

Markson cleared his throat. "A thought, lads – and, er, lass."

Everyone turned to the mortal, whose ear tips turned pink under their scrutiny. "Do you have a plan?" Finley said doubtfully.

"Me? Why, no, not really. But I think there's something you're forgetting. Something you might utilize." When no one sprang in with the answer, the old man sighed. "What I mean is the repelling charm you put on me."

Fenn shook his head. "That is nontransferable, I fear."

"That's nay what I meant."

Finley sat up straight, his eyes sparkling with mischief. "You know, that's not a bad thought. Not by half. It would be a great danger, though, my good man."

Intrigued, Verve turned her gaze to Fenn, who continued to frown. "Can he make the passage to Letorheas?"

"He is a middling," said Finley. "How else would he be able to tolerate being around so much magic? Not to mention the repelling charm sticking to him so well. So yes, he can make the passage safely."

The mere suggestion of any potential danger was causing Fenn irritation. He jumped to his feet and started to walk away but stopped with his back to them as he took in deep, shaky breaths.

Something told Verve he just needed a moment to think, so she didn't press him further but instead kept her words and attention focused on Finley and Markson. "Could the charm be manipulated to keep Dacre away from my aunt?"

"With someone as powerful as Fenn at the reins? Yes, it is more than possible."

Verve didn't need to look to know her husband's shoulders were tensed. "But?" she asked Finley, for she sensed some doubt there yet.

"It might make our presence detectable. It would be very conspicuous if a large amount of fae simply turned and started leaving the palace without permission. Fenn would have to draw the charm in very close to Markson." He sighed and got to his feet. "I'm afraid the two would have to remain near each other, if Fenn is to concentrate on so great a task. The charm cannot simply be drawn near to Markson and expected to remain there. It has to be consciously held in place." Finley's boot scuffed at the ground as Verve watched Fenn's rigid back.

"Then he and Markson free my aunt together while you cause a distraction and I siphon off Dacre."

"That is quite a risk," said Finley. "If he lost concentration for a second, one of them could be exposed. An alarm would be sounded, and, well, there are ways around a repelling charm if someone knows it's there in their midst. Three people is the maximum, and even *that* is questionable."

Fenn now turned and regarded Verve, his left eye twitching. "I don't know if I can even manage three people."

"Then practice," said Verve, trying to keep the hard edge of resolve she felt from creeping into her voice. "You can do it."

He closed his eyes and hung his head as though ashamed. "I don't want to risk losing you, Verve. Please, don't ask me to agree to this plan."

"The Fire Queen does confront the Traitor King," said Finley. "It is written in all of the prophecies, false and otherwise."

Fenn's eyes snapped open. "And in all of those prophecies, is she successful?" It didn't sound like defeat in his voice, not quite. Rather, the tenor of his words made Verve think he was grasping desperately for hope.

"Half," Finley admitted. "In some tales, she succumbs to the Traitor King's power and rules by his side. Others tell of her losing everything but living. Two prophecies say she sacrifices herself and perishes. There are lost predictions. I'd imagine this Dacre fellow has a few of them in his vast library and that they have been his constant study. But the point is that she must confront the Traitor King. It is more than destiny. It is the fate of entire worlds at stake."

"Can it wait?" asked Markson.

The smile Finley wore now was sad. "Oh, undoubtedly. But her aunt might perish, and the blame would most definitely rest, in part, on her shoulders. And I don't think you want to live the remainder of eternity with a bitter wife, Fenn."

It appeared that Fenn was not in agreement. He stared into Verve's eyes, searching them for something, most likely a reason for him to say no. Whatever he saw, it made him shudder and look away. At long last he sighed and said, "If we are to do this, we do this right. No unnecessary risks. Finley, you won't let my wife out of your sight for a moment while we are in enemy territory. And Verve..." He swallowed. "I want you to kill me if we're caught."

Chapter Eighteen

Shortly after that declaration, Fenn made himself scarce, no doubt avoiding the argument he knew Verve would cause. *Kill him?* How could he expect her to do such a thing?

The thought of killing Fenn made her insides twist and the mark on her chest burn. She knew she would have to promise him if she were to get him to co-operate. But that would mean lying, because of course she would never follow through with it. *Please don't let him force me into a blood vow.*

"Verity?"

Verve whipped her head around to face Finley and Markson, the latter of whom was picking morosely at his tattered coat. "What is it?"

"The first thing to know about true shape-changing as opposed to illusion-casting," said Finley quietly, "is that it is a personal invasion of privacy. You only need to see the face and the general shape of the person to accomplish the change, but once you are in another person's form, you will know things about their body that you ought not. For example, if they have a secret pain, such as a bad hip, you will feel that pain also and will walk with their limp. Or if there is a deformity that clothing covers, you will also be privy to that information. If the person you're imitating doesn't want that information known, it is your duty to keep that knowledge to yourself. Or, if they are a wicked person, to use that knowledge for your gain." Finley gestured at Verve then pointed in the direction Fenn had gone. "It's easier to invoke the change when you know the person intimately, so might I suggest you first try with your husband's form."

"No," said Verve. "I'm not taking on his shape."

Markson spoke. "What happens to your clothing when you change your shape?"

"If you're smaller than your mark, then the clothing is torn to pieces. If you're bigger than your mark, you'll find yourself suddenly swimming in your clothing. But if you're talented and quick enough, you can seamlessly magick your attire into matching the right appearance and the right size. Like so." Finley twisted his neck to the left and back, his skin pulsing for a brief moment with light before he stood as Rillian, tall and menacing. Indeed, he was wearing the last outfit Verve had seen the fae in before his demise.

Verve shuddered. "I don't see any strange look about you. Your face...fits."

"That's because it's a true shape-change, not an illusion," said Finley. His voice had changed to Rillian's, and Verve wondered if the change came with the shift or if it was something separate she would have to learn.

"Dacre isn't a shape-changer but an illusionist," she said slowly, and then she felt her face fall. "At least, he wasn't before he absorbed more magic in Ithalamore." Indeed, he could have many new abilities now that Verve didn't know about. The thought was not an encouraging one.

Finley bobbed his head. "He could have any number of new powers, but we're not going to dwell on that right now. At the moment, we're focusing on you and *your* powers. You have many, but most are weak or undeveloped."

"Can that be fixed?"

"We'll have to be selective of what needs to be developed if we're to be ready in time for the fete. Now, Verity, the second thing you need to know about shape-changing is that it is alarming and disorienting at first. The art itself goes against nature and shouldn't be. You will feel repulsed and violated initially, but as you develop this talent, you'll become more and more immune to the negative sensations." He got to his feet. "First, close your eyes and envision the form you wish to take. It must be someone you've seen in person, not a drawing or painting, no matter how good it is. Otherwise you'll end up looking like a drawing yourself, at best."

For the next few minutes, Finley had her imagine the person whose form she meant to take. At first she had suggested trying the form she meant to use in their plan – the one cousin she knew, Charlotte, she had decided, who looked quite similar to Ainsley – but Finley quickly suggested she imitate someone whose form she would never take in front of Dacre.

"You will get the first change wrong, and once you get a form wrong, it's difficult for some to correct in later iterations, though you might be the exception. Think of a deceased friend or relative you wish to imitate. You won't need to pretend to be them later, so it's the best way to practice."

Verve fought down a squawk of protest. The only form she could think of now was her dear deceased younger sister, Helena, and she didn't feel right about becoming the poor girl. "I can't think of anyone deceased," she lied. An image of her elder sister came to mind, and she at once rejected that as well.

Finley cleared his throat. "Ver— *Verve*, may I be honest with you? You're not going to be good at this if you're not willing to make yourself uncomfortable, physically or emotionally. And you need to be good at this…fast. We don't have weeks to practice this. We have two days at best in Etterhean time. At worst? A few hours."

His words sent shivers down her spine. "Right. I'll try anything if it helps our cause." Again she closed her eyes, searching her mind for the image of someone she could turn into. "I could turn into my aunt."

"Not if she's the one we're going to rescue. You might need to take her shape for a while, should the need arise, and that image will have to be faultless as well." He was quiet for a moment, his expression thoughtful as Verve continued to think of people besides her family whose forms she would be willing to take and distort. Finley soon interrupted her and laughed. When she opened her eyes, he smirked and said, "If you're worried about desecrating a beloved family member's or friend's form, why not change into someone you hate?"

That wasn't appealing either. But what other option did she have? "All right. I picture them in my mind and then what?" Verve closed her eyes and formed the image of Dacre in her mind, filling herself with instant disgust.

"Examine them from all angles. I want you to really see them first. Then you need to feel and hear them. After that, well—"

Verve's skin tingled unpleasantly as she thought of becoming the man she hated. There was a loud ripping sound, followed by pain in her joints and a sense of unease. The distance from her head to the ground had suddenly increased, and she found it difficult to balance. "Ack!" Her voice still sounded her own but had dropped an octave.

"Very good. You're taking to this quickly. But you're only halfway transformed." Finley words were brimming with mirth, which he was doing a poor job of disguising, if he was trying at all.

"Can I become stuck in another form?" she asked.

"That's not unheard of, but rare. It's more likely you'll lose concentration and – ah, there you go."

Without warning, Verve had shrunk down to her usual height, her joints and skin making apocalyptic popping noises. She was thankful when Finley reached out and steadied her before she could fall flat on her face. "That was…strange."

"The first time is always the most disorienting," he said. "Now, try picturing the person longer *before* you feel your way to becoming them."

For the next two hours, Verve shifted in and out of different variations of Dacre's form, never quite succeeding in leaving her own body's shape entirely. Sometimes she was Dacre from the chest up, other times from the waist down. One time she managed everything but his face, much to Finley's apparent amusement. With each attempt, her clothing became more and more torn, until it reached the point where she was forced to stop their practice and transform her dress into something larger that would accommodate both forms.

After what might've been her fiftieth attempt, Finley stopped her. "All right, enough of that shape. You've done enough iterations of him to tell me you're ready to try something else."

Now Fenn had rejoined their group, his jaw clenched and his eyes lighter than they should be. It was obvious he was terrified.

Verve gave him a reassuring smile, but he was either unwilling or unable to return it. Again whirls of emotion surrounded him, and she had to fight the urge to pluck them out of the air and devour them.

"That might help, actually," Finley startled her by saying.

"What?" Verve asked.

"It's obvious you're distracted by his emotions. Why not take a few, grief-eater?" He gestured to Fenn, who frowned as he watched Verve.

The whole thought of eating emotions was still strange to Verve, and she didn't see why it would help her with shape-changing. Self-conscious, she cleared her throat and attempted to turn her attention away from her husband. "What form should I try next?"

"Try first as I have said," said Finley. "If your husband is willing, why not relieve him of some of those unwanted feelings?"

Still Verve hesitated, until Fenn said, "It's all right, Verve." He appeared mildly interested by whatever his uncle was after, but Verve did her best to ignore the glance that passed between the two of them as she reached out toward Fenn.

Snatching the emotions proved less difficult than it had for her in the past, and she stuffed them into her mouth before she could be embarrassed by her actions. Verve swallowed and turned to Finley.

"Change," he said.

Verve blinked. "Into who?"

"Remember how it felt and simply fall into whatever shape you will." Before she could react, Finley lunged and knocked her off her stone seat.

Verve had just been remembering how it felt to shape-change, and so startled was she that her body and magic acted without her mind's intervention. Again her clothing tightened as she unintentionally shape-changed.

Finley chuckled, and even Fenn, whose expression had gone slack and calm moments earlier, seemed amused. "Well, I'd call that a success."

Markson swore. "I'll be! They're identical."

"Let her see herself before she changes back," Fenn suggested, lips twitching.

From nothing, Finley conjured a mirror and directed it at Verve, who was pulling herself to her feet. Or, rather, her husband's feet. The man looking back at her in the mirror was most definitely Fenn, but for the eyes. They had stubbornly remained blue. "It worked," she said, startling herself with her suddenly deep tone. She slapped a hand over her own mouth at the sound, causing the men to laugh even harder. Their amusement raked the coals of her temper, and the flames in the fire behind her jumped. But irritation quickly gave way to surprise as she shrank back to her regular form without warning.

"And that is why you cannot entertain strong emotions when in another's form." Finley's expression had grown grim, as had Fenn's. "If you shift in front of Dacre, you'd better hope you can get to him and siphon before he can immobilize you. Now, try again, but this time pay attention to the eyes." He sat back down and gestured at Verve to commence. Beside him, Fenn had grown agitated again.

★ ★ ★

Verve practiced deliberately taking Fenn's form until the sun had sunk beyond the horizon and the birds began to sing their evening songs. She went without food and drink the entire time, something that concerned Fenn, who kept suggesting they take a break so she could rest.

"We don't have time for that," Finley said the fifth time Fenn attempted to intervene. "She has to be able to do this in any condition."

Fenn seemed ready to argue until Verve put up a staying hand. "I'm all right. I'll rest later."

Finally, Verve was so bone-tired that she could barely manage to move, let alone change her form. "I'm done for now," she said, her voice nigh identical to Fenn's. She had improved much over the last hour, though her eyes would not reach the correct shade of black.

"Wait, don't change back yet," said Finley.

Verve stared at him. "Why?"

"See how long you can remain in your husband's form. It would be good practice." He was stifling a yawn, by the sounds of things.

"I'm sorry, but it just feels – wrong." And with that, she shrank and slipped back into her own shape with a sigh of relief. "When am I going to take Charlotte's shape? She's the one I really need to practice." Verve staggered toward the blankets she'd left in a mound earlier that day, ready to collapse and sleep as one dead.

"You should eat something before you lie down," said Fenn.

He reached for some bread and fruit, but Finley stopped him, saying, "Meat and cheese. She needs protein after that sort of magic."

Verve lowered herself onto the blankets. It was almost too difficult just to keep her eyes open, but when Fenn brought her a hunk of cheese and a cold sausage, she tore into them with more vigor than she thought currently possible.

Once she had finished, Fenn passed her the canteen, which she drained, and then handed her another link and a bit of fish. These she ate with a little less gusto before thanking him and lying down. No sooner had her head touched that ground than she fell asleep and started to dream.

A dark shape ran through an unfamiliar wood. The apparition might have been a woman who ran, or perhaps a boy, but whatever their gender, it was apparent to Verve that they were not human.

As if knowing someone watched their progress, the figure secured their cloak's hood and doubled their speed. Whatever they might be, the creature was fast.

"Wait!" Verve heard herself cry. Her own form came into view, racing toward the hooded form.

"Leave me alone, Verve." The voice belonged to Dav.

"It was an accident. I swear I didn't want to kill anyone."

At that, Dav slowed to a walk but didn't look back. "You really should leave me alone." But her voice sounded uncertain, like she was teetering on the edge of something. Perhaps it was forgiveness; Verve could only hope.

"Please, Davinia. We're all we have left. D-don't you leave me too."

Now Dav stopped in her tracks and her shoulders sagged under the weight of a soft sigh. She turned. "You have your husband. Shouldn't you be happy enough with just him?" Her words were bitter, and she glared at Verve.

Verve winced, both her dream-self and the one sleeping in reality. "Fenn doesn't know me like you do. He never can. You and I share a bond – one that no one can break. We're sisters."

Dav's lip twitched as she wiped at her eyes, but she seemed to be fighting whatever she was feeling. "Now that you've rescued Aunt Springer and defeated Dacre, what are you going to do?"

"We can do anything we want," said Verve. "We could return home and go back to how things were."

That made Dav snort with amusement. "We can't go home now, silly. Things are just getting interesting. Don't tell me you really want to go back to the way things were. We were always at each other's throats, remember?"

Verve groaned. "Fine, we'll stay. And we'll work on our relationship." She approached Dav and threaded an arm through hers. "But you'll have to tell me how you managed to never get caught by Dacre or his men."

Dav's smile widened. "It wasn't all that difficult to avoid him. Letorheas is, after all, a very big place." She leaned against Verve, and it felt so very good to know that they were going to be all right.

They stood there in silence for a time, watching the night sky. In her sleep, happiness and hope bloomed in Verve's breast, and then the dream shifted.

She was back at Dacre's summer home, the one where she had been held captive all those months ago. The mansion sat behind her, and she saw herself leaning over the stream that flowed through the property. It had been said that the waters held power. One might look into them and see days gone by or days yet to come. Verve and her dreaming-self peered into the gently rippling stream.

The waters showed nothing at first. After a few minutes, Verve was inclined to turn away and escape this dream for another; she didn't harbor any happy memories from this time, and she wondered why her future-self – at least, she assumed it was her future-self – tarried.

Light flashed in her peripheral vision, and she faced the water once more. Her future-self knelt and stared into the stream, tears running down her face and rippling into the vision she beheld. "I'm sorry," her future-self whispered at the image.

Head cocked to the side, Verve squinted and tried to make out what her other self was seeing, only to at once reel back in horror and confusion. The image in the water was a face, one pale and still in death, but that was not what baffled Verve. "Why are you mourning *him*?" she demanded.

Her future-self continued to sob over the sight of Dacre's face. The waters stirred, light flashed once more, and a hand rose out from its depths.

"Watch out!" she warned, but her cry went unheeded.

Just as a hand closed around the other's wrist, Verve was torn from her slumber by a scream that seemed to shake the foundations of the earth.

Chapter Nineteen

Verve sat up with a gasp. The moon had set, and daylight was winging its way to the mortal lands. "What was that?" Already the dream was fading. She looked around the camp, prepared to confront danger, but was surprised to find that Finley and Markson were yet asleep.

Only Fenn was awake. He lay by her side and was so quiet and still, Verve hadn't noticed him until that moment. "You were dreaming." His hand reached up and brushed a strand of hair out of her face.

"I don't think it was a dream."

"You think you had a vision?" When she didn't respond, just nodded, he sat up as well, as though suddenly on high alert. "You haven't mentioned having any visions since returning from the Sky Realm. Tell me what you saw."

"Give me a moment." Verve closed her eyes and attempted to recall what she had seen and heard, but her memory was proving resistant.

Now Fenn positively vibrated with alarm. "Your memory is normally impeccable."

She opened one eye. "It has its flaws. When I'm distraught, it sometimes doesn't work as it should. But I think it was a good vision... for the most part." She relayed what she could remember, of her words with Dav and their happy reconciliation, the vision slowly returning to her. But when the dream shifted, it was as if she had hit an invisible wall. "I think it ended there."

Fenn eyed her askance but didn't press her for more information. He remained quiet for several minutes, his body visually pulsing with many conflicting emotions, as though he couldn't make up his mind how he felt. "It sounds like a dream," he said at length. Fenn held up his hand to waylay the argument her lips were forming. "That wasn't a vision of the past, unless there are some important things you aren't telling me. And it's not of the present, because you haven't left this camp all night."

"What of the future?" she said, heart racing. "It must be sometime down the road."

But Fenn was already shaking his head. "To this point, your premonitions have been audible only. Why would that change now?" He raked a hand back through his hair, disheveling it, and his emotions settled on confused mixed with weary.

Verve reached up and smoothed out his dark waves, and his eyes flickered closed. "It was so vivid, Fenn. It couldn't have just been a dream." Why she needed him to believe her, she couldn't exactly say. Perhaps it was because the vision had been so full of hope, hope that she wanted him to share in the success of their rescue mission. Or maybe it was because she was tired of being doubted and simply desired to be right about something…*any*thing.

Whatever the reason, Fenn remained skeptical. "Are you certain you're not just *wishing* for a sign?" he whispered as Finley stirred.

"This *is* a sign, Fenn. We're going to rescue my aunt, I'm going to defeat Dacre, and everything is going to be right in the world. It has to be." *I've lost too much for this not to be true.*

Fenn leaned down and brushed his lips against hers, much to Verve's irritation. It was obvious he was dismissing her and would remain apprehensive about the whole thing. He pulled back, eyes twinkling with understanding. "Perhaps you'll prove me wrong yet. Until then, you need to keep practicing your shape-changing until you can do it in your sleep."

"You're not going to continue to object to things, then?"

The face he made might have been amusing, had things not been so serious. "Oh, I will absolutely keep objecting to your plans until everything is resolved. Dacre's not going to kill your aunt. It isn't at all in his best interest. He wants you to fall in love with him, Verve. If he's responsible for her death, that's never going to happen."

Verve rolled her eyes and got to her feet. "It's never going to happen anyway." But she remembered Dacre's attempt to use persuasive magic on her in Ithalamore, and her certainty wavered.

No doubt sensing her shifting mood, Fenn continued. "Please, give this more thought."

"We don't have the luxury of time to think. We have to act."

Finley groaned and sat up. "She's right, you know." He nodded toward the food supply and got to his feet, swaying for a moment as he was clearly only just awake. "Eat something, both of you. There is no reliable way of telling time in Letorheas when in another realm. I'll have to return shortly to see what day it is there. And when I come back to camp, you'll know it is I by my first words to you."

"And what might they be?" Verve tossed a log into the pit and then let it catch fire by way of her fingertips.

"I'll simply say, 'Less arguing, more kissing, that's what you two need'. Now, if you'll excuse me." Finley left the immediate area, his footsteps heavy with annoyance, leaving Verve to flush and Fenn to smirk.

Markson groaned at this point and sat up. "Did I miss anything exciting?" He took one look at Fenn and shook his head. "You are too much the pessimist, lad. It'll all turn out as it ought. You'll see."

★ ★ ★

For the next three hours, Verve practiced transforming into Ainsley. She would wait for Finley's clearance to start attempting Cousin Charlotte's form, as he had far more experience than she in these matters and seemed to know what he was talking about. This time, however, shape-changing felt more like a violation of her sister's memory than anything, and it was a relief when Fenn interrupted with a call for the noon meal.

There was little protein left, but he offered her what there was, and Verve devoured it all in several large bites. "How long has Finley been gone?" She downed the entire contents of the canteen and went to refill it, only for Fenn to seize the vessel and do the magic for her.

"For Finley? It's impossible to say." Fenn took a swig of water and passed it on to Markson.

Verve frowned. If something happened to Finley, or if he betrayed them, they had no contingency plan. That was a worry.

"I'm sure he's fine," said Fenn, interrupting her troubled thoughts. The truth was in his eyes, though; he was concerned as well.

"Do we go after him?"

Fenn's brows rose. "Now? It hasn't been that long."

"You still don't fully trust him."

"He'll have ample opportunity to prove himself." Fenn gestured to the fire. "Perhaps you ought to work on your fire magic."

But Verve shook her head. "It's no good when I'm like this." She fought the compulsion to wring her hands, instead opting to clutch them together in front of her. *Why this dread now? You were feeling so confident not long ago.* Silently chastising herself didn't have the desired effect. Her heart rate sped up to almost that of a mortal's, something Fenn was fast to take note of.

"Perhaps we should move camp. Would that make you feel more at ease?"

"No," said Verve.

They grew silent, listening for the telltale signs that a gateway had been opened. There was nothing, just the sound of birds singing their earky-afternoon songs and squirrels chittering as they ran through the treetops.

Three hours soon became four. The only one among them who did not grow anxious was Markson. The old veteran took to darning his socks, attempting and failing to engage Verve and Fenn in conversation. When he had finished this task, he hoisted a log onto the camp's makeshift chopping block and went about splitting wood.

Now it was five hours. Surely Finley was all right. Five hours in Etterhea could be just one in Letorheas, Fenn reasoned to her. Time was not consistent there.

Verve grunted in acknowledgment and went back to transforming herself, this time attempting to look like Mother. The shape was thinner than the others she had tried and more fragile. Mother had never complained of rheumatism or the numerous other ailments Verve discovered were riddling her body. It was almost enough to distract Verve from her worries…almost.

Six hours, seven, eight… Time blurred while they continued to wait for Finley's return. Several times Fenn went to the tree his uncle had used as a gateway. He checked and rechecked the boundary, making certain he hadn't portaled through another hawthorn in the vicinity. Verve went with him during these rounds, though she knew it to be pointless; if Finley had returned, they would have heard him. She gave up shape-changing practice and gathered their supplies into three great heaps, on the off chance they needed to flee.

It was at the twelfth hour that Fenn turned to the other two, his expression grim. "Something's happened."

"You said time moved differently there, lad. Could it be that you're arriving at a conclusion too early?"

"Time moves at a different pace, yes, but this is excessive. We need to leave." Fenn swung the canteen strap over his shoulder and was gathering bedding when Verve stopped him with a word.

"No."

He stared at her, his expression hard. "Verve, if he betrays us, the area surrounding could be swarming with Dacre's men before nightfall. Repelling charms are not perfect."

"I know, but think about it. They would be here by now." She waited for him to argue. When Fenn didn't respond, Verve continued. "Finley must be in a difficult position, or else he would have returned. He's probably waiting, hoping we'll come to his rescue or that we have the wisdom to go ahead and execute our plan."

Markson grunted. "The lass makes sense. This Dacre fellow of yours, he doesn't strike me as the sort with much patience. If he knew where to find Miss Verity, he'd already be in these here woods surrounding us." He rubbed a hand over the white stubble on his jaw. "Strike first and strike hard."

Verve drew in a shaky breath, willing Fenn to agree. To her surprise, he slowly nodded.

"I see you are determined." His words were tight with the anxiety Verve saw whirling around him. He clenched and unclenched his jaw.

"If we are to do this, we'd better do it now. I doubt it is as you say, that he is waiting for us to rescue him. It is more likely he is being tortured for information as we speak. So if we want a chance, we need to move."

That surprised Verve. She had expected more resistance from her husband.

Fenn gave her a strange smile that he no doubt had hoped to look reassuring. "He'd expect for us to wait for him longer. We must not live up to that expectation."

"Then I will change into Cousin Charlotte and… What?" she asked, for her husband was shaking his head.

"Finley knows you're going as Charlotte. You need another form, should he have betrayed us. Preferably one you are very familiar with."

★ ★ ★

The camp was a flurry of activity. Since everything had already been gathered into a pile, Fenn and Markson only had the task of making certain it all was able to catch fire. They scattered dry hay from the bedding around the heartier objects, such as the canteen and the footlocker, hoping that enough heat could be created to at least melt them. That way, Fenn had reasoned, tracking would be at least *almost* impossible to accomplish for any foe.

While they worked, Verve pictured Davinia in her mind's eye, concentrating on every detail she knew of her sister so that she would get the image right. She tried not to be distracted by the men's terse words as they worked; Verve knew full well that distractions would abound once they set foot in Letorheas, so she needed to have a handle on herself and her magic before then. Once she had pictured Dav and was certain she had the image firmly implanted in her mind, Verve imagined her sister's voice.

"We're ready," said Fenn. "While you're lighting it, I'll set up the hexes. We'll just need to be careful to avoid them on our way to the hawthorn."

Verve gave him a tight nod, and he and Markson quickly retreated. As soon as she directed her attention at the mound of possessions, they at once caught fire, and the blaze shot up to the treetops, burning at such an intense heat that Fenn was forced to shield Markson and himself. This was so no tracker would be able to use their possessions to trace them.

Bringing the fire under control proved a little more difficult, but as the pile of belongings were now ash and molten metal, there was nothing left to burn. Verve soon took the fire back into her own veins and allowed it to dissipate there.

"Cool down a moment," Fenn warned as she took a step toward where he was spell-casting. "You're glowing."

The fire in her veins leapt and threatened to spill onto the ground in front of her, but she seized control and ceased to glow. "Should I shift now or…?"

Fenn dipped his head. "You'll need to do so here in case we emerge where there are other fae. Do you have a good image of Davinia?" He ceased raising hexes, though the air where they lingered glowed and reeked of his magic.

Verve ran her hands down her thighs. "Yes."

"It's not too late to change plans."

"Yes, it is." Verve looked Fenn squarely in the eyes, and relief washed over her when he again failed to argue with her. Then, trembling with nerves, she held on to the image of a mortal Dav in her mind's eye and allowed the shape-changing magic to take hold. Her body fought it at first, as though it knew about her contentious relationship with the girl, but she forced her form to obey and shift, gritting her teeth as her eyes burned.

Nearby, Fenn sucked in a deep breath and whistled. "That has got to be your best attempt at a shape yet."

"I'll be," said Markson at the same time.

Perhaps they were saying that to bring Verve some form of comfort. If that was the case, it didn't work. The world around her seemed to close in, and she had to take a few steadying breaths through her nose before she opened her eyes. When she looked again, Fenn nodded. Markson grimaced.

"What?" she asked Markson, her tone harsher than she meant it to be. Verve jumped in surprise at the sound of her youngest sister's voice coming out of her own mouth.

"Your magic, love," said Fenn. "You need to do a more thorough job of muting it."

"Right." Hastily she focused on her power retreating deep down inside herself and ran a hand over her face to help hide the appearance of power. She must have done it to Fenn's satisfaction, for he sighed in apparent relief.

Fenn took her hand in his and he led her and Markson around the hexes he had set up. "These will discourage anyone from attempting to find something to track us by." His tone was light enough, but his eyes had lightened, informing Verve of his true feelings, as though the whirling colors surrounding him would not. He pulled on her hand and increased his pace. "Take Markson's hand. Once we pass into Letorheas, I'll have to adjust the repelling charm if anyone's nearby."

Verve snatched Markson's hand in her own sweaty one, making certain to be as gentle as possible. Her magic might be muted, but her strength would still require controlling.

"If you need to find me in the palace, feel for a sense of unease and a slight physical pressure on your face."

"My face?"

"It will feel a bit like someone's trying to turn your head away from me, should you know what you're looking for." They had reached the hawthorn tree at this point, though Fenn did nothing to indicate he meant to create a gateway. "I'll cast invisibility over us, as a precaution, but if you are to confront Dacre, you'll need to wait until you know I am nearby."

At once she shook her head. "I might only get one chance at it. No, whether you're there or not, I'm siphoning."

Fenn tensed and seemed ready to argue, but Markson groaned.

"Are we going to do this, or are you two going to have another row?"

The look Fenn gave Verve made it apparent to her that his request was still in play. Instead of coming out and saying that she wasn't going to kill him if they were caught – they *wouldn't* be caught, of that she would make certain – she gave him a noncommittal shrug, which he could interpret any way that he chose.

Perhaps satisfied, Fenn turned to the tree and placed his hand on the smooth bark. The hawthorn trembled beneath his touch, and a high, reedy voice begged Fenn not to harm it. "Will you grant us safe passage to Givebend in Letorheas?" he asked, patting the trunk as though it were an old friend.

There was a slight pause, and then the tree sighed. *"You will not harm me, then, like your companion threatened?"*

Verve exchanged a look with her husband, who answered for them all, "You have my word. But please, make haste, we haven't a moment to spare."

At this, the hawthorn shook its branches. *"Much happening in Letorheas. Very much badness. I would stay here, little fae."*

"What's happening in Letorheas?" Verve demanded.

The tree strained away from the sound of her voice. *"Begging your pardon, Your Majesty. Why not create a gateway of your own? No need to involve one of your tree friends in such danger."*

"We don't have time for this," said Verve to Fenn, who shook his head and held up a hand for her to be patient.

While she fretted, Fenn went ahead and cast invisibility over them in a tight bubble, leaving them visible to each other and yet invisible to anyone outside of the immediate area. "What's happening in Letorheas?" he repeated.

"Good fae burn trees, bad fae punish good fae. It's a right mess. And the weather! Why, they have had nary a drop of rain since you last left them, Majesty." The hawthorn's tone had soured on the final word of its complaint, and its voice stretched so thin, she believed it felt its brethren's thirst.

Verve held back a sigh. "I'm sorry they are suffering. But if you prevent us from returning to Letorheas, they will suffer all the more."

"You'll make it rain, then?"

She nodded, then, realizing the tree would perhaps not know – could hawthorns see? – said, "Yes, I'll see to it that it rains as soon as possible once the three of us are safely back in Letorheas. Will that work as a bargain?"

The trunk split beneath Fenn's hand, the branches overhead wending and winding until a gateway had formed that led into the world of the fae. *"Take your passage, then. But be on your guard, little Fire Queen. You are hunted."*

Already Verve could hear the sounds of fae moving about in the land beyond, and she waited until Fenn had drawn the repelling charm closer to the three of them before following him through the gateway. At once the tree sealed the passage behind her, and the world grew quieter as the nearby fae moved a-ways off, repulsed by the charm.

Beside her, Markson had begun to tremble. "S-so this is what it feels like. Magic everywhere. Fit to rip me to bits."

Fenn laid a hand on the man's shoulder – whether to comfort or restrain him from bolting, Verve couldn't be certain. "We're within five miles of the palace. If you want to turn back, this is our last opportunity, as you'll no doubt be spotted as soon as I remove invisibility."

She ignored that bit and instead took in her surroundings. The air was dry and crackled with unspent magic. Charms had been scattered about, lighting the air with multicolored pinpricks here and there as if the landscape were a distorted rainbow. Thankfully, from what Verve could sense of the magic, none of it would give away their location but was meant to confound, upset, and discourage anyone attempting to make their way to the palace.

Overhead, the sky darkened, as though sensing she had returned and was ready to empty its stores over the land. "No," Verve said, fearful that the rain would give her return away. In response to her voice, the clouds scattered, the sky lightened, and the sun scowled down on them.

"Be careful," said Fenn. His face was tight with concentration, and his eyes had grown dark once more.

Verve raised her hand to his cheek and nodded. She wished to say something, anything, that might reassure him. But no words occurred to her, and the longer she lingered, the more she knew his resolve – and magic – would waver. So she gave him one last look, turned, and walked toward the palace without glancing back.

Chapter Twenty

It wasn't long before Verve knew she'd been sighted by several fae. Voices echoed in the distance, murmurs of excitement and doubt. The strength of Fenn's repelling charm was strong enough to give her a small headache, and she'd had it as soon as she had stepped out of the protective bubble, emerging visible while he and Markson remained unseen. Hopefully no one else would be aware of the men's presence, charm or not.

For one mile Verve trekked onward, and no one approached her, though she passed preparations of a scouting party in the west. These fae she ignored for the moment, focusing instead on seeming mortal, lost, and helpless.

The terrain was full of enormous bright red tree roots, spilling out through the soil and making the going hazardous. Of all things, they started to pull out of her way as she went, and she had to expend some light magic in order to discourage them from giving her away. Trees, she knew, didn't react to just anyone. And these seemed eager to please her, perhaps in hopes of receiving more water for them or their bracken brethren.

Something invisible brushed against her right shoulder, a touch that set her teeth on edge and made her want to turn around. Verve took a moment and paused. Should she press forward, despite this obvious warning charm? Mortal or immortal, Dav would have felt it and shied away. Verve at length decided to adjust her course, and veered instead for the north-west. If she ran into any more charms or hexes, she would simply retrace her steps until someone found her.

The party sent out to intercept her grew quieter, and the air reeked of Dacre's magic, coffee and chocolate. If the Traitor King were among their number, this might be more difficult. For one thing, she didn't feel quite prepared. And for another, his guard would be up outside of the palace walls…or, at least, that's what Verve assumed.

Verve moved into a clearing full of purple spikes of grass, strangely aware of her heart thundering in her ears. As she pretended to look around in confusion, she did her best to calm herself, in fear that her true level of panic would alert Dacre's men that she was hiding something.

Feigning ignorance was more difficult than Finley had warned her. She paid no obvious attention to the men sneaking up on her, their presence too soft for even fae ears to discern. They came from different directions, and ahead she sensed a snare lying in wait for her. To avoid any inconvenience it might cause, Verve adjusted her path so that she wouldn't make contact with it. Her lower lip trembled. "Where am I?" she murmured. Thankfully, her voice still sounded identical to Dav's, something she had worried about.

A twig snapped behind her, but Verve knew it was a ruse to get her to turn. The biggest threat lay ahead, and as soon as she turned her back to it, the real difficulties would begin. "Hello?" she called out. Her voice broke of its own accord, so it sounded genuine.

There was the sound of horse hooves behind her, another fabrication, but Verve knew she would have to react or else appear unnatural, so she sucked in a shallow breath and turned. A scream ripped itself from her throat as she was seized from behind and blindfolded. She fought them, or rather, pretended to, as they bound her wrists with ropes. Thankfully she had through-sight, which she used to observe her captors.

Someone on her right sighed with relief as she was subdued. "Reports were wrong," he said to someone straight ahead of them. "She's still mortal."

Verve tugged at her bonds with weak movements, until a blade was laid across her throat. She whimpered and let her knees tremble.

"Put that away," said a formidable woman. From the sound of things, this fae was in charge. "You're going to get us all killed."

"But—" one of the men began as the blade was lowered.

"Not a scratch on her. That was his order, and it is mine as well."

The woman stepped forward. When the fae spoke again, her voice softened. "What is your name, child?"

The fae in front of her was dressed as what might pass as a soldier, though it was no uniform Verve had ever seen among the ranks of man: stiff black fabric with thick plates of chain mail worn over top. There were no weapons on her person, but an excess of magic rippled through the woman's body, waiting to burst forth at the slightest provocation. It was as visible to Verve as the men behind her, whose blades they were only just replacing in their respective sheaths.

Verve jerked her head around. "I-I..." She swallowed down a sob. "I didn't do anything!" She squirmed and the two males holding on to her tightened their grip.

"Easy," said the woman in charge. She glared at her inferiors until they released Verve's arms and stepped back. "Are you the young woman we've been searching for?" Hands folded in front of her, the fae studied Verve as though trying to figure out some great puzzle.

"I don't know," said Verve. "I just want to go home. Please, tell me how to leave this place."

The woman actually had the nerve to reach out and brush a blond curl out of Verve's face. "If you answer a few questions, we'll make sure you are safely sent back to Etterhea – your realm. Can you be brave for a bit longer while we sort this all out?"

At first Verve hesitated. She didn't want to seem too co-operative. Then, sensing a deep restlessness in the men behind her, she slowly nodded. Hopefully Fenn and Markson were in their positions by now, ready to break into the palace. The distant sounds of revelers reached Verve's ears, and many clashing residual bursts filled the air as well. If the fete had begun already, would it be too late for Aunt Springer?

"Excellent." Of all things, the woman came alongside Verve and placed a hand on her shoulder. "Now, if you would be so good as to come with us, we'll interview you." She turned to the nearest soldier. "Remove that rag from her eyes. Where we are is no secret now."

Two of the men exchanged looks as their comrade hastily pulled the blindfold from Verve's eyes. "Sorry, Captain."

"And I don't think we'll be needing these either." The captain snapped her fingers and the bonds tying Verve's hands behind her back withered into dust.

Verve let out a small whimper and rubbed her wrists vigorously. She cringed as the captain threaded an arm through one of hers, obviously attempting to assert control. "What do you want to know?"

"Not here where any ears can hear," said the captain cheerfully. "We need to move you to a secure location first. Then we'll see if you are what is sought." She tugged on Verve gently but firmly, and it took all of Verve's self-control not to lash out at her.

They exited the woods surrounding the palace grounds at a brisk pace that didn't slow as they passed through metal gates. Guards stood watch on either side, but there were so many people about that it was clear they weren't paying close attention to the comings and goings of any creature. One woman in bright red livery nodded to the captain and then disappeared into the crowd on the right.

"Stay close," said the captain, as though she would afford Verve any other option. "And try not to listen too closely to any music. I fear things here can be rather disorienting to your kind."

Verve didn't respond but put on the charade of having difficulty keeping up with the fae escorting her. The males seemed to tire of this quickly, as there were muttered complaints behind her back and the ones in front of her didn't even try to slow their pace. As they walked, Verve took in her surroundings, hoping to find a sign of Fenn or sense the repelling charm. *No, it's a good thing I can't tell. If I could, Dacre might be able to as well.*

The captain squeezed Verve's shoulder and steered her around a crowd of tents, her posture tensing. As if in response to her unease, the males closed rank around them, magic flickering at their fingertips.

"Keep your head down," the captain murmured. Her grasp on Verve tightened further still, and Verve cringed, knowing it would hurt a mortal.

Voices rose in raucous laughter, deafening to the ear. Male and female alike sang unfamiliar tunes, and small explosions interrupted any silence that might be found. Red smoke hung thickly about their ankles, though it wasn't apparent what the source was until they reached a stone-flagged path that led past a grand stone staircase. Wyvern-like creatures the size of hunting dogs prowled about, spitting sparks at those who dared to tread too closely.

"They are to celebrate the Middling Season," said the captain, startling Verve from her observations. "The Fire Queen, our good king's counterpart, is expected to arrive any day now."

Verve fought a shudder. "What is the—"

"Shh. Please, no speaking until we are safely within the palace walls." She forced Verve past the small wyverns and through a small garden that reeked of coffee and chocolate. The flowers bowed their heads as Verve approached, but thankfully no one seemed to notice. Or, if they did, perhaps it was a regular occurrence and Verve didn't need to worry that these particular plants were responding to her.

They turned, ceasing to walk parallel with the palace, and took a downward-sloping path to a set of stairs. They took the steps down toward a faded red door that opened into a large, empty room. The temperature dropped dramatically and the humidity increased tenfold when they entered.

Verve's stomach lurched as the door was shut and barred behind the last guard. "I-I want to go home," she managed to choke out once more.

The captain motioned for her to be seated in a high-backed chair that hadn't been there a moment before. "Please, you must be exhausted. Be seated and rest."

Verve eyed the chair with trepidation. Was it a trap? She thought of reaching out with magic, to see if it would affect her negatively, but she knew the others might sense power if she were to use too much of it. Instead, she decided on a happy middle ground: she moved toward the chair but remained standing, facing her captors head-on. If Dacre wasn't aware that 'Dav' was his prisoner yet, would Fenn be able to slip in with Markson? They *needed* a distraction for this to work.

Much to her relief, the captain didn't insist that she sit. Instead, she studied Verve as though wishing to tease out some secret through observation alone. Twice she released subtle tendrils of magic from her fingers and allowed them to reach out to Verve. Each time, they brushed against Verve's skin and then returned to their mistress. It didn't hurt nor did it feel invasive. Verve wondered what the magic was telling the other woman.

At long last, the captain spoke. "What are you called, child?"

Thankfully, Verve was aware that the woman was no longer speaking what would be Dav's native tongue, testing her no doubt. She allowed her face to remain blank of expression.

The captain repeated the question in Dav and Verve's language.

"D-Davinia Springer," said Verve. She affected Dav's mannerisms, raising her slightly too-large nose in the air and staring haughtily into the other creature's eyes.

"We have to be certain." It was a man who had spoken, the one standing on the captain's right side. He kept opening and closing his fists, and rivulets of sweat ran down his collar, which he took a moment to loosen before returning to his nervous habit.

Verve didn't give them time to doubt further. When the captain stared straight back into her eyes, Verve let her gaze drop and she said to her shoes, "Who are you? No, *what* are you and why am I here?"

"How did you come to be in our realm, Davinia Springer?" Again she chose a different tongue, and again Verve feigned confusion.

"I don't believe she understands you," said the same fae from before, his unease still palpable.

"I'm just making certain." The captain approached Verve, hands outstretched, and touched her fingers to the latter's cheeks. She frowned. "Well, it's not an illusion. This is her face."

Verve could have fainted from relief. She kept her mouth closed and pulled away from the woman's cold touch.

"Who brought you to this realm, Davinia?"

"Some dreadful man with pointed ears and too-dark eyes," she whispered.

One of the fae's mouths formed the words 'Rogue Prince', but the captain had no reaction to Verve's description. "Did this man call himself anything?"

"He said I was to call him Fin or some other ridiculous thing, and that he was…my brother now." She frowned, pretending that the memory confused or upset her.

The fae before her exchanged meaningful looks. "Are we certain?" asked the fae on the captain's right. He had stopped fidgeting and was standing at attention now, his voice sharp and his eyes alert. "If we bring His Majesty anything other than the Fire Queen or her sister, Tricea, our lives are forfeit."

The captain folded her arms across her chest and tapped her long fingers as one lost in thought. Her gaze bored into Verve. "If she's an imposter, he'll know."

"Tri—"

She held up a hand. "The king will know and reward us, for if she is not the Fire Queen's sister, she is at least an ally and can be interrogated for information. We bring her before the king at once. If you value your lives, speak no word of this interview to him or anyone else."

"Temperamental tyrant," one fae muttered, and the captain gave him a glare.

"I'll pretend I didn't hear that," she said. Wasting no time, she spun Verve around and took her by the right arm.

Finally, thought Verve, though her nerves tingled with dread. "Where are you taking me?" She resisted a little, as they were leading her into a dark hall, which would have certainly alarmed Dav, so it was in character.

The captain gave her arm a reassuring squeeze. "We're going to see someone who can help find your sister."

Verve snorted, and she noted the others tense. "Why do you want to find *her*?" She was certain to add disdain to her tone, and she knew the others were not happy with her for that.

Someone cleared their throat in the short silence that followed, and at length the captain said, "Mind your tongue and how you speak of your sister from this point onward. Your very life might depend on it." Her hold on Verve's arm tightened and she quickened her pace, forcing Verve to stumble after her.

They wended their way through poorly lit halls, up steep staircases and ones that wound forever downward, across wide, open rooms littered with tapestries that moved in an unfelt breeze, and then stopped at the threshold of a room so bright it took Verve's eyes a minute to adjust. When she could see clearly, she wished she had had longer to think through her plan.

Hundreds of fae heartbeats resounded against the forefront of merry voices, all raised in delighted chatter. The conversation running from person to person varied in tone and in tenor, but the content all revolved around the festivities and who had had the pleasure of seeing His Majesty and the elusive Fire Queen. Some speculated as to her whereabouts, though everything was kept positive and veered clear of criticism or doubt as to where her loyalties lay.

The grand room itself was resplendent in whites and golds, the marbled floor beneath bare feet shined within an inch of its life. Servants in cream livery moved in silence from person to person, trays with a sparkling purple drink in crystal glasses balanced in their hands. Verve noted the iron bands around their wrists and frowned. Focusing her eyes, she noticed they were similar to the magic-canceling manacles worn by the prisoners she'd freed for Igraine. They might make good allies – if they were, in fact, in disagreement with the Traitor King. If she could find a way to free them without anyone noticing magic leaving her...

"I know this must be overwhelming," said the captain into Verve's ear. "Keep your head down once more and say nothing until the king speaks to you. Do you know how to curtsy?"

Dav did, so Verve quickly nodded.

"Good girl. Don't try to break free from me in this crowd. There are those who don't like mortals and won't be as kind to you as I have been." She patted Verve's arm and led her through the crowd, which paid them little mind.

Though Verve did as the captain said, she was able to search the crowd around her from the corners of her eyes. Still she did not sense a repulsion indicating Fenn's presence, and again she reassured herself that that was a good thing. Movement to the right drew her attention and she started to look up until the captain cleared her throat pointedly and pulled Verve along at a faster pace.

"What's this?" asked a familiar voice, one that caused Verve to break out in gooseflesh. Tubsman, a transporter who worked for Dacre, had joined the captain and the soldiers surrounding them.

The captain tucked a smile into the corner of her mouth, one that Verve watched with some interest until the captain frowned. "Linwood."

"Captain," said Tubsman in the same neutral tone.

They reached a tall set of ornately decorated doors, beside which stood four guards, two on either side. One of the guards, a female fae with auburn hair, stepped forward and put out a hand to stay them. "The king is not seeing anyone at the moment."

"He'll see us for this," said the captain, nodding at Verve.

Now the crowd spread out across the floor began taking not-so-covert looks in their direction, only to turn away when the captain took notice and glared at them. The guard at the door was unmoved.

Tubsman clucked his tongue. "Surely His Majesty will see the captain. She has served him well and would not request an audience unless it was of great importance."

Verve took a chance and peeked at him sideways. She had to school her face into a neutral expression when she noted the additional scars and disfigurements on his once blemish-free face. The gash running down his eye had been from Dacre; Verve recalled having seen it in a vision. But the way his skin sagged and hung off the bone on the right side of his face was new. She shuddered when he caught her peeking.

"I would thank you, Linwood Tubsman, but your help might prove my hindrance in this case." The captain gave him a pitying smile and turned her attention to the guard watching the exchange. "Please tell His Majesty that I come bearing a gift. One that he has had his eye on for the last few months."

That seemed to perk up the guard. Her spine straightened, and surprise flashed in her eyes. She turned to Verve before nodding to her companions and hastening through the doors. A great silencing spell must have been raised, because Verve couldn't hear a word that was being said on the other side, nor could she detect any heartbeats or breathings.

Soon enough, the guard returned and motioned for her fellows to part the way. She held the door open for the captain and Verve, but put up her hand when the others along with Tubsman attempted to follow in after. "His Majesty will see the captain and her guest and that is all."

There were murmurs of relief among the ranks of the captain's men, but Tubsman seemed positively offended. "Did you mention that I wished to speak with His Majesty?" the transporter demanded.

Verve didn't get to hear the guard's response because the door snapped shut behind them and she was propelled forward. Now she didn't attempt to calm her frenzied heartbeat. The amount of power in this room would surely be evident even to the most non-magical person in existence. Magic thrummed in the air and pushed up against Verve, threatening to squeeze the air out of her lungs. Her own power reared its head, a dog sniffing the air. Hastily she pushed it down, willing it to remain quiet and unobserved. Everything smelled potently of chocolate and coffee, Dacre's residual burst.

"It's all right," whispered the captain, though she sounded intimidated herself. "Just breathe normally."

Oh dear. Now that the fae had mentioned it, Verve had not breathed for the past fifteen seconds at least. She made a show of slowing and drawing in a few deep breaths, which made her want to throw up. The magic was so strong, she could actually taste it.

"Compose yourself and do not be afraid."

Verve didn't dare look up or ahead, where there were five sets of beating hearts. She didn't trust herself not to react strongly when she saw Dacre again, and she needed the entire walk to prepare herself. *I'm not going to fly at him. That would be foolish. And I'm not going to flee...no matter what he says or does. His magic is mine.* As they grew closer, the talking ceased altogether, and some sort of magic was released, judging by the intensification of the residual bursts hanging in the air. *Fortification spells*, she noted. Whatever magic Dacre already had in place, he was seeking to strengthen it. The only way out or in would be by his say-so.

The captain stopped suddenly, and Verve, who had not been paying attention, stumbled to a halt as well and nearly fell over. Four fae chuckled at her clumsiness, presumably, and the captain made a bow. "Curtsy," she hissed at Verve, who hastily dipped into a pathetic attempt at one.

Silence fell over the room, and Verve knew Dacre watched her intently from his throne on the dais. Soon a wave of magic spiraled forward and brushed against her, teasing and testing. He wanted her to know he was in charge here. "Look at me," he said, barely above a whisper.

Verve hesitated. This shape's eyes had been difficult to shift to the right shade. Would Dacre notice? He had met Davinia on several occasions.

"No one is going to harm you, Davinia," he said, sitting forward on his throne.

The captain nudged her, and Dacre scowled. "Sorry, Your Majesty." She took a deliberate step away, leaving Verve alone and exposed.

This was the moment of truth. Slowly Verve raised her head and cringed when she looked Dacre full in the face. Power robed him, leaked out of his every pore. Its magnitude exceeded hers, of that she was certain. This might not be as easy as she had hoped. Quickly her eyes darted away.

"Tell me how you came to be here." His voice was kind, conversational, but she felt an eagerness about him as he nodded to the men on his right, who hastened toward the nearest doors.

Verve's throat bobbed and her mouth went dry when she tried to form the words she had practiced in her mind. "You mean this place here or—" She gestured around vaguely, and Dacre watched the movements like a hawk.

He drummed his fingers on the arms of his wooden throne and tilted his head to the side. "Has anyone explained the realms to you?"

She nodded, her eyes roving, unwilling to meet his again. "Yes. H-he said something that sounded like Et-ear-ree-ah." Each syllable she pronounced slowly, as she imagined Dav doing. "He said I would be safer here instead."

Dacre had stilled. "He? I'm assuming you mean a fae like me?"

"Yes." Again his magic reached out toward her, though she tried to pretend she didn't notice it. Power wove around her ankles, like a cat happily greeting a friend. She knew he was attempting to soothe her nerves, but it did nothing to ease her. *How am I going to touch him without arousing suspicion? Maybe if I tripped...*

"This male fae who took you from Etterhea – your realm, that is – what did he look like?"

Verve frowned. "Dark eyes, dark hair. And he was tall. Very tall."

This seemed to amuse Dacre; his lips twitched upward. "Indeed. So, he took you from your home and brought you to Letorheas, and then...?"

She fidgeted, her hands twisting a bit of her dress, and his focus homed in on the action. When she stopped, he leaned forward, his breath hitching. Verve shook her head and feigned distress. "Why do you need to know all this?" Her voice broke and he stilled. "I just want to go home."

"You do not address His Majesty that way," the captain said, and Dacre was on his feet.

"Careful," he purred. "We don't want to frighten our guest." He wore a black cloak, which he shrugged off and tossed over his arm with a casual flick of the wrist. "Are you cold? You seem cold." Dacre took one step down from his throne and then another, his movements lithe and slow.

A thrill of terror washed over Verve as he moved nearer. His hands were gloved, and his arms covered by long sleeves. There was nowhere she could touch him to siphon magic without appearing too forward. "Please, I didn't mean to trespass here."

Dacre moved into her space and unfurled the cloak to its full length, spinning it out suddenly so that it covered all but her head. In Dav's form, Verve was swimming in it. "You're quite pretty, you know." He took her face in one of his hands and stroked her jaw absently before releasing her and backing away. "But you're nowhere near as devastating as your elder sister, I fear."

Verve's stomach twisted as he licked his lips. "Ainsley is – *was* very pretty, but devastating is a strange way of putting it – begging your pardon."

His laughter sent his magic skittering across her skin once more, warming her against her wishes. Dacre clasped his hands in front of him. "I meant your eldest sister, *but one*. Now, she...her beauty is unsurpassed." His eyes twinkled. "Will you tell me where I might find her?" He reached out and swept a strand of hair back over her shoulder.

"What do you want with her?" The door to Dacre's right opened and the two fae guards from earlier stole back inside. They nodded at their king and took their positions next to his dais.

Dacre's eyebrows rose. "I was under the impression that Verve wasn't a favorite of yours," he said.

"Whatever ill she's done, she's still my sister."

There was another burst of laughter. What was so funny to him? Dacre shook his head and gestured to the space next to her, where a chair appeared out of nowhere, accompanied by a residual burst smelling of both coffee and chocolate. "Sit...please. You seem tired."

Verve spared the chair a quick glance, remembering too late to appear dazed. Her version of Dav was supposedly, after all, not accustomed to magic still...at least, that was the story she had made up in her mind. "N-no, thank you," she said, causing him to smirk. This interview was not going well. She needed to find a way to get him to take the gloves off, and fast. Her magic did not like being tamped down for so long. It was begging to be released, more than it should have.

Dacre looked pointedly at the chair, which slid across the floor and knocked against the backs of her knees, successfully tilting her into its seat. She was about to scramble out of it, afraid of putting herself in a vulnerable position, but he hastily conjured one of his own and sat in it across from her, their knees almost touching. "Tell me where your sister is." His voice was soft yet serious, and she knew at once he was using compulsive magic.

Thankfully, it brushed against her without effect, but she couldn't let him know that. Verve willed her face to go blank as she said, "I haven't seen her in months. She disappeared after Hel – elena died." *Blast!* She was the only one who called Helena 'Hel'. Her tripping over the name, however, went unnoticed.

"I was sad to hear of her death." His lips turned downward. When he spoke again, his voice was soft, strangely kind. "I hope you don't blame your sister for it."

That was still a fresh wound, and Verve shuddered. She gulped, but he said nothing of it and still showed no sign of thinking anything was amiss. This gave her courage. "Thank you," she offered. "I would probably tell you where Verity was, if I didn't think she was in trouble, and if I knew."

He cocked his head slightly. "Would you?" He leaned back with a sigh, tugged at his gloves for one hope-inducing moment, and then let them be, instead folding his hands together. "She's not in any trouble. Quite the opposite, in fact."

Verve held her fury in check as his eyes danced with mirth. "Oh? What does that mean?"

The maddening man sat forward again quite suddenly. "She's all that's missing from the puzzle at the moment. It's very important, Davinia, that I find her soon. Are you certain you don't know of her current whereabouts?"

Should she throw him a bone? Send him running in the wrong direction? No, that wasn't an option. She had already pretended to be affected by his compelling magic and it would make him suspicious if she suddenly gave him information now. "I'm sorry."

"That's a shame. I need her here, not only because I've missed her terribly and am worried for her safety, but because I love her and want her ruling at my side."

Verve struggled to keep her expression composed. It was her power he wanted as much as anything. She knew he had suspected her of being the Fire Queen from the moment they'd met...well, if not from that exact moment, then shortly after he had kidnapped her. Memories of him holding her under water and forcing her first transformation arose in her mind like a venomous snake, and she had to bite her tongue before she could come out with a waspish retort.

"Do you know of anyone who might know Verve's whereabouts?" When she took too long to respond, Dacre started rambling. "You see, I was so close to finding your sister months upon months ago. She'd taken up residence in a small cottage, and Tubsman – one of my servants – found it, only for her to run off before I could arrive. I've been out riding just now, searching for Verve." He nodded at the gloves. "I saw you noted my strange attire several times – oh, don't feel embarrassed for looking. It is strange. But they mute my magic during physical contact. It's important, since my power now frightens my horse, Ravitt. I think you'd like him." Dacre's smile broadened for some reason. "But I don't think – that is, I *hope* my magic doesn't frighten you."

The door to the left opened once more, but she paid it little mind. Verve held absolutely still as Dacre held out his hand for her, as though to shake. When she failed to react, he snatched her right one in his and kissed it...just as something metal slipped around her neck from behind and then audibly snapped into place.

Chapter Twenty-One

It was a strange sensation, having her magic repressed by such unnatural means. Verve clawed at the collar, which burned cold against her flesh. "What have you done?" she said to Dacre, and was horrified to hear her own voice come out of her mouth instead of Dav's.

Dacre moved quickly, pulling her hands away from her neck, where she had begun to claw. "Careful." He was strong... *too* strong.

There was a commotion, and a certain blond-haired girl circled around Verve and came to stand at Dacre's elbow.

"So, you found her," said the real Dav, who must have sneaked in when the door opened last. She sounded...excited. "You're going to punish her like you said?"

"Not now, Davinia." Dacre's voice was tight, strained. "Will someone get the little traitor out of here?"

Ignoring the presence of her sister – what did he mean by 'traitor'? – Verve pulled against his iron grip in vain. Terror overtook her. She bucked and writhed and screamed her anguish, while her magic fought against the magic-canceling collar. There was a satisfying grinding sound, telling her that her power was fighting the restraint. But before it could break free, a second band was clamped around her neck. At once the painful burning sensation ceased, and her magic went silent.

"Calm yourself," Dacre said as she continued to fight him. "Verve."

From the corner of her eye, Verve noticed Dav shaking off two fae who were attempting to escort her from the room. "Unhand me! I want to watch."

When Verve's kicks missed Dacre entirely and his hold on her tightened, she swore at him and attempted to bite his wrist. "Let me loose!"

He did no such thing, instead drawing her into his body and holding her mortifyingly close. "Someone, bring me a sedative," he ordered.

Hot, angry tears spilled down her cheeks. How had things gone so wrong so quickly? And did Dav have something to do with it? "No."

Dacre chuckled. "I'm so glad you're here and alive. Your act would have been convincing if I didn't already have the real Davinia Springer at my disposal, feeding me information— *Easy*." He steadied Verve, who was attempting to sink from his grip. "Verve, you need to take deep breaths. No, stop struggling." He turned to one of his men and snapped his fingers, not to cast a spell but to summon their attention.

"I don't think a sedative's a good idea," said one of his nearest men. The fae did not approach his master, his eyes fixed in apparent terror on Verve.

"Why is that?"

She yanked against him, and her wrist bones snapped with a sickening crack. Pain she hadn't experienced since her last transformation overwhelmed her, and her magic, being repressed, neither healed nor muted the pain. Verve howled like a wild creature, even after Dacre hastily fed magic into her body, taking the pain away and repairing the bones.

"I asked why a sedative is a bad idea!"

The servant stumbled backward, his eyes widening before he had the sense to look away from Verve. "She, um, well— When your magic is restrained like that, sedatives can be harmful. Not in the long term, mind. There's a theory that—"

A wave of coffee-scented magic struck the poor servant in the chest, and he went sailing against the far wall, where he lay unmoving and with glassy, vacant eyes. Verve didn't have to ask to know that the creature was dead.

"Shh," Dacre whispered. Then, perhaps seeing she wouldn't settle down anytime soon, he drew a fistful of magic into his hand and gently pressed it against Verve's forehead.

A dull calm settled on her and she ceased to struggle. Vaguely she was aware of being enraged and petrified, but whatever Dacre had done to her had pushed those feelings into a corner of her mind, away from where peace dwelt. Verve hiccoughed once, twice, and the last of the tears left in her eyes rolled down her cheeks in thin rivulets.

Dacre wiped the moisture away. "There we are." He pulled back and surveyed her as his guards watched. "This spell isn't going to hold for long. She's too powerful, even with the collars in place." Amusement filled his voice, and at his words, the guards took slow steps toward them. "It's all right. My queen has just had a long day and needs to rest." As if to reassure them of the power he had over Verve, Dacre released her momentarily, and she found herself collapsing. He caught her before she could hit the floor, lifted her, and carried her out of the throne room through a back door she hadn't noticed before.

Dav cried out in protest all the while, sounding angrier and angrier by the moment, until the door slammed shut in her face.

"We'll have to be quick with the ceremony," said a woman flanking Dacre on the right.

"I'm well aware." The words were spoken through Dacre's teeth as he bore Verve with haste through golden hallways that glittered in the light from dozens of bejeweled wall sconces. When her head rolled back, he slowed, adjusted her, and then kissed her eyelids closed. "It's just a marriage bond. We should be able to disenchant her, yes?"

The woman hesitated as the pace quickened yet again. "Theoretically, yes. But she's the Fire Queen."

"And I am her king."

Dispassionately, Verve wondered where they were taking her and what would happen when they got there. She yawned and peeped at her surroundings with one eye and ceased caring.

"But her mate is the Rogue Prince. He's always had excess power running through his veins. Their bond—"

"Will be broken."

The silence that followed made it obvious that the woman didn't share his confidence but didn't wish to argue. Instead, her jaw tightened and she bobbed her head once, almost dismissively.

Their pace slowed and the group took a left turn, walked several paces, and then went right. The room that they entered was bright, lit with sunlight seeping in through an overhead skylight.

Verve scrunched her eyes more closed as she was deposited on something cold and hard in the beam of sunlight. She tried to sit up, but Dacre attached the metal collars around her neck to a chain, limiting her movement. Next, her arms were stretched out and fastened to the raised stone surface, and that was when fear slowly trickled back into her mind.

"Your blood, sire," said the woman. She passed Dacre a thin, silver blade with runes carved into its hilt.

Dacre snatched the dagger, his eyes alight with excitement. He sliced the palm of his left hand and then held the dripping wound over Verve's mouth, which she snapped shut. Undeterred, the hateful fae used magic to force her jaw open, which it did with surprising force.

Choking, Verve tried her best not to swallow any of the sickly-sweet blood, but the wound continued to gush and Dacre held his hand steadily over her lips until she knew she had swallowed a good deal of it. Nausea overcame her as he forced her jaw shut once more and then stroked her neck, encouraging her to swallow the rest of what had landed in her mouth.

"Now hers," said the woman fae. She disappeared from Verve's view as Dacre sat on the stone dais.

"Don't do this."

"I'm sorry, Verve." He didn't sound it. Dacre stroked her cheek for a moment before slicing her right palm open.

Verve hissed in pain and tried to move as Dacre brought his lips to her wound and drank greedily of her blood, his tongue probing the cut as though he were determined to get as much out of her as possible. Now she was lightheaded. Stars swam in her vision and magic pulsed all around them, strong, hot, and electric.

After some time, Dacre lifted his head. "Why can't I smell her magic?" he demanded of the other fae around them. The room reeked of coffee and chocolate.

"I don't know," the female replied. "But this was just the introductory magic, meant to weaken the bond. You'll need to finish before she rids her body of your blood." Again she entered Verve's line of sight, this time clutching a large vial with a glass stopper. The vial was full of golden liquid, and it glinted in the sunlight as it was passed to Dacre.

He took the potion – for what else could it be? – and swirled it around and murmured a strange incantation. The vessel lit up like the midday sun, and the smell of coffee intensified.

"You need to drink more than she does, if you are to maintain dominance."

Dacre grunted, unstoppered the vial, and drank more than half of its contents in several large gulps.

Struggling against her bonds, Verve looked around her for someone who might be sympathetic to her cause, and tried to make eye contact. No one would even spare her a glance. Perhaps it was wishful thinking on her part, but a few seemed guilty. One started to turn toward Verve, only to shake their head and move out of sight. Verve screamed in frustration and rage as Dacre once more swirled the vessel and muttered an incantation. She thought he was going to pour the liquid down her throat, so hastily she clamped her mouth shut.

But Dacre did not bring the vial near her mouth. Instead he took the ceremonial dagger from his servant and cut open Verve's dress at the bodice, right over her heart. He wore a pained expression as he raised the dagger in the air, but then he frowned and looked down at her exposed chest. "What is that?" He stared at the female servant, who peered down at where Verve knew Fenn's mark rested.

The female tsked. "Well, that complicates matters."

"What?" Dacre demanded.

"They're not just soul-bound." She nodded at the mark, which Dacre quickly covered as the others in the room started to take interest. "I'm guessing he wears her mark as well. It's old, physical magic, but we'd need him as well in order to break it."

"So this would be for naught?" Dacre tilted the vial as if in suggestion.

"I'm afraid so."

Dacre stoppered the bottle and thrust it at his servant. He stood in silence for a moment, staring at Verve with a thoughtful look on his face. "The Rogue Prince can't be far." Something in his expression shifted as he leaned down and freed Verve from the wrist restraints and detached the collars from the dais.

Verve attempted to roll away from him but was caught and lifted once more, though she clawed at his face and struggled as much as her strength would allow. No one paid her any mind, not even Dacre, whom she spewed all sorts of abuse at.

"She must know where he is. We should interrogate her," said the female servant.

Dacre stopped midstride. "No one is going to question her but me. You will not lay a finger on her, is that understood?"

The servant huffed. "I didn't mean to imply that I would harm her, Your Majesty."

At that moment, Verve lashed out at the female, who stood too close for her own good, and clawed at the creature's arm. Silver blood dripped down the woman's bicep, and Verve was satisfied to note the panic in her eyes.

Dacre sighed. "Sleep, Verve." Again he drew magic into his hand and pressed it into her brow.

Verve's body went limp.

Chapter Twenty-Two

"Come on, Verve."

Verve stirred at the sound of her name, but her head was heavy and filled with what felt like lead. She couldn't think around it, this strange presence. Her eyes attempted to open, but they, too, proved heavy and unable to move.

Frustration overcame her better senses, and Verve reached for her magic, prepared to fight whatever was pinning her down. But her magic wasn't there. All she received for her effort was a splitting headache and a pain that shot through her ribs like a burning lance.

Then she remembered.

The spell Dacre had put on her had hardly been enough to render her unconscious. If she recalled correctly, no fewer than ten fae had been forced to cast the same magic against her at the same time after his first attempt. It had worked, which explained the heaviness and fuzzy-headedness. As for her magic… Yes, the collars were still there. On top of that, bands had been added to her wrists and ankles. She didn't have to look to see them, sensing their magic-repressing powers' presence.

"Try. You have to try. Find a way."

The words were but a distant echo in her mind now, and Fenn's mark burned unpleasantly before ceasing. With the pain, the voice also faded. But with their absence, some of her strength returned.

Verve opened her eyes and blinked in confusion at her surroundings. She was not tied down to anything: her hands were free to run over the soft cushion beneath her, and she could sit up, which she did with deliberate slowness. The room was plain but large. Where there might have once been heavy curtains, sunlight poured through tall glass panes. Smooth gray stones made up the walls, and above was a molded white ceiling with a gold-and-crystal chandelier hanging over the bed. As if in response to her observation, the candles flared to life with blue light and flickered in an unfelt breeze.

Her stomach twisted into knots, and her head throbbed as she threw her legs over the edge of the tall bed and slid to the cold marble floor. *What a peculiar room*, she found herself thinking. She was trying very hard to not think of Dav.

There were no rugs and no furniture besides the bed and a metal chair, whose arms were fitted with manacles. A shiver ran up her spine as she moved in search of a door.

Though she searched and searched, Verve could find no hint of a doorway. She ran her hands along the walls, dug her nails into every crack that looked like it might conceal the outline of a door, but nothing revealed itself.

As panic burbled up inside of her, Verve closed her eyes and tried to better clear her head. Rooms had doors. They just did, otherwise how would anyone come and go from them? *I'm not taking magic into account. Think!*

If she had been put in this room by magical means, then it would take magic to get out.

Verve held her wrist manacles to her eyes, searching for a seam, something she could gain purchase with – even if it were her teeth – and force the bands to open. There seemed to be something, but it wasn't a seam, merely a small keyhole. *Well, that's something. I can work with a keyhole.* Indeed, locks didn't seem to be immune to mortal lockpicks; she'd discovered this during her imprisonment at Dacre's house. Yes, if she could find a pin that was the right size, she could pick the locks on her other magic-repressing restraints, which all seemed to bear a keyhole, and have a decent chance of saving herself. There was one problem, however.

No matter how hard she looked, there was no pin to be found. Verve got on her hands and knees and felt around for something, anything, she might use to pick the locks, going as far as to crawl under the four-poster bed and run her hands on the reverse side of the mattress. There was wire just there, poking through the slats that held up the box-spring bed.

If she could find something with which to cut off a long enough piece…

Footsteps echoed in the near distance, just as Verve bumped her head on the underside of the mattress. With a yelp, she scooted out from under the bed.

The approaching feet stilled, and Verve strained to hear what might be happening outside the room. Unfortunately, all of her enhanced senses had been dulled by the bands imprisoning her magic. She waited for the telltale *snick* of a lock being turned, followed by the door whining open on its hinges, but neither sound reached her.

Instead, the wall opposite the single window flickered, and through the stone blocks emerged a young woman, one who Verve at once recognized. Behind the new arrival, the wall ceased to blink in and out, and the two stared at each other, horror appearing perhaps on *both* their faces.

"Elaia?" Verve croaked. The fae had helped her months ago, right before Verve had been forced to travel to the Lands of the Dead.

She was thinner now, gaunt even, and circles like bruises underlined her eyes. The fae said nothing to Verve but she raised her hand to pull down the neckline of her dress, revealing a collar of her own.

"I'm sorry."

Of all things, Elaia shrugged and moved toward the far-right wall, where a wardrobe suddenly materialized. She opened the mahogany door and quietly rifled through its contents while Verve watched her with growing unease.

Is she working for Dacre now? No, that couldn't be. At least, not of her own free will. "Where's Ardyth?" The two had seemed inseparable back in Githtariel, the town where Verve had been meant to find sanctuary. She received no response, so she tried again. "Elaia, what happened to Ardyth?"

Elaia cringed but did not turn around until she had pulled out a long bottle-blue dress with flowing gossamer sleeves and a plunging neckline. The fae held the dress up to the light streaming in through the window and then laid it down on the bed.

"Is she back in Githtariel?"

The creature's shoulders stiffened, but she said nothing and returned once more to the wardrobe, this time producing a pair of slippers that matched the dress. These she set on the floor before turning, approaching the wall opposite the window, and then vanishing into thin air.

Wasting no time, Verve rushed at the wardrobe, hoping to find something in there that might prove useful, but it disappeared as well. She cursed, and then heard someone clear their throat behind her.

"Are you hungry?" asked the newcomer, a mortal girl Verve recognized from her hometown in Etterhea. She carried a tray toward the bed, waited a moment, and then a small round table and chair appeared where she had stood moments before. Sally set the tray of steaming food on the table, and then placed a golden goblet next to it. "I hope it's to your liking." Her glassy eyes and vapid expression alerted Verve to the fact that she was one of Dacre's Trusted.

Warily she approached the young woman, whose expression never wavered, and reached out to tap her face, hoping it might wake her. "Are you still in there?" Verve whispered.

Sally blinked. "Why don't you sit and eat?" She hastened to the table and pulled out the chair for Verve, whose last thought was on food.

"What happened to you?" Verve knew the answer but thought engaging her in conversation might loosen Dacre's hold on the girl's mind.

The smile stretched thinner across Sally's face. "Please, eat. You'll offend Chef Chao if you don't."

Offered so casually, the name of the mortal man who had once helped her was like a blow across the face. Verve reared backward. "What did you say?"

"I think you know, Verve." Sally smirked and pulled the chair out a little farther. "Eat or I will be in great trouble with the master. So will your friend Chao-Schulz, and your sister, and every other person you know here."

Verve stared in horror at the girl's darkening eyes. Was this Dacre in the room with her now? No, it didn't seem to be. Sally shook her head suddenly, and her eyes lightened once more as she pointed to the seat in front of her. She was merely being controlled and told what to say and do.

"Sit, please," said Sally.

What should Verve do? Is she lying? He wouldn't actually hurt people... would he? The moments passed as she recalled what he'd done to Fenn in Ithalamore, and what he had threatened to do to her aunt. Verve shot Sally a glare meant for Dacre and edged around the table before sitting and jerking the chair forward with more force than was necessary. "What do you want?"

Sally appeared perplexed. "Why, for you to break your fast." She gestured to the spread on the table, which had multiplied while Verve wasn't paying attention. There was a silver tureen of fruit that must be indigenous to Letorheas – red, blue, purple, and green berries, and melon slices that Verve had never seen in the course of her life; a tray of pastries and a few pats of bright yellow butter; several types of bread in loaves; baked apples swam in a sea of crème anglaise in a clear trifle bowl; smoked sausages, a rarity in this world, for most of the fae did not consume meat; a pot of honey; and a mug of steaming-hot tea. It all smelled delicious, and Verve's traitorous stomach rumbled.

"And if I'm not hungry?" said Verve.

The young woman smirked. "Oh, Verve. You really haven't changed." Her tone had turned strangely fond. She tucked a stray strand of hair behind Verve's ear and pulled away. "Do you need anything?"

"For you to drop dead."

Sally feigned a hurt look and pressed her hand to the space over her heart. "You wound me."

Verve clenched the silver fork in her hand until her knuckles turned white, then stabbed a piece of red melon from its tureen and popped it into her mouth. "Go away," she said around the melon.

"I will soon enough, but not yet." Sally rounded the table and a chair materialized across from Verve. She sat. "It was easy, you know."

She didn't ask what she – or, rather, what *Dacre* meant by that. He offered the answer anyway.

"Giving you that sliver of hope, is what I meant. I'm sorry, Verve, but you will never reconcile with your sister. She really does hate you."

So, Fenn had been right. Verve shouldn't have trusted the so-called vision she'd had of making things right with Dav. But that Dacre had actually been able to violate her mind like that; it was terrifying. Searching for courage she didn't feel, Verve sat up a little straighter and said, "If you hurt her—"

"I wouldn't dream of it. Not after she's been so helpful to me. Well, and because she means something to you still, I daresay. Even after she gave me insight into how you might act." Sally's smile was smug, and Verve wished to slap it off her face. Before she could contemplate more violence, the subject turned rather abruptly. "Where is Fenn?" Casually she lifted a sweet roll from the plate in front of her and tossed it from hand to hand.

"In Etterhea."

Through the girl, Dacre raised his eyebrows and looked pointedly at the table in front of them. "You never were a good liar, I'm sad to say."

Verve shrugged and, scowling, stabbed a small purple berry and added that to her mouth. "Only in your demented fantasies would I ever *dream* of telling you anything."

The girl's eyes darkened and magic slowly seeped into the room, filling it with overwhelming aromas of the bitterest coffee and the most cloyingly sweet chocolate. "Perhaps. But I don't think you realize the lengths I'll go to in order to get what I want. And what I want right now is for you to tell me exactly where the Rogue Prince is before I'm forced to drag the truth out of you."

Verve eyed Sally sharply as the girl licked her own fingers. For a moment Verve forgot that it was a foe in a friend's form before her. Verve lifted the mug of tea from its spot on the table and threw it at Dacre's puppet.

Dacre's magic batted the mug away harmlessly before it could reach Sally, his laughter rippling through Verve's mind. "He's close, isn't he?"

Verve rose from the table, but Sally was too fast. Dacre used the girl to gently but firmly force her back into the chair. At once something soft but persistent rubbed up against her consciousness, begging to be let in. "Stay out."

"Tell me where Fenn is first and I will leave your mind alone." Sally's fingertips rested against Verve's temples and she rubbed gently.

Verve brought up her hands and dug her nails into Sally's flesh, all thought of sparing the poor girl cast aside. "Mark my words, Dacre, I'm going to kill you."

"Of course you are." It was Dacre's voice in the shell of her ear, and it dripped with amusement. When had he slipped into the room? It didn't matter now; he pushed Sally aside and placed his own hands on either side of Verve's head, though she writhed and screamed curses at him. "How close is he, Verve?"

She resisted as best she could, but without magic at her disposal, Dacre easily infiltrated her mind and probed her thoughts. "Don't," she grunted.

"He came here with a mortal, did he?" Dacre chuckled. "It's interesting to see what sort of company he's keeping these days."

The room spun and slowly disappeared. To her horror, she realized Dacre was more than discerning her thoughts and memories: he was seeing them with his own eyes and forcing her to realize them with him.

Now she and Dacre stood in the cottage where she and Fenn had lived those short five weeks together. Verve jumped when her husband burst through the front door, bearing a bedraggled figure that was glowing strangely.

"When was this? Did he hurt you?" asked Dacre, sounding concerned. Before she could respond, he sighed and, raising his left hand, he made the scene play out more quickly in front of them. "This was after your return from Ithalamore, wasn't it?" He grinned when she ground her teeth, and stopped the memory. They were in the back bedroom together now, where her memory-self and Fenn lay entwined.

"You don't even know your own last name," Memory-Fenn was saying, "which is a further testament of how little I've shared with you." There was a pause where he leaned in and kissed her memory-self – which made Dacre tense. "It's not Larknott, love. That was my father's name. Though few know it, I took my mother's. If you choose to take the name, it's Letorheas."

Now Dacre positively vibrated with excitement. "That's new information." Back in the real world, his fingers dug a little more firmly into Verve's temples. "If that's true, and I have no reason to doubt your impeccable memory and his eagerness to impress you, this will be so much easier."

In her mind, she gave Dacre a shove, throwing him momentarily off-balance, before the scene faded and she returned to reality with a shudder. "Stay out of my head!" Verve leapt out of her seat and struck Dacre across the face. Sally was nowhere now to be seen.

Dacre grabbed Verve by the wrists and smirked. "Names really do have power, Verve. And now that I have his true one, I can easily find him. Thank you for that." He released Verve and pulled away, eyes flashing.

"Leave him alone." *Perhaps the repelling charm will afford Fenn some protection. That is, if Markson's still alive.* Verve grimaced.

"A repelling charm on a mortal?"

Verve stilled, her stomach clenching as her heart took off at a gallop. "Don't hurt him." When Dacre turned, Verve ran to him and grabbed him by the shoulder. "Please." Her hands wrung his arm, but she was easily yet gently removed, and Dacre strode toward the wall opposite the window.

"Someone will be here to help you bathe and dress shortly." He nodded to the table. "You need to nourish yourself in the meantime. Try not to worry." With that said, Dacre vanished.

Trembling and face burning, Verve picked up the teapot and threw it to the ground. The shards disappeared in the blinking of an eye, as did the pot's contents. Wasting no more time, she picked up the table knife – a mostly dull and harmless-looking thing – and threw herself again under the bed. The knife had fine teeth on its edge, so she set about sawing at the coil of wire, praying and cursing as metal grated on metal. Progress was nonexistent. The wire, thin though it was, did nothing but grow hot beneath her touch. She sawed harder and kept sawing until rough hands seized her by the ankles and hauled her out, her skirts riding up to her armpits as she was dragged.

Two unfamiliar women towered over her. One of the fae wore a collar around her neck, and the other bore no signs that she was doing anything other than acting of her own free will. The former wouldn't meet Verve's eye, but the latter held out a hand for Verve and smirked. "Inspecting for bedbugs, are we?" She pointed at the knife, which Verve clenched all the more tightly in her fist. The woman tutted. "Come now, you really don't want me using my magic. Not here. Not now."

"Are you threatening me?" Verve snapped.

The fae chortled. "Why, pray tell, would I do a silly thing like that? The knife, Your Majesty." When Verve did not yield it, the woman bent down and pried it from Verve's grip and tossed it aside.

Verve crawled backward, meaning to retreat under the bed, but both of the fae women took her by the arms and raised her to her feet. "Let me loose."

"Our orders are to help you bathe and dress. There'll be no setting you loose except into a tub of soaking water." Her nose wrinkled up as she inspected Verve more closely. "You've been around a mortal or two, I'd wager. And a high fae. Goodness! His scent is all over you."

At those words, the collared fae's eyebrows rose, but still she would say nothing. Perhaps it was Verve's imagination, but the soft pat she received on the shoulder from this fae seemed to be meant to reassure her. Could she be on Verve's side?

Maybe she just wants me to calm down so she can do her job and then get out of here. Verve renewed her attempts to free herself, only to be tapped lightly on the face, not hard enough to sting, but enough to get her attention.

"Really. You need to get cleaned up and then dressed. The quicker, the better." She leaned over Verve to whisper conspiratorially to the other fae, "I hear the Rogue Prince is within His Majesty's sights. He should be subdued before nightfall."

"No!" Verve cried out, but the fae women paid her no mind, dragging her to the far-left wall, where a large metal tub with clawed feet appeared.

"Strip her."

The collared fae did as was asked, removing Verve's blouse, skirt, and starting on her underthings, all while Verve struggled. Strangely, the other fae had turned her back and was tidying up the room.

"No need to hurt her, Your Majesty. She doesn't wish to be here any more than you do."

If shaming Verve into co-operating had been the desired effect, it worked. The collared fae managed to finish undressing Verve and then took her by the arm and led her to the tub, which steamed and emitted the aromas of lavender and lemongrass.

'Please don't land me in more trouble,' the fae's eyes seemed to say, and Verve didn't have the heart to cause her grief.

"Perhaps we can help each other," said Verve mostly to the collared fae, but with hopes the free one would change her mind as well.

But the latter shook her head. "That's not going to happen, Your Majesty. We're sorry to disappoint you." She waved dismissively in Verve's direction, and the other fae lifted her into the hot water.

Verve yelped and tried to jump out but was held down. Thankfully, her body quickly adjusted to the high temperature of the water, which turned a strange brownish gray as she sat there. She tried to think of an argument that might change their minds, but nothing brilliant occurred to her, so she spoke the first thought that came to her. "Dacre's not going to win. You don't want to be on the losing side, do you?"

"On the losing side? My dear, you do realize that the king has won already, don't you?" The free fae laughed as the collared one scrubbed Verve down with soap and a sponge. "You're the one in a collar, so I'd be careful about whom I called a loser."

"This isn't over."

"Oh, but it most decidedly is. Think about it, Your Majesty. You are exactly where he wants you: your magic is repressed and soon to be put under his control—"

The world went silent as she was dunked under the water, held down for a moment, before breaching the surface with a gasp. "You don't know that."

"Once he breaks the bond between you and the Rogue Prince, you'll have little choice. Can you imagine? Two powerful beings joining their magic together? It's never been done in the course of history." The fae turned now and watched Verve intently, as though waiting for a reaction.

Verve frowned. "Join power? What does that mean?"

"Why, don't you know?" Her ensuing laugh echoed off the empty walls, and Verve resisted the urge to clap her hands over her own ears. The fae smirked. "He'll have full access to your magic and his own at the same time, and you – well, if you co-operate during the ceremony, it sounds as though you'll have access to some of his. It's as good as done, so you might as well get used to the idea."

The other fae chose that moment to dunk Verve under once more, then again, before pulling her out of the tub and wrapping her in a large white towel. Now she would hardly look at Verve, her expression pained.

"Oh, don't look so forlorn. Don't you want to be on the winning side?"

Verve met the other fae's eyes as she was rubbed down. "I would rather be on the side of what's good and right."

"And it's up to you, Fire Queen, to decide what is good and right?" Her face twisted into a sneer, though her eyes twinkled. Something was...strange about this fae.

"How is forcing me into this acceptable? How will you be able to live with yourself when Dacre takes over this realm and then another? When he's killed someone you care about all because they said or did something that displeased him, don't come crying to me and expect compassion." Verve thought of the fae who had been trying to assist Dacre, the one who had met his end all because Dacre had grown impatient. She shuddered at the thought of such a man in charge of the fates of Letorheas and other realms.

Again the fae turned away, this time giving her attention to making the bed, which she did by hand instead of employing magic to do the work for her. "Finish dressing her and get out." She nodded at the collared fae, who dropped the towel and went about getting Verve into the blue dress.

Arguing with her is getting me nowhere. This one's mind is made up. Verve winced as she was laced into the gown. She needed an ally, one whose power wasn't under lock and key like her own. Perhaps it would be wise to go after a Trusted. They could be harmed, being mortal still. Maybe she could threaten one into helping her.

Such a thought made Verve feel ill, but she was fast running out of time. Even now, shouts of triumph were taken up outside her window. Her heart lurched as she imagined the reason for their celebration. Had Dacre bested Fenn?

Verve was so absorbed in her thoughts that she barely took note of the collared fae quitting the room, leaving her alone with the antagonistic one. She jumped when the creature snapped her fingers in front of her face.

"His Majesty loves you very much, you know." The fae went to the table and pulled one of the table knives from its spot. "You'll learn to love him in return."

"Never."

The fae looked into Verve's eyes, her own brimming with meaning as she made a charade of pretending to cut her own finger and holding it over the inside of her wrist. "There's no way out of here, Your Majesty. Guards are everywhere." Her eyebrows rose meaningfully and again she kept up the gesturing with the knife. "Your magic is under his power." She nodded at the manacles on Verve's wrist.

"What—"

She held a finger to her lips and then slit her own thumb with the supposedly dull blade. "Power may run through your veins...but it all soon will be his." Drip by drip, she allowed her silver blood to fall onto the inside of her wrist, all in one spot, before hastily licking it up, as though to hide the evidence. "You're a smart young woman who learns her lessons, I believe." Now she appeared positively exasperated as she gestured to Verve's own wrists, then pointed at the knife.

Verve drew in a sharp breath as the fae winked. "You're awful and he's awful." Could the woman truly be on her side? Her mind raced as she tried to put together what the charade had meant. The woman must have swapped this knife for a sharp one, though it did not appear to have anything other than a dull edge with some small teeth.

"I'll be back to collect you shortly, along with others." The last part sounded like a warning, and she left the room to Verve's parting remark, "This isn't over."

Verve took the knife and studied it, placed the tip against her finger. It was dull there, dull and thick. There would be no picking her locks with it. Why had the fae cut herself?

A memory flickered to life in Verve's mind. Her friend Olive stood before her, in Verve's mind's eye, and shrugged. *"Magic is in your blood, and blood is in your magic. You can't separate the two."*

Why would Dacre take such care that the room was free of objects that she might harm herself with?

Eager, Verve ran the blade across her right thumb and let silver blood collect there. Power thrummed in that small pool, and she allowed it to drip down into the keyhole of her left hand's manacle. There was a tug in her stomach, but also outside of herself, and she sweated and strained as she attempted to manipulate the power. The magic wormed its way through the hole until it opened, soundlessly. It was not as quick or as painless as directing the magic through the regular means, but she at once set about freeing her right wrist as well. With the removal of both restraints, Verve's power swam a little closer to the surface. If she wanted to maintain the element of surprise, she knew she would have to wrestle it back down quickly once she was master again.

The manacles on her right and left ankles followed, and she made certain to silently set them aside. Now it was time to attempt the two collars encircling her neck. Unable as she was to see the keyholes for these, Verve's fingers frantically ran over the cold metal of the bottom collar until, at last, she discovered what she sought. At once she wounded herself again, ignoring her growing dizziness as she fed her blood into the lock and allowed her power to do its work. Now her magic was pumping hard in her veins, practically singing with the need to be released. The last collar cracked under the strain, and Verve hastily pulled the fragments from her throat.

Her blood burned as she wrestled her power in silence, her teeth clenched so tightly she was surprised they didn't crack. It took a moment for her magic to calm, and when it did, she shoved it down deep inside herself and ran a hand down her face as she pushed the appearance of her mortal-self into place.

Wasting no time, Verve searched for a place to hide the restraints, and settled on shoving them under the mattress. Her immortal hearing alerted her to the approach of several fae, ones that were talking excitedly of a ceremony.

Her heart beat a frantic tattoo as she looked down at her free arms. Whoever was coming to collect her would notice at once, and that would ruin her chances, so she hastily conjured harmless imitations of the magic-canceling bands around her ankles, wrists, and neck. *Please don't let them notice any difference.* Just as the wall opposite the window flickered, Verve remembered the knife and only had time to make the blood on it vanish.

Ten fae, all female, entered the room side by side, magic in their hands, ready and waiting. The knife in Verve's hand sailed out of her grasp and into that of the captain who had found her in the woods and brought her hence.

Verve tensed, expecting to have to fight her way out, but the captain – Tricea, Verve reminded herself – didn't act afraid. "You don't have to do this."

Boldly she approached Verve and snatched her right hand in her own while the others stared on, quivering with what appeared to be terror. The captain inspected the manacles while Verve forced herself to remain calm and put up only a minimal resistance. With a nod, the captain straightened. "All seems to be in order." The women under her command didn't relax. "Oh, for pity's sake. She's suppressed. You have nothing to fear." There was an air of unease about the woman, and visible waves of apprehension drifted around her.

Verve repeated herself as she was taken by the arms and led toward the wall, which flickered once more and allowed them to pass through. She was then surrounded by the other fae. All kept their distance but were close enough that if she should try anything, they would be ready. The halls were quiet, save for the steady beating hearts of a dozen or more fae. To Verve's consternation, she sensed Fenn's among them. Markson's heartbeat was nowhere to be found.

"What do you have to gain from catering to Dacre's every whim?" Verve said below her breath.

The captain winced. "His Majesty can hear every word you are saying. Mind your tongue, please." Her grip on Verve tightened by a hair as she marched her through the winding halls, turning left, and then right, circling back, going up stairs and going down stairs, until Verve knew she would never find her way back without using magical means.

"So what if he can hear what I'm saying? This is wrong, and I think you know it."

"I've chosen my side, Your Majesty. I think it is time you accepted your place in all this." With that said, the captain passed Verve off to one of her inferiors, and approached a set of golden double doors. She paused a moment and raised her fist to knock, but a low voice called from within, "Enter."

The doors swung open of their own accord, and Verve was herded inside a large room with a high ceiling. Against the far wall was a stone platform upon which sat a great throne sculpted out of black marble. At its side sat a lesser, wooden throne, more a fine chair, really. In the middle of the room was a wooden dais with three stone seats set upon it, spaced so close together, one would have to walk sideways to enter the middle where Dacre stood. Behind him and to the left sat Dav, her face pale and her eyes simmering with rage. Her gaze met Verve's before darting away. Good. Perhaps the little brat felt guilty for her part in this catastrophe.

"I must remind you to be careful with your words, Tricea. This is, after all, your queen." Dacre's voice came from everywhere and hurt Verve's ears, though she tried her best to act unaffected.

"My apologies, Your Majesty," said the captain.

A shaft of sunlight shone down upon Dacre, and as he moved out into the shade of the room, those surrounding the dais parted for him. "It's not going to hurt, Verve. This will be over quickly enough." He snapped his fingers, and two guards dragged Fenn from the other side of the room near the thrones.

Verve cried out and nearly forgot her plan as she spied the thick collar clamped around her husband's neck. When he looked up, she was mortified to see the gash running down the length of his face. "What have you done to him?" *Not yet. You've got to play the part still.*

Dacre approached her slowly, his eyes alert and cautious. "It's just a scratch, love."

She balled her fists at her side as Dacre reached out and took her face in his gloved right hand. Even through the leather his power pressed up against her, eager to explore and claim. Verve spat in his face, but he simply smirked at her.

"Your part in this will be relatively small," he breathed, his eyes on her lips. "First you will remove your claim on the Rogue Prince, which will free him to remove his claim on you."

"I'm not—"

He placed a finger to her lips. "I know you don't plan on cooperating, which is why I will work the magic through you." Dacre leaned in and spoke directly into the shell of her ear, "All you have to do is sit there and hold my hand for a little while. The blood exchange will come later, but I'll keep the pain at bay." His lips pressed against her temple, and before she could wrench away, he was leading her to the dais, where Fenn was being forced to sit.

Fenn stretched and strained against the fae holding him, desperation leaking out of his every pore as he caught Verve's eye. He cried out as one of his captors clubbed the side of his face with their fist.

"Don't you hit him," Verve warned. "I don't forget, and I rarely forgive."

That seemed to amuse Dacre for some reason, his lips twitching. But he raised his hand, and the offending fae stepped down from the dais, their head bowed. "My apologies, Verve. They forget he's suppressed and can't harm them." His eyes flickered meaningfully at her throat, and for one horrible moment, Verve thought he was going to inspect the collars more closely and discover them to be a fake. Thankfully, Dacre's eyes rose to meet hers, no trace of suspicion in their depths – none that she could discern, anyway.

Verve chanced another glance at Dav, but the girl refused to look at her at all this time. It was apparent now that she did not wish to be here.

Leaning away from Dacre, Verve stared him down and said, "Get her out of here." As angry as she was with her youngest sister, Verve didn't want her to witness what was about to happen.

Dacre shook his head. "I think she needs to witness the consequences of what she did, to see where my heart truly lies."

It was impossible to control her racing heart that threatened to escape her chest. Verve put up a small struggle as she was forced to sit, but Dacre hastily attached her collar to the stone seat by some magical means. "You don't have to do this," she cried out. She tried to keep her gaze off his gloves, off his darkening eyes, off Fenn, lest she give away the game.

"Who am I to deny prophecy?" was his response.

Verve snorted with rage as he took her hand in his gloved one. Perhaps this wasn't going to work, after all. "Then we are simply pawns of fate?"

Dacre shook his head emphatically. "No, not at all. We are its exploiters, at the very least. The writers of it, at the most. We bend destiny, fate, whatever you want to call it, to our will, you and I." His thumb stroked the back of her hand before he turned to someone unseen behind them. "Can we begin?"

That someone cleared their throat. "Sire, the glove."

"It has to come off, does it? I won't hurt her, will I?"

Verve noted that his left hand, which he reached to Fenn's, was bare. Should she make a leap for it, if Dacre refused to uncover the one he offered her? She tensed, ready to spring, but the voice from behind them, one strangely familiar, said,

"I soul-bound them with both their hands bare, Your Majesty. In order for this to work, I'm afraid you'll have to touch her flesh to your own." It was the fae priest who had wed her to Fenn who spoke now. He did not sound well. "It won't do her any permanent damage."

Dacre hissed through his teeth. "But it will hurt?"

"It would hurt less if you removed the wraith-bonds." When Dacre looked over his shoulder to glare, the fae backed away several paces. "I'm just speaking the truth, Your Majesty."

Fenn was beside himself now, trying to escape. His eyes were icy blue, and his emotions swirled around him so thickly, Verve had trouble seeing anything else.

If only I could reassure him! She knew, however, that there was no possible way to do so without alerting Dacre. Tears filled her eyes and she sobbed.

"It'll be over quickly enough," said Dacre with a sigh. With apparent reluctance, he slid the glove from his right hand and grasped Verve's hand in his own.

The force of his magic rammed into Verve, threatening to drown her in its struggle to claim her. Perhaps it wasn't Dacre who wanted her so much; perhaps it was his magic. Around her the world changed colors for a brief moment. Everything was tinged in red hues, and Dacre stood out in stark contrast to all.

He watched her, concern marring his features. His lips moved, making sounds that did not reach Verve's ears, and he squeezed her hand, hard.

Verve shook her head as dizziness washed over her in waves. Like a drowning sailor, she was aware of the magic rising up inside of her, struggling to meet his, but she hastily anchored it inside herself and searched within for her siphoning ability.

Dacre's hand left hers before she could find that particular magic, and she slumped forward in a near faint. "Verve." He tapped her face gently. "Verve, can you hear me?"

"Perhaps we should postpone this until Her Majesty is feeling better," said the priest.

Opposite Verve, Fenn had gone quiet and still. When she managed to look up at him, and her vision cleared, she was alarmed to see how pale his face had gone and how vacant his eyes were. "Stop. You're hurting him," she whimpered.

"Shh," said Dacre. "You're fine, Verve. We'll get this over with, and then you can go lie down." He reached out once more and took her hand in his, sending electric-like shocks running up her arm.

Verve ground her teeth and clenched her eyes shut as she resisted the siren song his magic sang to her own. Again and again it called out, *You are mine. Mine.* She ignored it as she rifled through her own power, searching for... Her mind went blank for a moment.

Dacre had begun chanting. The words were strange, spoken haltingly, but she reacted instantly to them.

Unwittingly, her head snapped to face Dacre, and he held her gaze as he continued to say the words offered to him by the priest. *Stop!* a small part of Verve cried out in the back of her mind as the magic from Dacre traveled through her and made its way to Fenn, threatening to rip her own essence from her husband, her mate, her friend.

Something made Dacre stumble over the words, and he sounded pained. "What was that?" he demanded.

"I-I don't know. Possibly her magic is resisting your own," the priest offered.

Verve took that moment to draw in a steadying breath and tried to pull her sweaty hand out of Dacre's. When that didn't work, she dropped Fenn's hand, which she did not remember grabbing, and found inside herself what she had been looking for.

The first thing she siphoned, after using her assessing magic on him, was his ability to discern magic, hoping he would then be unable to detect what she was doing. Her magic embraced the new addition, and his own store eagerly gave of itself to hers.

Dacre resumed chanting, and Verve knew she had to work more quickly.

Desperately she siphoned at random, taking some of his large store of speed and strength, before other abilities let themselves be known and raced to join her magic. Spell-casting was an enormous, seemingly bottomless magic of his, and it was the one her own magic sucked in greedily. Nameless hex and curse-casting abilities flooded her being, threatening to tear her apart in their haste.

Again Dacre stumbled over his words, and he dropped her hand as one burned. He shook his head, eyes closed as though trying to rid himself of a dizzy spell, and when he looked into her eyes once more, he cursed and rose suddenly. "Verve, what have you done?" His words were a harsh whisper, and she had no other warning before he attacked her with a bolt of white light.

Verve groaned as it struck her in the chest and caused her limbs to go numb. Before she could recover, something cold slipped around her neck, but whoever was attempting to restrain her was easily thrown off before a new collar could be clamped into place.

She ripped the fake collar from around her neck, freeing herself from the chain that was restraining it. It gave her a small sense of satisfaction, seeing comprehension dawning on Dacre's face and the panic that was rising in its place.

He lobbed a ball of fire at her, an experiment, and she caught it midflight, fed air and power into it, and threw it right back at him, where he caused it to burst into a million pieces of glass, which he aimed at Fenn.

With little effort, Verve turned the glass into sand, and it blew around him harmlessly. She dodged a spell meant to immobilize her, leaping over the stone chair tops and dashing around in a wide circle as hex after hex was cast in her direction. Each spell missed her by inches, alerting Verve to the fact that Dacre was driving her where he wanted her. Instead of continuing her current course, Verve froze mid-step and threw out a shield around herself.

Dacre rent the shield in two. "So. You're a siphon now. Interesting." He ducked as she threw a whip of pure heat and hatred at him. It lashed at the dais and nearly caught Fenn, though Verve redirected it at the last moment so it merely singed the air near him and then came down upon the middle of the dais with a resounding crack.

Fenn. She needed to free him so he could help her.

"Oh, I don't think so." Dacre threw out a shield of his own, preventing Verve from reaching her objective.

She stopped just shy of hitting the wall of magic that encased Dacre and Fenn, and watched helplessly as the former approached her husband, a dagger in his hands. "Don't touch him."

The look Dacre gave her was positively predatory. "Surrender and I'll think about sparing him."

Verve attacked the shield with everything she had, but each spell bounced off it and rebounded on her and the room. Fae screamed and ran for cover, heedless of their king's cries for them to hold their positions. She absorbed her own attacks and let them build within her blood and strengthen her as she prepared to unleash fire on the room. Burning the world down was perhaps not the wisest of ideas, but if Dacre cared at all for the palace, this would get his attention.

But just as she was about to release all hell, Verve heard a fae heartbeat approach her, felt a gentle tap on her shoulder. The priest stood at her elbow and bowed, even as Dacre formed killing magic in his hands.

"Verity," said the priest, his voice sounding nothing like his own. "He's connected to it." He winked and stepped back before Verve could lash out at him.

Her mind raced as she stepped away, and the fire she had been preparing faltered. What did he mean by that? And who was he that he would help her?

With a shout, the priest dodged the curse that Dacre sent his way, his form shifting into a friendly one. Where he landed now stood Finley.

Verve could have cried in relief, but Dacre was not beaten. The Traitor King reached out with a bolt of black light, striking Fenn's uncle squarely in the chest. He fell over, dead apparently. "No!" She stepped forward, but Finley was swallowed up by Dacre's shield, preventing her from going to him.

Dav, whom Verve hadn't seen in minutes, was also encased in Dacre's protective bubble. She must have moved nearer to him while no one was paying attention.

"It's over, Verve," said Dacre. "I have the upper hand." He held a blade to Fenn's throat, even though they both knew it wouldn't kill a fae. It still could hurt him and slow him down.

Think, Verve. He could kill Fenn with a glance. Why hasn't he? It made little sense. Unless he was hoping to use Fenn as bait. She prowled nearer to Dacre's shield until its warmth pressed uncomfortably against her skin. *Think.* Verve closed her eyes and used through-sight, scanning the whole scene from every angle.

Magic leaked out of Dacre, reaching toward the shield. He was trembling – perhaps from exhaustion or perhaps from his own magic's desire to escape. Dacre was a more powerful being than Verve; that much was obvious. But maybe, just maybe, he couldn't kill Fenn without killing her, and that would give her the advantage after all.

But what did Finley mean when he said, 'He's connected to it'?

Dacre lashed out once more with magic, striking Verve's hand, which she had raised. It stung, and she withdrew with a cry. "Don't hurt yourself, love." His voice was gentle but mocking.

Her eyes flew open. *Of course!* Hope blossomed along with agony as another one of Dacre's spells hit her.

"S-stop," said Dav, her voice soft beneath the roar of the magic.

Dacre paid the girl no mind. "I'm being serious. Don't make me hurt you."

Verve's eyes narrowed. Without hesitation, she placed her hands on his shield, ignoring the pain that seared her palms.

Dacre sighed. "Verve, there's no reason to hurt yourself like that. You're not going to break through my shield."

There! Power wriggled beneath her touch, feeding through his shield and sinking into the skin of her hands. She bore the pain as he reinforced the shield with more magic, obviously unaware that he was simply offering her power. A scream tore itself from her lips as she held on to the protective orb. Her poor body couldn't decide which was worse: bearing the brunt of Dacre's defenses or taking them in for her own stores. *I need to siphon faster.*

Indeed, Dacre's eyes widened, and he drew the shield in closer to himself. Through with Fenn, he raised the knife and slit Fenn's throat, just as Dav jumped on his back and clamped her hands around his neck.

"Get off me, pest!" With ease he tossed Dav from his person, just as Verve sprang forward. Dacre must have been anticipating this, as he let loose a plethora of powerful spells in her direction. Several missed, but most of them struck her in the chest. Oh, did it burn. But she allowed the magic he had expended to seep into her skin and gathered it into the well within herself.

"That's not possible." Dacre ceased lobbing magic at Verve, instead retreating several steps as she raced to her husband's and sister's aid.

Fenn still wore a collar and was incapable of using magic to defend himself or recover from the damage Dacre had done to him. Verve knelt, preparing to speed up his healing, but Dav placed a hand on her arm.

"He's getting away."

Hastily, Verve snapped off the collar around Fenn's neck and threw it to the ground. As she had practiced many times with Fenn in the past, Verve ran after Dacre and lashed out with a rope of light, knocking him off his feet.

He at once recovered and sent a lasso of his own at her, but Verve simply grabbed it and held on, coiling it around her hands. More power rippled through the rope and into her waiting hands.

Now Dacre's face darkened with rage. He drew magic the color of night into his hands and aimed it for Dav.

Verve didn't think but ran between the killing spell and her sister. Time seemed to slow.

Dacre cried out in dismay and attempted to push her out of the spell's intended path, but she was faster. And yet she barely reached Dav in time.

There wasn't a moment to lose, and yet she lost it. The spell in its full, evil potency struck her in the side. Her lungs emptied themselves of air, and her body grew icy cold in an instant.

Verve's eyes rolled back in her head, the world grew dark, and she fell in a perfect arc, hitting the floor as her spirit squirmed to free itself from its shell.

Chapter Twenty-Three

Dav was at her side in an instant, screaming and crying for Verve to return to life. Verve tried, but she couldn't.

Then Dacre was there, pushing Dav aside and cradling Verve in his arms. "You are not dead." He sounded furious, his words spitting through his teeth. "Verve, you are not dead."

And yet, there was no pulse in her body. She felt no one holding her, no one pumping their hands on her chest and attempting to breathe life back into her lungs. Somehow she knew these things were happening, but to feel or behold them? At the moment, it was beyond her. Suddenly there was light, brighter than her wildest imaginings, and yet there was also a terrible darkness that threatened to swallow her whole. She drifted there in limbo, uncertain as to what she should or could do.

Light coiled around the fingers of her right hand – that much she could see now as she lay there. But darkness engulfed her left. So, she was still in her body, somehow. But why couldn't she move?

"It's not a choice, the road we walk," whispered a voice as cold as death. *Igraine.*

Verve tried stirring, but her limbs were too heavy, as was her head. She was so tired, her eyes wouldn't even open, though more and more was coming into focus.

Igraine leaned over Verve, ignoring Dacre entirely. "You're in an alternate state, Verity. As am I, which is why the others cannot see or hear what's truly going on."

"I'm not dead?"

The woman shrugged. "You're not exactly dead. But you're not quite alive either."

Verve groaned. If she was not quite alive, why did it still hurt so much, then? "What's happened to me?"

"You've thwarted every prophecy I've ever read, and that is many." Igraine gestured to the lightness and darkness that Verve was emitting. "You cannot kill the Fire Queen, not really. Oh, that was killing magic you threw yourself in front of just now. But it went in you rather than through you."

Now Verve's head had begun to ache. "What does that mean?"

Igraine smirked. "It means, Fire Queen, that you absorbed it, just like you absorbed all the other magic the Traitor King threw at you." She waited, her expression smug as though she could see Verve's thoughts whirling around in her brain.

"So, he can't kill anyone anymore? I siphoned it?"

The potion-maker simply nodded.

"But why am I lying here like this, unable to move? A-and you said I wasn't wholly alive. What does that mean?"

"It means, child," said Igraine, "that you hold death in your hands now, of every mortal and immortal alike." She grew silent for some time, and then surprised Verve by repeating a poem that had haunted her for two years now:

"She wades 'neath shallow shores,
Her worth soon to prove.
Child of the flame,
Of blade and bone,
She divides and kills,
Unites and raises.
She is of us and other,
Of all and none,
The once-brittle child,
O she of middling ground."

Then Igraine grinned. "It makes sense now. If you control death, you control life. You're the blade, the weapon. That prophecy really had very little to do with the Cunning Blade, after all."

Verve found herself growing more and more confused as the moments passed. "So the light is life, the dark is death. What do I do with them?"

"Do? Child, you can do whatever you want." Igraine rose, and her figure shimmered briefly over Verve and vanished, but not before her parting words reached Verve. "I suggest you regain control of your body. That much power you're currently holding is enough to bring down the palace."

With a shudder and a cough, Verve's sense of feeling returned to her limbs.

Dacre gripped her so tightly it hurt. He didn't seem to notice what she now held in her hands, and it was a wonder, for the power was great and begged to be released. "You're all right," he breathed, hastily removing himself out from under her. Had he really only just remembered how dangerous being in contact with her was?

She could have laughed. It made no difference, the distance he put between them. Verve took the white and black lights and blended them together in her hands, then sent them spiraling toward Dacre, who finally had the sense to run.

His flight was futile. The combined magic latched on to him, turned him to face Verve as she sucked every last drop of power from his body through the connection. She didn't stop, not when he fought and screamed for mercy, even though she was tempted. "You showed your servants no mercy."

"Verve, please. I love you!"

She continued to siphon, speeding up the process as much as she could. "You never showed Fenn any mercy."

"Th-that's not true," he said, crimson tears pouring from his eyes. "I spared him. For you. Only for you. And your sister."

Verve shook her head. "You tried to kill her but hit me instead."

Dacre sobbed. He was now quite helpless, with little magic left in his veins. "Please, Verve, love. I'm sorry." He hiccoughed as the last dregs of his power fled his body and entered Verve with a sickening crash.

There was a sound louder than cannon fire. Her body erupted in flames as the power settled on her, and with a shout she released the killing magic into Dacre, who dropped instantly and was still. A sob tore itself from her throat, one of relief and sorrow. But her mind was at once on more pressing matters.

Fenn. Where is Fenn? And Dav?

All was so bright and yet so dark. She looked around for her love, only to find him bleeding silver everywhere. "Fenn, I need you."

He moaned but appeared too weak to move. "N-not going anywhere."

She forced a laugh, even as she continued to burn and threatened to explode. "It's too much for me, Fenn. Way too much for me to handle." The words were pushed through her lips with effort, her voice strained and strange to her own ears.

Fenn winced, his eyes still blue with terror. "That is a lot of magic, Verve."

"Yes, and you're going to have to take some of it."

"What? No, I can't."

Verve started to tremble, and the very ground beneath them shook. Pillars surrounding the outer wall crumbled into nothing. The ceiling spat dust down on them and threatened to collapse. Cracks formed in the marble floor, racing outward from Verve, chasing Dav from the room with a scream. In seconds, all that remained was Verve, Fenn, and the dais on which they were precariously positioned. "I'm sorry, Fenn. It's going to eat me alive." In truth, she did not trust herself with so much magic, and he seemed to understand the words she wasn't saying.

"Please, Verve. I have so much power already."

But she knew his resolve was fading as he watched her suffer. Gently, she reached down to him and placed a burning finger to his lips. "Please, Fenn. Help me bear it. I don't want to do this alone."

Cold water ran down his cheeks and found her finger, taking some of the heat out of her flames. "All right, but not much. I can't—"

Verve couldn't wait a moment longer. She didn't have time to sort through the abilities that she could give him, didn't have the strength to do anything but gift. Power after power slipped from her fingers and fled into Fenn's mouth, flew down his throat, and settled in his own store of magic.

To his credit, he didn't scream but held on to Verve's gaze as she poured the stolen magic into him. That it pained him was obvious, though she tried to make it as easy as possible for him to accept.

"I'm sorry," she whispered, and then pressed her lips against his as the last of the magic she needed to rid herself of settled in his bones.

Fenn shuddered mightily, biting Verve's lip so hard that he drew blood.

She pulled back with a gasp and panted. "How do you feel?" There was still so much magic within her, and yet there was more space now, enough room for it to stretch its limbs and move comfortably without her feeling like a sausage skin ready to burst. *What sweet relief this is!*

He didn't respond at first but stared at her, a dazed look upon his face. He reached for her. "I-I don't think I can hold a drop more." His eyes flickered closed and he groaned. "Is your sister all right?"

Dav was nowhere to be seen, but her heartbeat sounded sure and strong among the raised voices outside. "Yes."

Fenn swallowed. "Is Finley dead?"

Verve's heart thumped painfully. "I-I think so."

"Markson's dead too. We have to—" Fenn attempted to sit up, only to collapse once more. The floor shuddered beneath him as he struck it. "Finley saved us with his words." His voice was so heartbroken, that it moved Verve to action.

She rose and searched through the rubble for him. Sure enough, Finley lay where she had seen him fall, and was now half-buried beneath debris from the ceiling. Verve threw the wood and plaster away from his form, and her right hand, the one pulsing with white light, throbbed painfully. "I think I could bring him back."

"You don't have to bring me back," said Finley, his eyes flickering open.

Verve screamed, which caused both males to cover their ears. "W-what do you mean, you're not dead?"

Finley chuckled. "I'll try not to take offense at your disappointment."

She ignored the jest and threw a fistful of sparks at him. "You scared me half to death." As she watched, Finley raised himself into a sitting position and pulled open his shirt, revealing a thick plate of armor with an inky black ripple marring its surface. "You knew what was going to happen."

"Knew? Well, yes, I could see some moments, flashes, really. You didn't take *all* of my foresight, if you will recall."

Fenn sat up as well and pushed some debris from off his legs. "When you left," he began slowly, "you had no intention of coming back." He sounded like he was barely in control of his temper. "We worried for you. You could've ruined all our plans, had you been caught."

Verve cleared her throat, not wishing to witness another row, not so soon after the all-out battle she'd taken part in. On instinct, her eyes flickered to where Dacre's body lay, but she hastily looked away again. "So you hid among the fae until we arrived?" When Finley said nothing but nodded, she threw more sparks at him. "And you didn't help my aunt escape in all that time? Finley! She could have *died*."

"I'm doubtful of that possibility."

The couple exchanged a look before Fenn said with a sigh, "He never had her."

"Oh, he knew where she was. But she's not a middling, and Dacre didn't have a death wish. If he had attempted to pull her through a gateway, she would have perished. And you, being as you are, would no doubt have given him hell for it." For someone who had come precariously close to dying, Finley seemed far too merry.

And Verve – Verve was exhausted. She could barely keep her eyes open, never mind remain standing. Swaying, Verve was grateful when Finley leapt up and caught her before she could hit the ground.

"Easy there, Your Majesty."

"I've got to..." Her words slurred and the world swayed.

"You haven't got to do anything but rest until your power fully settles on you."

Surprisingly, a sob escaped Verve's lips and her eyes once more found Dacre. "B-burn his body, would you? Just to make sure?"

Finley dipped his head. "As the Fire Queen wishes, so it will be."

Fenn groaned. "It's a mess."

Verve knew what he meant. Not the throne room and palace – which was a disaster area – but Letorheas itself and perhaps parts of Etterhea. The worlds had suffered in their short rule beneath the Traitor King. "And I have to clean it all up."

Fenn pulled himself to his knees. "Not alone, together."

Her eyes found the sole throne that had survived the fight between her and Dacre. As if drawn by a magnet, she made her way toward it, and Finley released her. "Together." The seat was made of wood, a mockery of the fine marble throne that had been meant for the Traitor King but which was now in ruins. *So it begins.*

"Are you ready?" Fenn asked.

Strangely, she thought so. Without answering, she ascended the stone steps. Lightning flashed without. Rain battered the roof. Verve stumbled a few times on her way, her body sluggish and glutted from all the magic she held, but she knew her place now and found it hard to resist.

Mortal and immortal, death and life, fire and water – she was all these things. This was meant for her, a burden, yes, but one to share. Then, with one last look at her mate, the Fire Queen gave in and took her throne.

Epilogue

Time is a peculiar thing.

Seconds fall like delicate petals from flowers, spilling over into minutes, hours, days, weeks, months, years, and decades. But for the fae, time moves even more strangely. For what is a year but a second when you're immortal? And what is a second to someone who was once mortal and is now so much more?

She forgets the seconds, the Fire Queen, Firstblood of the No Lands, Ambassador to the Realms. They mean little to her except for two months out of every year. Then every second stretches an eternity as she waits for her love to return.

The throne room is empty and has been for fifty-nine days, twenty-three hours, fifty-six minutes, and three seconds. No one, not fae, human, nor elf has seen her, not even her beloved sister, to whom she has reconciled. Some speculate that their queen is in hiding, though from what they cannot be certain. Others say she is not hiding but becomes rather lost when the Rogue Prince serves his sentence as assistant to the queen of death, a role that some argue she should fill, given her strange powers.

Five miles away from Strattavus Palace, in a lone glade with wilting plants and drooping tree boughs, the air ripples and warms. It's as if nature is sighing. The trees perk up. The flowers raise their weary heads. And bees buzz once more as a breeze picks up, swirls dead leaves from the forest ground, and a tear forms in the ether.

Laughter burbles from somewhere unseen, and then, all at once, she is standing there, alone and alert. The Fire Queen peers around her, listening. When she doesn't find what she's looking for, she takes to pacing and quickly grows agitated.

Plants tremble in response to her feelings, or perhaps to the fire licking her fingertips. "I'm sorry," she whispers, and the fire dies. Nature sighs in relief but remains tense as a nearby hawthorn forms a gateway.

The queen turns in slow circles and then stops.

A shadowy figure emerges from the tree and pauses. His breathing hitches as he takes in the woman before him. "You've grown taller."

She turns to him, a radiant yet playful smile on her face. "Or perhaps you have shrunk."

He can take it no more. The Rogue Prince runs to his queen and lifts her off the ground in a tight embrace until she squawks in protest. "Sorry! I forget."

"No need to brag about being stronger than me again."

The grin he affords her is a lazy one as he sets her down on her feet but continues to hold her hands. "I wouldn't dream about bragging to you." He leans down and presses his lips against hers, drawing away all too soon, much to the Fire Queen's annoyance.

She swats at him. "You're late."

"Actually, I'm early. By two minutes this time. Igraine didn't bat an eye when I left." When his mate peers up at him, concerned, he smooths out her brow and says, "With you in control of life and death, she really hasn't got a good argument for forcing us to keep the bargain. I believe she's close to agreeing to amend it."

The queen reaches up and touches his face. "Good." And then she's walking away.

The prince is close on her heels. He snags an arm around her waist, and she lets him, before he brings her to a halt. "I missed you."

"I missed you so much more."

"I seriously doubt that," he grumbles. "Where do you go...when I'm not here?"

She pulls against him and then stops. "Who says I'm not here where I ought to be?"

He is silent, not judging but waiting for the truth.

"I am nowhere. I–I live in the places between when you are gone." Her voice wavers over these words, and she is at once crushed into his chest.

"I worried that might be so."

"I made sure it rained plenty before I disappeared. And that the people were fed and well and that the realms were all in good order." She squeezes his middle and attempts to pull back. He is having none of that. "Fenn."

His sigh ripples through her hair as he stoops once more. Thankfully, he doesn't press her further. There are some wounds that will take more time to heal, just as she found with the rift between her and her sister. Just as she's finding with the extent of the damage done by not one but two tyrants' reigns.

"We should return," she says.

The prince pauses. "*Should* we?"

She gives him a playful shove. "Yes. We have responsibilities to attend to, I suppose. Besides, it seems like it's going to rain."

"You make the weather."

The air crackles, and thunder rumbles in the distance. "Race you back to the palace!"

They don't make it that far. He grabs her once more and, laughing, they tumble to the ground, lie back, and watch the clouds come rolling in.

Acknowledgments

To my street team, these three in particular:
Traveling Cloak,
Amanda Yarsa,
&
Kelly Mantin.
Thank you for reading my books and leaving honest reviews!

And last, but never least:
A big thank you to Don D'Auria and the rest of the fantastic crew at Flame Tree Press!

About the Author

Beth Overmyer is the author of the fantasy trilogy *The Goblets Immortal*. *Booklist* described book one as 'packed full of adventure' with an ending that leaves readers 'anxiously awaiting a sequel'. Beth's short fiction has appeared in the magazines *The Lorelei Signal* and *Big Pulp*, and in various anthologies. Her short story 'Red' received an honorable mention in *Allegory*'s 2010 spring/summer issue. Previous Flame Tree Press books of hers include the trilogy *The Goblets Immortal*, *Holes in the Veil* and *Death's Key*, and the first two books in the *Blade and Bone* series: *Brittle* and *Tempered Glass*.

Beth was born and raised near Oberlin, Ohio, and she hasn't moved far. The charming college town is a favorite haunt of hers for daydreaming when writing and planning fantasy novels. When not writing, Beth can be found reading fantasy novels, cozy mysteries, and almost any book she can get on the craft of putting words on the page.

You can find Beth online at @Bethyo and bethovermyer.com.

FLAME TREE PRESS
FICTION WITHOUT FRONTIERS
Award-Winning Authors & Original Voices

Flame Tree Press is the trade fiction imprint of Flame Tree Publishing, focusing on excellent writing in horror and the supernatural, crime and mystery, science fiction and fantasy. Our aim is to explore beyond the boundaries of the everyday, with tales from both award-winning authors and original voices.

•

Also by Beth Overmyer:
Brittle
Tempered Glass
The Goblets Immortal
Holes in the Veil
Death's Key

You may also enjoy:
The Sentient by Nadia Afifi
Junction by Daniel M. Bensen
Keeper of Sorrows by Rachel Fikes
Silent Key by Laurel Hightower
The Widening Gyre by Michael R. Johnston
The Heart of Winter by Shona Kinsella
The Sky Woman by J.D. Moyer
The Guardian by J.D. Moyer
One Eye Opened in That Other Place by Christi Nogle
The Last Feather by Shameez Patel Papathanasiou
The Eternal Shadow by Shameez Patel Papathanasiou
The First King by Shameez Patel Papathanasiou
Tinderbox by W.A. Simpson
Tarotmancer by W.A. Simpson
The Hatter's Daughter by W.A. Simpson
A Killing Fire by Faye Snowden
A Killing Rain by Faye Snowden
A Sword of Bronze and Ashes by Anna Smith Spark
Idolatry by Aditya Sudarshan
The Roamers by Francesco Verso
Whisperwood by Alex Woodroe
Of Kings, Queens & Colonies by Johnny Worthen

•

Join our mailing list for free short stories, new release details, news about our authors and special promotions:

flametreepress.com